HarperTeen is an imprint of HarperCollins Publishers.

The Antidote

Copyright © 2019 by Shelley Sackier

All rights reserved. Printed in the United States of America.

No part of this book may be used or reproduced in any manner whatsoever

without written permission except in the case of brief quotations embodied

in critical articles and reviews. For information address HarperCollins

Children's Books, a division of HarperCollins Publishers,

195 Broadway, New York, NY 10007.

www.epicreads.com

Library of Congress Control Number: 2018946000

ISBN 978-0-06-245347-1

Typography by Jessie Gang

18 19 20 21 22 PC/LSCH 10 9 8 7 6 5 4 3 2 1

❖

First Edition

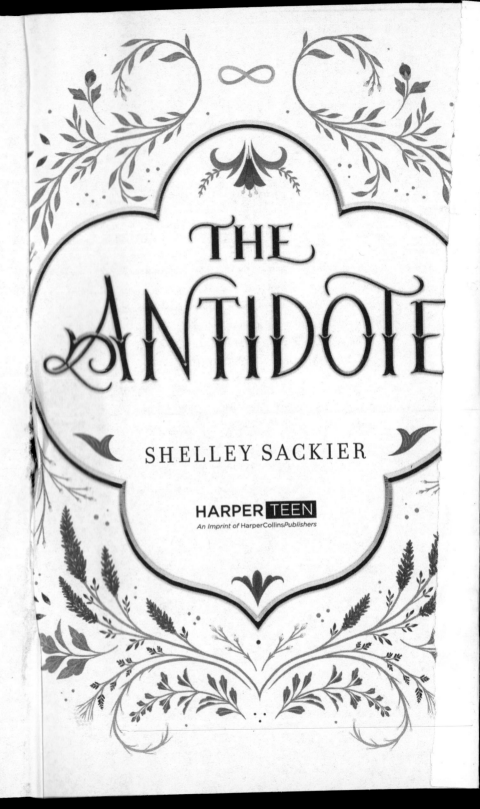

THE ANTIDOTE

SHELLEY SACKIER

HARPER TEEN

An Imprint of HarperCollinsPublishers

*To the long line of women in my family—the true
Savvas—both living and passed—who have made my
eyes widen with surprise at all the magic they have
imparted from their stills and with their skills.
But mostly to my mom, who still sees magic everywhere.*

BOOK ONE: FIRELI

PROLOGUE

THE FINE HAIR ACROSS HER FOREARMS PRICKLED beneath the soft satin of her sleeves. Evanora could not trust her eyes. They pearled and doubled her vision.

But she *could* trust her ears. And the words that spiraled within their bony labyrinth caused her breath to shorten, her hands to clench, her heart to drum with unsteadying strength.

She clutched at the top of the brick wall, barely hidden, and watched the iridescent bubble of her bright future pop and disappear.

The man she loved whispered words of devotion to someone else.

The man who she'd believed was her equal—a match with such potent possibility. Together their skills were unrivaled.

You've changed my whole world, Evanora heard him say, and she could not stifle the sob that welled up from within her.

The other young woman twisted to look over her shoulder, eyes wide with panic. She snatched the sheath of silk at her feet to raise the hemline of her dress and dashed out of the garden, leaving the man staring at Evanora, rueful regret in his gaze.

He raised his hands apologetically, prayerfully. "I'm sorry."

Evanora rushed toward him, her words tumbling out. "I can change your mind. Give me a chance!"

He reached out to put a hand on her arm. "I am decided and cannot be swayed. Forgive me, Evvie."

"It is forbidden by the realm's statutes. You cannot be together—your magic and her . . . bloodline," Evanora choked out. "Rules are rules."

The man's eyes sparkled before he closed them, hiding his contrition. "I know the law, but it must be cast aside in this case. For she is now with child. I cannot abandon her when I have been the one to make it so. There are no rules that can abolish my feelings, and certainly none that will dissolve my responsibility. I *love* her, and I will be there for her—and the child—no matter what."

The man's resolute, dark features configured themselves into a look asking for compassion and mercy. But Evanora felt a tearing in her chest, not of fabric but of flesh. The spear of pain radiated through to her limbs—made her heave in search for breath. Her body choked with need to break the vise that pulled its corset strings inflexibly fast. *A child!*

It should have been hers.

A bright-eyed boy toddled into the garden, his sweet, cherubic voice calling out in delight at finding the man.

"Azamar!"

But Azamar did not turn toward the child. Instead, his eyes

followed the line of Evanora's approaching form, taking in her gripping fists, her rising, bellowing breaths, and the forward thrusting of her chin. He honed in on her lips—whispering, soughing, rustling with softly edged words that strung together and quickly filled the air with a crackling, electric prickle. He pulled back as Evanora's hands made a swirl in the air above her.

Azamar turned and shouted at the boy, who dashed to cling to the man's leg as leaves and petals swirled in an eddying vortex about their feet.

Evanora unclasped the cork from a vial of glass and wheeled to empty its contents. A shimmering, ebony powder pirouetted through the air, whirring around Azamar and the boy as they stood frozen in a garden full of forget-me-nots. Azamar tried shielding the boy, but Evanora was lightning fast.

She spoke, her voice quivering and cracking with the great strain of the ache she could not hold back. "I may not be able to alter your feelings or the obligation you now bear, but as one who firmly abides by the realm's rules for our people's safety, I *can*, at least, amend your access. If you must love them, then you must love them from afar!"

With a twist of her hands, the black dust filled the air, darkening the space between them.

Evanora could not have heard the pleading she knew was present, as her ears were deaf to everything but her pain.

She ran.

From the scene. From Azamar. From the hasty curse she would carry as a stifling cloak, as black as the void of loss that collapsed around her.

She had left herself unguarded. It would not happen again.

CHAPTER
ONE

"I KNOW THIS MUST BE DIFFICULT FOR YOU—YOU'VE suffered an abuse of skills that has our community still rippling with outrage. But I'm doing everything I can. I hope you know that." Savva stroked Xavi's hair and looked deep into his eyes.

The eight-year-old prince of Fireli looked back at the bedraggled castle healer, his brows furrowing together, his eyes squinting in confusion. "What's difficult?"

Savva picked up his hand and squeezed it, wincing slightly as her joints grappled with the onset of arthritis. "I'm sorry, Your Highness, I was speaking to . . ." She trailed off, sighing, and then mumbled, "Someone else."

Xavi looked about the lush castle gardens and searched for anyone hiding within the verdant beds of blooming flowers and feathery grasses. He saw no one. "Mother said you might be able to make me feel less . . . peculiar."

Savva looked skyward. "Yes. Come back to the stillroom with me. Your situation is very complicated. It's better that I work on you there than—"

"Am I going to die?" he asked gravely.

Savva's head snapped back and she peered at him solemnly. "No."

Then she put her hands on either side of his head, covering his ears. It was an attempt to keep him from hearing her, but her gnarled fingers left gaps. "I will get you back. And the stone. And Fireli will live on." She released her hands and looked off into the distant hills, toward the kingdom's borderlands with their neighbor, Gwyndom. She raised a hand to her mouth and whispered from behind it, "The consortium will help figure this out. We still have time, my love. At least until he's twenty-two."

"DON'T CHEAT, XAVI. REMEMBER YOU PROMISED NOT to cheat."

"Rye," Xavi said to his eight-year-old brother as they sat across a chessboard from each other in their mother's softly lit sitting room, his face full of humor and patience, "I've never cheated. And I *will* never cheat. When will you learn to trust me?"

"Why is it you're always winning?" Rye complained.

Xavi snorted. "Maybe because I'm paying attention to the game and not distracted by searching for Fee."

Rye's eyebrows fused as one and Fee giggled, popping out from behind the lush velvet sofa Rye perched upon.

"I heard that!" she gushed. "And your face is red, Rye."

"Leave us alone, Ophelia," Rye groused, tucking his head toward his chest. But she knew he didn't really want her to go, because what

Xavi said was true. Rye *was* always scanning for her.

She ambled toward the queen's writing table and the shelves holding thick leather-bound books and trinkets of bewitching designs. The queen was deeply immersed in her duties, writing and occasionally toying with the feathers on the edge of her quill.

"Your necklace is very pretty," Fee announced, standing in front of the queen's desk.

The queen glanced up and smiled. "Thank you, Fee. It's a gemstone called an opal."

"It's all pearly and smooth. And big. Like Xavi's teeth when he smiles."

The queen looked amused. "The Kingdom of Fireli used to have one more than twice this size a time ago."

"What happened to it?"

Fee and the queen both turned to see Savva at the door to her chamber. The queen motioned her over and answered distractedly, "Lost, I'm afraid. I've no idea where it is."

"Mother says lost things are usually right under your nose. I'll check beneath your desk." Fee darted under the curtained sheets that skirted the table as Savva approached the queen.

"Thank you for coming," the queen said in a subdued voice. "My concern is the same. Xavi seems much too lethargic for a boy of ten."

Fee saw Savva's weathered leather shoes shift as they poked beneath the table's skirt. "Might the prince be pushed too heavily in his studies, Your Majesty?" the healer asked.

The queen clucked her tongue in response. "No. He learns at his own pace—although his appetite is voracious in that regard. Are you not in the least bit concerned?"

Fee toyed with Savva's shoelaces, and Savva pulled her foot back immediately and looked beneath the skirt. "Fee!" she scolded. "Come out of there."

"I was searching for milady's big opal. She said she's lost her necklace."

Savva pulled at Fee's skinny arm until she was standing upright in front of them again.

"Don't reprimand her, Savva. She's done nothing wrong." The look the queen gave the healer held a thousand unsaid words, and Fee studied the queen's face to make sense of it.

"I'm sorry, Your Majesty. Giving him the opal was keeping in tradition with the healers. His *disappearance* is distressing, but I will never stop trying to recover it for our kingdom."

The queen sighed and glanced over at Fee. "Darling, you've a rent in your trousers—which you shouldn't be wearing in the first place. And it appears that your knee has been skinned. Perhaps you should go back with Savva to her stillroom for treatment?"

Savva pointed to an aloe vera plant on a table by the fireplace where two women bustled to stoke the flames and add more wood. "Break off a spear and spread it on the abrasion."

Fee did as told, plopping down on the carpet by the two servants. One of them looked back to see Fee snap off a pale green spike. "Oh no," she gushed, darting toward Fee. "This is the queen's plant. You mustn't toy with it. She'll be cross if she sees it marred."

Fee pouted, and felt a thread of heat for yet another finger-wagging. "I can fix it," she said in a huff. She then touched the tip of the broken aloe spear and the missing three inches sprouted to fill the empty gap.

The woman gasped, and Fee saw Savva rush toward the servant.

"Did you—What was—" the woman stuttered as Savva put an arm around her, leading her to the door.

"A simple trick she learned from the two boys—nothing more. I really should scold her for upsetting you, but she's just an impish six-year-old."

Fee shrugged at the frazzled woman and at Savva, whose lips were pressed into a worried line of unease. Grown-ups were tricky. But she caught Rye's eye and decided to go back to the boys and their chess game. Two friends who were never ruffled and always up for fun.

CHAPTER
THREE

"FIRELI'S MINES BRING OUR KINGDOM SECURITY AND wealth. The precious metals culled from those caves allow us the ability to trade freely with the three other kingdoms of Aethusa. Our excess is essential as a bargaining tool to purchase that which we need but which is produced in other quarters of the realm." The tutor's voice floated down to where Fee sat beneath the open window. Rye and Xavi were captive to their lessons. At not quite seven, she was not permitted to join their schooling sessions, but instead, grew fidgety in the garden below, each passing minute adding to her displeasure.

She wanted to be with them. And was galled she was forced to wait.

Fee looked about at the flowers surrounding her. She plucked at the edges of a gangling vine growing low to the ground and encouraged it to intertwine in and around her fingers, threading through them and up her arm. She pressed the vine upon the stone wall beneath the window and glanced up, instructing the creeping plant to shoot up and into the classroom.

"And of course, the people of Fireli are quite fond of pointing out that the mine is where we found our kingdom's core stone—a small touch of folklore whimsy within your history lesson today."

Fee heard the sudden scraping of a chair and looked up to see Xavi's face above her in the window, full of warning. He tossed out the vine, shook his head, and firmly shut the window.

Fee sighed. Xavi, too, was beginning to lose his sense of humor when it came to her plant pranks.

Out of the corner of her eye, Fee suddenly spotted a woman crouching behind the feathery plumes of green ornamental grasses. The woman smiled broadly, so Fee scrambled along the ground to where she perched.

She peered up at the woman's face. "What's the matter with your eyes?"

"What do you mean?"

"They're two different colors. One is green and the other yellow. Are you ill?"

The woman laughed. "No."

"Then how did you make them do that?" Fee leaned in and placed a tiny finger upon the woman's cheekbone to pull down the skin. "I want to do that too."

The woman tittered again and grabbed Fee's little hand, giving it a kiss. "I was simply born that way, Fee."

Fee's eyes widened. "How do you know my name?"

"Many people know your name." She pointed at the vine snaking around Fee's arm. "Is it fun to do that?"

Fee grinned with delight and nodded.

"I imagine so." Then she leaned in and said secretly, "Best not do it very often. And never in front of anyone else, okay?"

Fee's eyes went wide and she answered back loudly, "Why not?"

The woman gave Fee a pat on the head. "Because it makes people decidedly upset. Now be good." The garden went suddenly dark—blackened as night—and was then sunlit again. The woman was gone. Faster than the blink of her two-colored eyes.

Curious, Fee thought.

She shrugged and returned to her post.

"What are you reading, Rye?" Fee asked. She was hanging upside down from one of the widespread oak trees in the garden, tossing tiny acorns at Rye's book from the fistful she'd gathered. He had been ignoring her, absorbed with the writing.

Xavi leaned over to peer at the title. "Where did you find that book? I thought Father had purposefully thrown it away."

"Sir Rollins insisted I read it. He said everyone who will be working in government needs to be warned against the realm's history with sorcery, so that evil cannot have another chance to gain a footing." Rye buried his head farther into the pages, unaware of the small, sprouting acorn beside him. Reaching out tiny rootlets, it buried itself in the earth and sent up two shiny green leaves, unfurling toward the sky.

Xavi reached over and plucked out the miniscule sapling and then glared up warningly at Fee. "Seriously, Rye. Father said that book is pure propaganda. Nothing but fearmongering."

Fee pitched a nut at Xavi. "I don't know what that means. Stop using such fancy words."

He looked up at her. "Your face is turning purple, Fee. Come down here, and I'll tell you both the real story of magic within the realm."

She leapt down and roosted beside Rye, both of them peering up at Xavi.

"Long ago, there lived a gardener who fell in love with a barren woman. One day they visited a wish-granting old shrew who lived in the woodlands. They brought all the money they had and begged the old hag to bestow upon them a child. She agreed, but on one condition: she could only grant them twins—one filled with goodness, the other with greed, as this was how the balance of nature worked. Neither would succumb to their base temperament as long as they were raised side by side and loved equally. But what the witch did not say—"

"I knew there was a catch," Rye said pointedly. "There's always a catch."

Xavi continued. "What the witch did not say was that although the couple would conceive and have two children, the wife would die in childbirth."

Fee made a little gasp, and Rye turned to her with knowing eyes. "They should *never* have trusted the old witch."

"May I continue?" Xavi asked. "The man could not bear to see the infants, as the twins were a constant reminder of what he had lost. He sent them away and never made contact again.

"But the deal had been broken. They were raised by others who did not know that one would be difficult and the other a delight. Sadly, they were not loved equally. They grew into their true natures—and they both displayed magical gifts—using them in ways that suited their dispositions.

"The twins had children of their own eventually, creating generations of offspring with natural magic in their blood, but also great goodness or greed. Most people with magic knew they were the progeny of one line or the other. Those from the malevolent line fed only the appetites that suited them and left destruction in their wakes. People with no magic grew so fearful of anyone with it—helpful or hurtful—they banded together throughout the realm to rid the kingdoms of any possibility of evil—even the slimmest threat."

Rye jumped in. "The book says they're just waiting for a chance to rise up and rule us all. And Sir Rollins said that if it happens we will all fight to survive—that no king could save us. That we'd have to fend for ourselves."

Xavi groaned. "That book and Sir Rollins are wrong. The history we have from *reliable* sources, Rye, tells us that sadly, long ago, these people's numbers were unfairly decimated."

"But we *are* purged of them, right?" Rye said.

"You have nothing to fear, Rye." Xavi gave his brother's knee a pat.

"I never said I was afraid." Rye wiped off his knee. "I'm just glad the witches are banished. Now we just have to make sure they never come back."

FEE STOOD IN THE CAVE, HER HANDS ON HER TINY hips. This game of make-believe was not going very well, but she wasn't ready to give up. "You are cured. Now get up, Husband, and fetch me some flowers for our dinner table." The fixed and determined look she gave Rye, whose ten-year-old mouth frowned with unwillingness, was clearly not enough to move him from where he lay, contentedly snoozing in the back of the cave on an old straw pallet.

She thrust out her chin, directing it toward Xavi, deciding to involve him in her playact as well. "Tell him, Sultan. Tell him he must do as his wife instructs or he'll be riddled with pockmarks from the witch's spell I shall cast."

Xavi, sitting at the mouth of the cave and leaning against the wall, glanced up from the heavy book perched atop his knees. He chortled quietly, fingering the amulet around his neck as he allowed his gaze to fall back to the inky words. "I command you do as your wife demands, you ignoble peasant. I, for one, would never cross a near-eight-year-old conjurer with such wrathful skills." He looked up to wink at Fee, who still frowned.

"See?" Fee poked the pallet with a collection of dried reeds and grasses she'd bound together as a makeshift broom. One small vine snaked out from the end of the sweeper and curled around Rye's bony wrist, giving him a tug.

Rye cracked open an eyelid, allowing Fee to see the jade-colored iris beneath it. It hinted at further malcontent, and then irritation when he saw the vine. He ripped it off and frowned as Fee prodded at the pallet with her grass-stained, slippered foot.

She continued with her complaint, pointing to Xavi. "Even the great Sultan of . . . of Shadowdale has summoned you to rise."

"Why must you encourage her, Xavi?" Rye growled, closing the eye and turning his face toward the wall.

"You must address him as 'Your Greatness,' Husband. Remember, he has the power to have you beheaded if you ignore his words."

Rye snorted, but didn't move. "I'd like to see him try. Go ahead, oh Great One. Bring me to the block. At least I'll be free from the wretched nagging of my *wife*. And don't forget"—he held up a finger—"we burn witches to the very core of their bestial bones in this realm."

Fee folded her skinny arms across her chest and blew out a heated puff of air. She leaned down and put her small face close to Rye's. "You will live to regret this, Husband. I am off to prepare my spell."

"I am not your husband yet, Ophelia. But I'm filled to the brim with misery for the future."

Xavi chuckled again, but did not look up. "That's not what you said last night, brother, when you told me she smelled like all your favorite foods put together."

"Shut up, Xavi," Rye said gruffly. "I was just pointing out that she needed a bath."

Fee narrowed her eyes at the boy on the pallet, the muscles in her little fists growing rigid as she squeezed them. "Rye!"

His response was muffled chortling.

Her thin shoulders slumped and she turned to one wall of the cave, running a narrow finger along it. The lichen effortlessly fell away to reveal a vein of coppery brilliance. "Have you ever seen the kingdom's core stone, Xavi?"

She glanced over to see him shake his head, but not look up. "No, Fee, and I don't think anyone I know has."

"The core stones are an apocryphal story, Ophelia. There are no magic rocks in these old caves. That's just a legend," Rye said sleepily.

"Is that true, Xavi? Is it all pretend?"

Xavi searched the ceiling for an answer. "Well, I suppose some people still have faith in it. It is a rather romantic notion believing that long ago the realm of Aethusa was split into four powerful kingdoms because one precious gemstone was found in each land."

"Not just precious gemstones, Xavi, *magical*," Fee interjected.

One corner of his mouth turned up. "I think the only magic they provided was aiding the growth of strong and productive kingdoms. Via their wealth, and the wealth of the people who uncovered gems by mining their own lands."

"*I* still think they're magical. That's what one of Savva's books in the stillroom says. And it also says that since the beginning of each kingdom, each stone was granted to only one person. That person was the protector of the stone. Who has ours?"

Xavi shook his head and smiled at her. "Be careful what you read in Savva's stillroom, Fee. Many of her books are fusty and old-fangled. And I've no idea who—if there is such a person—is the protector of Fireli's core stone. Or any kingdom's stone, for that matter." He sighed and bent his head to his book. "It might be as Rye says—that it's all part of Aethusa folklore."

Fee studied the pearly white opals that edged Xavi's tunic—a tribute to Fireli's core stone. "Well, you sure do seem to wear a lot of fairy-tale costumes then. Just like the king's and queen's. Maybe one of *you* two are the protector. Maybe you're wearing the core stone right now—and don't even know it!"

Rye grumbled from the back wall. "Each province displays fake core stones everywhere you look."

"Why aren't ours red? Like the name of our kingdom? Don't these caves make fire-colored opals, Xavi?"

"If they do, I've not seen any yet."

Fee closed her eyes, lost in wistfulness. "I bet our core stone is fiery red."

Rye tsked. "They're just emblems of each territory. Like flags or mottos. It's silly advertising, Ophelia. That's it. Period."

Fee frowned. She wasn't at all in the mood for Rye's grumpy pessimism. She walked to the mouth of the cave to peer out beyond where their horses plucked sweet clusters of clover out of the ground. "Do you hear that?" she asked the boys. She scanned the horizon of lush green meadows and long-grassed salt marshes, her eyes following the flight of a disturbed flock of squawking fowl. They settled on an approaching line of horses.

"Someone's coming, Xavi. A lot of someones." She faced him with an inquisitive air.

He turned from his book with a cursory glance, but then stopped when he caught sight of what she'd announced. He dropped the pendant to his chest and put the book aside. "Soldiers. We must be wanted. Have I forgotten something today, Rye? Are we supposed to be somewhere? Sir Rollins is going to kill me if I've neglected a duty."

Rye mumbled sullenly from his still position, "You are always supposed to be somewhere, Xavi. And rarely anywhere fun."

"This has been fun," Fee chirped. "Except for the part when Rye refused to play any longer." She dropped to sit in front of Xavi, her small skirt billowing like a parachute around her legs as she settled. Beneath it she wore a pair of boy's breeches—her preferred mode of dress, as they kept her legs from getting skinned as she shimmied up trees and slid down ravines. But there were rules in place regarding proper attire, so she'd stumbled upon this work-around.

Xavi flashed her a warm smile and tussled the ebony-colored hair that fell all about her deeply freckled face. "Breathing the same air as you, Fee, is a guarantee that fun is in abundance."

A balloon of pride rose in Fee's chest, and her left wrist tingled with warmth. She looked down at her strange birthmark and kneaded it with her other hand.

"I'm very good at making fun happen," she giggled.

Xavi winked. "You're very good at many things, Fee."

She gave him a smile that she hoped would reveal the newly lost tooth she'd forgotten to tell him about.

Xavi stood—a little tiredly—and tucked his book inside his leather satchel. He brushed the remnants of the earthen floor from his riding breeches and tugged his leather tunic into place. "Best we move to meet them, Rye. It looks as if they're in a hurry."

They gathered their few belongings and unrolled the entrance-hiding, moss-covered mat that Fee made each time the three of them came to the old stone cave. It was their special place, and theirs alone. All three of them sought to keep it that way.

Securing their pouches onto their horse, Rye bent his already tall frame and made a foothold low enough for Fee to use.

"No, thank you," she said, her features vexed with reproach. "I shall do it myself." She scrambled to grab hold of the horn at the front of the saddle, struggling to pull her small body up the side of the giant animal.

Rye looked up to Xavi, who had already mounted, and saw him shake his head. The quiet warning did not stop Rye from rolling his eyes and sighing.

"Stop your big puffy breathing, Rye. I can do this by myself." She grunted with one last surge of effort and hauled her leg over the saddle. Smiling triumphantly, she felt the flushing warmth spread from the point of her birthmark. She looked down her slight nose at Rye, her eyes crinkling with merriment, fixing her lips into a tiny purse. "Need help?"

Rye catapulted himself into the saddle behind Fee and leaned around her to grab the reins. "No," he responded in clipped tones, and clicked the horse to follow Xavi's.

They hadn't galloped toward the onrush of soldiers for more

than a swift minute before the men were upon them. Xavi pulled up short, and the soldiers made a hasty half circle around the three children.

A man in a sleek gray pearled uniform saluted Xavi. "Your Highness . . . you're to come with us . . . at once." His speech was labored, and although he tried to project authority, it was clearly undercut by tremendous unease.

Xavi took a slow breath and held it, the air inflating his chest. "What has happened, Captain Whittard?"

A shadow fell over the man's features. "Illness has befallen the kingdom, milord—it's racing throughout the castle. People are dropping dead from disease as we speak. We are to take you to Savva's stillroom immediately. She's prepared a remedy."

Fee watched Xavi swallow discreetly. He raised his head to meet the level gaze of the soldier, a tall order for a not yet twelve-year-old boy. "And my parents?"

The soldier needn't have answered, for grief spread across his face. "Their Majesties, too, have been afflicted, and are now hastily making preparations for you and your brother. Miss Ophelia's parents are also ill. Fast measures are being taken for the rest of the children in the castle. I'm afraid—"

"We must go to them at once," Xavi interrupted.

"No, milord! We cannot. We've been given orders to protect you at all costs. You must follow us directly. I'm sorry."

"Sorry?" Xavi questioned him.

The soldier bowed his head to stare at the coppery dust of the road. "I fear it is already too late. And you are not to be exposed. God save the king and queen."

A thread of alarm whirled through Fee's body. She wanted to see her parents—and those of Xavi and Rye. "I shall help Savva. I shall help in preparing the cures. And I *will* save the king and queen."

Rye took hold of Fee's elbow. "Ophelia. There is nothing you could possibly do."

Fee twisted to look up into Rye's face and saw his features reflecting his lack of faith. She narrowed her eyes. "I can get there faster without you weighing us down." She spun around and dug her heels into the horse's side. The horse reared and rocketed forward, catching Rye off guard, and he slid off the back of the animal.

She flew past the soldiers and tore through the fields toward her parents and the king and queen. *At this rate,* she told herself, *I shall get there before God, and there will be no need of Him to save anyone.*

CHAPTER

FIVE

THE HORSES WERE CLUSTERED IN THE COURTYARD, the last of the carriages rushing off in the distance, disappearing in a golden film of sunshine-dappled dust. They carried the final few children away from Fireli, and all who remained were Xavi, Rye, and Fee. The two brothers had said their sober farewells—the last twenty-four hours showing the great, cracking strain each boy was feeling over losing his parents and, now, one another. Rye was being forced to leave—to follow the exodus of Fireli's youth—insurance that once the epidemic had passed, there would still be young men and women to replenish the kingdom, and a monarch in reserve should they need it.

Xavi had tried to give Rye the talisman from around his neck, as a means of remembrance, but Savva had stopped him.

"No." She'd put up a hand in warning. "The bulla is not the

ideal gift. Perhaps instead . . . a pen. For your letters."

The guards were mounting their horses, preparing to lead Rye to one of the three other kingdoms, to a land empty of familiar rituals, friendships, and memories.

Fee looked at him with reddened eyes. "Savva says ten years will pass quickly, Rye," she said, trying to show her bravery. She handed him three small flowers—forget-me-nots—and then tucked a thin glass vial that had been wrapped with a paper note and ribbon into his tunic pocket.

He turned toward his horse, put a foot in the stirrup, and then pulled it out again. He walked back to Fee and said in a quiet voice, "You do *not* smell like all my favorite foods, Ophelia. . . . You smell like lilacs."

He mounted his horse and was off, surrounded by guards. They were soon swallowed in the late-evening light, and the last thing Fee remembered seeing was the shine of his coppery, burnished hair glinting through a shaft of sunlight.

"Up! Up into the loft and be still!" Savva hissed, pushing at Fee to move faster on the ladder.

"Savva?" came the wavering voice again through the thick-planked stillroom door. "I have spilled my medicine and need more. Are you there?"

"One moment," Savva called out before putting up a finger to remind Fee to be silent.

Fee unrolled to lie flat upon her mattress and listened with quiet curiosity as the healer opened the door for her patient in the stillroom below.

"Oh," Savva said in a low voice of surprise. "I thought you were—"

"Yes, I know."

Fee noticed the voice had changed—it was not at all like the shaking tones of the elderly who usually came to visit.

"I thought it best to look and act like one of them so I'd not draw attention."

Fee's ears pricked and she slid off her bed and slithered along the floorboards to peek through a small crack by the ladder. It had been a full year since she'd heard anyone whose voice did not quiver with age, apart from Xavi's.

"How is she?" the woman asked, drawing back the heavy hood of her cloak. She uncurled herself from the round-backed posture she'd adopted, and stood surprisingly tall and willowy thin.

Savva glanced upward toward the loft, an eye trained on the fissure Fee peered through. "We are managing. She is stubborn, but still grieving."

The young woman nodded. "Is it working?"

"When she takes it. As long as she takes it."

"And the prince?"

Savva shook her head. "He will soon be thirteen. Nothing shows signs of working thus far, but remember, it is Fee who is mixing his curatives. There is much for her to learn and so much I cannot teach her."

"Has anyone seen her? Does she adhere to the rules?" the woman leaned in to ask quietly. Her voice was mellifluous, like the wind rustling through the delicate meadow reeds.

Savva released a long sigh. "She sees only Xavi. But fights me daily on this ruling." Savva raised her voice to a level unmistakably meant for Fee to hear. "She has been told repeatedly that because she was especially affected by the plague, she could easily reinfect the weakened souls that have survived, and if seen by anyone but me or Xavi, the result would be an immediate removal from the only home she's known and her best friend. I do not think she will gamble with such a loss."

The woman put a hand over Savva's. "We are thinking of you both. We are thinking of you all. Every one of us would give anything to help . . . if it were possible." She pulled the hood to hide her face and opened the stillroom door. "Don't give up. There is still time."

Savva sank to the bench in the middle of the stillroom, bent her head over the table, and wept.

CHAPTER
SIX

FEE HADN'T TAKEN HER TONIC TODAY. SHE'D PRE-tended she did, but when Savva wasn't looking she'd poured it into the "waste" pot—the dented copper crock that held all their scraps and would be emptied outside at the end of the day, behind the old stillroom.

For nearly ten years she'd choked down that daily bitter dram. It clawed at her throat as she knocked back the vial. But it wasn't the taste that brought on the struggle. She knew the medicines she and Savva made in their stillroom had very little appeal. That wasn't the point. If you came to them, and you were ill, they would do their damnedest to heal you. Because that's who they were: the castle healers.

Correction. Savva was the castle healer. Fee was her invisible apprentice.

She hadn't taken the tonic because . . . because she knew what it felt like *not* to.

Everyone was supposed to. And every single day. It was one of their unbreakable rules. Three proclamations had been posted for the kingdom's constituents to follow. They were referred to as Fireli's Three Seclusion Rules:

1. You must never leave the castle grounds of Fireli, or the confines of your hamlet if you live outside the castle.
2. You must never use more than the barest of Fireli's meager resources.
3. You must always take your antidote.

So everyone did. Except Fee. Occasionally.

Sometimes she and Xavi would take theirs together—as somehow the phrase *misery loves company* would provide a measure of solace and solidarity—but he'd never miss the opportunity to tease her about it.

"Oh, for heaven's sake, Fee. Just swallow the damn thing and be done with it," he'd chuckled yesterday. "The face you make is one more reminiscent of a seven-year-old and not a seven*teen*-year-old."

She glared at him. "Why can't you cast out some supreme command that gives us permission to end the Seclusion Rules one month early?" she huffed.

"Because if incumbent kings wish to realize their new role as *acting* monarch, they best take the advice of the physician who explained what it will take to live to see that day." He rolled his eyes. "It's one more month, Fee. Then the epidemic will be over, and our kingdom can rejoin the other three. No more isolation. And no more antidotes. I plan to make sure I reach my twenty-second birthday so that I may do my duty and help restore Fireli. So do as I do and just take the damn tonic." He tugged on the long, dark braid that fell over her shoulder.

"Is that a command from my soon-to-be king?" She eyed him mockingly.

"No. It's a plea from your current best friend. I'd like for *you* to live to see my twenty-second birthday too, you goose."

When Fee looked at Xavi her heart grew heavy with doubt and worry—two intangible ingredients that somehow thickly brewed within her stomach whenever she stopped to assess his health. He was sick. And growing more so daily. His skin was pallid, his eyes drowsy with fatigue. And some days it seemed he barely had energy to walk from one end of the castle garden to the other.

She pulled herself from her stupor and turned to face Savva, watching her mentor's puckered lips frown familiarly as she stooped over the liquids she was measuring. Fee's unsuccessful efforts generated more work for Savva, and the resulting exasperation left her peevish and gruff. "Xavi's tonic is not working. And it doesn't make any sense. Surely he needs something stronger—he's marching straight toward death." Fee picked up a tiny seed between her fingers, eyed it up close, and watched as a delicate green shoot snaked its way through a small split in its seams. Savva turned toward her and Fee quickly pinched the seed to stop its growth, pulling her hand behind her back.

Her weathered face sported one raised, hair-prickling brow as Savva rasped out, "The prince is not dying because he is ill. The prince is dying because of *you*."

Fee's lungs were struck with a paralyzing angst, but after a reflective pause, she narrowed her eyes and broke through the vise binding them.

"Explain to me how?" she insisted, biting through the words as if she had to tear each one apart from the last. "Do I not work at your side every day to find a remedy to his ailment?"

Savva said nothing.

"Have I not read through endless volumes of text to uncover some cure?"

The old healer stood steadfast.

"Am I not writing down every word you utter and committing them to memory?"

Savva glanced to the dented copper crock.

Fee felt her body tremble with willful defiance.

"*Everyone* must take their antidote, Fee. It will keep them safe from reinfection."

"Skipping my medicine a day here or there has no effect on Xavi," she said through clenched teeth.

Savva met her gaze and Fee felt the heat of it. "If you do not take your tonic, it will kill him."

"How?" Fee demanded.

"Keep a rein on your temper, Fee." Savva pointed to the pot. "Empty it, clean your instruments, and then go to bed. I have put another dose on the ladder to the loft. Take it. Now, good night, Fee." Her words had started off brusque, but they'd ended tenderly. She always forgave Fee for her outbursts—and always cautioned her to be more even-keeled.

But her ire was often impossible to withhold. From the moment Fee had been assigned to study with the healer—to prepare for the time when she would take the old medicine woman's place—Savva doled out as much criticism of Fee's work as diagnoses to her patients. And the words stayed with her, as heavy as a woolen cloak she could not shake off, burdensome and considerable.

CHAPTER

SEVEN

"YOU MUST REPLACE THE DEVIL'S DUNG, CHILD, AS that which is currently in this jar has grown stale and ineffective." Savva's quivering hands replaced the cork that stoppered the large glass jar holding what Fee had labeled *asafetida*. And even though Fee had swapped the common-name labels years ago for their proper Latin terms, Savva refused to refer to the herbs and roots by anything other than what suited her most—archaic recipe names that she prescribed as cures to the grief-stricken survivors of the kingdom's epidemic.

"You must find roots no thicker than a man's thumb. Since it takes several months to draw every drop of milky juice from each plant, we must prepare now. But the resulting gum-resin will serve us well come winter."

Fee sighed and jotted a reminder in the notebook beside her.

"Have you heard me, child?" Savva questioned, raising her

tremulous voice, which struggled for clarity a little more each day.

"Um-hm," Fee answered, her eyes darting back and forth, dividing her attention between two of three open books on the table in front of her.

"And Jesuits' bark. The stores are growing thin on that shelf too. You must find me the longest quills. Not like the last batch you brought back with the mottled grey patches. They must be fibrous and splintery with no adhering lichens, do you understand?" Savva rapped her gnarled knuckles on the smooth, thick block of wood that served as their preparation table and that stood between the old healer and Fee—a physical representation of the years of contrast in life and weathering.

Fee quickly made another memo beside the first entry in her notebook.

Cinchona

She returned to her studies and had not even gotten through the first line of text when she heard Savva sigh as she came around the blending table to stand at her shoulder. Fee raised her head. She took a deep breath in and stared straight across the stillroom at the door, her gaze so full of sharp vexation it could likely bore a hole through the ancient, scarred wood.

"Yes?" Fee said.

Savva's knotted finger pointed to the book beneath Fee. "I would not trust half of the entries in that compendium. The elder Uledrin's *Flora Homeopathica* is much more thorough than his son's. He speaks not only of the plant's healing properties, but of its true potential energy. Study his instead."

Fee swiveled to stare at the woman. She had been focusing on this face for over a dozen years. Enough time to know every crease and pleat in her skin. Every bump and ridge that protruded from the planes of sharp bone. The sprouting hairs on her chin and the darkening moles on her cheek. All familiar and as predictable as the one expression that appeared repeatedly. Like the spring rains, or the call of the whippoorwill that began without fail at sundown. The old woman's features were molded into one single visage from morning through midnight.

Anxiety.

Occasionally, Fee saw something beneath it as well. Hidden behind Savva's cloudy eyes was a note of sorrow. Clearly Fee wasn't what Savva wanted her to be. But *what* she wanted Fee to be was ambiguous. Apart from one thing: obedient.

Fee shut the inferior book and put it aside, which must have suited Savva, for she wandered back to the shelves to inspect the powders, tinctures, and balms. Nearly everything that lined the shelves of the stillroom had been prepared by Fee. All the ointments, the infusions, the herbals and soaps. The tonics, the salves, the lotions and liniments. She'd readied them herself, hundreds of times, and all under the critical, diagnostic eyes of Savva—the old woman who had outlived most everyone in the kingdom.

She'd outlived the two most important people in Fee's life— her mother and father—and the two most important people in the lives of the kingdom's inhabitants: the king and queen, the parents of Prince Xavi and his younger brother, Prince Rye.

"You shall find Uledrin's reference book on the lowest shelf closest to the window, child. And again, *do not* forget your tonic." Savva shuffled toward the stillroom door.

Irritation bloomed throughout Fee's chest. *That's the last book I'll ever touch.* She stared at a small pot of ivy on the table in front of her. She nodded at the tiny tendrils, nudging them to reach across the bench for the old woman, thinking for a heartless split second how much she wished to bind Savva's mouth. To keep Savva from reminding her about the tonic again by just wrapping the greenery around her like some vined botanical muzzle.

But then she quickly pulled the tendrils back, appalled at herself.

Savva raised a finger and glanced back. "I shall return before dinner to resume my inventory. Until then, make haste with your studies, and do not open the door for *anyone*.

"Remember, knowledge is power, Fee. There is so much for you to learn, and one day I pray you will learn it as you should."

Had Savva just called her . . . unteachable?

Fee refused to meet the gaze of her mentor, determined to steep in her sour mood.

The door shut with a quiet click, and Fee turned to face the wall lined with books and manuals.

Another afternoon filled with memorizing dead people's receipts for curing infection and affliction. It was enough to make her wish for an illness herself so that she might lie down and close her eyes to the soporific words for eternity. There was something so exhausting in reading about cures rather than creating them.

But perhaps somewhere in the dusty pile of papers lay the answer to unlock Xavi's problem and free him from disease. For how in the world was their new king going to restore the health of the kingdom if that very kingdom was hell-bent on making sure he never had the chance to try?

CHAPTER
EIGHT

FEE GAZED OUT THE FASTENED WINDOW SHE'D SPENT
ten years often wishing to be on the other side of. The honeyed
glow of the afternoon spread like a liquid blanket of bullion,
warming the room with soft ribbons of light. Reasonably,
she could venture out to hunt down the herbs on Savva's list.
There'd be no sound cause for criticism if Fee set her studies
aside to accomplish a task she'd been assigned. Perhaps she could
spend a few minutes perched in her favorite tree, listening to the
sweet notes of birdsong—a deep contrast to the raspy tones of
Savva's reprimands.

She chewed on one of her knuckles and stared at the glowing
emerald grass basking in the sunlight beyond the window. Just one
hour outside, to give her mind a rest.

A soft rap on the door startled her mid-yawn, but she stayed silent and did not move.

"Fee?" came Xavi's voice.

Her muscles loosened. "Yes?" she called out softly.

"Good God, Fee, are you still in here? I was hoping to find that you'd finished for the afternoon and were on your way to see me." Xavi stuck his fair-haired head around the door and peered into the room. "I see my optimism is for naught."

Despite her weariness, Fee felt the corners of her mouth lift. "Xavi," she breathed out, the tension in her shoulders releasing for the first time in the last six hours.

"Time to leave the tomb, sweet Fee." He stepped in, looked about, and batted a hand around in front of him. "I admire your determined commitment to study, but the air in here is stifling. I'm surprised you've enough oxygen to make it from one breath to the next. And I'm guessing the irritable quibbler is using twice as much as you if she's casting out one criticism after another as she is wont to do. Sucking in large lungfuls of air only to spit out a string of reproving words." He half smiled. It brightened his weary eyes.

Fee sighed, and Xavi pointed at the table. "Not every answer can be discovered within the pages before you." He pulled back his shoulders. "Come on. I'm in need of a walk."

Fee glanced down at her books. "Savva—"

"As if Savva would defy her king."

"You aren't her king yet, Xavi."

He cast a hand in the air. "Close enough to count for now. Hurry up. I *command* it." He grinned and nodded his head toward the door.

Now she had no choice, Fee told herself. She'd been given orders from a higher authority. The fact that the higher authority was her best and only friend might be grounds for reproof from the medicine woman when she found out, but at this very moment, Fee was willing to risk the censure for an hour of treasured amusement.

"Yes, milord," she said with a slight bow. "Accompanying you on your daily constitutional would be my honor."

"Not to mention your duty," he added, holding the door wide for her.

Fee chortled, made a short detour to the shelf that had her tonic, quickly downed it, and then rushed out of the stillroom into the sunlight. Just stepping outside was like surfacing—breaking through the heavy weight of water and filling her lungs with restorative air. She sighed with contentment as the sun shone on her face, and then recognized the tiny buzzing energy that made her fingers tingle about the same time each afternoon. But within moments, she felt the tonic at work, smothering the sensation, a wet blanket over flame.

"What has she been on about today, then?" Xavi asked. "Have you not pulverized the herbs finely enough? Not squeezed enough oil from an oil-less root? She's not been encouraging you to recite any uh . . . curious incantations?" he said a little uncomfortably.

Fee snorted and rolled her eyes at him. "Yes, yes, and no. There's no incantation in this stillroom, or anywhere the patients are—you know that. Savva is nothing but a simple healer."

Xavi tried to hold in his own snort. "Simple*minded* I might believe." He stopped and turned to face Fee. "Do you know that just yesterday she asked me if I was at least *comfortable, stuck as I was*?"

"Xavi, we're both terribly worried that you're not recovering."

"I'm not *ill*," he said, brushing off her concern. "Just tired. I'm tired like everyone else."

"Your level of fatigue surpasses the rest of us. And there are some days when you are near collapse."

"I am grateful to be alive," he said with a calm smile.

Fee glared at him with fierce determination. "No. Clearly you're under enormous stress—your marriage next month, your birthday, and most important, your coronation." She bent down to snap off a stalk of lavender. She ran her fingertip over the unopened buds; they pushed their tiny purple petals free at her touch. She handed the stalk to Xavi, who'd suddenly drooped to sit on the garden bench beneath them. "Squish it all between your fingers. The scent will help wi—"

"Fee," he said, looking up at her. "I know you find your unusual talent entertaining, but—" He swallowed and closed his eyes, taking a moment to regain his strength. "But you must refrain from doing it in front of anyone—especially when they return. There is still a great deal of ignorance and fear when people think of . . ."

"I'm not like one of *them*, and you know it, Xavi," Fee said, her fists curling inward.

"They say it's been a hundred years since sorcery was erased from the realm. I can't imagine what it must have been like. So many hunted down for the great slaughter." He caught her eye. "Be careful, Fee."

She thought about the countless hours of grinding herbs and pounding seeds, or standing over the hot copper pots as they belched out steam, distilling Savva's ancient recipes into tonics for the ill. And she thought about how occasionally she had the energy to cheat and use her *unusual talent*, as Xavi had put it, to hurry up the process by quickly growing or sprouting her ingredients. She loved her work—despite Savva's unhappiness with her. And she *was* careful. *Very* careful. Especially around Savva. Fee was determined to keep her shortcuts to herself, as in the past—especially as a young child— Savva had been swift to come down hard on her.

"I can't imagine they were all horrible." He nudged Fee with his elbow.

"Who?" Fee asked, looking at him.

"The witches. Yet the statutes still exist. Magic is still banned within the realm."

Fee's mind conjured up an image of black-cloaked wizards and warty-chinned women who twirled about, warbling in front of bonfires. If such people did exist, they did no more in Fireli, where guileless people shuffled about, all of them barely living—as if they were place markers in a world put on hold.

She looked down at the ground, refusing to meet his eyes. "I do not practice magic."

Xavi tapped the lavender stalk in her hand until she looked up. His eyes held a plea.

"Your Royal Highness!" a shout came from over the hidden garden wall.

Fee leapt up onto the bench and vaulted into the tree branches above them, scurrying high enough not to be seen. A breathless, elderly man limped through the bricked archway.

"Sir Rollins demands you meet with him this instant!"

"Why?" Xavi said, not hiding his irritation.

The old man bent over, his hands on his knees, panting. "He did not say, Your Highness. He never does."

Xavi stood and patted the man on the shoulder. "I'm sorry

you've expended so much energy on his behalf. You have my permission to walk back *slowly*. Get a drink, take a nap if you want, and then report to Sir Rollins that I will get there when I *get* there."

The man chuckled uncomfortably, and gave Xavi a worrisome glance before hobbling back toward the castle.

Xavi looked up. "It's safe. He's gone. You can come down."

Fee caught the dark-cloaked form of Savva beyond another one of the crumbling garden walls and replied, "No. Go to Sir Rollins—and be quick about it." She made a subtle nod toward the old healer. "If you are less than fifteen minutes, you'll find me up in the ancient withering oak tree across from the lavender garden. I'll be the one trying to be mistaken for a leaf."

"And if I am not?" Xavi asked, sighing with resignation.

"Then eventually you will find me where you always find me."

Xavi raised a brow in question.

Fee smirked and said, "Under Savva's thumb."

CHAPTER
NINE

"SORRY I COULDN'T RETURN YESTERDAY, BUT I BELIEVE you are well acquainted with Sir Rollins's farcical urgency." Xavi bit into an apple Fee had handed him, then took her by the elbow and directed her down a neglected path.

"I hope it wasn't something serious, Xavi."

He shrugged. "There are an endless number of problems and a shocking absence of answers." He swept aside a few fallen flower stalks as they wound their way throughout the unkempt castle gardens. "Like why can't I find anyone capable of taming these unruly grounds?" He reached out to run his hands through the feather-veined fronds of a willow tree's branches. "No one compares to the fellow we had when I first started playing out here. Do you remember him?"

Fee cocked her head in thought.

"No, of course you wouldn't. You weren't alive then. But he was marvelous. A most prized gardener. Jet-black hair, a smile as warm as the sun, and always time to play a game with me. I think his name was Azamar."

"Did he die in the epidemic?"

"Disappeared long before it. I was rather too young to remember—only four or so—but I wish to God we had him back." He nudged a large stone into alignment with its border. "In truth, the gardens are the least of my worries."

She met his eyes, and saw that twenty-one years of preparation for service to this kingdom had permanently etched lines onto his winsome face and deepened the half-moon shadows beneath his dove-grey eyes. "Why? What is it?"

"The ministry meeting did not go well."

"Define well," Fee said, stopping to snip a few twigs of lemon balm and chamomile for Savva's afternoon tea—she needed a peace offering for her surly mood, and these herbs felt particularly fresh beneath Fee's fingertips, giving off a tingling vibration of intense potency.

Xavi sneezed and absentmindedly rubbed the tip of his nose with his sleeve. "By *well* I mean it did not go as Sir Rollins wanted. The council should be moving toward a consensus regarding mining—do we reopen or keep the caves sealed? But with each gathering the sides widen to an unbridgeable gulf."

"Have *you* come to a decision, Xavi? After all, you will have the final word." Fee pocketed the herbs within the pouch of her apron. It was a difficult topic—the mining. They'd been told it was the cause of the great disease that swept through Fireli. A maelstrom of wind was said to have carried a devastating contagion from within the caves across the kingdom. It killed more than half the population, leaving the kingdom's workforce decimated and most children wretchedly orphaned and quickly sent away. Rye had been sent with them. The mines were sealed by the government and the people told it would be ten years before the abhorrent plague would no longer be a threat.

Xavi shook his head and pulled at the old amulet strung around his neck. "We must have something to contribute to the realm's three other kingdoms. We have survived until now on their aid and our own meager crops. Those kingdoms are expecting we will replenish their dwindling reserves.

"Sir Rollins insists the caves must be mined or we will face wrath from all other quarters of the realm. Our metals are desperately needed, and our neighbors are growing more impatient with the vexing delay." He blew out a lungful of air that spoke of near defeat. "I am afraid, Fee. I still cannot decide. Sir Rollins insists we are free from danger."

Fee squished down the sliver of distaste at the mention of the regent's name. The man who had been hastily appointed by the king and queen on their deathbeds—who, for the last ten years, had made all the decisions for the kingdom until Xavi came of age. "Don't let him push you, Xavi," Fee counseled. "Remember, it is ultimately your decision, not Sir Rollins's."

His brows rose, and his sideways glance was unconvinced.

"What about Rye?" she asked. "Have you sought his opinion?"

"His weekly letter is late." Xavi chuckled. It was a soft sound of disbelief. "Can it really be that we three will finally reunite? I cannot picture what he must look like after nearly ten years."

Fee met his eyes briefly.

"Forgive me, Fee. It must be even more disconcerting for you. I imagine you have countless worries where Rye is concerned. Most people do not have their spouses chosen for them at birth."

"You did."

"Future kings and queens are always paired then, but their siblings have never been bound. I understand our parents' logic—that the three of us remain fixed together—but I think their decision might have been made during a night of too much wine and too little oversight. In fact, I swear I remember overhearing a conversation where Rye announced to our parents that he intended to marry you. He couldn't have been more than eight or nine, and he hated being teased about it. It might have all been done in fun."

"Are you suggesting they might have unbound us had they lived to see us now?" Fee looked toward the far-off undulating hills that marked Fireli's borders with Gwyndom, the kingdom where Rye now lived.

"Perhaps," he said, and then quickly went on. "Don't worry, Fee. I'm sure Rye is no longer uncooperative and ill-natured. God knows *we've* certainly changed." Xavi's eyes could not hide the sadness that leaked through into his words.

"I remember having such hope for this kingdom—back when I was a naïve boy with whimsical notions. I thought I'd be a visionary and sagacious king, but . . ." He rubbed at his bloodshot, red-rimmed eyes. "Well, we were lucky to have escaped the epidemic."

Fee bit her lip. "Despite what you told me when I was little, I still hear people blaming all our misfortunes, including their own personal aches and illness, on their belief that someone stole our kingdom's core stone."

He puffed. "I highly doubt any rock is going to make one whit of difference."

Fee smiled wistfully, tapping on the engraved gold disc that sat in the hollow of Xavi's throat. "What about this one? Is your talisman fresh out of luck these days?"

He stiffened. "I used to feel so certain that someone was looking out for me—guiding my hand if I was unsteady. Savva gave this to me ages ago—probably just a placebo to make me feel better. She calls it a bulla." He toyed with it absentmindedly. "Can good-luck charms be drained of their bounty? Lately, I've just been feeling more uncomfortable in my own skin. Like it doesn't belong to me anymore—does that sound crazy?"

"I think you're nervous of the new person you're about to become. Surely that can cause such discomfort."

"No. It's more than discomfort. It's self-control. Willpower maybe?" he said uncertainly. "I sometimes feel like my decisions are not necessarily *my* decisions."

Fee bumped her shoulder against his. "It definitely sounds like Sir Rollins is getting into your head. Just like Savva gets under my skin. She is so rigidly controlling."

"Wait." He raised a hand. "It's time I put a stop to this. We have had great fun at Savva's expense, but she is not to blame. She may push you, but I believe it is because she sees tremendous potential in you."

Fee's gaze fell to the ground as if the soil acted like a magnet. "Perhaps," she said grudgingly, and fell onto a rickety garden bench. "But I couldn't save our parents. I believed I could. I was too confident—too brash. I deserve every moment of Savva's disapproval."

Xavi looked at her solemnly. "Fee. She cares for you. Deeply. I can see that even if you cannot."

"I've done my best to be who she wishes—and not let who I really am leak out."

"You cannot hide who you are," he said, sitting down beside her. He drew her chin to face him, scanned her features from brow bone to jaw, turning it slightly as he inspected. "And thank God you also lack her appearance."

Fee swatted his hand away, and he broke into laughter. "Except, of course, when you don your disguise." He scratched his head and sat back. "I've nearly forgotten how atrociously frightening it is to see that face appear at my door. It's probably time, don't you think?"

She stifled a laugh herself, recalling the myriad evenings she'd dressed as Savva to escape the stillroom and make her way around the castle, always to visit Xavi. No one bothered the old healer—she was given free rein of travel. Although she was the castle physic, her character cowed most people into giving her a wide berth. It was years ago when Fee and Xavi had realized that by creating the perfect costume, Fee could enjoy that same freedom, if they were careful.

Xavi spanked his knees and stood. "It's decided then. Find it. Slap it on. And then make your way to my study after dinner. Just for old times' sake, Fee. Before everything changes."

He left Fee sitting on the bench, asking herself if it was truly feasible to find a shred of the person she used to be—that plucky, unburdened girl who believed anything was possible.

The girl who believed in herself.

CHAPTER
TEN

FEE TRACED THE DELICATE EMBLEM THAT SWIRLED IN an infinite loop on the translucent skin at the inside of her wrist. She neglected the open books in front of her, choosing to focus on the strange marking that had appeared at her birth.

It used to flush with heat—at strange, unpredictable times—but at some point in the past, it suddenly stopped. It could not have been long after the plague had swept through the castle. It just grew quiet, no longer glowing with crimson color when triggered.

She'd asked Savva about it dozens of times, but the healer brought no relief for her bewilderment. She was certain Savva's thoughts had been written down in *The Book of Denizens*, though.

The Book was a healer's most guarded annals of health. A book Fee had no permission to access. Yet.

Each kingdom possessed one—an account where one page was dedicated to each citizen. Inscribed upon that page were the most important details about that person, recorded by the kingdom's healer and utilized by only the monarchs should there arise a situation where they needed to interact with the individual and where understanding their subject's full nature might help with negotiations, settling disputes, or general guidance if asked for advisement. It was a well-shielded book and never to be placed in the hands of anyone save the monarch or the healer who wrote in it.

"You wouldn't believe some of the peculiarities I've read about in *The Book*, Fee," Xavi had told her years ago. "Good lord, I'd no idea the number of ailments with which people suffer."

But Fee would believe it. And although she might not know exactly what it was each patient who came to see Savva endured, Savva had taught her from a very early age how to read the signs.

"Body language can be much more revealing than speech. One must see all the signals communicated. A patient may come in to report one thing, but the body broadcasts something else entirely."

Fee could read the body, but oh, how she burned to see inside that book. Just one tiny peek behind the thick leather bindings bejeweled with opals. Surely it held insight as to Fee's quirky gift and an explanation as to why her birthmark had gone silent and dark.

For now, she could only treat the ailments of others by secretly making their curatives. Whatever their need, Fee came to their aid.

I itch. This burns. Do you have anything for inflammation and rash? they would ask Savva.

Yes. Fee made treatments for them all. She could help ease their redness, their rawness, their irritants and stings. She could make it all go away. But she had nothing to make an absent part of her *come back*.

She dug a fingernail into the sensitive flesh at her wrist and then scraped it across the birthmark. Only she'd grazed herself a little too hard and tiny spots of blood appeared within the path of the abrasion. Fee hissed with a sharp intake of breath and looked up from the anti-itch compound she was researching to see Savva staring appraisingly, her tiny black eyes like those of a small, curious bird.

Fee winced and rubbed at the scratch she'd created.

"Do you really miss it, child? Is an agitative birthmark necessary to affirm what you should already know?"

"You are forever chastising me for what I don't already know," Fee said caustically.

The old woman's features grew pained. "I only remind you that time is of the essence." She pointed toward the bookshelf, and likely, Fee thought—although she refused to look—directly at her dusty, prized reference volume. Savva stood, took one of the gas lanterns lighting the textbooks in front of them, and scuffled toward the door.

When Fee was convinced Savva had left, she unrolled herself to lie flat upon the bench. She stared up at the flickering, uncertain light the remaining gas lamps cast upon the thatched roof ceiling and said, "Even with infinite minutes, I will never be good enough . . . for you."

Fee pushed the mole a smidge higher on her cheekbone and readjusted the bulbous nose that needed to sit crookedly upon her face. If she were stopped by a guard, he might ask that she remove the hood of her cloak to identify herself—more out of the elderly's fear of the unknown than as protocol. As easy as it had been to whip up the mask that was the old healer disguise—a costume Fee had perfected during the last five or six years—she'd never been foolishly risky, for Savva had repeatedly made clear the consequences of anyone discovering Fee existed: banishment from Fireli.

She moved through the subterranean passages beneath the castle's great footprint with muted, nimble steps, double-quick when alone in the dimly torchlit hallways, but punctiliously whenever passing someone so that her gait reflected Savva's physical limitations.

When she reached Xavi's private suite of rooms, Sir Rollins was pulling the door closed behind him. The ashen-faced man, whose expression had long been permanently pressed into that of high anxiety, swallowed at seeing Fee. He caught her by the arm with a somewhat shaky hand and pulled her aside from the sentry who stood at the entrance to Xavi's rooms.

"I trust there are no issues, Mistress Savva—nothing you feel compelled to communicate to the prince that is . . . out of the ordinary?" He eyed Fee with a wary, timorous gaze.

Fee slowly shook her head, but kept her eyes focused on the floor, careful not to allow her expression of bewilderment to be seen.

"Excellent. As we are nearing the end of the quarantine, remember that Prince Xavi needs to be guided *appropriately*. Good night." He dashed down the hall and left Fee in a thoroughly puzzled state, but she wasn't gifted time to consider the exchange, as the sentry opened the cumbersome wooden door to allow her through.

Xavi looked up from a vast mahogany table, polished to a thick sheen but mostly covered in papers and strewn with books. He pressed his lips inward, assessing the scene in front of him.

Fee stood motionless.

He rose slowly, his eyes narrowing. "Mistress Savva, you have news for me this evening?"

The door closed behind her. Fee broke out in a wide grin and pulled off the hood of her cloak. She unbuttoned it and tossed it onto the back of a deep leather chair.

Xavi rubbed at his eyes and sat back down. "You really are an atrociously frightful, but convincing, old quack."

She made a small snort and pulled off the artificial nose and wig, being careful not to damage either as she placed them in an empty spot upon the table. She poured herself a cup of tea from the service in front of him. Although not radiating heat, the liquid was still warm enough that Fee could make out the oscillating scents of spearmint and ginseng—lively, bright, and deeply earthy.

There was a tap at the door. Fee dashed behind a curtain as Xavi announced, "Come in."

Peeking from between the folds, Fee watched an elderly woman bring in a few logs of wood, letting them fall from her arms onto the grate.

"No need for a fire tonight, Mistress Kemble."

"Shall I tidy before you retire, or turn down your bed, milord?"

Fee heard Xavi chuckle. "I'm quite fine. I suggest you call it a night and find your own."

The old woman gave him a matronly smile and left.

Fee came out from behind the curtains and picked up her cup of tea. "Speaking of fires, which ones are you wrestling with this evening?" she asked, snagging one of the confections spread out on a tray next to the tea. She popped it into her mouth and then sat across from him in her favorite well-worn chair. Folding her legs up beneath her and sinking into its warm leather folds, she smiled bliss-fully as the white, powdery sweet melted across her tongue.

"New schooling procedures," Xavi said, stacking his papers. "They must be enacted once all the children are permitted to return to the castle next month. A great unleashing of 'policies for the public' for when we are a fully functioning kingdom once again. Although, that will require money, and Fireli is nearly destitute. Sir Rollins just left after telling me that the king's coffers are cobwebbed and barren. I've no idea how we shall pay for everyone's return. We barely have enough to sustain the few ghostly souls that maintain this massive stone hut as it is."

"My memories from when the kingdom was teeming with life are so sketchy, but I have this hopeful vision of bustling, spirited people in the near future."

Xavi's face shadowed. "I think nearly a decade of silence has torn at the edges of what we all knew as normal life. It's as if at one point the earth we walked on split beneath our feet and pulled away, leaving some giant, growing divide of *before* and *after*." He rubbed at his chin. "Ten years is a long time to separate a person from their homeland. Sir Rollins repeatedly pays tribute to Gwyndom's healer, Mistress Goodsong, admiring how rapidly she executed the quar-antine. Rye has mentioned her on many an occasion in his letters. But what we need right now is for our youth to return and fill the kingdom."

Fee puffed her retort. "They're hardly all that youthful any longer, Xavi. Many of them will be finished with school and on the verge of adulthood."

He shrugged. "And so they will soon marry and fill our quarter of Aethusa with babies once again. Savva saved as many people as she could, Fee. There just wasn't enough medicine. And not enough time."

His words clashed with discord. Fee recalled rushing back to the castle, fighting to enter through its gate as it was in the midst of a savage windstorm. The wind whipped, a raging gale of chaos, and Fee crawled past people writhing on the ground, clutching at their throats for air, scratching at their eyes from the burn. She dragged herself to the stillroom and found that desperate villagers had laid waste to it, leaving broken bottles and medicines all about. Yet every inch of it was brimming with children—parents shoving their offspring through the door to get them inoculated. She'd slithered around crushed glass and scores of feet, beneath the tables and chairs, just to reach Savva. The healer—clearly in pain and wholly overwhelmed—immediately dosed her with the antidote and then demanded she make more with the paltry supplies they had left whilst the healer vaccinated as many as she could.

Countless people died. Xavi was right. There wasn't enough time.

Both sets of their parents had sacrificed themselves to save the children. People were frantic and screaming for help. They quickly succumbed to the poisonous black dust. By the time the king and queen finally choked down the reserve dose of the medicine set aside for them, as was protocol for reigning monarchs, they'd been overcome.

What hadn't been destroyed by disease had been ravaged by the squall. The survivors stumbled about in a daze, blinking unseeingly at the catastrophic wreckage. The ground was littered with people, their faces twisted and frozen in anguish.

Xavi sighed with his head in his hands, his defeated breath blowing a few papers off the many stacks surrounding him and pulling her out of her reverie.

"There are some days, Fee, when I want to crumble." He looked up at her, his eyes overwrought. "Do you miss them all as much as I do?"

Her throat constricted, dry and uncooperative.

"I *will* bring Fireli back." He pulled up a scrap of paper to show Fee his scribbles. "Now, enough of our maudlin moments. Look here. I'm noodling over a new Fireli motto: *audemus patria nostra defendere*. What do you think?"

Fee's face pinched, and she chuckled. "I think your Latin skills are still pitiable. I'm pretty sure it should say: *audemus patriam nostram defendere*. But you were close, if that matters. And yes, I like the sound of *We dare to defend our homeland*. It has a confident ring to it."

She returned the paper, determined not to dampen his fragile enthusiasm. "If anyone can make that happen, it is you, Xavi. Now, what else keeps you up this late?"

He pulled a letter out of the pile of papers before him, a broad smile spreading across his features. "Our weekly missive from Rye."

It was exactly what they both needed, for Rye's letters were filled with fascinating tidbits of his travels, his friendships, and his adventures. It was like reading one chapter a week from an ongoing book neither of them wanted to finish. Although coming to the part where it said *The End* would mean something significant for them both.

For Xavi, it would announce the conclusion of the great quarantine and the beginning of his reign as the new king of

Fireli when he reached his twenty-second birthday.

For Fee, it meant marriage. The end of the closest bond she'd ever held with one person, as it would be replaced with another. Xavi was her brother in every way that mattered. But Rye would be her husband—the thought of it loomed unnervingly.

Xavi's coronation would be in one month's time, and Rye would return to serve as his right-hand advisor. Everything would change. The kingdom, the faces around them, their friendship. And she would be released from her deplorable isolation. Finally.

"Read it," Fee said, unable to restrain the note of impatience in her voice.

Dear Xavi,

I write to you today from the inside of Gwyndom's annual cabinet meeting. The annual board of governors has gathered to hash out the kingdom's budget and calendar. Blah, blah, blah.

They are boring, argumentative, and continue to serve the most dreadful fare. Naught but soft puddings and easily masticated foods. It is a reflection of the subjects debated as well, for nothing that is bandied about is anything fulfilling once completed. Stripped of mental and physical nourishment, my head spins with sleepiness, thus, I am writing to you and feigning I am taking copious notes.

Do not be cross with me, Xavi. Even you would slump.

Your future mother-in-law sits across from me; her placid expression mirrors my own. It is impossible to tell the thoughts behind her countenance as her features neither rise in amusement nor fall with displeasure. It is a visage I have come to decipher as one meant to either hinder her enemies from reading her true feelings and using them against her, or to fool the cabinet into believing she is awake but, in fact, has learned the talent of sleeping with her eyes open. Regardless, three years of interacting with her gives me the confidence to speak with authority:

Queen Islay is not the warm and welcoming type.

And speaking of new family members, her daughter is packing her trunks as I write. I find it difficult to believe your betrothed can have as extensive a wardrobe as she does. You may need to have blueprints drawn extending the existing castle walls. I'm certain more room will be requested upon Quinn's arrival.

I suppose there was one event of note this week. Gossip has filled Gwyndom's halls with the story that the Kingdom of Oldshire found a practicing witch. Some say she was not only stripped of her citizenship, but physically accosted to the point where she was nearly deprived of her life. The details are gruesome, although probably inflated. Still, it helps us all sleep sounder knowing the heinous activity has been squelched.

I continue to hear endless notes of concern from the other two kingdoms regarding peoples' decision to return home to Fireli or remain where they are. We are fed stories each day as to the disintegration of our once great kingdom, and we are encouraged to face the truth that assimilation into our current kingdoms of residence might be our best option. But *to once more see the lush grasslands and undulating hills from my youth is a thought that has sustained me for these many years of separation. I won't be deterred.*

Ah, I have been discovered. I must endeavor to engage with the council.

Until next week, brother.

Yours,

Rye

Xavi quickly looked up and caught Fee's expectant gaze. He shook his head. She wanted another line at the end, a line that had been there solidly for at least half the time Rye had started writing weekly letters. It had always said:

Send my love to the feisty Ophelia.

Instead, Xavi sighed and finished with:

PS Have you settled your thoughts on the subject of mining yet? It is the talk of many and the worry of more.

Xavi lowered the letter. His shoulders sank with it.

Fee was long ago resigned to the idea that Rye had stopped addressing her in his letters. It had been the only acknowledgment she'd had that he still recognized her presence, as he'd never responded to the dozens upon dozens of letters she'd written to him over the last decade.

Not one.

But she never gave up, and each month wrote him a long missive telling him of any tiny snatches of news. Xavi did the same—he never left out news of Fee.

Dismissing the tiny prickle of rejection, she said, "You still have time to decide before announcing your decision, Xavi." Fee wanted to reach out and put a hand over his, to soothe him from the mounting stress that pulled at his face, marring any serenity that might fleetingly settle there.

"I feel I cannot breathe because of it." He rubbed at the deep groove of worry across his brow. "What if the mines are still full of toxins, Fee? Should we not look at other options for trade—maybe go back to our agrarian roots and just farm the land? Is it not possible that with the return of our peers and friends—this . . . this *educated* youth—we could create a new plan for our kingdom's future?"

Fee desperately wanted to declare they could, but they both knew that was not a sound guarantee.

"Perhaps your beliefs are not unreasonable, Xavi, but what of the expectations of the other three kingdoms? They all contribute something equally valuable, and we must have something to trade." Gwyndom had successfully mined their lands for precious gems and apparently made a kingdom flush with wealth. Oldshire held vast tracts of timber, and Thornbridge's lands were honeycombed with rock quarries. "Are you aware of how they will take to the announcement that the metal mines will be permanently closed?"

"The other kingdoms have no concerns for the safety of Fireli's people." He rose and moved to the bookshelf behind him. The shelf that contained all the writings and documents, ledgers and diaries from past rulers—hundreds of years' worth of archived information.

And, Fee noted—enviously—it contained *The Book of Denizens*. The register that identified every person's most important particulars: their birthdate, sex, allergies, diseases, and parentage. Whatever the healer thought relevant. Countless times, Fee would watch from the loft as Savva scratched notes onto the thin velum before returning the book to the shelves in Xavi's library.

Oh, what she wouldn't give to have a peek inside that book—to know what Xavi already did. But she would never ask.

Never.

"When does the princess arrive?" she asked.

Still scanning the bookshelf, Xavi's face brightened. "Princess Quinn comes in one week's time."

Fee noted the tiny flush. "Not looking forward to meeting your betrothed, are you, Xavi?" she teased.

He tried composing his features, but Fee could see his eagerness and smiled as he carried on. "I feel confident that over these last many years, between the exchanges of letters, the two of us have grown to know one another to a comfortable measure. She appears to write with reason and clarity."

Fee rolled her eyes. "Reason and clarity? How utterly romantic. Let's hope she's a scholar with her Latin as well—to help you with *your* reason and clarity."

"I'm sure I don't know what you speak of, Fee, as my Latin skills are quite respectable in some circles."

Fee put her teacup down on the great table and began refastening her disguise. Raising the hood of her cloak, she hunched her shoulders and pointed a finger at her best friend. "If my Latin skills were as respectable as yours," she said, mimicking Savva's wavering voice, "I'd unwittingly turn all of my patients into a toad."

Xavi chuckled and made a small bow in Fee's direction. "Good night, milady. Safe travels home. Oh," he said, reaching toward the table, "and don't forget your mole."

CHAPTER
ELEVEN

FEE CRUSHED THE LAVENDER BUDS BETWEEN HER FIN-
gertips. The heady, sharp scent filled her nose: piney, floral, and
bitingly fragrant. Although she'd spent the last two hours in the
castle garden harvesting the stalks, the camphor notes still swirled
around her, pungent and calming. She centered her keen focus on
the tiny purple germs and made them dance about in her palm—
then looked about quickly to make sure Savva was nowhere in sight.

She took in a great lungful of the perfume emanating from her
hand and sat down to rest, leaning back onto the wild, soft grasses
beneath her. She closed her eyes to the bright summer sunshine, taking a few stolen moments to daydream.

The sounds of her parents' voices had faded long ago, ghostly
murmurs that echoed in the castle's cobwebbed corners and vacuous
halls. The recollection of their image grew dim, each day's strong

sunlight bleaching away the color and details. Only the fragile trimmings of their conversations remained.

Savva will be your life's mentor, Fee, her mother had told her when she was only six and standing on the threshold of schooling. *We believe you will never grow weary of the allurement within the healing arts. You will serve your head and heart with the quest for scholarship but also the needs of the people of this kingdom. It is a great honor to be chosen to study in the stillroom.*

She hadn't understood much of what her mother had said at the time, for as a frolicsome child, her concerns revolved around directing everyday delights with Xavi and Rye, playing house or playing healer. Having been told her future early on—revealing both her spouse and her profession—only added to the certainty of Fee's nature.

"When I am the castle healer, Xavi," she would say, "I shall make people pay me with sweets. They may not have my cures unless my coffers are full of confections I adore."

Xavi would tug at her ear, evoking an impish grin. "And when I am king, I shall allow it. Even though you'll end up toothless and fat."

"I will not be forced to marry a gummy butterball, Ophelia," Rye had complained as the three of them walked through a grove of apple trees in search of an afternoon snack. "I won't have anyone pushing me around and telling me what to do. Least of all, someone who cannot see the value and necessity of teeth."

"Rye!" Fee had complained, and flicked a finger at a small root in front of his foot, making it rise slightly to catch his shoe. He fell forward and landed hard, a rush of air forced out of his lungs. He shot her a venomous look as he scrambled to find his feet.

She'd scurried up one of the apple trees to keep a safe distance from Rye and made a puckish face at him.

"Perhaps it's a little early for determining how you wish to be paid, Fee," Xavi had said, giving Rye a look of reproach. "I suggest you simply focus on becoming the brightest healer Aethusa will ever come to know."

This was a phrase that thrummed through her veins repeatedly. Her only desire was to see it come true. But her failure at curing Xavi completely shriveled her confidence.

Fee stretched in the grass, recalling those blissful days before the plague had grabbed hold of them. The last few days of innocence and self-possession.

Things were not turning out exactly as Fee had once imagined they would. For one thing, no one paid her in sweets. No one paid her at all. She worked under the watchful direction of Savva, who had not only refused to give her a coin for her labor, but neither paid her a compliment for her efforts. And the only time Fee was given sweets was when visiting Xavi's private study, where he always kept an open box of the white, powdery confection that Princess Quinn sent every week—a token of her affection and honeyed disposition.

Marrying Rye was another matter for unease, although one that had been easy to put off because he wasn't, in essence, a real person to her anymore. He was a series of weekly letters. He was a story. He was fiction. But in one short month, the fairy tale would end, and reality would knock on their doors in the form of people— potentially scores of them, demanding to be engaged with.

Or engaged *to*.

Fee gathered the two baskets filled with lavender stalks, the heads, condensed together, creating the mesmerizing color of a deep, inky bruise. Would Rye still see her as he once had—a scrappy girl with unending nerve—or had his view changed?

It might explain his suspended mention of her. Maybe the old *feisty Ophelia* wasn't what he wanted anymore. Maybe, since having been schooled by sagacious tutors throughout the realm during the last ten years, he'd decided to overrule his parents' wishes. Or perhaps Rye knew what she was beginning to suspect—that she could not fulfil her parents' aspirations to *serve the needs of the people of this kingdom*. Perhaps he wanted someone more capable. Really, how clever and proficient was she, if she was unable to cure his brother? And *that brother* the most important patient within their entire kingdom.

Fee stretched to reach the jar of dried powder on one of the still-room's highest shelves and then scooped out a full measure of the herb she'd labeled *Ruta graveolens*: ground leaves previously stamped with the name *herb of grace* when Savva had been in charge of the shelves.

It was the main ingredient in the tonic everyone in the castle was required to ingest daily—everyone apart from Xavi and Fee.

"How is this helpful against a reinfection of the plague?" Fee had asked Savva years ago—when at last much of what she was memorizing in her homeopathica books was beginning to make sense. "It's nothing more than an antispasmodic."

"And antimicrobial," Savva had said, absorbed in some other book.

Fee shook her head. It hadn't made sense. "But how is this supposed to—"

Savva cut her off. "Make the week's supply of the antidote for our patients and then begin work on Xavi's."

Fee had grumbled at being brushed off. Their patients were getting nothing more than a strong tea to help with arthritis. She would bellyache about it later to Xavi. After Savva would leave the stillroom and lock her in. And after she would pick the lock and dress like Savva to wander the halls of the castle toward Xavi.

Xavi's tonic was also a mystery. And one that she alone was forced to figure out. Savva never helped in the preparation. Only guided her toward chapters that addressed human vigor and endurance.

Fee's medicine was the most mysterious of them all. Savva made it whenever Fee was sent to gather supplies from the medicinal gardens—a small field behind the stillroom where no one else from the castle visited.

"Why is mine different?" she'd asked when first ordered to take it.

"You, especially, were highly infected. You are a carrier of the contagion. We must suppress it from resurfacing. But most important, we must keep you away from the others."

"And not Xavi? Am I not a danger to him?"

Savva pulled Fee into a quick embrace before holding her small shoulders out at a distance. "Xavi benefits from you more than he is threatened by you."

Fee finished making the brew for the elderly and decided against taking her antidote tonight. It left her sluggish, and what she truly craved was adventure—something she and Xavi were sorely desperate for, but had found little of.

She hunted for her Savva disguise. To hell with the books, the remedies, and the teas. They needed excitement. And Fee knew just where to seek it. But going there would mean breaking one of the Three Seclusion Rules.

You must never leave the castle grounds of Fireli.

The source of this delight was definitely beyond the castle's perimeter—and also the reason for the quarantine in the first place.

Their cave. They hadn't been there in a decade.

This evening—the last before Princess Quinn would arrive— they'd try to find a sliver of their youth. She hoped their youth would recognize them.

"YOU HAD BETTER KEEP EVERYTHING CROSSED THAT Savva does not take an evening stroll about the castle, Fee. For any of the three guardsmen we duped into believing you were bringing me to the stillroom for treatment would likely question her as to the outcome."

Fee rolled her eyes at Xavi and continued walking through the dark along the deeply neglected path her feet used to effortlessly travel. "Sometimes it's difficult having you as a friend. You're such a rule follower." He'd had great difficulty clambering over the castle wall behind the ground's small orchard. Fee wondered, how foolish had she been? Could Xavi even make it to the cave?

He made a choking snort of amusement. "Yes, in comparison to you, sweet Fee, I am practically saint-worthy. But some rules are vital. Plus, what would you have Fireli's king do? Make them *and* break them?"

She turned around and smiled devilishly. "Couldn't we?"

He spun her shoulders forward and clucked his tongue. "No."

Fee shrugged resignedly and heard Xavi's labored breath behind her, a writhing spiral of turmoil encircling her thoughts.

In front of them were the rocks they needed to climb to reach the cave's entrance. Fee looked back at Xavi and, suddenly, feeling anxiety mushrooming in her stomach, she measured whether he could scale them. He glanced up at the rocks with a weary but determined face. "Wait a moment," she said, grabbing hold of a young liana. She stretched the long-stemmed, woody vine in the direction of the cave's mouth and spurred it to rapidly unfurl across the rocks, swiftly growing higher and anchoring itself within the rutted cracks along the way. "There we go," Fee said, proudly dusting her hands and turning back to Xavi. "That should help with the cli—" She stopped dead as she saw him sink to his knees. "Xavi?" she whispered, kneeling beside him.

He weakly shook his head. "I need to rest. I . . . I thought I could do it, Fee, but . . . I'm sorry."

She forced him to sit. "I don't know what I was thinking dragging you all the way out here, knowing you're . . ." She thought the word *depleted*, but couldn't bring herself to say it.

He pushed away her concern. "I'm simply already exhausted, Fee, and nothing more. My overworked head has been unable to leave the question of what's to come. My thoughts for tomorrow's ministry session are scattered across my desk and I cannot make sense of half of them."

Fee watched Xavi mindlessly rub at the back of his neck. *Failure,* she thought, staring at him with dismay. *He's afraid of failing this kingdom and its people.*

She sat next to him and shivered, staring out across the summer grasses. They rippled with the cool night breeze as if a giant, invisible hand were running its fingers through its weft and weave. "I'm sorry, Xavi. I know how stressful it's been for you."

He looked toward the star-filled heavens. "I must be persuasive—convince the ministry I am capable—but they have been cowed by Sir Rollins for far too long. I fear tomorrow I will be forced to go along with him, as no one yet holds my ideas in high esteem." He sneezed and rubbed his nose with the back of his sleeve.

"Well," Fee said wryly, "to be frank, the only thing I see lacking to make you a well-respected monarch is a proper handkerchief, but, if we are to be serious"—the tone of her voice changed, finding a mixture of optimism and wistfulness—"tomorrow is the start of all that. Princess Quinn arrives, and the two of you will begin planning a wonderful life. You will make a fine king, Xavi. And I'm sure your parents chose an exceptional partner for you."

Xavi slowly found his feet and made a purposeful effort to smile. "I hope you hold no worries, Fee. You'll always remain my closest confidante."

Fee brushed off the dirt on her trousers. Deep within her bones she knew this could not be true. Not with the changes that waited upon their return to the castle.

Xavi pulled her into an affectionate hug. "You are such a goose. *Do not worry.*" He swept a hand up toward the cave. "We'll make it up there again one day—you'll see. Tonight I'm just—"

His words were cut short by a high-pitched yelp and the flurry of limbs mixed with a cloud of dust rolling down from the ridgetop to rest at their feet.

Their mouths dropped open, stupefied with fear over being

discovered, when a teenaged girl scrambled to find her footing, repeatedly apologizing while attempting to adjust her clothing.

She wrestled her skirt of braided leather straps and her blouse made of closely cropped green grass into place, but refused to make eye contact. She hurriedly backed up a few steps. "So sorry. Dear me. This spells trouble. Carry on. I was just . . . checking."

The dark was beginning to swallow her up, when with one quick pivot, she turned and dashed off into the night.

Xavi and Fee stood staring into the space where she'd disappeared. "Are we in trouble?" Fee whispered.

She heard Xavi take a shaky breath in. "I don't . . . think so. But we did just see the same . . ." He turned to face her.

Fee nodded mutely.

"Come back to my study," he said slowly. "If we are in trouble we shall be in trouble together. And if we are not then I am left wondering if the mines are still toxic with hallucinogens."

Sneaking back into Xavi's room was easier than sneaking out of it, as most of the guards were long in the tooth and repeatedly fell asleep on the job once the dinner hour had past. Rare was the occasion when Fee would come across someone in the castle who *wasn't* snoozing when no one was looking. Most inhabitants had at least two, if not three, positions they carried in order to keep the castle running—even if *running* was a debatable term.

The return trip took longer, as Xavi's pace slowed considerably, and twice Fee insisted they stop so that she could "fix her shoe," or pick a quick handful of *Spigelia* for the stillroom. But the urgency to return and not be found out again spurred them on.

They tiptoed past Xavi's private study sentry, whose head rested on his chest, a soft snore emanating from his crumpled form. Fee stifled a giggle as Xavi opened the door and then felt her smile go slack as she stepped across the threshold and tried to comprehend the scene.

A young woman with hair so blond it appeared gilded stood behind Xavi's desk, a cup of tea in her hands. Her violet eyes—the same shade as the garden of Fee's lavender—came to rest on Xavi after having made a brief but thorough assessment of Fee. The young lady put her cup down and moved around the large wooden writing table. Her scrutinizing expression softened into a smile of hospitality, as if welcoming visitors into her home for the first time.

"Prince Xavi?" she said, putting her hands out to receive him, her voice downy soft.

Xavi's face was cast with the shadow of bewilderment. "Princess Quinn? Wh-what are you doing here?" He then pulled back. "I mean, welcome!" He took her outstretched hands and placed a kiss upon one of them. He pulled back just in time to sneeze and stopped a second one by hastily tucking his nose into his sleeve.

Fee cringed inwardly, imagining the first impression that likely made. She *must* find him a proper handkerchief.

Fee followed Xavi's eyes as he scanned his desk. She knew he must be unnerved at the state of disarray the princess had observed. "Please, do sit down," he encouraged her, pointing to the chair Fee normally occupied when visiting. But the princess simply stared at Fee and said, "And who is this?"

"I'm sorry. Where are my manners?" Xavi fumbled. "This is . . . Fee."

Fee stepped forward and made a small curtsey, her heart hammering wildly for the second time that night.

Princess Quinn raised her face to meet Fee's eyes after resting on the trousers Fee sported, and the barest of a schooled smile turned up the corners of her lips. "Fee?" she echoed, tilting her head to look back at Xavi. "Your senior citizens appear remarkably youthful. I thought all minors had been forced to leave the kingdom."

Xavi faltered. "Ah yes . . . Well, she's only just arrived—early, like you—working in the stillroom. But I believe I've mentioned her in my letters, milady."

Her face flushed pinkly and she looked toward the floor. "Your letters. They've meant a great deal to me. I've kept every one. I tuck them straight into my treasury." She glanced back toward Fee. "And yes, Fee. You'd described her as your *little* sister."

It was Xavi's face that now reddened. "Ah, well, all grown up now, of course. But for all intents and purposes, that's about accurate. Perhaps Rye told you of the countless hours we've all spent together, playing as children up in one of the mining caves. We were as close to family as could be, under the circumstances."

The princess gazed at him intensely, a hand to her heart. "And tragic circumstances they were, my lord." She slowly made her way to the chair, her lush skirts of swishing taffeta rustling as she moved. Lowering herself into the chair, she continued, "We've heard so much of the misfortune from your former residents—and, of course, from Prince Rye. I'm determined to be of assistance."

"Yes, assistance," Xavi said distractedly, rubbing at one temple. "I'll be glad of it, although I wasn't expecting it tonight. Why have you come early? I feel somewhat rattled that I was not here to greet you and have no idea if you received any reception whatsoever. Did you come with an entourage?"

The princess's eyes briefly lit with puzzlement, but then her features settled into what appeared to be a practiced and perfected arrangement. "Your Sir Rollins received me and brought me here. I do believe he is in search of you now. I wanted to surprise you." Her eyes flickered toward Fee and the phrase *It certainly appears I have* hung in the air above them all, unspoken.

Xavi's eyes scanned the room and did not catch the princess's intimation toward Fee, but Fee's mind raced with what being discovered a second time tonight might mean. Xavi responded with, "I'm sorry. The state of my study is atrocious. We should have been more prepared. A proper greeting."

The princess turned back to him. "I came this evening with no one other than my lady's maid, two guards, and the coachmen, of course." The princess waved a dismissive hand in the air. "Everyone else will arrive tomorrow morning. Make a fuss of it then if you feel it necessary."

"Of course we do. The people of Fireli will see you a proper welcome—or die trying," he added with an uncomfortable chuckle. "And as it is late, and I've already displayed the worst of appropriate etiquette, we must get you settled."

"Already?" Lines of perplexity appeared on the princess's forehead.

Xavi moved toward the door. "I'll call for an attendant to see you to your rooms. You must be weary from the journey."

The princess raised a hand, and Fee noted the jeweled silk cuff secured around her wrist, a snug bracelet of dashing finery. She fought with the tight smile around her lips. "No need. Perhaps Fee would accompany me to my suite, since it is *very* late."

She rose from her chair with one fluid motion, and Fee stole a glance at Xavi, who gave her a subtle nod of concession. He did his best to cover the angst that slipped through his façade, but Fee could not put a finger on why he should struggle so.

The princess nodded at Fee to follow and then made a polite curtsey in front of Xavi, drawing herself up with fresh enthusiasm.

"I am so pleased to finally meet you. And I look forward to tomorrow when I will see the depth and breadth of Fireli. I know it will thrive and flourish once again. We shall breathe new life into this kingdom." She paused and cast him a glance full of humor. "On our lives, we shall."

By the time Fee had escorted the princess to the door of her suite, there was a small legion of people waiting. Obviously, Xavi had sounded an alert and roused as many as possible to make sure that the princess's reception—although late—would at least be an effort to regain lost ground. Somehow, the people believed Fee to be one of the princess's attendants—oddly dressed as she was—and paid little heed.

Fee could see from the open doorway several elderly women shuffling about lighting gas lamps and candles, unpacking the few trunks brought up from the princess's coach, and turning back the best bed linens the castle could locate. One woman fumbled with a tray of spiced bread and wine on a low table before the fireplace, where another struggled to build up the flames.

Fee's heart twisted at the thought of Xavi judging himself so poorly for having been caught unprepared. And there was the larger matter that Fee wrestled with herself—the fact that it had been *her* idea to pull Xavi away from his study in the first place.

"Do come in, Fee," the princess said, sweeping a hand toward the threshold of the late queen's chambers.

It felt odd, Fee noted, the thought of stepping into Xavi's mother's room—a place she used to frequent as a child, going there with Xavi and Rye on countless occasions. But this part of the castle had been in disuse for years and only recently cleaned in preparation for Xavi's new bride and Fireli's new queen.

"As you said, Your Highness, it's late, and I'm sure there are myriad things you will want to attend to before tomorrow. No doubt I am already missed in the stillroom and should get back. But here." Fee held out a cup of freshly poured tea from the tray. "I know this to be one of Savva's best sleeping brews for a restful night."

The princess reached for the cup but then froze and suddenly pulled back with a sharp intake of breath. Her eyes moved from Fee's outstretched hands to her face, as if disassembling her features, her own having gone pale as bone.

"Are you all right, milady?" Fee asked worriedly.

The princess took a step backward and put up a hand, struggling to regain her composure. "The stillroom," she finally continued distractedly. "You work with the castle healer?"

Fee nodded politely, but focused on the signs of distress in front of her. "I do . . . yes," Fee fumbled. "With Mistress Savva, Fireli's healer."

The princess slowly straightened. "I have heard her name spoken endless times with admiration, specifically by our own healer,

Mistress Goodsong. Xavi is lucky to have Mistress Savva attend to him and the kingdom. She will doubtless be a fine tutor. I feel certain Xavi will be . . . *fortunate* to have you as well." She winced, her face grimacing ever so slightly for a split second before settling back into serene composure. "After your training, of course."

"Are you sure you're well, milady?" Fee asked.

The princess at last took the outstretched cup of tea and drank deeply from it. "I will be."

Fee lowered her eyes and studied the intricate design of the princess's beautiful traveling gown—a great contrast of dress between the two of them. The glowing soft, coral colors, the folds of sumptuous fabrics reminiscent of the sun at dusk. Fee's outfit, by comparison, was solely faded dark blue, her short-sleeved blouse now stained with the efforts of the day's work along with the mucky impressions from their trek to the cave.

Fee had never experienced a moment of discomfort regarding her clothing when around Savva and in the stillroom, but now she felt wholly self-conscious, suddenly recalling the years of disapproval she fought when shedding her frocks in favor of breeches.

"So, we are to be sisters through marriage, are we not?" the princess said coolly from the rim of her teacup.

"It was arranged once upon a time," Fee said, trailing off.

"Prince Rye has spent nearly the last three years in Gwyndom. There are many maidens in my kingdom who will weep bitterly to discover he is to be wed."

"It's been a very long time since I have seen the prince. I expect it will take some time getting used to him again."

The princess smiled wryly. "I doubt it will be a taxing enterprise."

She cast a glance to where her lady's maid stood waiting in her bed-chamber and then faced Fee once more. "I have so many questions about Fireli. Perhaps it has greatly changed since you've been . . . gone."

The word came out of the princess's mouth with a small, almost imperceptible effort, making Fee's heart skip a beat. The princess continued. "But maybe not, and you will be so kind as to fill me in on every detail."

"Of course, milady—that is, if Savva allows me the time, as I'm sure there is much my new mentor will assign me."

Fee made a small curtsey, a gesture that filled her with unease.

Making her way down the dimly lit corridor toward the castle exit, Fee was aware of a growing discomfort stemming from the princess's parting words: *Perhaps it has greatly changed since you've been . . . gone.*

Had she figured them out? Did she know that Fee had resided here since the plague? Did it matter, as everyone would shortly return? Fee brushed it off. For the last ten years, Fireli had been caught in a time warp where every day had been the same. They needed change—*craved* change. They were on the brink of it. Finally, the winds were shifting.

Finally, a breath of fresh air.

Fee walked the torchlit garden path toward the stillroom door, wholly absorbed in her thoughts about tomorrow and the vast changes about to take place. The princess had the disposition of a young woman heavily schooled in stately rhetoric and quick assessment. She hoped the new queen would find the people of Fireli to be generous and appreciative, even if her new surroundings did not quite measure up to her standards. What an ordeal to find yourself supplanted into another person's home and told you will soon be running it!

It would be absurd to covet the life of a monarch, as it was one sharply molded by generations before you and held to high principles of such conduct and protocol, it surely must be like having a corset sewn to the bones of your ribs, impossible to unlace and remove.

Fee felt a wave of optimism wash through her, resolute that she would do whatever she could to make the princess feel welcomed. Perhaps, over time, they could become friends.

Rounding the stone path to the stillroom's entrance, she reached for the latch on the door.

"Go inside, but do not light the lamps, Fee."

She started and drew in a quick breath before realizing it was Xavi's voice that had spoken from the dark.

"What? What's going on, Xavi?" she whispered.

"Just go inside. I'm right behind you."

She opened the door and stepped aside to allow Xavi a quick dart through the cottage door. She left the heavy wooden slab ajar so they had some light from the torch that burned a few steps from the stillroom threshold.

"What is it? Are you ill?" Panic ran up her spine. Her mind immediately inventoried what she had available on her shelves.

"I do feel unwell—but it's not been brought on by disease, Fee."

"Dear God, what's happened, Xavi?"

He grabbed her by the shoulders, and she studied his face in half shadows, the flickering torchlight quivering across his features. "Do you recall that I told you that my paperwork for tomorrow's meeting was on my desk—the one with all my scattered thoughts?"

Fee nodded.

"Some of it did not make sense. To *me*."

"Did not make sense? What do you mean?"

"I can only say that what I wrote and what I know are two separate things."

"I don't understand."

"I don't either. I was beginning to be swayed by some of Sir Rollins's arguments—that the mines were the key to our recovery, but then"—he looked up toward the ceiling—"out of nowhere, I began drafting reasons why the mines should never reopen. Technical reasons, Fee. Reasons that could only be backed up with *medically based* arguments. I don't understand half the words I wrote."

Fee shook her head. "I'm still not following."

He stared at her, his face full of anxiety. "Those papers are now *gone*." He dropped his hands. "If my words end up in the hands of the ministry tomorrow, they'll ask me what I meant, and I'll have no answer. They'll think I'm mad—unfit for the crown!"

Fee's heart skipped in rhythm, her mouth falling open.

"But worse—if anyone outside of Fireli has read it, they would think I'm refusing to open the mines. They'd be compelled to alert the three other kingdoms. We'd be denying them what they are demanding of us. *Demanding*, Fee. We have no defenses to stand our ground. Any of them could easily seize what they want. They just need to declare . . ."

Fee gasped. "War?"

They stared at each other a moment longer before both saying the same words together.

"The princess."

CHAPTER
THIRTEEN

FEE SLEPT FITFULLY AFTER XAVI'S DEPARTURE. "WHAT will you do?" Fee had asked. "You can't just march into the princess's new quarters and accuse her of rifling through your desk and stealing your papers. Imagine the damage that would inflict on your relationship, and that with her kingdom, whether it turned out to be her or not."

"You're right," Xavi had said, pinching the bridge of his nose. "I can see no other choice than to carry on tomorrow as planned— although, I'm not entirely sure what my *plan* really is."

"Why not push the council meeting forward? It might save your skin—that is, if the princess did take your notes, and she intends to alert the three other kingdoms first thing in the morning. Your other worry," Fee had said with a false air of confidence, "is not a concern."

Xavi had given her an unconvincing glance, groaned, and ran a hand through his hair. "Oh good God, I hope we are quick enough."

If the princess were quicker, Fee knew they'd be woken in their beds by the blades of three vengeful kingdoms' worth of soldiers.

But they hadn't risen to the sight of soldiers, and the castle grounds remained eerily quiet as Fee spent the first few hours grinding herbs at the worktable. With frayed nerves, she toiled with the mortar and pestle, mashing the dried leaves into tiny aromatic fragments, then jarring and labeling them for Savva to dispense to their patients.

Every knock on the door had Fee jumping in her skin before scrambling up to her loft. She'd received several elevated-eyebrow glances from Savva already—alert as she was to unseen vibrations. Fee grew determined to better control herself.

Late in the morning, as Fee was pouring grain alcohol into the dark brown glass bottles that held the buds of lavender, rose petals, wintergreen leaves, and balsam needles, she heard another announcement at the door, this one firmer than most.

Fee quickly scaled the ladder and lay quietly waiting as Savva answered the call.

"Good morning, Your Royal Highness," Fee heard Savva say. "I hope you slept well. How is it I can be of service?"

Your Royal Highness? Fee slipped to the knot in the floorboard to see.

The princess's regal frame, stately and lithe, was outfitted in a flowing lightweight silk gown. Blue-green fabric with thin ribbons of gold trailing down the bodice to the floor gave her the appearance of a mermaid rising out of the sun-streaked sea. Fee stared at her, not only stirred by the dazzling imagery, but stunned that the princess would come here to seek them out.

Savva peered at the young woman, drinking her in with eyes that hungered for details. The princess did the same with the stillroom, taking in every element, resting on all corners and their contents.

"I would like to speak with Fee."

"Fee?" Savva's eyes widened.

"Yes. Your apprentice. The one I met last night."

Savva remained silent for the space of half a dozen heartbeats. "Fee is occupied with work, Your Highness. How may I assist you?" The words were softer, lacking Savva's customary gruffness.

The princess's face did not break with surprise or anger at the hindrance. She simply turned her royal veneer toward the old woman. "I will not delay her progress long. May we have a moment alone, please?"

Fee felt a lump in her throat.

Savva continued to stare appraisingly at Princess Quinn, who moved toward the long table in the middle of the room. She sat carefully on the bench so as not to snag the silk of her gown on the gnarled, old wood.

Savva twisted to look over her shoulder and up at the loft. "Fee? Could you stop your work and come down?"

Fee descended the ladder and knew her face revealed her guilt. The old healer returned a cautionary look and headed outside, closing the door after her.

"Yes, milady?" Afraid her dithering anxiety would betray her, Fee grabbed hold of two instruments on the table so her hands would not shake.

The princess scanned the shelves behind Fee, mute in her appraisal, and at last leveled a measured gaze. Her features were so cold they sent a shiver through Fee. "Our physicians appear to be worlds apart."

"In what way, Your Highness?" Fee said tentatively.

Fee heard the faintest exhalation of breath come from across the table, and the princess's eyebrows arched with subtle effect. "In every way. We are not treated with herbs and potions any longer. There is no stillroom, apart from that which makes the castle spirits."

Fee forgot herself and moved swiftly toward the table, sliding in to sit across from the princess. "Really? What is medicine like in Gwyndom? Do you have need of healers at all any longer?" Her mind raced at the possibility that life in the other kingdoms was not a duplicate of her own.

"Yes, of course. We still fall ill and seek treatment, but our medical care has . . . evolved. Mistress Goodsong is apparently remarkably skilled, as people are most devoted to our healer. Her cures are not made from ground plants and steeping teas, but as I am here"—she paused, and again her glance flickered across the shelves—"I shall have to make do with what is available."

Part of Fee grew warm with the criticism. "I give you my word we shall do our best to accommodate your needs. Is that why you've come? To discuss your ailments and find what we have to address them?"

The princess stood, and Fee watched as she made her way behind the workbench and toward the many shelves of jars. "You are familiar with all of these substances?"

"I am, milady. Is there something in particular you seek?"

"Two things. Last night, I could not sleep. I wrestle with distress beyond measure."

"Oh?" Fee felt her heart hammering like a fist behind a wall. She could not think what else to say. She waited for the disastrous news that the princess had discovered Xavi's notes and had taken action.

"So I seek some sleep aid—at least for the next several nights—as I'm certain one of the issues will take a few days to get sorted."

Fee could barely move air through her throat in order to utter the words "Issues, milady?"

The princess turned to face Fee, locking eyes with her. "Rats," she whispered. "They scurry through the walls. Which is the other reason for my visit. I need a deterrent for the rodents, if you please." She closed her eyes as if trying to block out the visual of the memory.

Breath rushed out of Fee. It felt as if someone had removed the choke hold around her throat. "Oh, milady, how awful," she burst out. "Yes, of course. I can have both remedies prepared and sent to your suite immediately."

"Is the castle rampant with them?"

"As you can see," Fee said, gesturing to the large wooden barrel in the corner of the stillroom marked *acid arsenicus pulv*, "we have a ready supply of treatment."

The princess's eyes lit with recognition. "Yes, how peculiar. Mistress Goodsong insisted I ask for it straightaway, as she warned me against diseases from a castle somewhat dilapidated and rodent-ridden. I thought it would appear rude if I made the request to Xavi last night."

Fee swallowed the obvious barb. "I apologize for the odious reception. I imagine it's tainted your opinion of Fireli."

"Well," the princess began as she moved toward the stillroom door, "I did come unannounced, and my early appearance clearly caught the people of Fireli unaware. But the more disappointing matter has actually been with the king, and not his kingdom."

Fee's head whipped around. "In what way, milady?" *No, no, no,* Fee's voice repeated inside her head.

"I was told to expect a reception this morning—meant to introduce me to the people of Fireli, but instead, a note was placed upon my breakfast tray indicating that the schedule had changed. A government council meeting was taking its place. Perhaps Xavi is indifferent to my arrival and our kingdoms' union." Her eyes grew softly focused as she stared beyond Fee.

"No—the schedule change was my idea," Fee blurted out. "I mean"—she fumbled—"Xavi—he is under such pressure."

The princess's eyes barely narrowed. "Your idea?"

Fee scrambled with her explanation—she must convince the princess that Xavi and Fireli were not defiant. "The reception has been moved to this evening—a more grand event. Xavi is most enthusiastic about your appearance, I assure you. And he plans to spare no efforts in making you feel welcome in your new home. He's spoken of it often and *eagerly*."

The princess raised an eyebrow. "To you?"

"Uh . . . to everyone, Your Highness," Fee added hastily. "He speaks of his betrothed and the future of Fireli with great fervor. You simply caught him by surprise last night."

Princess Quinn opened the door and turned to look over her shoulder. "Yes, last night was full of surprises."

The door shut with a definitive click, and Fee wondered if she'd done enough to cure the princess of her suspicions.

She released herself upon the workbench, staring up at the shelves of elixirs. "I have pacifying words, sleep aids, and rat poison in abundance. But nothing that will take the sting out of the tongue-lashing I am about to receive from Savva."

CHAPTER

FOURTEEN

THE EVENING BANQUET, MEANT TO HONOR THE SOON-
to-be queen, left Fee repeatedly with her mouth agape: the sight of so
many people all together, the sound of those people all buzzing with
chatter, and the taste of the food they had gathered for the feast. Fee
indulged in it all and did her best to quell the thin thread of worry
that it might be snatched away by sipping the red wine in her hand.

Her eyes wandered about the sparing but festively decorated
hall, and she tried to conjure an image from her past—any one of
many from when Xavi and Rye's parents ruled Fireli, and celebratory
feasts were commonplace.

There were fresh flowers on the long banquet tables, which the
grounds around the stillroom oddly held in abundance, regardless
of the season. The linens might have been shabby, but the food they
rested beneath was warm and savory. Plates held small portions of

fish thanks to the elderly men who still had the energy to cast a net or rod across the castle grounds' pond, and fresh fruits and vegetables from the overgrown castle gardens, where those who could still bend to plant and weed worked during the day. They had few hunters, as it required fair eyesight to spot an animal and manageable strength to bring the kill home, so bagging a prize was an occurrence few and far between. But extra efforts had been made for tonight.

Fireli's residents had grown accustomed to a frugal lifestyle. Meals had been subdued, activities restrained, and conversation mostly muted. It was as if the castle had still cloaked itself in the dark mourning garments it had slipped its arms through nearly a decade ago. Tonight though, Fireli was determined to climb out of its fog.

"She is a vision of pure composure, is she not?" Sir Rollins said in quiet, crisp undertones at Fee's side. She'd been seated beside Fireli's regent for the evening and had struggled to make conversation with the man for the last hour.

You will go, but be silent, Savva had instructed her earlier. The outrage she'd expected the healer to project did not appear, but in its stead were directions—succinct and specific.

Do not offer your name. Nod toward the princess if asked where you came from. If you must speak, say you have been assigned to the princess as her personal physic and are working in concert with me.

And lastly, an omen: *I am left unsettled, Fee. I'm uncertain whether I should be bolstered by your ingenuity at skirting around our mandates or fearful for your future because of that same gumption. Best you be prepared for battle.*

She'd left Savva, befuddled, but now looked down the banquet table to where Princess Quinn sat beside Xavi. The beautiful young woman's hair, intricately braided, was swept up into an arrangement where a few tendrils grazed the shoulders of her garnet-colored gown. The candlelight, suffusing the room with soft illumination, caught on the tiny beads of sparkling gold, winking with elegance.

"Indeed, Sir Rollins. She appears quite comfortable being the center of attention."

"Not to mention worldly. Necessary traits if you are to be crowned a monarch of one of Aethusa's kingdoms," he added.

She turned to face him. "Surely once the moratorium on travel has been lifted, Prince Xavi will tour the remaining territories of the realm. I would imagine he's done endless hours of research on Gwyndom, Oldshire, and Thornbridge, yes?"

Sir Rollins tsked and fiddled with a prodigious ring on his middle finger—a rich, pearly opal. "Reading about a place is a far cry from actually knowing it. His lordship has buried himself within his library for nearly ten years. Perhaps now he will rely more heavily upon those of us with true life experience."

Fee's fist clenched around the stem of her wine goblet.

You will go, but be silent.

"My monthly trips have given me great insight—"

"Your monthly trips?" Fee interrupted.

He took a large swig from his wine goblet and gestured with his hand over his shoulder. "In the past, in the past. I used to travel greatly. But the young prince has complained bitterly in the face of the necessary sequestration. He has not been easy on any of his ministers, and I fear we shall find him butting heads with his advisors in the future too."

Fee looked at Sir Rollins's plate and fixated on the forkful of fresh spinach he raised to his mouth. She made it wither and go putrid just before reaching his tongue.

He swallowed uncomfortably, quickly reaching again for his wine. Finally dabbing at his mouth, he said, "This does not bode well for the princess, whose kingdom's early aid was instrumental in keeping us alive."

Fee knew part of the man's complaint to be untrue. Xavi understood the necessity of the quarantine and would not have argued against it, but there were countless issues she could easily see him find fault with and wish to debate. She was certain Xavi would have researched and contemplated every decision needing to be made. It wasn't to spurn authority, it was in order to earn it. She turned away from Sir Rollins as the buzz of conversation within the hall went silent. Xavi stood and raised his goblet.

"People of Fireli," he began, a small hitch in his usually steady voice, "I take this moment to properly introduce the newest resident of our kingdom. We have long awaited the day when grace would shine upon us again, and I believe the constituents of our home have been doubly blessed by not only the presence of such elegance but the clear intelligence behind it. I hope all of you will embrace a young woman who will walk beside me and help govern this land. Together we shall make it prosper for ourselves and our children. We shall breathe life into Fireli once more.

"Good ladies and gentlemen, may I present Princess Quinn of Gwyndom!" Xavi raised his glass an inch higher and turned to smile warmly at the young woman. "To your good health and our fine future."

Shouts of *hear, hear!* crested through the crowd, a lively ripple of movement as people raised their goblets to drink in agreement.

Fee watched Xavi lower himself to his chair and draw out a handkerchief from the inside of his doublet, swiping it across his brow. *At least,* Fee thought, *he's not using his sleeve.* His smile faltered as he turned to the princess and took up quiet conversation beside her. If he'd been nervous, then he'd found a way to shake it off in his tribute, as his words eventually grew steady and sure. But something was off. Fee was certain of it.

She hadn't quite made it through to the end of the meal, when the rustic fruit-and-berry pies were to be served, before receiving a note from Savva. The delights of the pastries' jammy insides, the fruit freshly plucked from their small orchard and the pies baked that morning, would have to be skipped, as Fee was to return to the stillroom immediately.

She made her excuses and bid her dinner companions good night, gazing longingly at the servers walking in carrying the sweet-crusted tarts. She sighed, thrilled to have been given a glimpse of life as she'd once remembered it, and made her way back to work.

As she stepped through the stillroom door, Savva greeted her with a sly glance toward the workbench. It was piled high with freshly harvested leaves and stems. It also displayed Fee's standard *Flora Homeopathica*, opened to the page Savva had marked as *Herbe du Diable*—the devil's herb—better known to Fee as *Atropa belladonna*.

Clearly, her evening would be spent expressing juice and mixing spirits to make a popular ointment they kept on hand for those patients who suffered from sciatic nerve pain. When Fee raised an eyebrow to silently inquire, Savva said, "The princess brought three carriages full of heavy trunks. I am fresh out of supplies to help those who were put in charge of them. I imagine tomorrow will bring an additional wave of discomfort to those overtaxed muscles. So do not tarry, child."

She did not. She worked relentlessly, long past when Savva herself retired, and deep into the night, when even the crickets beneath her open windows grew weary of their nightly pursuits.

As she finished tidying the stillroom and prepared to climb the ladder to her bed in the loft, the candlelit stillness was interrupted by a tentative knock on the door.

"Fee?" She heard a voice from behind the wood. "Savva? Is someone there?"

It was the princess.

"Coming," she called, backing down the ladder.

"It's Xavi," the princess said as Fee opened the door. "I've come for peppermint tea—something for his stomach. I think he's come down with the flu."

Fee moved swiftly to the shelves and said over her shoulder, "Tell me his symptoms."

The princess recounted his afflictions as if reluctant to part with them. "His stomach is in pain. He is nauseated, dizzy, and very thirsty."

Fee pulled things down from the shelves, the ingredients nearly leaping into her hands and echoing the urgency she felt: a sachet full of peppermint leaves to brew, crystalized ginger, and oil of oregano. Uncorking the stopper in the glass vial of oil, she sniffed its contents and placed it in front of the princess. "Here. It's an antiviral and an antibiotic. Take the vial with you. Make him drink one drop in a glass of water every couple of hours."

Fee placed the small bag of crystalized ginger beside the bottle. "This will also help with his nausea. Has he a fever? He did not seem himself at dinner. I wondered if something was the matter, but I wrote it off as simply the stress from—"

"Stress from . . . ?" the princess echoed.

Fee had been about to say *stress from the missing papers*, but caught herself. "Stress from the excitement of your arrival, milady."

Fee gathered the remainder of her curatives and said, "Perhaps I should see him. Make sure it's nothing worse."

The princess reached across for the small sack. "He has no need of you, thank you. I'm here to tend to him."

And before Fee could object, the princess left.

Three days had passed, each one giving rise to further concern for Fee whenever she looked in on Xavi. Although he remained upright, it was with great difficulty.

After the third day of unsuccessful attempts to keep anything solid in his stomach, Savva had instructed him to ingest nothing apart from the brews she provided. With each batch she instructed Fee to steep, the old woman then sent her running to replace Xavi's last treatment with something new.

Princess Quinn hovered and made the occasional visit to the stillroom, endlessly inquiring after Xavi's recovery from the perspective of his healers.

On the fourth day, it appeared he'd finally turned the corner. He was pale and thin but feeling much recovered. Fee received a message to come to his library and, showing Savva the official request, happily left the stillroom and her studies to see her best friend.

The sentry opened the door to reveal not only Xavi sitting behind his mahogany desk but Princess Quinn in a chair—a new chair—on the opposite side of it. The battered leather seat Fee had spent years sinking into, with its softened grooves and form-fitting depressions, had been removed.

Xavi smiled warmly, but weakly, and Fee quickly made a polite bob to the princess before addressing him. "You're looking much better," she said, feeling the anxiety from the last three days ebb away.

"Many thanks to you, which is why I called you here in the middle of your workday. I won't keep you long. It was Quinn's idea, actually."

Fee looked to the young woman. "My mother," the princess began in clipped tones, "instructed me to always thank people properly." The princess reached beside her chair, produced a box, and held it out. "For your help with Xavi."

"Confections." Xavi winked and tapped at the similar box on his desk.

"This is very kind of you, Your Royal Highness, and although not necessary, I will appreciate—or rather savor—every last bite." Fee took the box and turned to Xavi, smiling with the thought that perhaps the three of them were at last moving in the right direction. "I aim to make this last as long as possible, Xavi."

"See that you do, Fee," he said wryly. "At last, no one to pinch my supply."

"A small price to pay for a healer at your beck and call, is it not, *milord*?" Fee stifled a laugh and, turning to see what she hoped would be an agreeable face, noticed the princess's placid expression. She was not amused.

Fee quickly repeated her thanks and made her way out of Xavi's study and back to the many hours of study in front of her.

Upon Fee's arrival, her gift caused Savva's face to spread with curiosity. Fee placed the parcel on the table and sat before her books, hoping to dive into her studies without a parade of questions.

"Assessment is key when trying to unravel a puzzle, child."

Fee kept her head down, her finger tracing the lines as she absorbed the material in front of her.

Used to reduce natural and morbid vomiting . . .

Helpful for patients suffering from darting pains . . .

"Your life's work will be more than the simple matter of mixing elixirs and grinding herbs, Fee."

The fine, powdery, spun-like substance, when introduced to the eye, may cause severe inflammation.

Eruptions at each corner of the mouth, swelling of the glands, and ulceration of the lips.

Savva's voice interrupted her reading again. "Our task is one of solving mysteries. Often we are presented with an incomplete set of clues, and if they are misread, we may come to a conclusion that is wholly inaccurate."

Fee looked up and sighed, long and loudly. Obviously, she would not learn anything that might be of future use to cure Xavi—or anyone else—if Savva was bound and determined to lecture.

She turned to find Savva at the window, hunched over a small plant she was potting and taking advantage of the strong sunlight to aid her weakening vision. Fee selected one stem from the pile of freshly picked begonias and held it in the air. She fixated on the flower and found a small thrill with the sound of the begonia head popping off its stem.

Savva straightened for a moment, then bent back over her work and said, "Please."

Fee stopped dead, a cold stone falling hard into the pit of her stomach. *The woman has eyes in the back of her head!*

"Please put these somewhere special," the healer said, leaving the window and coming to stand before her. She placed the small potted plant in the center of the table, in front of Fee. It held a spray of freshly planted tiny buds: five-petaled, robin's-egg-blue blossoms with an eye of yellow winking in its center.

Myosotis—forget-me-nots.

Tomorrow was the anniversary of the day her parents died. When a vast number of Fireli's residents died. When life as they knew it changed immeasurably. They would spend time remembering and grieving, but also looking hopefully toward the future.

"Experience will be a book you must review from time to time. The collection of knowledge combined with your memories will be invaluable. Remember, child, you may never find all the answers to life's secrets, but it doesn't mean you should give up searching for them. Perhaps somewhere, you will find yourself as well."

Fee looked up at Savva, pulling the beheaded begonia down into her lap. "What answers do you believe I'm searching for?"

The old healer's lips curled at the edges with a knowing smile. "Your questions are growing in numbers. It's easy enough to see them. You want to know why the princess is so cold to you. You wish to know why Xavi is not improving—or at least maintaining health like the rest of Fireli's residents. But most important, you question your worth in this stillroom."

Fee sank lower on the bench with each statement Savva spoke. It was as if the healer had a tiny hammer that effectively pushed her farther into a sinking hole she'd been trying to climb out of. She detested being so transparent.

Savva put a warm, trembling hand on top of Fee's and smiled patiently. "You are Xavi's fighting chance. Do not give up." She pointed toward Fee's daily tonic. "Take yours, and work on his. Sometimes the answers are right in front of us, child. For that is the best place to hide secrets."

CHAPTER

FIFTEEN

FEE DOWNED HER DAILY ANTIDOTE BEFORE GETTING
into bed and then lay on her stomach, her cheek against the cool pil-
lowcase covering the old goose-down-stuffed cushion. She stared at
the tiny, flickering candle on the table below the loft, watching the
flame dance in the faint breeze from an open window. Its light shone
on the forget-me-nots, which, as soon as Savva had left the stillroom
to find her own bed, Fee made blossom into a tiny spray of lush flowers to temper her misery.

She wanted someone to blame.

You should have been more prepared! Fee had shouted at Savva
on a particularly difficult day of remembrance when she'd been
thirteen. *Why was there so little medicine to treat people?* she'd cried.
Savva's response was a face full of culpability. Fee's words had been
sharp and injurious. She'd never said them again.

Although the rest of the castle held a memorial to mark the

somber day, Fee had never been allowed to join the others. Savva helped her mourn in private. The yearly collecting of blossoms and burning of the tribute candle were meant to stir her memory, to honor her past, to summon her parents. But with the memories came the pain, and within the ache was the rush of criticism. Surrounding it all was the essence of shame.

"It's called *survivor's guilt*," Xavi had explained one day when as teenagers they sat together in the stillroom, late at night, their tribute candles burning side by side on the old wooden table. "I suffer it as well."

"Savva does not wish to speak of it. She prefers we keep it locked within the stoppered jars upon the shelves, that I grind it with her pestle to a fine powder or paste at the bottom of her mortar, and then drown it with nerve-blunting grain alcohol where it cannot surface and catch its breath."

Xavi's expression had revealed strong disapproval. "You cannot silence your emotions. Or keep them in tightly sealed compartments. Not for long, anyway. Perhaps Savva is different, but you are *not* Savva."

Fee had looked over Xavi's shoulder at the shelves full of remedies. How many times had she bottled and stoppered some concoction incorrectly—some unforeseen burbling reaction slowly taking place within the jars that ended up exploding out of their containers? Perhaps it was like this with imprisoned emotions too.

She pulled a faded, patched-up quilt over her head to chase away the thoughts. Being alone—sequestered from everyone for so long—strained the walls of those captive feelings. At times, this stillroom was a dark and soulless place. But it was also a refuge. Her sanctuary. And it was where she could fight death—refusing to let it steal what it wanted most of all: the people she loved.

She closed her eyes and let the vision of the candles, the blossoms, and Xavi grow muted and vague. This lightless, monotone world was a familiar cocoon. It was safe. It was simple.

It was home.

Xavi was ill again.

It had now been a full week of him growing slowly sicker. His skin paling, his lips drying, the nausea growing. Fee was gripped with panic at her constant defeat in overcoming his ailment.

She scanned hundreds of pages, read through dozens of books and myriad ledgers filled with homemade recipes that had been tested, tried, and honed throughout the years. Concoctions that had been handed down from one healer's generation to another's. But she could find nothing new. Nothing that made hope spring from the pages.

"Savva, I've nowhere left to look. Nothing remains in these books that will kill off that which is making Xavi suffer."

Savva looked at Fee and held up her hand. "You are looking at the problem from the wrong direction, Fee. Our work as healers is not an effort to destroy that which does harm to a body, but rather to multiply that which brings *life* to it. Search with that in mind."

"Help me. You know so much more than I do," Fee said, her choler beginning to rise. "I don't understand why you just point and lecture. Don't you care?" she cried out, snapping the covers of a book together.

"I care about Xavi's health more than you could possibly understand. But there are certain medicines I can no longer touch or create. Many compounds would disable me quickly, and I'd be of no use to you." Savva came to stand in front of Fee and put her hands on Fee's shoulders. "Now . . . funnel your anger into focus."

Savva sent Fee to deliver the teas and tinctures to Xavi. The princess was always there on the receiving end, his constant companion. The occasional peek Fee was given showed Xavi dull of speech and heavy-lidded. At the end of the seventh full day, Savva announced to Fee that she was delivering his medicine herself, and that Fee would accompany her.

They were greeted by the princess, her features revealing an overwrought countenance, her comments, a lack of faith.

"It appears your treatments are falling short."

Xavi was propped up on a long chaise lounge, papers in his lap, an array of ointments overburdening the small table beside him. His face was sallow but he managed a feeble smile.

Savva turned to the princess. "May I see him alone, please?"

"Why?" the princess asked, incredulous.

"Occasionally patients feel discomfort discussing some of their . . . symptoms."

Princess Quinn flushed with pink. "Perhaps it is not that he has held back information. Perhaps you're using antiquated methods of treatment. I feel I should call for Gwyndom's healer, as Mistress Goodsong is most capable. I wonder if even Xavi is losing faith in your abilities?"

Fee gripped her hands into an angry ball. That couldn't be true. Surely, the one person who always assured her she was on the right path was not doubting her—especially since she had Savva at her side. Fee swallowed the outcry she wished to release and instead noted Savva's features radiating a degree of fretfulness Fee had never seen her display. The old healer hesitated and then gestured toward the threshold. "If it is what you wish, milady, but for the moment . . . please." She glanced toward the door.

The princess glared at Savva with a cool gaze of surrender and then turned to face Fee. "I shall be right outside if anyone has need of me." She left and, after hearing the door click, Fee went to sit beside Savva, to watch as the healer palpated and studied her patient. When Savva was finished, she picked up one of Xavi's teacups, emptied the remaining contents back into the teapot, and carefully pocketed the fragile cup. She placed a hand upon his head briefly and then struggled to rise. "I shall return with a different medicine, milord, but until then, rest. Trust that we will resolve this problem. Both of you must have faith."

Fee wondered if she meant *both of you* as in both she and Xavi, or *both of you* as in the *princess* and Xavi. It probably didn't matter at this point, as the words rang hollow in Fee's ears and they were most likely intended to buoy the prince.

They'd traveled only a short distance down the hallway before the healer turned to Fee and tapped her temple. "I left my satchel on the prince's desk. Please fetch it, and meet me immediately in the stillroom."

Fee scurried back to Xavi's study. She knocked and, upon entering, found Xavi already sleeping and the princess reading a book by his side. Fee pointed to the bag and moved to get it quickly. When she turned back, she watched the princess reach for one of Xavi's confections, pop it into the teapot, and add more hot water.

Something clicked in Fee's head, and instantly she stifled her sharp intake of breath.

She raced down the corridor and the long spiral staircase toward the door that led to the gardens and the stillroom. It was just as Savva had told her. *Sometimes the answers are right in front of us. For that is the best place to hide secrets.*

She tore down the garden path toward the stillroom, cutting across the weedy gardens and overgrown lawns. When Fee finally burst through the door and into the cottage, she found Savva hunched over the workbench, a large gas lamp pooling a halo of bright yellow light around her workspace.

Fee rushed to where the healer stooped, and spotted the open box of confections next to her on the table.

"How did you know?" she asked Savva.

"I was not one hundred percent certain until I studied the dregs at the bottom of the teacup. Come here. Run your finger along the inside, and then look at it under the glass." She handed Fee the ivory-handled magnifier. The remnants were gritty, like grains of fine sand.

"What is it?"

Savva turned toward the barrel in the corner, and Fee gasped. *Arsenic.*

It felt as if she'd been kicked in her belly, her guts twisting with realization. "I—I gave it to her, Savva. It was me. She said she heard rats in the walls and couldn't sleep. Dear God, what have I done?"

The old woman turned to Fee, aghast. "You may have given the poison to the princess, but it was *she* who chose what to do with it. Do not cloud your mental state. Lives depend upon your ability to act with intellect and an even keel of emotions."

Fee knew Savva had tried to dissolve her guilt, but it remained steadfast, stuck in the knot of tangles that tightened in her stomach. "So what do we do—I mean, firstly, we have to save Xavi, right?"

Savva wiped her fingers of the residue onto the apron tied around her drab gray skirt. She shook her head again and moved to the shelves behind her. "Xavi shall survive this, as long as we act quickly and our treatment is not interfered with."

Fee closed her eyes. "The princess dusted the confections?" She then turned quickly to look at the pink box—the one from which she'd been eating—and slowly raised a hand to her throat.

Savva shook her head. "I've just tested them."

"Nothing? Just Xavi's batch?"

"It appears so."

"I saw her put it in his tea."

"She might have gotten away with this method except that she did not dissolve the poison appropriately for disguise. One must vigorously boil the arsenic for at least one half hour within a liquid, and it appears she simply stirred it into the pot itself."

"We must tell Xavi—and the castle guards—to apprehend the princess," Fee said, trying to hold back the panicky thought of her best friend lying in his study at this very moment and being fed more poison.

The healer held up a crooked finger. "No, for there are two issues to consider. The first is that it might not *be* the princess. She may be ignorant of the toxic nature of the sweets."

Fee nodded slowly.

Savva held up another finger. "Second, if it *is* the princess who's poisoned Xavi with the intent to kill him, there is a reason for it—likely planned and supported by others behind her. Others we cannot see. We must find them out first, or we will be walking into a snake pit of inestimable trouble."

Fee thought back to Xavi's papers, dread spreading within her like the spilling of oil on old wood, seeping into every fissure and crevice. She told the healer of their first meeting with the princess—how Xavi panicked when discovering a theft had occurred and painted a picture for Fee of potential disaster.

Savva stood very still, her lips pressing inward, and then, finally, nodded. "It is possible that the princess read his papers, sent them to Gwyndom, and then received instructions as to what next steps to take. Or she may be nothing more than a pawn in a greater game."

"But what do we do now, Savva? We must act quickly, for Xavi's life is at stake."

Savva pulled several jars and glass vials down from the shelving and collected stock ingredients from inside the cupboards below them. "Place the large kettle on to boil, child. I am assured that Xavi will not ingest anything until we see him next, as I warned him not to."

Fee felt her features twist with tension. "We cannot simply cure him of the injury and then let him fend for himself. That's hardly solving the problem."

Savva rolled up the sleeves of her stained and fraying blouse. "We have a small window in which to brew the potion that will give us what we need to illuminate the true culprit in this crime. Then we may act accordingly."

"What is it that we need?"

"Time."

"And how are we to get it?"

The healer pulled a stopper out of a small glass bottle and squeezed two drops of oily liquid into a brown vial. "First, we must kill Xavi."

CHAPTER
SIXTEEN

"I KNOW IT ISN'T THE SAFEST PLAN, NOR THE MOST ideal, but it's the best we could come up with." Fee stared down at Xavi, kneeling beside him as he lay stretched out, weakened and pallid, his eyes looking back up at her, incredulous.

"Death? Ideal?" he whispered, too limp to even move his limbs.

"It's not *true* death, Xavi. And it's our only means of escape. The potion is meant to slow your respiration, minimize your heart rate, and cool the temperature of your skin. It's meant to deceive those viewing you superficially—likely the princess and Sir Rollins, possibly a few others from the ministry council. Enough to call Savva for her official examination and pronouncement."

His eyes remained large and fearful. "And then what? I am to be buried?"

"No," Fee said quickly. "You would be moved to the stillroom, where the deceased are always brought, where Savva and I prepare them for burial. And in your case, there would be an expected 'lying in state' period of time."

"Are you saying I am to be kept in this half-dead state for days on end?"

Fee put a reassuring hand on Xavi's arm. She could feel him struggling to lift it. "Not at all. As soon as you are brought to the stillroom, Savva will administer an antidote, and then we'll move you to our cave, where you will have a chance to recover without the threat of future poisoning—or some other manner of assassination attempt." She looked at him pleadingly. "It will buy us time, Xavi, and save your life."

"That is if I don't die of the cure first."

"You must trust us. You are not safe here."

He glanced around the room, his gaze falling on the box of confections at the windowsill, the teapot on the table, and finally Fee's face. "I do trust you," he said feebly. "With my very life. I always have."

Fee thought about the charm Xavi wore around his neck and tucked beneath his linen shirt. "Hold on to that trust, Xavi, and do not forget that we are here to protect you—just like your talisman."

He seemed on the verge of saying something but then changed his mind and simply nodded.

Fee breathed out in relief. "We should move quickly."

"Wait," he said, trying to reach for her hand. "Fee . . . if I don't make it out of this"—he swallowed with difficulty—"you must promise me to stop allowing your unusual *abilities* to surface." He looked into her eyes, a desperate plea behind them. "You heard what

Rye wrote—about the witch hunt in Oldshire. You know what it is they do to people with such skills. If I am no longer here to look after you, I have no doubt that Sir Rollins will act according to old laws. And if Rye takes my place, he may be forced to—or even *believe* it is right to—do the same." He clutched her hand. "I know sometimes you cannot help it but . . . take heed."

She felt a chill across her skin and tried to steady her expression into one of calm complaisance. She would think on his words, of course, but right now, she needed to get Xavi to the other side of this nightmare.

She nodded and pulled the vial out of her apron pocket, putting it into Xavi's hand, curling his fingers around it. "Take this. The liquid will act swiftly. Do not swallow it until you are alone."

Xavi nodded, his face wretchedly pained but determined.

"This will all be over shortly. As soon as you are pronounced dead, Rye will be sent for. He will help sort this out, Xavi. And we will do it all before we welcome home the returning citizens of Fireli. We will save both you and this kingdom."

Xavi locked eyes with Fee and uttered the words Princess Quinn had spoken on their first meeting: "On our lives."

The kingdom was shattered. Word spread as rapidly as the disease that had swept through it a decade before. Fireli's remaining inhabitants cried bitterly, speaking of the long shadow cast across the land, but in payment for what wrongdoing? No one could say. Was it the absence of the kingdom's core stone? Had the realm been cursed?

Princess Quinn had discovered Xavi, as hoped. For three merciless hours, Fee had paced the length of the stillroom, unable to focus on the tasks Savva had assigned her. She fumbled with jars, spilled a week's worth of black elderberry cough syrup, and mislabeled two crocks of steeping oils. Savva shook her head and shooed her away.

When finally a guard came, Fee slid onto the bench and in front of her books, desperate to appear fully immersed in work.

"Mistress Savva!" the guard cried, flinging the door wide. "The prince!"

The healer appraised the guard coolly. "What of him? Illness or injury?"

The guard's face was ashen. "Neither, mistress. I was told he is deceased."

Savva whipped around to face him. "You were *told*? How did he die—and did you see him?"

The guard shook his head. "From disease, they say. He was found lying in his study."

Savva eyed him with scrutiny. "But who has made this pronouncement?" she asked, gathering vials and bottles into her traveling satchel.

"I believe Sir Rollins."

"I trust no one but my own eyes. Quickly—lead me to him."

Fee was awestruck at her mentor's playacting. She followed Savva and the guard up to Xavi's study, where six or seven council members clustered and spoke in hushed tones. The princess stood among them, her pallid face and posture the perfect blend between shock and fortitude. Savva pushed past the throng to the daybed where Xavi was lying.

His face was colorless, his eyes closed, and a blanket had been drawn to his chin. Fee could make out no discernible rise and fall of his chest. Savva put one hand on his neck and the other upon the inside of his wrist to feel for a pulse. She remained still for a full minute while Fee's heart hammered away, booming within its cage and surely interfering with Savva's ability to detect any faint rhythm from beneath Xavi's skin.

What if Savva had given him the wrong dose? What if he was truly dead and *they* had been the ones to kill him?

Savva glanced up at Fee and nodded gravely, then rose and made her way toward where the elder council members and the princess waited. Fee collapsed to her knees and lay her head upon Xavi's arm. Although to the others it would appear she was weeping with the anguish of losing a patient, it was in fact the only way to hide her relief. The release was short-lived though, as she and Savva still needed to have Xavi delivered to the stillroom and then spirited away to the cave for safekeeping.

"Bring him to the stillroom," she heard Savva direct. "Be careful with the prince, and disturb nothing upon his body, for before I prepare him for viewing and burial, I must examine him for that which caused his death."

Fee turned to watch the reaction among the group, wondering if the princess would object, but she remained as solid as if molded in plaster, as regal as if in a parade.

"Might I stay to accompany him down, Savva? I cannot bear to leave his side," Fee said, looking up, eyes brimming with tears.

Savva gave a terse nod and turned back to Sir Rollins. "Have him brought to me immediately."

The pathway from Xavi's study to the stillroom was lined with nearly all the castle's inhabitants, men and women continually casting out to grab at Fee, who accompanied the body.

What has happened? The gods cruelly toy with us again. Fireli is no more!

She looked at them miserably and plowed on.

Savva had the table prepared, and when they were at last alone, she turned to Fee and put a hand on her arm, squeezing it with her frail fingers. "Do not fret, child. The drug will wear off shortly. In the meantime, help me assemble the last of the supplies for when he is recovering in the cave on his own." Savva looked off into the distance beyond Fee and mumbled, "The sooner we have them relocated, the greater their chances grow for survival, as staying here is not an option."

"What do you mean *them*? Is someone going to stay with Xavi?"

Savva didn't answer. She worked busily, lining up supplies, and Fee filled two bags with the healer's provisions. They would travel under cover of night, as the kingdom would be blanketed in mourning tonight, with no one fit to do their jobs and post watch at the guard stations. For what was the purpose now? There was no future king to guard. There was only waiting until the new heir to the castle appeared. This meant that now was their best chance for escape.

Xavi began to stir as they finished their tasks, and Fee rushed to his side with a cup of water. She helped him to sit up and wrapped his shoulders in the wool blanket he'd been placed upon.

"How are we feeling?" Savva asked, searching his face and reading his features. She came around to take his pulse.

He shivered and put his free hand to his head. "Well, I can't speak for anyone else, but personally I feel as if I've risen from my grave." He peered groggily about the stillroom. "From the looks of it, it appears you've pulled it off. Congratulations. I am still alive—if just barely."

Savva gently pressed him to lie flat again and returned to the workbench. "Best we not celebrate prematurely, milord. We must see ourselves successfully through the next part of the escape before I can breathe easier."

"At this point," Xavi said sluggishly, "I am simply grateful to be breathing at all." His eyes fluttered closed.

Fee squeezed his hand and whispered, "I told you everything would work out. You still have your guardian angel. And Savva's bulla is probably working in your favor as well."

Xavi shook his head weakly. "It was none of those things. It was the proper use of *Atropa belladonna*. Or perhaps she used a neurotoxin from an *Atelopus*. You should know that."

Fee pulled back. "What did you say?"

Xavi blinked back the cloudiness in his eyes and then mumbled lethargically, "I said . . . oh, I can't remember. It doesn't matter. Right now, I'll take good fortune in any form offered. Wake me when it is time to move. I cannot keep my thoughts straight, Fee. But know how grateful I . . ." His words trailed off, and Fee pulled the blanket back up to his chin. How would he know the contents of his death elixir? she wondered. There was no time to puzzle it out.

"Go to the kitchens and gather food," Savva instructed her. "Then you must saddle two horses and have them ready for us to ride. Trust no one, child. Go with haste and care—use your stealth. For more than Xavi's life depends upon it."

CHAPTER
SEVENTEEN

THE ANEMIC CALL OF THE CASTLE TRUMPET CAUGHT
on the wind, and Fee straightened from her task, straining to hear
the cry. She looked toward the sound where the sun was setting. She
squinted, and could just make out a band of riders coming toward
her, their silhouettes obscured by the dust the horses were kicking
up in their race to reach her. She was at the very edge of the castle
grounds—as far as they were allowed to stray before breaking one of
the Seclusion Rules.

She reached down for the basket that held the long, purple-
blossomed stalks of digitalis she'd harvested for the past hour. She
was prepared to play the part of a girl filled with grief over the loss
of her king and patient. They would tell her the body she and Savva
had prepared for viewing had been stolen, and she would display
shock at the news.

Six horsemen galloped to where she stood in the bountiful flower field and slackened to a stop, surrounding her on all sides. Fee did not recognize the horses, nor the men who sat upon them. One, though, had a face that stirred a memory, awakening something that had been dormant for nearly a decade. Her heart quickened as she looked up into a pair of jade-colored eyes and a face that had grown from that of a mischief-making mutineer into one of a sharp, observant statesman.

Rye.

Fee's face broke into a wide, embracing visage of relief, her whole body bursting with joy.

He slid off his horse, finding the ground beneath him with practiced ease, and moved toward her with the pace of a wary, calculating hunter, scanning her from top to bottom. When he reached within a foot of where she stood, Fee dropped her basket and leapt toward him, arms outstretched.

"Rye!" she called.

But he caught her arms midair before they could wrap around his neck, and then they were immediately hooked by one of the men who'd come to stand behind her, unmercifully restrained, and pinned at the small of her back.

"Ophelia?" came the deep voice of a boy she once knew. One eyebrow quirked in question, coolly and painfully inquiring.

"Rye?" she said, wincing with the brutal assault. "Rye, what is going on?"

The soldier grappling her arms imprisoned her wrists within a steel bracelet, the click of captivity a keen and panicking sound.

"Are you Ophelia de Vale, the child of Peregrine and Annabelle de Vale of the Kingdom of Fireli?" Rye asked, his face growing stolid, his body stiffening.

"You more than anyone know that I am. What is this?" Fee asked, her eyes searching his face for any remnant of recognition.

"You are under arrest for the murder of my brother, Prince Xavi Chin-Ranton of Fireli, and for the theft of his body. Come without struggle and perhaps you shall see a measure of mercy."

"What?" Fee said, her mouth falling open, her body writhing against the constraints. "Surely you don't believe—"

"It is advisable that you cooperate, Ophelia." His eyes grew dark, his left hand tightening into a rock-solid fist. He looked away and spoke to the man holding Fee in custody. "Take her to the castle stockade. I will follow shortly to question her."

"Rye," Fee pleaded. "Wait, please! You've made a terrible mistake."

The muscles at Rye's jaw twitched as he turned to face her again. "I believe what you meant to say is that *you've* made a terrible mistake, Ophelia. One that will haunt us both for the rest of our lives—although your torment will fortunately be short-lived, as assassins are quick to meet their execution." He pointed toward the castle. "Take her now."

Fee sat on the dirty straw tick mattress at the back of the cell, the stone walls slick with wet moss, the air smelling of mildew, stagnant water, and mold. She shivered in the dark and pulled her knees up to her chest—grateful for the extra warmth provided by the trousers under her skirt.

How could Rye believe she would kill her best friend, his

brother—and worse, their king? Someone was clearly leading Rye down the wrong path—directing attention away from the one who truly wanted Xavi dead. If she could speak with him alone, she'd be able to tell him the whole story. Rye would know that Xavi was safe and would help them solve the crisis in the kingdom. He would be grateful, filled with relief, and embrace Fee as he should have when he first came to seek her out.

The small cell in which she waited had a thin slit in the corner of the room where the ceiling and wall met. A glassless window, with stubby, paint-flecked iron bars that showed an inch of ground and three of sky, was as good as a clock for Fee, and she estimated the time of day by watching the shadows move across the grass beyond the short metal rods.

When the shadows faded to blend in with the night sky, Fee searched the sliver of heavens to catch a glimpse of the moon rising. She needed to keep track of the hours, to maintain a task for her mind. Allowing it to go still left it unguarded. And then panic would rush in. She would scramble up to the rails at the window and cry for help, or grasp the tall iron rods that served as the fourth wall of her prison and shake them, a flood of hysteria coursing through her as she shouted for attention. *Xavi needed her!*

She sat on the floor, calculating his food, his water, his medicine. How long he could survive without assistance.

She quickly came to realize there was no lock to pick—just a pulley system that operated the door from much farther down the hallway.

She nodded off eventually, her head resting atop her knees, but each time her muscles relaxed to give in to sleep, she jerked awake, the sensation of falling wrenching her back into consciousness.

The sounds of booted feet jolted her from her drowsy state, and she leapt from the mattress, grasping the cell's cast-iron bars. Flickering torchlight grew stronger as she heard footsteps descending the stairs, and as the cold stone hallway lit with growing illumination, Fee counted three rats scattering for the inky shadows and the safety of invisibility.

Two guards, the personification of twin thickset oak trees, moved to stand with their torches on either side of the wide wall of solid rods. The scent of burning tar accompanied them, filling Fee's nose with an acrid whiff. Rye came behind them, his tall frame erect with purpose. Fee did not know this man, this grown version of the boy she desperately needed to see. She pulled back from the bars, shivering from both the cold and the unfamiliarity before her.

"Ophelia," he said, his low, resonant voice deadened with exhaustion.

"Rye? We must speak alone," Fee said, glancing from one guard to the other.

Rye's eyes narrowed in the dimly lit surroundings, and Fee caught sight of his left hand clenching with swift rigidity. "I think not. I have come to officially question you, and procedure requires there be a witness present."

"Surely the guards could give us a moment to speak—just one quick minute before the official interview."

Rye shook his head. "I'm not speaking of my guards." Fee turned at the sound of a new set of footsteps, light and clipped. Straining to see down the hallway toward the staircase, she saw the folds of falling silk gathered in two bunches by manicured hands slowly come into view and, a moment later, the self-possessed features of Princess Quinn.

"I am here, Rye." Fee noted the lack of formal address. "Could we finish this quickly? It's terribly cold. And there's much that needs to be done." She cast a sideways glance at Fee. "The Kingdom of Fireli depends upon your ability to bring about swift justice."

Fee gasped. How could this young woman possess such authority? "Rye," she began, "you must listen to me."

"You will address him as *milord*," the princess said with a note of umbrage.

He held up a hand and took a deep breath. "I am determined to follow protocol, Ophelia. Do not attempt to divert due process."

"Divert it?" Fee repeated. "I've not seen a shred of it yet. I am only aware of being apprehended without a reasonable explanation and accused of a crime I have not committed—by any stretch of the imagination."

Rye wrapped his hands around the bars of the cell. "The governing bodies of Fireli, given appropriate and legal authority to act to the benefit of its people, need offer no reasonable explanation when apprehending a suspected assassin—although one has been thoroughly discussed. And if I remember correctly, Ophelia, your imagination has never fallen short of extraordinary."

Fee felt her mouth go slack with shock. "Do you seriously believe I have done what you're accusing me of doing? That I'm even capable of it?"

Rye's left hand constricted around the iron rod he grasped.

"You mustn't be waylaid by the girl's canny pleas, Rye," Princess Quinn said. "She is beyond measure with her cleverness, and what happened to poor Xavi is incomprehensible. I implore you to begin the questioning. There is no time to be spared."

Fee's gut twisted and, by the looks of it, Rye must have seen the gruesome pang reflected on her face. He looked to the ground. "Yes," he whispered, and then straightened. "When was the last time you saw Xavi Chin-Ranton, the prince of Fireli, alive?"

This question couldn't be answered. Revealing the truth to Rye in front of the princess and the guards would put Xavi in certain danger. And even though the words were aching for release, Fee held on to them—to save the life of her king, even if it meant she was putting hers in peril.

"The day before last—the day of his death," she choked out, shaking her head at the wretched torture of having to speak a lie to Rye—one that surely filled him with a throbbing pain, like touching a supremely sensitive wound, the nerve endings biting and raw. "Rye," she said, hoping that just the sound of her saying his name might evoke a thread of benevolence. But he carried on.

"And up until that point, you and Mistress Savva, Fireli's healer, were in charge of his care whilst he was ill?"

Princess Quinn stepped forward. "They visited his study repeatedly to bring him potions that only increased his illness."

"Rye," Fee said, searching his face. *Where is the boy?*

"Once the body had been delivered to the stillroom to prepare for viewing and burial, how do you account for your whereabouts?"

"You found her alone in a flower field, Rye, attempting to establish some reasonable distance from the crime—in fact, as far from the castle as was deemed allowable. No one saw her from the moment the prince's body was delivered to the stillroom until you tracked her down."

Rye gave the princess a sideways glance. "That is not damning evidence, Quinn. Regardless, is this accurate, Ophelia?" The look on his face was one that Fee read as hopeful she could provide an alternate version.

"Savva will tell you exactly where I've been, which"—and here Fee swung her gaze from Rye to the princess—"up until the moment she sent me out to gather stalks of foxglove, had been directly at her side."

Rye's head tipped toward the floor. "We cannot ask Mistress Savva."

"Why not?" Fee asked.

"Your healer cannot answer questions currently or, quite possibly, ever again," Princess Quinn said.

"What has happened to Savva, Rye?"

He pressed his fingers to his eyes. "She has taken a spill. Someone found her at the bottom of your stillroom's stepladder. She must have been reaching for something on one of the upper shelves and lost her balance."

Quinn added, "It is most unfortunate that she is unconscious in the castle infirmary with no physic to aid her."

"What?" Fee choked. "Rye, please, release me. I have to help!"

"Don't be ridiculous," the princess said coolly. "You are the prime suspect in the slaying of Fireli's future king. You are also charged with the theft of his body to prevent any efforts that would distinguish the reason for his death. And, as of yesterday afternoon, when your healer was found lying unconscious on the stillroom floor, the general consensus has been that it was not only possible but highly likely that *you* were the one to manufacture her current state, as she is the only other individual within Fireli that could identify you as the murderer and thief of the man I was to marry."

Fee felt as if someone had sliced her open and gutted her insides. She could not catch her breath. She grabbed the bars and looked beseechingly at Rye. "Surely this woman cannot come into our kingdom and take charge? Only you would have the authority to deny me the grace of granting my plea to help Savva. Whatever reason could I have for acting so calculating and ruthless? My God, Rye— you know me better than this! We were going to be married!"

"And there we have it. You have confessed to the motive," Princess Quinn said, removing her hands from the bars and dusting them off. "I think you've illustrated exactly the reason behind your madness."

Fee looked at her, wholly baffled. "Why?"

"Because you wanted to be queen."

CHAPTER
EIGHTEEN

HER ARMS AND LEGS WERE LEADEN, HER HEAD REFUSED to lift. Fee saw no point in opening her eyes to follow the thin ray of sunlight or the squat bars' shadows as they fell across the ground. Time halted due to the creep of overwhelming exhaustion. Like a piece of wood, she'd been left shaven down to a flat plane, where no thoughts or emotions could catch a foothold and settle in.

She had felt much the same nearly ten years ago when Savva told her that her parents had died, and the kingdom had been turned upside down. There was no want for reflection. Life had stopped— at least the lives that had made hers meaningful.

And now she wanted the license to leave this one behind. To stop responding to breath. To extinguish the demand for consciousness. A thought would occasionally slither into her head. She would acknowledge it, and then mindfully turn her back on it. Her consciousness was hidden away in a murky, softly edged place.

It was a familiar home. One that rarely needed dusting from disuse.

Fee heard the small iron flap on the barred wall slide open and detected the sound of the metal meal tray grating along the cobblestone floor. She didn't stir. She'd lost count of the number of times that door had opened and one full tray had been exchanged for the previously untouched one. There was no need to nourish life at this point. If she was imprisoned, she couldn't help Savva. If Savva was injured and unconscious, they couldn't minister to Xavi. If no one helped Xavi, he would die.

They might as well all die.

The morning after Rye and the princess left, Fee was greeted with a formal letter stating the charge of murder and an official notification created by Sir Rollins and the cabinet ministry, signed by Rye, breaking, officially, their lifelong engagement.

As if that needed clarity.

Fee nearly pleaded for an audience with him, to loose the story and have him save Xavi. She would have, except one niggling fact refused to allow her to do so.

Rye was so changed—he was such an utterly different person than the one Fee had known. And he seemed remarkably close to Princess Quinn. Rye's brother's death would mean his own ascension to the throne.

What if Rye is a coconspirator?

It was a heart-wrenching thought. And one she attempted to drive away, but with each hour of pacing, she grew more uncertain.

Perhaps the years abroad had left Rye hungry for power, or bitter from the banishment. Maybe he'd been schooled to believe he would be a better ruler than Xavi ever could be. Who was to say he was not a pawn in a greater game to overthrow and replace the ruler with a figurehead who could be easily controlled by others?

And so she'd sunk to the lowest place possible. A place where light, faith, and hope were choked of any growth. A place she'd become so deeply embedded in, she did not recognize the sound of Rye's voice, repeatedly calling her name, until it was accompanied by the jarring sounds of metal on metal. He banged on the bars with the tin cup from her tray full of uneaten food.

"Ophelia," she finally heard him say.

Fee sat up, uncurling herself from the tight ball she'd been wrapped in. She turned to look at him, sensing it must have been sometime in the hours long after midnight.

"Ophelia," he repeated.

"What?" she croaked.

"I cannot sleep."

She shook her head. Slowly. With astonishment. "I have not known sleep for days." There was a tiny flame of heat that flickered to life in her belly, and she wanted to say something caustic about how *his* slumber was the farthest thing from her mind.

"I feel I must speak with you. I am compelled."

She raised an eyebrow in the dark. "Speak with me or hurl more accusations—which is it?"

"The former, if you're willing."

"And if I am not?"

She heard the shrug of fabric. "Then I go to my grave with

unanswered questions."

Fee puffed with bitterness. "Pacify your angst with the thought that at least your grave is not freshly dug and ready for you."

There was silence between them, a stretch so long that Fee leaned her head upon the wall and closed her eyes with weariness.

"I want to know of him."

She pressed her lips together, a final act of defiance. Why should she share anything with him when he'd acted so callously? So devoid of mercy?

He spoke again. "You owe that much to me. You see, I don't understand any of it. Why did he have to die? Why must we have no man to mourn? Why has someone like you done something such as this?"

"Someone like me?"

"Like the girl I used to know. The one who I once knew cared for my brother just as much as I knew she cared for me."

She could not hold back. "And with all this weighing on your mind, you still dismiss a heavy doubt that points toward my innocence?"

"How can I not when there is a weightier body of testimony that points toward your guilt?"

"Testimony—but no evidence."

He could not suppress a sigh. "What would you do in my stead, Ophelia?"

"I would likely not shoot first and ask questions later. In fact, most of the questions you asked were not even answered by me. Or does my voice count for nothing in this sham of an inquiry?"

Rye did not respond immediately. And Fee thought perhaps

she'd struck a nerve.

It didn't matter. She couldn't trust him. For if she told Rye that Xavi was still alive, and where he was, there was a chance—no matter how slight—that it would put Xavi's life in increased danger, if not end it. All she had was hope that fortune would allow him to survive this ordeal on his own.

"What was he . . . what was he like?" came Rye's voice out of the dark at last. It was a quiet question. An imploring one.

"Empathetic," Fee answered in a whisper. Then she rolled back into a ball, closed her eyes, and said no more.

Rye came again the next night. He carried a small candle this time, so Fee could make out his face. "Ophelia," he said, his voice tight with restraint. "Tell me what to do for Mistress Savva."

Fee looked up at him from the pallet. She raised herself to sit, struggling with the weakness of not eating. Fuzzy-headed, for a moment Fee doubted she was having a real conversation with Rye, as there were times when delusions seemed to rule her conscious hours—the repeated hallucination that Savva would enter and tell her she'd recovered and sorted everything out, that Rye would appear and release her from this cage, begging for forgiveness after discovering the truth, or that Xavi would walk down the steps, alive, capable, and in command. But they were bubbles that popped with the vile, bitter taste of consciousness.

Rye's jaw muscles twitched as he bit down on his words. "I suggest you not waste our time. If you have any shred of humanity left, you will give me instructions on how to help the healer. If you refuse, I am left to further confirm my suspicions that you were responsible for her current position, and that she holds some secret of your guilt. What. Must. I. Do?" His last words were quietly spat out.

A boil of fury heated her breath, and she wrestled with the overwhelming desire to refuse him. But giving the old healer aid was the lynchpin in finding a shred of hope for Xavi.

She swallowed her choler. "There are drops you can place upon her tongue. A tincture that must be made, which may help with the inflammation within her brain, if there is any." Fee rubbed at her head, trying to stimulate the recall of which treatment she'd need. "Will you be doing this yourself?"

He nodded gravely. "And held accountable, no doubt, if you decide to act with malicious intent."

Fee glared at him with all the wrath she could muster. "I shall give you instructions—but I demand an action in return. If my ministrations prove that I have honestly given aid to my mentor, you will take this as a sign of my innocence and act on my behalf. I must be released in order to further tend to her and any other suffering individuals within Fireli."

He scrutinized her for a long moment and then gave her a small nod.

She sat back, took a deep breath, and visualized the stillroom. "At the back of the room, behind the wooden workbench, you will find the wall stretches with four long shelves. To the right of the shelves are the apothecary drawers—each are meticulously labeled, so you must pay careful attention and collect exactly what I tell you. Will you bring everything to me?"

"I will."

For the next five minutes, Fee scoured the recesses of her

brain, searching for long-stored information regarding swelling and edema, anti-inflammatories, and vasodilation. "You must also bring a clean jar and a glass eyedropper. How quickly can you act?"

"I'll be back within the hour."

She answered him coldly, "I'll be here."

One by one, Rye slipped the ingredients between the rusty bars, the last item a second candle for Fee to illuminate her filthy workspace. Her hands felt supremely sensitive—all pins and needles—as she took each jar from him. She would blame it on the damp cold of the cell except she'd experienced this feeling before—whenever she'd skip taking her antidote for a day—but never this intense. A disquieting voice in her head wondered if she truly was free of the plague's toxins. Was she still a carrier?

She sat on the stone floor, measuring meticulously.

Vaccinium macrocarpon

Ginkgo biloba

Curcuma longa

Boswellia

Linum usitatissimum

Drop by drop she weighed her work, probing her memory for snippets of knowledge until, at last, she lowered the glass eyedropper into the liquid and screwed it tightly into place.

"Here," she said stiffly, and placed the medicine in Rye's hand. "Three drops on her tongue. *Every* hour."

In the quiet of her cell, long after he'd left, Fee sat on the pallet, listening to the sound of dripping water. Her mind mentally scanned the shelves and drawers of the apothecary supplies. She reviewed the lines of text she'd recalled to create the prescription for Savva. Her lungs filled with a little more air, her head raised a fraction of an inch. Her instincts had guided her and left no filament of doubt.

From the depths of the numb and soulless place she'd been residing in for the last several days, she felt a small flush of warmth greet her, unfamiliar because of its absence but longed for because of its insight.

She needed no candle to study the phenomenon, for she was keenly aware of the symptoms of manifestation as, apparently, the ancient memory of her own biology responded with immediate recognition. The long-dormant titillation that came with such surety about herself was a resurrection she believed hardly possible.

Encircling one wrist with the hand of the other, she smiled, chafing at the sudden flush of gratitude, as it was tightly braided with irony. The tiny, kindled flame of heat had returned.

At last, she felt her birthmark.

Alas, it would be an unfairly short reunion.

CHAPTER
NINETEEN

"WHAT DID HE LIKE TO READ?" RYE ASKED, LEANING stiffly against the wall on the opposite side of the bars.

Fee's lips drew closed, purse-string tight, part of her steadfastly determined to hold on to the sharp edges of her temper. But, with the memory of Xavi, she shut her eyes and felt herself warm. She spoke as if only to an empty room. "Anything bound between two covers. His appetite for literature was insatiable.

"I doubt there's a book within his study whose spine was not cracked and pages not dog-eared. He absorbed it all, every word, every letter, each philosophy, and all the laws. His passion was this kingdom and its people. He loved Fireli, and he could not wait to be its king." Her voice grew soft as she lost herself in the description and, suddenly becoming aware of her languor, she picked up a fold of fabric and worried a hole in her filthy skirt.

Rye studied her; Fee could feel it even though she stared elsewhere.

"And now, Ophelia, Fireli will never see that day. Parts of me still resist believing it."

Rye continued. "I thought I had steeled myself to your cold apathy years ago, but I've been proven wrong. The knife you wield is capable of deeper cuts. Mortal ones."

"I cannot follow your line of logic. In fact, I cannot fathom why you would not show some sliver of compassion as I sit here begging for it."

"Perhaps it's because you denied that same compassion to *me* for the years I have been away."

She ground her teeth at the wrongful accusation. "I . . . did . . . not . . . kill him, Rye."

"Did you ever see him read *The Book*?"

Fee glanced up sharply. "No. But I'm certain he has, for he spoke of it. He knew each constituent of Fireli better than he knew himself."

"I aim to follow through with his wishes. Unlike you, he was an active scribe and has left copious notes on his thoughts for the kingdom. And of course, he revealed many of his ideas in his letters to me. I plan to honor him, Ophelia."

Unlike me? Fee thought, befuddled. How could Rye make such an inaccurate assessment of her? She had books filled with the pages of her academic pursuits, but she refused to defend herself and kept on topic. "I hope you will," she said shortly. "There is nothing Xavi would have wished for more than the ability to see Fireli restored to greatness."

"Apart from making it happen by his own hand," Rye answered caustically. He pulled a handkerchief from his pocket and wiped at his forehead.

Fee gaped at him. "I find your allegations utterly contemptible, Rye. You are immeasurably unjust."

Rye shrugged. "Perhaps. You know I am to be married now. It is being arranged in concert with the coronation."

Fee would not look at him. "To whom?"

"Quinn."

She swallowed, but her throat would not cooperate, and she fought the feeling of it being compressed by unseen fingers. "Congratulations, Rye," she pushed out. "I wish you"—her tongue went rigid with unwillingness—"every happiness."

"I have known her a long time—three years, to be exact, for I spent the other six or seven in the other two kingdoms. Fireli's ministry and that of Gwyndom agree it is fitting, if not serendipitous."

"Serendipitous?"

Rye cleared his throat and met her incredulous gaze. "Perhaps not the finest choice of words, but I believe they see the situation as the best option—as would the kingdom's healer, Mistress Goodsong, who has been as mindful as a mother to both of us. She would argue that we are accustomed to one another from living in the same kingdom. I imagine both governments feel it is as good a fit as can be found."

Fee had been led to believe that she and Rye were the ones who fit, but she pushed aside her own sorrow and instead thought of poor Xavi. The tiny stabs of pain must have shown upon her face.

"From the perspective of Quinn's comfort," he quickly inserted.

Rye swiped the handkerchief across his brow again, and Fee wondered if he was nervous—uneasy with either his false incrimination or his part in this façade. For certainly he could not be overheated. This dank cell beneath the castle kept a constant temperature that cut through her clothing with a shivery chill.

"Tell me of Savva. What have you seen today?" She needed to change the subject.

Rye's mouth tightened briefly. "Nothing much, Ophelia. She mumbles occasionally, incoherently. No better, but no worse, if the latter assessment brings a small measure of comfort."

Fee sighed and put her head into her hands. "As if my comfort is of any concern to you, Rye."

"I understand the import of her recovery—"

"No," Fee interrupted, a crushing sense of doom billowing within her chest, "you can't *possibly* understand the significance."

"I know your life depends upon it."

"It's not just my—" The sound of hefty footfalls on the steps interrupted her near confession.

Rye scrambled to his feet. Two heavily armed guards came into view, followed by the stately form of Princess Quinn, the lush fabric of her dress brushing against the slick stone walls.

"Have you managed an admission of guilt yet, Rye?" the princess asked. "It is such a contemptible task, and one that must be a thousand times more personally loathsome, knowing that you must speak with a girl who murdered your brother."

Despite the dim illumination of candlelight, Fee knew that Rye had flushed with heat, as he swept his cloth from temple to temple, breathing out with some discomfort.

Fee herself felt a staggering wave of rage, wanting to bare her teeth and release the deep-bellied growl that roiled within her. All this chatter. Had Rye been attempting to soften her into submission?

"I wanted to speak with Ophelia about my brother's ambitions for Fireli, to make sure she would know—whether guilty of murder or no—my aim for this kingdom."

"Ah," Princess Quinn said, raising herself a half inch taller. "Yes, I'm sure Sir Rollins and the ministry will be pleased to have aligning agendas."

Rye gave one short jerk of his head. "I'm not entirely sure Sir Rollins will find *all* of it harmonious."

The princess arched a brow. "Are you speaking of the mines again? I thought you'd settled this matter with Sir Rollins."

"Except, I've come across more information. I've changed my mind."

The princess's head tilted. "Isn't that odd? Xavi had also changed his mind at the eleventh hour." Fee watched the young woman's gaze as it made a swift assessment of her and Rye. "I think we've spent enough time here. You have demonstrated to the girl that despite her best efforts to purloin a position of power, Fireli will be ruled by those who truly deserve the station of leadership."

"*The girl* has a name, Quinn," Rye muttered, casting a glance back at Fee.

"She stole your brother's life and his person! I would advise you to toss aside your childhood sentiments. She is a killer of at least one person—possibly two—and refuses to reveal where she has put your brother's body. I will not dignify an individual as low as that with distinction."

Fee focused her eyes on the spray of tiny flowers tucked into the princess's hair and, without thinking, directed a froth of ire toward her. Tiny rootlets scrambled downward across her shoulder. The princess shrieked, batting at her collar in the dark.

"Mouse!" she cried, darting swiftly down the passage toward the staircase.

Rye looked back at Fee and paused, staring at her hard. Then he wrapped one hand around a bar and pleaded, "Where is he, Ophelia? What have you done with his body?"

Fee stared back, wondering why he'd never taken to calling her the shortened version of her name, why he'd always been so formal. Even as a boy. "I have not murdered Xavi. This will be proven true, Rye. And if I am put to death before you acknowledge that truth, I hope the weight of your decision will be a burden sewn to your very soul."

He pulled his hand from the bar as if it had been burned by her words and placed it upon his chest, curling it into a fist. His eyes could not hide the pain he felt. "Good night, Ophelia."

The following night it was not Rye's, but the princess's footsteps that sounded through the hallway. Fee had been sitting on the pallet counting how many drips fell in the corner and calculating how many drops Savva had left. Her vial of medicine would soon run out.

Fee did not rise, nor address the princess when at last the swish of her skirts settled in front of the bars. Instead, she stared straight ahead at the dark, mottled wall in front of her, watching the light from Princess Quinn's torch flicker upon it.

The princess sighed. "Tell us where he is. Make it easier on yourself."

Fee turned her face. "I think what you are suggesting is that I make it easier on *you*. I have not killed Xavi, and it is wholly unthinkable that you have put me here. You have taken away the one thing I can offer—the ability to care for Savva."

"What you have taken away from *me* pales in comparison. You've little right to complain."

Fee prickled. "You are mistaken if you believe there was anything inappropriate between Xavi and me."

"I don't," the princess said crisply. "But from where I stand it's clear you intend to strip me of any happiness and love, however possible."

What? Fee thought.

"And because of it, I suffer—or rather because of *you*, I suffer. I suffer simply because you exist. Or because someone wishes you *still* existed."

"Who is this someone?" Fee asked.

The princess spun on her heel and left, pulling the shred of light along with her. It forced Fee to sit in an ever-growing expanse of feeling *completely in the dark*.

"Fee. Psst. Wake up!" a voice hissed at her.

She groaned, curled tighter around her knees, and fell back to a state of semiconsciousness.

"Fee!" the voice hissed again. "Which cave is he in?"

"What?" Fee mumbled. She was delirious from lack of sleep.

"The cave? Is it the one Kizzy fell from—and then found the two of you at the bottom of?"

Fee's eyelids were leaden. She could not lift them to see. But she'd had these hallucinations before and paid them no heed.

"Kizzy?" she muttered.

"Never mind, and worry not. We will find him," the voice soothed. It was refined, the diction polished. Like someone who was speaking English to a foreigner just learning the language.

"Good. Thank you," she mumbled before losing herself to sleep, the figments of her imagination, and wishful illusions.

Well past midnight, Fee heard the sound of slow footsteps coming down the passage stairs. A thin, wavering candle lightened the stone hallway, and Rye's face came into view. Fee pulled back with shock.

His eyes were glassy, two bruising smudges beneath them revealing a lack of sleep. And his face shined with sweat while his shoulders hung with an invisible weight, emphasizing his labored breathing. "Ophelia, I have come . . . for Mistress Savva's medicine."

Fee stepped toward the bars. "Rye? What has happened?"

He licked at his dry lips. "Lack of sleep, I believe, and perhaps a touch of . . . influenza." He waved a hand. "Do not worry. I have kept up with your instructions for Mistress Savva's tinctures."

"But—but you yourself need care. And there is no one in the stillroom to provide it," Fee said with a note of grave concern. She fought with the internal tug-of-war that threatened to split her at the seams. Part of her wished to leave him—allow him to suffer without care—but there was another part of her, one where an ancient stirring of feelings would not allow her to ignore his distress. "Please," she said uneasily, "let me help you."

He rubbed at his head. "You needn't worry. Quinn has been relentless, forcing me to drink tea to keep hydrated, as I cannot seem to keep anything solid within my stomach."

A sickening jolt sprang up her spine. "What?" Fee cried. "Tea? No, Rye—you mustn't drink it!" She grabbed the bars between them and then reached out to grasp his shirt. "Has she given you anything else?"

He stumbled back and then reached for the wall, sliding partway down to the floor, blinking confusedly. "Nothing, although she's tried to entice me with the sweets she used to send to Xavi. She said the confection was the only thing that soothed his stomach."

Fee's heart nearly exploded out of her chest. "Oh God, Rye—she's poisoning you! Just as she did Xavi! You have to get me out of here. I need to get you medicine from the stillroom."

"Who's poisoning me?" he asked, his words sluggish and slow.

"The princess! Just as she did your brother!"

Rye pulled himself up to stand and clutched at the iron bars. He closed his eyes and rested his forehead against them. "Quinn killed Xavi?"

"No," Fee said in a rush, now alight with certainty that Rye was innocent. "He's alive—or at least he was until you arrested me. We have to go to him, Rye. He needs our help!"

His eyes popped open, and he croaked out the words, "Alive? Where?"

Fee put her hands over Rye's. "He's in our cave!"

CHAPTER
TWENTY

FEE HELPED RYE STUMBLE INTO THE STILLROOM. THE first thing she noticed was the great humming of an electric current—as if the room possessed tiny bolts of lightning inside its stoppered vials and jars rather than ground herbs and the essences of plants. The scent of green growth and life was overpowering. Ripe and vital, it quickened the flow of her blood. She craved the chance to explore, but knew her attentions were desperately needed elsewhere.

Groping about in the dark from one shelf to another, from one drawer to the next, she hastily assembled a small bag of medicines and fumbled at the back-wall bookshelf to locate the large, twine-bound copy of *Flora Homeopathica* Savva had always pressed her to read. "Fine. If she believed it so superior, then it should be the one volume I bring with us," she mumbled.

"I beg your pardon?" Rye croaked, propped up by the door. Fee had instructed him to scan the courtyard for movement.

She pulled the drawstring on the bag into a pinched knot and slung it over her shoulders. "Nothing. I was just thinking aloud. We must go."

"Wait," he said, trying to steady himself and reach out for her before she passed. "Somewhere deep inside, I knew you couldn't be guilty, but . . ."

Fee shook off his words. "We'll talk about it later, Rye." She grabbed his arm and, casting a quick glance left and right, clumsily moved him toward the castle gate.

"What are we to do about the guards?" Fee asked, her whole body tightening at the sudden realization that she'd never get through.

With a hand clutching his chest for breath, Rye rasped, "Let me . . . handle that. But you must stay hidden behind the stone rampart, and let me f-first speak to them alone."

They reached the castle's outer perimeter, the long stone wall where the kingdom's elderly night watches stood guard. Fee pulled back flat against the wall and listened to Rye struggle as he addressed the watchmen. "There is an emergency. You must round up as many men as available. The princess . . . must be arrested—she is the assailant we have been searching for."

One of the sentinels interrupted Rye. "But milord, she has just raced through the gates moments ago with two of her guardsmen. And Sir Rollins left shortly after that."

"Sir Rollins?" Rye echoed.

Fee's heart leapt with panic. Had someone discovered Xavi?

Come across him in some wide-sweeping search?

"She said a crisis had called her back to Gwyndom."

Rye pulled back sharply. "Then you must hurry. Gather up my men and as many able-bodied soldiers as Fireli still has. Meet me at the old cave above the salt marshes—the one I used to play in as a child. There is a chance Prince Xavi is still alive."

The watchmen hurried toward the castle and, turning back toward Fee, Rye panted, gasping for breath, "We must have horses. I will never make it on foot."

Fee put up a hand. "Stay here, I will get them." She dashed toward the castle stables but with a haste she felt might be futile. *If the princess has discovered our cave, there will be no need for rushing. Xavi's luck will have run out—as if he's had any to begin with.*

Reaching the cave, she put a hand upon the old woven mat that served as a crude and secret shroud and pulled back with surprise to see a lush wash of fresh moss fill the area beneath her hand. She looked down toward Rye to make sure he had not seen and then quickly cast aside the old screen. Savva had not allowed Fee to accompany her and Xavi to their old hideaway but, instead, instructed her to stay in the stillroom in case anyone came in search of them. Seeing the inside of the cave now was an experience that was both hopeful and crushing.

The memories of her youth greeted her in a rush—as if her eight-year-old self had been waiting at the back of the cave and now came racing to meet her with arms flung wide. But the recollections were lost through her fingertips before she could fully grasp them. Xavi was not here.

She had made Rye wait at the bottom of the bluff, the climb

unnecessary if Xavi were still in the cave, because they would have taken him directly back to the castle. She raced back to where Rye sat, slumped over the neck of his horse. He was beginning to slide from his saddle, and she rushed to stabilize him, but she only managed to break his fall as he slipped to the ground, unconscious. There was no way she could move him, and he needed help immediately.

She quickly gathered several armfuls of tall grasses from the dried-up bed of a salt marsh and made Rye as comfortable as possible. Fresh grasses sprang to life as she tucked them in around his head and shoulders.

After collecting a few twigs and scattered branches, she cleared an area to make a small campfire, only large enough to boil water for the teas she would make Rye drink. If she could wake him, the medicinal tonics would aid his recovery. That is, if he hadn't been given a fatal dose of Princess Quinn's poison.

As unsettling as this notion was, preparing Rye's remedy had her absorbed with fascination. The *special skills* Xavi had been warning her to keep hidden were flooding out of her every time she reached for something that had once sprung from the earth.

Her hands moved swiftly from one bottle to the next. She crushed pungent, spicy herbs with effortless speed, grinding dried flower heads and mixing a paste as she waited for the water to heat. With each preparation she finished, her sense of purpose strengthened, her skin prickling with scintillating warmth. At one point, she glanced down to see if she'd spilled some of the heating water across her arm but pulled back with a start, astonished to see her birthmark flushing with a warm, pink glow. The second time in the last few days.

When at last the infusions were ready, she lifted Rye's head, pressing a cool cloth along his brow to rouse him. His teeth chattered, and he moaned in a feverish haze as she forced the liquid past his lips. Hoping he'd swallowed a sufficient amount to begin counteracting the toxins, she began the preparations for the next medicines. Inventorying her bag, she counted what she'd have to search out: herbs, flowers, and seeds she hoped were within a short distance from where they were. As long as Rye was unconscious, she could make the occasional dash to gather her stock.

Four horses came an hour later. Three were from Rye's brigade, and the other was one of Fireli's watchmen—an elderly gentleman certainly not fit for battle, but at least still capable of riding a horse. She had hoped that none of Rye's men would be led here, as there had been no time to explain to Rye that more than just the princess could be involved in the takeover of Fireli.

With alarmed expressions, Rye's guards leapt from their mounts and charged toward them, shocked to see Fee at his side. They rushed to seize her but the elderly guard shouted out, "No! Prince Rye admitted to imprisoning the wrong person. He told me so himself before he left. Leave her be! The girl is innocent."

They stood back, uncertain and evaluating.

"You must get him up into the cave for me," Fee explained as calmly as if she were Savva giving strict orders. "Prince Rye is very ill. He needs shelter and medical care—the next forty-eight hours are critical."

"Surely he needs to return to Fireli. Why would you subject him to recovery in a cave?" one of the guardsmen asked pointedly.

"Travel to the castle would be too dangerous. I have everything I need here to treat him. Moving him farther may prove fatal." She could not tell them the whole truth, as even though they were Rye's men of arms, they were still Gwyndom's constituents. There was the niggling possibility they were somehow connected to both assassination attempts and, until Rye was fully conscious and capable of determining where their allegiance stood, she would not risk telling the men that Rye had been poisoned by Princess Quinn. In fact, all her senses prickled with anxiety at the knowledge that if the guards had been instructed to act according to the princess's instructions, they could easily overpower Fee and the elderly watchman right now. She scrambled for a believable ruse—anything to furnish her time.

"And unless you've been inoculated from the mining epidemic—as Rye, myself, and the Fireli watchman have—I highly advise that you make camp a few miles away. The quarrying caves are all about us and have yet to be determined as rid of their deadly toxins. Forty-eight hours. That should suffice. If we are in need of your help, I shall send our watchman to fetch you."

The men squinted, scanning the dark for the disease-ridden caves, then exchanged glances and took to carefully maneuvering Rye up the rocky incline and into the cave as instructed. They left quickly, pointing in the direction they would wait.

The next task was sending the Fireli watchman back to the castle with a fresh batch of medicine for Savva, along with instructions on how to administer it. Knowing she could not take care of the woman who had nursed her through the last grievous ten years nearly made her heart crack in two.

A few hours before dawn, Fee struggled to rouse Rye and forced another round of tea down his throat. Wrapping him tightly in a horse blanket against the feverish and unrelenting tremors, she at last put her head against the cave wall and allowed the worrisome thoughts of Xavi to creep into her head.

Where is he?

Had Savva not brought him to this place? Perhaps he was out floundering on his own, or worse.

She closed her eyes, feeling the tug of sleep, and tried picturing where he might be, determined to overpower the helpless feeling that she could do nothing for him.

Never mind, and worry not. We'll find him.

She sat bolt upright, the unfamiliar voice coming back to her. "Dear God, who will find him? Who did I tell? *Did* I tell?" Her mind raced, now fully doubting the conversation she'd dismissed as a dream in her cell.

Had it been the princess? One of her guards—for Fee was certain the voice had belonged to a man. Or no! Perhaps Sir Rollins?

She paced the cave for the next hour, convinced she'd doomed Xavi to death, and eventually, slid down the wall with exhaustion. She must have dozed off, for she woke to the first ray of sun hitting her squarely in the eye.

Wretched helplessness washed over her again, but she returned the small pan to the embers of her campfire and, after preparing Rye's medicine, waking him, and helping him swallow it, she made sure he was secure before leaving to hunt down more of what she needed outside. Nothing could be done about Xavi until Rye had recovered.

Fee pulled young stalks of burdock, yellow dock, and echinacea from the ground. They burst into blossoms at her touch. She dusted the dirt from their roots and placed them in her medicine bag. She located a patch of tall, stout, spiny milk thistle and separated the seeds from their lush purple flowering heads. Satisfied with her bounty, she returned to the stream where she'd first gathered water the night before.

Eyeing it hungrily and glancing up toward the cave, she rapidly stripped off her clothing and stepped into the cool water. She lay back into the burbling current, soaking every inch of her body and loosening her hair, saturating it with water. It was the first time she'd bathed in longer than a week. Once drenched and sodden, she pulled the lavender soap she'd nicked from the stillroom out of her medicine bag and scrubbed at the dirt and grime from the prison cell. She scoured her skin and hair, and rushed to wash her clothing, working to grind out the awful memories of being unjustly accused and unfairly imprisoned. She stepped out of the stream, squeezed the water from her laundered breeches and blouse, and swiftly redressed. She studied her surroundings while whipping her long black hair into another loose braid. Something was different. She scanned the sun-drenched hills and the openings to the mining caves. They'd been told that each had been boarded up and sealed—for their protection as well as for all of Aethusa's safety.

But these caves were open. And clearly . . . *active.*

Fee felt her jaw fall. Although she saw no people, equipment was scattered about. Someone had organized the mining. Someone other than the people within the Kingdom of Fireli. No one should have been here—not for several more weeks!

As her heartbeat pounded with this fresh discovery, she jerked at the thought that Rye would be in need of attention, and immediately made her way back.

He was still sleeping, but with the light shining through the mouth of the cave and reflecting off the tiny mineral flecks of pyrite and sphalerite, Fee had enough illumination to see that his skin tone was less pallid, and the half-moons beneath his eyes were lessening. She breathed a sigh of relief and settled onto the floor next to him, pulling Savva's book out of her medicine bag and placing it on her lap.

Rye rolled over, facing her. With his eyes still firmly shut, he mumbled, "So much better than the perfume you were using before."

"I beg your pardon?" Fee whispered, wondering if Rye was hallucinating or just talking in his sleep.

"Definitely an improvement," he muttered.

She bristled. "That's a rather rude thing to say after all I've endeavored to do for you."

He cracked open one eye. "I apologize. Somehow this cave has me slipping back into the comfortable cloak of youth and cheekiness."

No. She would not dismiss the many miserable days he put her through. This was not *her* Rye from long ago. "I thought perhaps ten years would round off some of your sharper edges, but I see you've only honed them to a finer point."

He closed the eye. "Whetted upon leather-bound books—my strop of knowledge."

"Well, I find your return to be a rather thorny homecoming. It certainly wasn't the warm embrace I was expecting."

Rye opened both eyes, but his features remained unreadable. "I was misled."

"You weren't the first." Fee watched the fingers of his left hand press into his palm. She wondered if Rye knew he had such an easy "tell." So many people did, believing others weren't watching or noticing. But that was a rule Savva drilled into her most—*observe everything.*

"She was very clever," Rye murmured. "Was positively despondent over the loss of Xavi. And I believed her feelings for him to be true."

"Rye," Fee began, "it's probable that Quinn is not the only person involved.

"I think," she continued, "I may have given someone else Xavi's location—by accident, from mumbling in my sleep. It might have been Sir Rollins. And if so, they've likely taken him to Gwyndom."

He brought a hand to his eyes, rubbing the sleep out of them. "Sir Rollins. Yes. He had jumped on the bandwagon that labeled you as guilty and reported that even though he'd no idea who you were at the princess's banquet, you'd raised his suspicions on that night nonetheless. Everything has been painted so expertly to look a certain way."

Fee nodded. "I have been pinned as some sort of mastermind—a woman conniving enough to kill her best friend in order to marry his brother and obtain a most coveted position. My appetite to rule a country must be of a ravenous sort.

"The question is," she mused, "*who* is the real person behind this scheme?"

Rye pulled himself to sit, wincing slightly with pain, or nausea, or both, Fee presumed. Part of her felt he deserved it, and she reined in her pity.

"Is it not reasonable to assume that Quinn's hunger to be queen was voracious enough that she would outline and execute a murder?"

"No. She would have been queen either way—there was no need to kill Xavi, and then you, for that matter. Something else has been the catalyst for removing both of you."

He met her eyes. "And do you know what it is?"

She nodded. "The mines."

"What of them?"

"Some . . . *part* of Xavi does not want them reopened—he's fearful that they're still contaminated."

"He'd written of that in his journals."

"Yes, well, that was discovered—despite his determined efforts not to reveal it yet."

Rye's bloodshot eyes widened.

"Precisely," Fee said.

"Such news would roil the four kingdoms. The other three would surely find some way to take over."

Fee nodded. "And with our defenses as meager as they are, there were clearly choices to gain control of the kingdom that did not involve dredging up bloody violence or killing off the rest of the inhabitants."

"Okay," Rye said, closing his eyes and rubbing at his forehead, "I can see how there'd be an uprising if everyone was denied our materials and would be forced to face a radical change to their lifestyles. And killing off Xavi would have solved that problem. But why me? Why would I have been the next in line for the guillotine?"

Fee snorted and rolled her eyes. "Because you are an *honorable* man." The words came out bitterly, forced passed her lips by vitriol.

Rye looked away and paused while Fee's words rang uncomfortably through the cave. "I *am* sorry, Ophelia. About all of it." They were silent for a moment and he added, "But I fear I'm still confused."

"Should you have honored what everyone thought were Xavi's wishes—as was your stated intention—*you* would stand in their way too."

Rye rubbed at the back of his neck. "We've got to get to Gwyndom. The rumors must be stopped before they cause three kingdoms to come to war over who will conquer Fireli and own the mining rights."

Fee shook her head. "It's too late for that."

"What do you mean?"

She looked out toward the opening of the cave. "Someone's already stolen them."

"The mining rights?"

She gestured with her chin outside. "The *mines*. My guess is that whilst Fireli has been under quarantine and we've diligently followed the Seclusion Rules—first and foremost not to stray from the castle's borders—someone else has been taking advantage of our lack of freedom and line of sight."

He rubbed at his chin. "I must get to Gwyndom. There isn't much time." Rye tried to stand, but struggled to get to his knees. Fee caught him by the shoulder as he stumbled, and she pressed him back down.

"I think we first need a plan and, before that, you definitely need sleep." She pointed to the straw tick mat. "You'll not make it to the mouth of this cave before tumbling to your death at the bottom of it—which is exactly what you deserve, in my opinion. But then I'll be stuck figuring out this whole mess on my own again, and falsely charged with the death of *two* brothers."

Rye collapsed dejectedly to the mat. "Now isn't this a twist of events. The last time we were here you were kicking at me to get up from this very spot."

Fee stared down at her hands. "I find that dismally sad, Rye, as over the last ten years I've not given that eight-year-old girl much thought."

"I used to give that eight-year-old girl a lot of thought. In fact, a great deal of it. And then . . . I learned to slam the door on all of it."

CHAPTER
TWENTY-ONE

RYE FELL ASLEEP ALMOST IMMEDIATELY, AND FEE SAT watching him, wishing he could have stayed awake long enough to answer the wretched, softly spoken *What?* she'd felt slip past her lips. Her stomach corkscrewed into an array of dizzying knots as she tried to decipher the meaning behind his last words. Certainly he'd never spoken these thoughts in his letters to Xavi—only the same tired last line, closing each missive.

Send my love to the feisty Ophelia.

Until they disappeared without explanation.

She took the time to study Rye. The jumble of emotions that churned within her was impossible to untangle, but it was easy to identify the main threads braiding together: fury—over his recent treatment, pity—for the pain he'd suffered from both the poisoning and the possible loss of his brother, and curiosity—the unfathomable pull that tugged her toward him. Surely it was a result of the long gap of time spent wondering how he was, where he was, and who he'd become. She did not want to yearn for him. She had to move beyond rejection.

She assessed the disorderly waves of russet hair that fell across his forehead, the strength of his brow and cheekbones that now protruded with angular extremes—no longer padded by the full roundness of boyhood. She measured the laugh lines around the corners of his eyes and lips, the length of his slim nose with a slight hitch in the center, wondering what had caused the break she—as a student of anatomy—could see had taken place. And she paused at great length to marvel at his mouth. The shape was one that begged to be traced with a finger.

But it was also one that had uttered cruel words in her direction. She could have been studying his mouth for a full minute before she realized that Rye was also watching her.

With a tiny but sharp intake of breath, she found his eyes, half open but apparently aware of the fact that she'd been staring at him. His heavy-lidded observation ceased, and his head fell to the side. Rye fell back asleep almost immediately, and Fee squeezed her own eyes shut and pressed her lips together, flooded with the heat of embarrassment. It was a risk she took and was caught taking. Perhaps he wouldn't remember.

She leaned back against the cave wall and pulled Savva's hefty medical manual into her lap. It was bound with fraying pieces of twine to keep it shut, and one by one, Fee untied them until the last of the bindings had come away. She cracked the spine of the book, expecting to see the first of a thousand pages filled with ancient, longhand scrawl, listing ingredients and preparation techniques, charcoal etchings of flowers, herbs, grasses, and seeds, and the myriad uses and warnings that came with each. Instead, she found a hollowed stashbox, the pages replaced with letters.

The majority of them were tied together—there must have been well over two hundred. Half of them were from Rye. And the others . . . were hers.

Fee's heart leapt in her chest, like a small fist banging from inside of her. She held her breath as she gaped at the stack and then hungrily ripped them open, reading one missive and putting it aside before devouring the next. The box held ten years' worth of letters. A decade of two separate one-sided conversations. One set from a girl who'd come to believe that she no longer mattered to the boy she kept writing to. And one from a boy who had been torn away from his brother, from his home and kingdom, and from the girl he'd been told was his future. A girl who was mute and possibly unfeeling to his desperate requests for correspondence. He'd grown up alone and lonely.

Fee wanted to curl around the letters and cry.

"Why would Savva have done this?" she whispered into her hand, staring at the sleeping form in front of her.

Fee tied the letters back into their bundles, resigned to not read them all, as with each one, she grew more despondent over the loss of them. She was about to place the bale of notes back into the stashbox when she spied an unattached letter at the bottom. It had her name scrawled across the top.

In Savva's tremulous handwriting.

Dearest Fee,

If you are reading this, one of two things has happened: either I am finally dead and you have been tasked with claiming the stillroom as your own—to do with as you see fit—or you have finally taken my advice and sought the wisdom of a healer I have pointed to time and again.

Regardless, you now have possession of something I have kept from you. Partly with good reason and partly because I had no other choice. Hear me out . . . and try to forgive me.

Things are not as they seem. You are not who you are. And that which you know is only a fraction of what you should.

I understand these words seem part of some horrific riddle, but the truth behind them was withheld from you purposefully—not by my decision, but one forced upon me.

I do not have the luxury of unraveling the above statements. I am compelled to take them to my grave. But I can direct you to others who are not bound as I am. And they will reveal that which I cannot.

Eventually.

Your life, before the deathly epidemic, had already been purposefully misdirected, but following the sickness, things took a drastic turn. New restrictions were placed upon us. Rules that were meant to protect and heal. Clearly, one of those rules affected you far more than the others, and for that I am aggrieved. But understand, hiding who you were might have been a wretched struggle, but that sacrifice helped keep Xavi alive.

No doubt my words are confusing. Eventually, things will change. The restrictions will be released. There is every chance I will not be around to explain what's happening, but there are others who can, and you must seek them out.

And of the letters, you ask?

Correspondence from outside of Fireli was to be denied to you specifically. Again, I am not at liberty to reveal why, but I followed the directives given to me with the intent to protect you for as long as I could.

I assume, if I am deceased, you are no longer taking your daily tonic, as I was the one to create and administer it. It was not—as I led you to believe—preventative medicine, but rather a numbing calmant. By now you are seeing the effects wear off and may be confused by this "new" person emerging from within you.

Forgive me if she is the person you'd longed to be for the last ten years.

Forgive me if she is not.

You may not be capable of recovering all that once was, but your skills of healing have the ability to restore more than you know. And that can be a cure in and of itself.

Seek the healers, Fee.

~Savva

Fee lowered the letter to her lap. A few of the muddled and malformed pieces of the last ten years now clicked together like a puzzle assembling itself, but the bulk of them had been cast off the table and scattered into the breeze, irretrievable and snatched from her grasp.

One thing was clear from Savva's letter, and only one. There was something about Fee that required—that *necessitated* her isolation.

But what? It had been kept from her—a secret all these years. She felt as though she had lived her whole life on one side of a door, on the other side of which was an entirely different world.

Savva had shaken and spun her around with a snarl of profound revelations and left no familiar tool with which to unravel them. *Seek the healers.* But who were they, and where?

She looked down at Rye, seeing him stir. A small smile curled the corners of his lips but when she didn't return it, he worked at pulling himself to sit.

"What is it?" he asked.

She held up a fistful of letters, and he stared at her, uncomprehending. "These," she murmured.

Fee saw a thread of pain slip across his face as he recognized his writing, and then a note of confusion creeped in as he spotted Fee's as well.

"I don't understand. Those are my letters and . . . yours?"

Fee nodded. "I never got yours . . . and you never got mine."

"How could that be?"

"Savva."

"But . . . why?"

She stuffed Savva's note into the stashbox and rebound the fake book with its twine. "I'm not sure, but I intend to find out"—she shut her eyes and took a lungful of air—"*after* we get you well and you help me find Xavi."

He looked utterly reluctant to leave the topic, but after assessing Fee he said, "We'll find him, Ophelia. Even if we must scour every inch of Aethusa. And then we will bring him back, and Xavi will be crowned the rightful king of Fireli. Soon enough, all will be exactly as our parents had planned for us."

She refused to meet his eyes. Could he truly mean *all* things his parents had planned? She poked at the glowing coals. "You need to drink, Rye. I would imagine your stomach is still tender. How are you feeling?"

"Impatient," he answered, downing the brew.

Fee shrugged. "Well, let me know when you're feeling hungry. For it's then that I'll know the medicines are working, and we can safely move. Until then, sleep. The brew will force it upon you regardless."

Rye scowled at her, and Fee saw the tiniest filament of the old Rye, a return of the impossible ten-year-old who'd left them. "You tricked me, Ophelia. Had I known the correct answer, I would have lied and provided it. As it is, having had half this tea, I am now of no use to you."

Fee pointed toward the mat. "I stand by my earlier assessment. You are too ill to be useful to anyone, and only time will alter that evaluation. Now sleep, Rye."

She looked down to see that he'd already succumbed to the potency of her tonic. Her stomach twisted as she thought about Rye's past without her and Xavi, and her heart quickened as she thought about Rye's future . . . with them.

When Rye next woke, Fee had a weak broth for him to drink, a chunk of bread for him to eat, and the beginnings of a plan. "I checked the surrounding caves, but there are no signs of Xavi. Even so, Savva would never have chosen anything but this one. Which means he was discovered and taken elsewhere. If we assume the worst, it's Gwyndom."

Rye's face grew dim. "If we are to assume the worst, Ophelia, then there's a very good chance they no longer have a problem on their hands regarding Xavi. They wanted him dead."

"Do you really believe they would kill him?"

"Fireli is ripe for the picking. With a weak government, no monarch to speak of, and inhabitants who are frail and few, there is likely not a kingdom in Aethusa that is not making plans at this moment. Now . . . tell me of *our* plans."

"Our plan is to first shake off any notions that Xavi is dead." She roughly gathered their things and shoved them into her saddlebag. "Next, the princess will fear that you've become aware of her assassination attempts on both you and Xavi. So you must be convincing enough—must persuade her that after your bout with some strange flu, you were given word of her crisis in Gwyndom.

"Then you must conjure up believable worry and offer your help. Keep her occupied. I, meanwhile, will stealthily hunt, in disguise, through Gwyndom for Xavi."

Rye nodded.

"Are you a fine enough actor?" Fee asked.

"I will have to be. What about you? Can you pull off being something like . . . my manservant?"

Fee smiled slyly. "I have been known to fool people with my impressions before."

"My clothing is too large for you."

She pulled a sack from her bag. "I have this—a guard uniform. It was handy for stealing around the kingdom. Don't worry. I shall tailor my gait and affect accordingly."

He eyed her outfit. "From what I recall, you'd always preferred ill-fitting dungarees."

Fee felt her face redden at the thought that Rye had even taken notice of what she had worn. "I actually quite . . . like trousers," she said haltingly.

"Hmm," Rye said, raising one brow.

She swiftly gathered the last of their belongings and helped Rye down the rocky path to where their horses waited, nibbling on the fragrant shoots of grass and clover beneath them.

"What do you plan to tell your *real* manservants?" Fee asked.

"As little as possible, for I'm uncertain whom to trust. All of the men are Gwyndom constituents assigned to me by Quinn's mother, Queen Islay." His left hand rolled into a tight ball—a habit that signaled his fear in the face of doubt. She wished she could grab hold of his hand and uncurl his fingers, but instead held out the reins of his horse.

Rather than reaching for them, Rye suddenly looked about, swiveling in an arc to study their surroundings, his nose rising slightly skyward. "Do you smell that? There must be a big patch of . . ."

Fee followed his gaze. "Of what?"

He reached for the reins and watched her silently for a few seconds, breathing in deeply and then shaking his head, a little embarrassed. "Never mind. It's probably just my light-headed state tampering with my senses."

Fee nearly burst out with the confession that not only was she smelling a thousand things more sharply than she had a week ago, but that colors were more vibrant, and the air around her crackled with skin-prickling magnetism. This must be what Savva meant when she said the effects of her *numbing calmant* would be wearing off. Was this the person Savva had tried to hide?

She held her tongue. Xavi would be horrified to see what new little talents she was discovering. But this wasn't the sorcery of old like he'd read to them about. She wasn't enchanting frogs and casting spells. And after hearing him read Rye's last letter, she was fully aware of Rye's opinion regarding "witches," and did not wish to encourage anyone to believe she was one of them.

Fee helped Rye into the saddle. Although mostly recovered, he still displayed weakness from the toxins. The thought of Xavi, ill and held captive with no one to care for him, made her stomach twist like an errant slipknot, impossible to loosen.

"You'll have to lead. I've never been beyond the borders of Fireli," Fee said, tightening the girth straps of Rye's saddle.

He looked down with surprise. "You've not?"

"We've been under quarantine, remember?"

"Of course." He nodded. "I can't imagine how difficult it's been for everyone here, for those who have never seen beyond the edges."

Fee settled into her saddle, and felt a hot puff of air escape. She'd not been allowed to feel the edges of anything for ten years. She'd been held prisoner smack dab in the middle of an insipid life, intentionally held back from the spectrum of experience available.

"I find it difficult to envision that you, Ophelia, did as you were told and behaved as instructed. Perhaps that was Xavi's even temperament rubbing off on you?"

"Hardly," she huffed. "It's a long story. Right now, I'd like to know everything about where we're going. What should I expect?"

"You should expect to be surprised, for it's wholly different from Fireli in ways you might find startling. Where Fireli is simple and modest—"

Fee interrupted him with a snort.

"Yes, well, through no fault of her own," he continued, "but by comparison Gwyndom is lavish and boastful. The kingdom displays its wealth at every opportunity: in its architecture, its *unusual* landscape, and the people. Imagine a world where an unseen wand has theatrically cast tinsel without reservation. Life is . . . indulgent."

"Do you miss it?" she asked, trying to stifle any note of envy.

"I missed home," Rye said miserably. "I missed everything about the kingdom and everything within it."

"We've hardly anything to offer in comparison, Rye."

"If I may clarify, it wasn't *things* I'd grown attached to. It was people. And none of them resided in any of the kingdoms I'd been forced to live in."

Fee twisted to look at him from her saddle. "I would have thought the excitement of seeing new lands and meeting new people would trump the version of Fireli's predictable, repetitious daily life."

"It didn't," he said flatly.

Fee studied Rye's face, still struggling at being both drawn to him and his familiarity, and indignant with him—for his disbelief.

"You'll be pleased to know that nothing has changed. We've had no money to lavishly construct grandiose architecture, our land has had to endure without the bountiful attention of surplus funds. And the people? They are the same. We've been inured to time."

Rye stopped his horse, causing Fee to pull back and turn to face him.

"No. You're wrong, Ophelia. From what I see, the entire kingdom is still shadowed by a wide net of sadness. The plague, our parents, Xavi, the mines. Fireli seems still cursed."

Fee set her jaw. "Then we have no other choice than to bring back the only cure—her capable king."

BOOK TWO: GWYNDOM

∞

PROLOGUE

SAVVA TOOK THE WOMAN IN, HER WEARY EYES ASSESS-
ing how much she'd changed in nearly eight full years. Her clothing,
sharply ironed—serviceable and simple. Her hair, tamed back with
some severity—a strict contrast to the softer style she'd employed
years ago. Her lips pursed with purposeful determination in place of
a mouth that used to suggest a sweet-natured disposition.

But the words that fell from those lips illuminated the true
change. This, Savva could identify effortlessly, without having to
employ any magical skill to assist her.

"You must realize how difficult this is for me, Savva," the
woman said as she moved inquisitively about the stillroom, running
her fingers across the scarred wooden butcher's block still scattered
with discarded herb stems.

"A life of solitude I was not expecting," she continued.

Savva took in a slow, calming breath, but felt her eyes narrow. She would show this woman no ounce of pity.

"I have tried everything. I've come to you . . . I'm *asking* you for help. We must work together to bring Azamar back."

"We?" Savva echoed.

Evanora raised her chin. "Gwyndom lacks what I need to complete the task myself."

"It is deficient because you made it so."

"You want him to return, do you not? It is in your best interest to provide me assistance."

Savva snorted. "I hold you wholly responsible and, currently, my spleen still stings with vitriol. I will work in solitude. I offer you nothing."

"I was doing what needed to be done. The law of Aethusa is clear. Azamar broke those laws—and *you* should hold some accountability for him. Therefore, you must help me. I need some of what your mines hold."

A series of rapid knocks on the stillroom's door caused them both to halt, breaking the heated gaze between them. Evanora moved to look outside the window as Savva opened the door. Her heart hammered upon seeing the upturned, hopeful faces of the inquiring couple before her.

"Sorry to bother, Savva. We've got a little problem."

Savva shook her head, trying not to look over her shoulder and back inside. "This is not a good time."

"It's a somewhat urgent matter, though," the young woman said, brushing past Savva and into the stillroom. Savva turned to see her walk toward the glass vials and stoppered jars, her eyes darting across the apothecary's shelves, oblivious to Evanora's presence at the window. "Surely you'll have something here."

The man gave Savva an apologetic glance and stepped inside. "Savva . . . it's Fee."

Savva's eyes went wide and she strained against the urge to glance at the other healer. "Is she ill?" Savva whispered.

"No. Not ill," the man said uncertainly, as the woman rushed back to the two of them.

"Not ill, but there is something that needs tending to," the woman said. "We've been racking our brains and can only conclude that Fee has somehow come upon some chemicals—a potent fertilizer perhaps. You know how she plays with Xavi and Rye—always so rough and determined to bring home the outdoors after exploration."

Savva put a hand on the man's shoulder, turning him. "Come back in a little while, please."

"I'm certain you must have some strong soap or salve," the woman said, gesturing toward the shelves. "Anything to wash the chemicals off—as she's . . . well . . ." The woman hesitated, and Savva pushed them toward the open door.

"Fee made a daisy chain sprout just by touching each unopened bud with her fingertips!" the man whispered loudly over his shoulder.

"Later!" Savva hissed, shoving the door closed with her aching shoulder.

"Whatever chemical she's come in contact with cannot be good for her skin, Savva. We must put an end to this. Please!" he pleaded, shouting through the door. "People are beginning to suspect she's—"

"Later!" Savva said loudly. She swallowed, straightened herself, and turned to face Evanora. The visage in front of her sent a jolt of terror through her stomach. She clutched the front of her apron.

Evanora's eyes, laden with rage, focused with precision and fixed on Savva. "That child was not granted breath in our realm. Aethusian law stated she'd no right to be born!" The ire that left her body was hot upon Savva's face as Evanora bore down upon her.

Evanora's hand shot out in front of her, her palm pushing unseen air.

It struck Savva like an oncoming wall, sending her sprawling to the floor backward, where she hit her head on the flagstone tiles.

Savva raised a shaky arm. "You mustn't do this. The child is of no concern. She knows nothing."

But Evanora came at her again, a whirl of wind that sent Savva spinning across the floor. Her back met the harsh wooden planks of the wall. Savva choked as her breath was expelled from her body. She looked up to see the madness in the healer's face, her lips twisting with a paroxysm of rage.

Savva clutched at the pendant around her neck and began whispering, mouthing words that came out as a gurgled struggle for air. She curled around her hands and rocked gently, bracing herself for the next assault.

"There are rules that must be followed, Savva. Some that suppress us, but others that protect us. And our people were *in agreement*—certain bloodlines must never be mixed! How could you have sheltered her? You are just as censurable as Azamar. The others will agree that you, too, must be scourged for your wrongdoings!"

Savva mumbled quickly in her huddled form, her hands rubbing the disc between her heated, trembling palms.

Evanora whipped a hand along a stretch of shelves holding the distillates. They flew off the flat wooden ledges and crashed to the floor, mixing their volatile chemicals together and creating a great cloud of gray smoke. Savva choked and heaved but still forced the strangled words past her lips.

Evanora growled, "I will find this child. I will bring her to the others. And for our safety, we will rid our realm of a corrupt and destructive force. It is what *must* be done!"

Savva looked up to see Evanora heading toward the stillroom door. She was drained of magic, having poured nearly every ounce of it into the bulla around her neck for safekeeping. "No," Savva gasped through the smoldering fumes. "I won't let you."

She struggled to find her feet and saw Evanora shake her head, then pull a vial from her apron pocket and uncork it.

The powder!

Savva recognized the ebony blight Evanora had used on Azamar. She would not be silenced. Would not be cast out of her kingdom. Fee needed her.

Savva reached out for a bottle on the workbench in front of her at the same time Evanora circled her hands above her head, the air above them whirring, a black funnel growing in strength. Savva tipped the bottle and reeled back as a wall of opalescent colors formed a bubble, encasing her body. She crouched and held the globe in place as the sooty powder pummeled against it, ricocheting off, deflected.

The barrage was unending, a brutal attack that howled in

her ears, vibrating, quaking, thrashing about her. Savva felt the last vestiges of magic slip from her body, the remaining essence of energy used to protect her life so that she might protect Fee's.

Suddenly, the bubble popped and Savva looked up. Evanora was gone, but so were the windows and doors. The force of the spell had blown open the stillroom, the diabolical dust spreading broadly on the breakneck currents radiating throughout the kingdom.

Savva's eyes went wide, and she stumbled in an attempt to stand. But she was injured and too weak. She peered up from the floor and placed her hands around the pendant, looking about at the shattered medicines and leaking volatile compounds.

"What have I done?" she repeated again and again. But the sounds of people outside, the chaos, the screaming, the fear and agony made it immediately crystal clear:

She'd shielded herself, but she'd also allowed the release of a murderous contagion.

CHAPTER
TWENTY-TWO

THE FIRST DAY OF TRAVEL TOWARD GWYNDOM WAS AN exercise in acquainting herself with the far reaches of Fireli's territory.

The salt marshes near the castle gave way to untouched meadows that had once been farms, barren since the epidemic. Fields that once held verdant crops had been reclaimed by nature and grew with desolate abandon. Grasses and wildflowers, both beautiful and neglected, swayed with native ease. Ducks skimmed the silky surfaces of quiet ponds, and birds perched in the hedges that lined their path, fluttering up into the pastel-blue sky as the horses disturbed their nesting habitats.

Only the guards assigned to Rye from Gwyndom—the ones Fee had sent away from the cave—joined them early in the day, leading the way. Fee rode her horse behind Rye and was now dressed head to toe in a Fireli soldier's uniform. Her dark hair was twisted and tucked beneath the broad cap, pulled down over much of her face. She stayed silent and as inconspicuous as possible, hoping Rye would not be questioned as to why she now accompanied them. But his guardsmen seemed focused on that which unfolded in front of them, not that which trailed behind.

The day's ride was a lengthy one, as in midsummer the sun remained high in the sky and provided extra hours of light. It also provided plenty of time for Fee to fret over Savva's welfare and the whereabouts of her best friend. She was as far removed as she could be from the two people who needed her most.

When the sun finally dipped beneath the horizon, Rye ordered the troop to set up camp and build a fire. Fee could see he was exhausted merely from keeping himself in the saddle.

"Why don't you sleep," she said quietly, "and I'll bring you dinner once we've finished making it. You still need to rest, Rye. In fact, I should probably gather a few things to brew. I'll wake you when I have the tonic completed."

He shook his head. "A fine example that would set. Never. I'll manage like the others until we all put our heads to rest."

"Still as hardheaded as when you were ten, I see."

He gave her a look from beneath his brow. "I do believe in kinder company it's referred to as *tenacity*."

Fee knew the criticism was not meant to wound her, but it did. She was about to offer a retort when she caught sight of one of Rye's guards approaching. Rye saw him too, and quickly pointed off toward the stream. "Go ahead, make the brew. Best to keep away from curious eyes."

When she returned, she found that Rye had directed the men to prepare two small fires—one for the guards of Gwyndom and the other for himself and Fee.

"I explained that I've been recovering from a nasty bout of influenza. That was all they needed to justify two camps, as they are jumpy enough spending time in a kingdom that has not yet been lifted from quarantine."

"That was clever thinking."

Rye raised an eyebrow. "Good God. Did you just grace me with a compliment?"

Fee shrugged dismissively. "Apparently I am more fatigued than I give myself credit for. Thank you for the word of warning. It shan't happen again."

"Yes," he chuckled. "I wouldn't want to get used to something like that."

It was clear that Rye wanted to say something else, but he swallowed the words. She saw him wrestle with the fingers on his left hand and then, after hesitating, step closer.

"Your hair is falling loose beneath the cap." He reached up and tucked the long strand in under the rim. Fee looked up at him. The firelight caught one of his vividly green eyes and separated the colors within it. It made her think of a glittering cat's-eye marble that had been one of her prized possessions as a child.

An emphatic cough announced the presence of someone else, and they both pulled back sharply, twisting to see one of Rye's guards, cap in hand, staring uncomfortably at the ground.

"Milord?" the soldier said tentatively.

Fee glowed with heat and felt a wave of anxiety flood through her body. Rye straightened his leather tunic and faced the soldier.

"Yes, Sergeant Pennington?"

The soldier swallowed and stepped forward. "One of the horses has gone lame, milord. An earlier laceration has grown infected. We'll likely have to leave him with a local farmer for treatment."

Fee cleared her throat for Rye's attention. He turned to look at her. She spoke softly. "I can tend him."

Rye raised an eyebrow, paused for a moment, and then turned back to the soldier. "Bring him to me. We shall see what we can do for him before night's end."

The sergeant nodded and stepped back out of the circle of light, leaving them alone once again.

"I've got some herbs in my saddlebag, I can make a poultice—" Fee began.

"Yes, of course. Do whatever you can." He spun from her and left. Taking the full measure of discomfort he carried from their last awkward interaction toward the woods and stream.

Fighting her own disquiet, she dashed off to where their horses were hobbled and pulled her medicine bag from her supplies. She tried not to think about the sergeant's disruption or what he might have interpreted. When she returned to the fire, the other horse was standing within the circle of light, favoring his left rear leg. Fee approached him calmly and, after pausing for a moment in front of his muzzle to offer her scent, she ran her hand up the long white blaze striping his face. She trailed it smoothly over his withers, down his thigh, and stopped at his hock, allowing the horse to grow settled with her touch.

She lifted his leg to examine his hoof and, seeing that all was intact, searched from hock to fetlock. She found the wound on the inside of his ankle. The horse was clearly sensitive to her treating the injury and tried repeatedly to pull away from her gentle probes, snorting and whinnying with discomfort, blowing air out his muzzle and from deep within his throat.

"I know you're nervous," she cooed. "Let me help, and in a few days you'll feel so much better."

She worked quietly to administer the dressing, first cleaning the wound, then gently packing the area with the tingling, pungent ground herbs she'd amassed and, finally, wrapping the fetlock in a snug bandage. At one point, she became aware of Rye and one of the soldiers watching her from a distance, but she paid no heed. An injured animal is unpredictable, and one needed to be prepared for any potential dangerous reaction to the doctoring.

What she couldn't help noticing, though, was that within a matter of minutes the horse had quieted. He no longer snorted with anxious pain, and even began to put weight on the injured foot. Astonished, but grateful she'd chosen the proper treatment, Fee became conscious of the prickling band of heat that encircled her wrist. She thrilled as she worked, feeling an overwhelming sense of certitude as she moved about her task.

Once finished, she returned to her initial quest to make Rye's medicine. He brought two plates of beans, a wedge of cheese, and chunks of bread, and the two of them sat quietly before the smoldering campfire, eating their dinner.

"Remarkable recovery . . . on the part of the horse," Rye said, not looking at her. "Isn't it?"

Fee's muscles suddenly went rigid with attention. She shrugged.

"Ophelia, perhaps it's best you go back to Fireli and wait there."

"Whatever for?" she asked, her head snapping up.

"Maybe I should do this on my own."

"A one-man parade?" She scoffed. "You will march into Gwyndom flanked by guards you mistrust and confront the princess—or even the entire government altogether—and demand to have them return the rightful king of Fireli *if* he's still alive, and *oh by the way, what's the deal with our mines?* Are you crazy, or even more pigheaded than I recall?"

Rye was silent, but his eyes simmered. "I was trying to . . . protect you."

She felt the staining blush of temper on her face. "You need help—specifically *my* help. You're still too unwell to travel on your own."

"Again," he began, his voice barely kept in check, "I'm thinking about *your* protection, Ophelia. I see the potential for grave danger in front of yo— us, and I'm trying to do what makes sense."

She eyed him carefully, growing both nervous and nettled at the real meaning behind his words. "I've been schooled by Savva with an oath to my duty as a healer, and a lifelong promise of protection to Xavi. I will not be deterred by *the potential for grave danger.*"

She stood and allowed the release of an uncensored tongue. "I am so very tired of being told what to do, Rye, and, finally, after a painfully long time, I am just beginning to know what it means to feel myself again. I will not go back—to either the castle we came from, or the girl I was. Drink that. Then go to sleep." She pointed to the small pan close to the fire, its contents emitting wisps of steam that mixed with the smoke from the wood. "Wake up tomorrow knowing that I am at your side, both for your sake—despite what you put me through—and for Xavi's.

"Good night."

The following morning the group rose early. They'd ride toward the borderlands between Gwyndom and Fireli, following Fee's morning ministrations to the injured horse. Wasting no time, Fee uncovered the dressing from the injured horse's leg, and found no evidence of the wound she'd tended to the night before. Nothing was amiss. He was *completely healed*. She was further caught off guard to discover Rye quietly observing her work over her shoulder.

"I had chalked it up to unreliable memory. Figments of a young boy's wild imagination," Rye murmured.

Fee refused to look at him, and instead worked to pack her herbs and the dressings she'd laid out in preparation. "I don't understand," she said stiffly.

"Neither did I at the time." He moved closer, his voice hushed. "When I first moved away, you gave me a curious vial full of sunflower seeds. You told me to plant one if ever I grew lonely. And I did. In less than twenty-four hours I had a full-blown broad-headed sunflower growing beneath my window. A cheerful face, yes, but hardly companionable." He looked at her, clearly trying to make sense of the situation, his face apprehensive. "Ophelia . . . are you some sort of—"

Fee jumped in. "You know as well as I do that I've always had a knack for plants and flowers and whatnot. Plus, the horse's wound was grossly overstated. And the seeds? From so long ago? Yes, I would chalk that up to youthful inventiveness. The mind can conjure up unbridled illusions if it believes it can be helpful. Don't forget, we'd all just lost our parents and our worlds were upended."

Fee finished packing but saw out of the corner of her eye Rye's left-hand fingers curling in on themselves. She quickly mounted her horse to stop any further conversation, but her mind fell back to the one she'd had with Xavi just weeks ago.

They say it's been a hundred years since sorcery was erased from the realm. I can't imagine what it must have been like. So many hunted down for the great slaughter. Be careful, Fee.

But surely her luck with herbs and healing would never be considered *witchcraft*. She simply had an aptitude for the medicinal arts, a curative craft, an acutely green thumb that made things grow. Rye wouldn't think to report her to any of the authorities.

But she suddenly didn't feel certain. And whatever warm flush she'd felt beneath the cotton sleeve at her wrist after laying eyes upon the freshly healed wound on the horse had now been replaced with the prickle of insecurity and angst. Time would tell.

She prayed Rye wouldn't.

CHAPTER
TWENTY-THREE

THE SCENERY CHANGED SWIFTLY FROM THE UNDULAT-
ing swell and dip of lush pastures, to the rise of ridges and sharp
slopes, the broad, leafy deciduous trees replaced by needled pines
with a spicy, sweet, and resin-like scent.

By early evening of the third day, as the sun fell beneath the
horizon, Fee began to feel the prickles of discomfort. The hills had
grown taller, their faces steeply angled, and the landscape had taken
on an imposing grandeur, illustrating a kingdom that commanded
respect and obeisance.

It did not matter that they were losing the illumination of day-
light, as the route they traveled had changed from a dusty footpath
to a broad and sizeable dirt road, and then into that which they
moved along right now: an exquisite cobblestoned thoroughfare,
lit with gas lamps that cast a buttery glow over every surface. The

houses grew larger and closer together with each mile nearer to the castle. And each bush, tree, or flower seemed utterly perfect. Fee was unsettled that they did not reach out to her. She could not smell nor sense them the way that she did the life force that encircled all living things back in Fireli.

"Rye?" she called out quietly. "It appears we have crossed the threshold from mortal lands. Is there something special about those who inhabit Gwyndom? Are they divine beings with celestial talents?"

Rye looked over his shoulder at her and puffed. "No, Ophelia. They are no more unique than you or I, apart from in their mind's eye."

"What does that mean?" she whispered.

"It means that Gwyndomites *believe* themselves to be superior because of the amount of wealth their kingdom possesses and displays, and, to them, prosperity translates to power."

Fee glanced about at the ornately designed houses of wood and stone, gold light pouring out of the bountiful glass-paned windows. "Doesn't it?"

Rye shook his head. "Only if your single means of measurement to define a worthy life is a unit of coin. It is not mine, but it is the standard here."

But to Fee, the images before her only underscored the idea that perhaps, in some way she'd yet to discover, the Gwyndomites truly were a superior race. And in less than one hour's journey farther on, that notion was firmly cemented in her head.

They came around the curve of a broad hill and caught sight of the kingdom's palace.

Fee gasped and every hair along her arms bristled. Six massive round towers enveloped the outside walls, and brightly colored flags lit from below whipped in the breeze at the tips of the turrets. Countless smaller minarets were tucked farther inward, punctuating the many roofs. Sleekly arched bridges connected each main tower, supported by stone that shimmered like burnished bronze. The coppery flecks glistened, highlighted by hundreds of torches and gas lamps that illuminated the castle.

A long drawbridge loomed over a dark, watery moat from the massive wood-and-iron gate at the entrance. Guards barred admission on either end, security measures clearly a matter of priority.

"Rye? Are you sure we can get away with this?" She pulled alongside him, leaning in to whisper as they drew closer to the bridge.

"Have you changed your mind? Are you saying you wish to go home?"

"I have not. And I do not." Although her words were true in her heart, the rest of her body rattled with indecision.

She saw his mouth set with mulish determination. "Then we've no other alternative, Ophelia. We must make this work. Keep your head down, and don't speak to anyone."

She nodded and reined her horse behind his again.

The soldiers in front of them were greeted with stiff but polite acknowledgment and, after a few words and gestures pointing back toward Rye, the smaller gate, giving access onto the bridge over the moat, was unlocked and raised. They crossed in pairs, Fee and Rye pulling up the rear. She kept her cap pulled low and was grateful for the cover of nightfall and the playing shadows of torchlight obscuring her features.

When they reached a set of immense iron-spiked doors, they stopped as the soldiers at the front explained once more who they led. Rye's party was granted immediate admittance. Once they crossed the threshold, a rush of servants came forward to aid them as they dismounted.

Fee fought the overpowering urge to glance up in awe at the towering structure before her, to ogle the grandeur of the architecture, but she kept her chin tucked close to her chest and, instead, took notice of the innumerable people moving about within the frenzied atmosphere Rye's arrival had created.

"Milord, you've returned," a voice boomed from across the courtyard. Heavily booted feet clicked purposefully across the herringbone-patterned redbrick ground. "We were given no warning, or we would have been ready to receive you." The man stopped a respectful distance in front of Rye and made a polite, if somewhat stiff, bow.

"There was not time to send word, Lord Drachen. I was told of the princess's plight and have come to her aid. Where is she?"

Fee peeked at the man to gauge his reaction and saw a flash of apprehension darken his face. His quick grey eyes, narrowly set within deep sockets, revealed sharp intelligence. The outfit he wore spoke of wealth and status: a burgundy silk jacket, trousers of fine black leather, and shiny knee-high boots, neatly outlined at the top with a rim of soft gray fur. His voice purred with earned authority.

"Princess Quinn is likely with the queen, milord, handling"— he cast a quick glance over his shoulders—"the apprehension and arrest of another witch, but if you allow us to resettle you into your suite, I'm certain they will be most grateful for your aid." Lord

Drachen clapped his hands sharply toward a cluster of servants, and Fee jumped at both the noise and Lord Drachen's pronouncement. The attendants scattered like unearthed beetles, gathering Rye's things from his horse and rushing off with them.

"I have brought my own manservant from Fireli. Set him up in the adjoining servant's room beside mine. I expect an audience in half an hour's time, Lord Drachen."

"Of course, milord. I shall see to everything." The man made a slight bow with his head and backed away, his last glance up at Rye revealing something Fee couldn't quite define. Wariness? Resentment? Worry?

A comely middle-aged woman, wearing a snow-white linen blouse and full skirt with a crisply ironed apron, glided smoothly toward them over the brick courtyard. With outstretched arms, she reached for Rye and pulled him into a warm, maternal embrace. She pushed him back to standing, still holding his ears to twist his face side to side as she assessed him.

"You've been ill," she announced in a voice that soothed like warm syrup, finally letting him go.

"It's nice to see you too, Mistress Goodsong."

"Perhaps food poisoning," she said as a matter of fact, her soft, wide brown eyes narrowing into focused slits.

Fee nearly leapt back at the woman's quick and accurate diagnosis, but Rye simply shook his head and chuckled. "Was it that obvious?"

Mistress Goodsong leaned in and looked down the bridge of her tiny, mushroom-capped nose. "Your eyes are bloodshot, and your skin has the pallor of old parchment paper. You've lost sleep and haven't been drinking enough fluids. You breathed in sharply as I bent you over, which means you've had intestinal distress and are still suffering from internal inflammation. I smell burdock and milk thistle..." She leaned in closer. "And echinacea." She closed her eyes and then pulled back to look at him. "But not any evening primrose oil or dandelion. Whatever medicine man you came upon along the road to aid your illness was obviously using ancient treatments— only mildly adequate."

Fee could see Rye holding back the urge to cast a glance her way and simply said, "Supplies were limited, I assume."

Mistress Goodsong spun on her heel, and Rye followed, motioning with his head that Fee was to come with them.

The woman put a finger up in the air as they moved swiftly across the courtyard and beneath a large arched passage into a long tunnel lined with torches. "A seven-day diet of nothing but brown rice, vegetables, and water will cleanse the liver and kidneys. I shall see to your *proper* treatment after delivering you to your room."

Fee was aghast, if not the tiniest bit affronted, at the woman's precise assessment. She did her best to keep abreast with the rapid pace of movement through the tunnel as they threaded their way among castle inhabitants coming from the opposite direction, including a long line of monks dressed in sweeping brown robes with deep, shadowy hoods. Obviously, this woman was Gwyndom's healer, a person she'd heard spoken of many times in reverent tones.

After ten further minutes of winding through the intricate maze of interwoven tunnels beneath the base of the castle, they finally began ascending—an endless spiral staircase that left Fee fighting for breath. When they popped out onto a landing dimly lit with torches, but devoid of other people, Fee felt safe enough to raise her eyes to look about. They moved down a narrow, plushly carpeted hallway and stopped at the midway point in front of a double set of large wooden doors.

Mistress Goodsong pulled a key from her pocket and had just inserted it into the door when she caught sight of Fee standing behind Rye. She pulled back sharply, having spied Fee for the first time. "Who are you?"

Rye put up a hand to silence her. He took the key, quickly unlocked the door, and ushered the healer inside. Then he gestured to Fee to step across the threshold. "After you, milady," he said stiffly.

Mistress Goodsong's face twisted with bewilderment as her eyes swept across Fee from north to south and up again, taking in her threadbare guardsman's uniform and too-large cap, still pulled down to cover most of her face. "Mi-milady?" she stuttered.

"Mistress Goodsong," Rye began after he'd closed the door and locked it, "may I present Fireli's healer, Ophelia de Vale." He nodded toward Fee, and she raised her chin to make eye contact with the other woman.

"Healer?" Mistress Goodsong repeated.

Rye walked toward Fee and plucked her cap from her head. Her thick black hair tumbled down around her shoulders. "Yes, healer. And for most of my life, the woman whom I was promised to marry."

Mistress Goodsong's gaze made a lightning-speed evaluation of Fee—the slightest widening of eyes when looking at her face—but she did not miss a beat. "You used the past tense, Prince Rye, which means one of three things: either you have changed your mind, in which case you are clearly more fool than I gave you credit for being—for despite her dishevelment and filth from the road, she is somewhat pleasing as well as intelligent—or *she* has changed her mind, in which case you're better off—for she has less intelligence than I just gave her credit for possessing." She paused, blinking and staring at him.

"You are wrong on both accounts, Mistress Goodsong. Your third deduction?" Rye said, keeping his face unreadable.

Fee looked quickly up at Rye. She had never seen him act so comfortably around anyone.

She sighed and tilted her head. "A forced marriage has been thrust upon you. But why?"

Rye turned casually to Fee and pretended to lower his voice conspiratorially. "I should have warned you. She is as keen as a hawk. Facts are like tiny moles scurrying stealthily beneath her, but nothing slips by unnoticed."

"And yet you insist on trying." She pointed toward a plush sofa in the richly furnished antechamber of Rye's castle living quarters. "Both of you look utterly exhausted. Sit. But I must press on with gathering the necessary details if I am to help heal my patients."

They did sit, gratefully. And Rye began the long tale revealing everything that had happened within the last couple of weeks. "When I'd been summoned home, there was no body, and Fee was the primary suspect in Xavi's murder. Then, after the news that I must marry Quinn, Fee discovered Quinn was poisoning *me*—just as she had Xavi. Quinn made a rapid escape at the same time we'd realized who was behind the assassination attempts, but possibly not before hearing Fee reveal that Xavi was still alive, and where he was."

Rye sighed and rubbed at his temples. "There was no sign of him in the caves, and we fear he's been kidnapped and taken here. On top of that, we learned that the mines have been in use, but we've no idea who's annexed them. So now we're here trying to engineer a plan. And would welcome your help."

Mistress Goodsong listened with static features but rapt attention. Fee understood immediately how Rye held the healer in such high esteem. Clearly, her mind was sharp, and it was a comfort to know Rye had had this person to give him counsel and affection.

"You are utterly convinced that *our* Quinn was behind the poisoning?" The healer's face did not scoff at the suggestion. Instead, she appeared to be absorbing the information.

Fee watched Rye's fingers slide into their revealing position. Mistress Goodsong had spotted it too. "You doubt," the healer asserted. "Not entirely, perhaps. But you leave room for the possibility that while Quinn was the vehicle, another force drove the events at hand."

Rye exhaled. Fee could tell it was a relief to be so well understood.

"So what is your plan?"

"To search Gwyndom Castle in hopes of finding Xavi." Fee jumped in.

"How will you do this unnoticed?"

"I will keep Princess Quinn occupied with marital plans," Rye admitted, "while Ophelia hunts the palace from top to bottom."

"You hope to convince the princess that you did not believe she was to blame for the poisoning?"

They nodded.

"And, finally, you hope to discover Prince Xavi alive, and have him verify the existence of two botched assassination attempts *and* a scheme to overthrow the Kingdom of Fireli in order to gain all the mining rights and a lion's share of power within the four kingdoms of Aethusa?"

Rye and Fee's eyes met. "Well, when you put it like that . . ." Rye swallowed and glanced uncomfortably back to Mistress Goodsong. "It does sound rather far-fetched."

"It's precisely what we intend to do," Fee said, straightening her shoulders and sitting forward on the silken couch. "And since it's abundantly clear that Rye trusts you with not only the details of our plan but with his life, then I must as well. We need your help, and I will beg for it if need be. We absolutely must find Xavi. His life depends upon it—that is, if he still has a life."

Mistress Goodsong studied Fee with a quizzical brow. She turned to Rye. "She is loyal and courageous—not to mention humble. Your parents tried to make a very good match."

Rye faced Fee. "I find it difficult to explain, but I cannot express how indebted I am to Mistress Goodsong. For the last three years, she has been both mother and father. She has been my guidance and advisor. She has been—and continues to be—there for me when I am in need. And"—he looked sheepishly at the healer—"I believe it may be with a frequency that is overwhelmingly tiresome."

"Nonsense, Rye. You are the son I never had, and I favor you with the intent to spoil. I am at your service always. You can trust this to be true. Alas, it is a pity—this . . . situation," she continued, now addressing them both. "But I will do what I must to help. How is it you plan to hide Ophelia and search for Xavi?"

"Please, call me Fee, Mistress Goodsong. Everyone does." *Everyone apart from Rye, for some reason.*

"The question remains the same," she said.

"I don't plan to hide her. I plan to *use* her. *She* will be the one searching for Xavi."

"Fee is not known here. There will be talk, and it will surely get back to Queen Islay and the princess."

"I thought we'd disguise her as one of the monks."

Fee looked up at Rye. "You mean the brown-robed men we passed in the tunnel?"

"Yes," Mistress Goodsong said, nodding. "They have unrestricted access. Mere fixtures we rarely take notice of. And, perhaps to your benefit, the castle is overwrought with the capture of this witch. They speak of it to the point of distraction. Their focus will be elsewhere."

Fee tried to swallow the sudden dryness in her throat and prayed that it was true, for if the rest of Gwyndom's constituents were anything like Mistress Goodsong, taking such keen notice of everything, they would never succeed.

The healer's face took on a scrupulous expression as she stared at Fee, but then fell with a sigh when she turned back to Rye.

"Yes, I'm certain Fee will capitalize on the freedom her disguise will provide, but Rye—" She clucked her tongue and shook her head slowly. "You must hope for all the strength a monk's prayers can deliver, as finding success with this venture will take nothing short of a miracle."

CHAPTER
TWENTY-FOUR

FEE PICKED UP THE SMALL WOODEN BOX ON THE BROAD table in Rye's sitting room and cracked the lid to peek inside. The box held five trinkets: a locket with a tiny inlaid portrait of Rye and Xavi's parents; Xavi's treasured pen, which he'd gifted to Rye before he departed with the strict instruction to write weekly and return it in good use; three dried forget-me-nots Fee had given Rye before he left; the empty glass vial that had once been filled with sunflower seeds; and finally, a worry stone with a groove worn smooth by ten thousand thumb strokes.

Fee felt her eyes blur as she rubbed the stone, imagining how awful it must have been for Rye all these years on his own.

"I wish you hadn't seen those. They're proof of what a sentimental sop I used to be."

Fee snapped the lid shut. She whirled to see Rye standing at an open door beside the fireplace, his expression dour and disconcerted. "I wasn't expecting company and obviously left in haste, otherwise I would have . . . well, kept those silly keepsakes out of sight."

"I don't think they're silly. And I don't think less of you for keeping them. I was just surprised they still held relevance."

A shadow passed over Rye's face, and Fee fumbled with her next words. "Of course, they probably still hold relevance. What a stupid thing to say. Or at least some of them still do—"

"Yes. Some of them still do, Ophelia," he said, staring at her.

Fee felt a rush of heat travel up her chest and into two bright spots of pulsating warmth on her cheeks. It was wholly frustrating, but the alternative—taking Savva's daily tonic to tamp down the fire of feeling anything—was an unthinkable choice. She'd never go back. She pressed on, set on recovering a thread of mental clarity.

"Have you managed to find a room for me to hide in?"

Rye gestured with his hand. "The adjoining one to my suite. As I mentioned to the man Lord Drachen in the courtyard, it's to be known that I've traveled with a manservant from Fireli. No one will think anything of it. And you needn't be seen much in that regard, as I'm always assigned a full detail of guardsmen whilst here. Most of the time you'll be outfitted in this." He held up a woolly brown robe. "Mistress Goodsong delivered it moments ago and said she'd be back with food and news." He gestured with his head. "You might as well settle in. I imagine you'd like to be free of that getup and scrape the layers of road dust from yourself. I'll call you when Mistress Goodsong returns. Then we can refine our plans."

She stepped past Rye in the doorway that connected their rooms. He put out a hand, grasping her arm and stopping her. "I know he's here, Ophelia. I believe I would feel it if he were dead. And I don't. He's every bit as alive as you and I. We're going to find him. And when we do, we are going to put Fireli back together again. All of us."

The room was sumptuous, unlike anything Fee had experienced before. The windows were hung with dressings of gauzy copper silk. She ran the material through her fingers, watching it slip from her grasp and pool at her feet. The carpets were deeply plush and cushioned her footfalls into silence. A wide four-poster bed angled out from one corner, draped from above with the matching gauze from the windows, and adorned with a hand-stitched embroidered coverlet, its hues of crimson, copper, and gold suffusing the space with opulent warmth.

Fee turned to see the fireplace that shared a chimney with Rye's sitting room. Inside, seasoned wood crackled and warmed the space around her. And the bedroom had an adjoining bath, which boasted a massive soaking tub that she calculated could fit three people.

"Is this how the wealthy people's *servants* live? For it seems they are treated well-nigh better than the man who will be Fireli's king. Surely if anyone in Fireli caught wind of the wealth showered upon Gwyndom's inhabitants they would wish themselves here in a heartbeat—and I wouldn't blame them." And then she recalled Xavi's concern whether Fireli could even entice the return of its discharged youth.

She shed her garments and gathered the stained and worn-out clothing into a pile. Standing before a mirrored wall, she took a quick assessment of what eight days in Fireli's prison, two in a cave, and three on the road with precious little to eat had done to her body. She was dirty, exhausted, and as hungry as a lion. How anyone could look at her and classify her as becoming was an impossible concept to embrace, but she'd take on the task of stripping herself of dirt.

She opened the faucet above the bathtub and watched swirling streams of hot water pour in a gush to fill the lower half. Submerging herself into the steaming water, she found a bar of heavily perfumed soap and a sea sponge beside it. She scrubbed; every square inch of skin was scoured until pink and free of filth. She worked the soap through her hair and over her neck and face and, when thoroughly covered in foaming, sweetly scented bubbles, she sank beneath the water line and rubbed herself free of it all.

She had never felt so clean.

Or so guilty.

She was used to the large copper bucket Savva kept behind the stillroom under the eaves of the thatched roof. Once a week they'd haul it inside, fill it bit by bit with the large kettles of water from the stove, and each take a bath, soaking in the quickly cooling water.

At least Savva allowed them to make lavender soap, since they were surrounded by a small field of the heady-scented flower. For that, she had always been grateful.

Drying herself with the luxurious towel strewn across the long arm of a brass rack, she searched for something to wear and suddenly realized she was without her small bag and the medicines within it. It also held her spare clothing. Glancing about the bedroom, she saw nothing but the monk's robe, and moved to pick it up.

The door to the corridor opened, and Mistress Goodsong entered, striding forward to stand before Fee, where she stopped and adopted a pose that radiated curiosity. "Now would be an appropriate time, Fee. I'm sure you'd prefer not to do this in front of Prince Rye."

Fee clutched at her towel. "Appropriate time for what?"

The healer's eyebrows rose.

Fee looked about the room feeling quite out of her depth, a sudden note of anxiety springing into her chest.

Mistress Goodsong tilted her head. "Yes, well, first things first, I suppose. I've brought you something to wear. You needn't house yourself in that garment when there's no want for it, child."

Grateful, Fee reached for the frock the healer held out and then gasped when the woman caught her with one hand and slid her fingers up the inside of Fee's arm until their wrists pressed together. The dress slipped to the floor as a wall of heat engulfed her. A roar filled the space within Fee's ears. Her knees weakened, threatening to collapse. And her breathing halted—the muscles surrounding her lungs gripping her chest in a crushing hug. Images flashed before her eyes like quick strikes of lightning illuminating her mind with bright and potent pictures.

Her parents.

The king and queen of Fireli.

Xavi and his study.

Fee lying in the lavender field, staring up at the hazy blue skies.

And Rye. His face as a young, reckless, headstrong boy, and that of him now but with an expression she'd never seen before . . . unbearable betrayal.

Pulling strength from this newfound place of shock, Fee wrenched her arm out of the grasp of Mistress Goodsong and stood, clutching her towel, eyes both startled and furious. But she was also frightened. "W-what did you do?" she whispered to the woman who stood before her as purposefully serene as the surface of a quiet, undisturbed pond.

"I took my patient's history. And, as a note of importance, it is considered common courtesy to acknowledge one of your thauma-turgical peers."

"My what?"

"A person like you. One who holds magic."

"No . . ." Fee exhaled.

Mistress Goodsong's eyes narrowed as she canvassed Fee's face and read her features. "You deny it?"

Fee was silent, hearing only her heart throbbing loudly within the cage of her chest. "You're a witch?" Fee asked hesitantly.

"As are *you*, Fee. No matter how much you refute it—which is a considerable amount based on that which I've gathered after view-ing your past."

Fee stumbled back, her legs giving out beneath her as she bumped into a small table. She finally found support against the wall beside it. Her mind raced to Xavi and his warnings. "I . . . I am not." She heaved and stuttered like a fool. "I am a nothing . . . just a healer—and only one who studies in apprenticeship. I assure you, *whomever* you are, what you did just now is wholly beyond my ken."

Mistress Goodsong took a big breath in and again keenly scruti-nized Fee from top to bottom. "For now," she remarked simply. "The others will be curious about you."

"What others do you speak of?"

"The other menders—healers, if you insist on calling them that.

It is generally agreed that we needn't use the term amongst ourselves. That designation is reserved for the Ordinary. *We* are hermetical menders—both earthly and mystic. We much prefer the description over that of 'witch.' But perhaps you already know this and are simply presenting yourself as an innocent? As some sort of ruse to deceive?"

"You are mistaken. I am *not* a witch—nor is Savva, my mentor. But you—"

Mistress Goodsong put up a finger. "I assure you I am not. Mistaken, that is," she quickly clarified. "And as far as Savva is concerned? She is one of the most powerful menders our kingdoms have ever known. Her, and her son."

"Savva has a son?"

"*Had*," Mistress Goodsong explained in patient tones, looking off in the distance. "He was Fireli's gardener, I believe, but it's been many years since anyone has heard from him. And of course, because of the quarantine, many years since anyone has interacted with Savva."

The healer paused and then slowly turned toward Fee. "Who are your parents? Did they not tell you of your magic?"

Fee swallowed, her head reeling. "They died . . . in the epidemic."

"Were there any others like you remaining in Fireli?"

"Like me?"

"Children. Those who held magic?"

Fee shook her head. "It was Xavi and me. We were the only two left."

The older woman did not tear her eyes from Fee, but bent to pick up the dress. She held it out again. "Where does your specialty lie?"

Seeing the blossoming confusion Fee must have presented, Mistress Goodsong added, "Are you telling me you've never had things happen to you that were—" She searched the ceiling. "—unexplainable? Hermetical menders have an unusual ability. to . . . *shift energy*. Usually with one particular specialty."

Fee cautiously reached for the frock and stopped as her mind whirled from one small event to another: the tiny knack that Fee had developed during the last ten years that seemed to alarm Savva so. The tiny knack that was growing startlingly fast.

She slid the dress over her head and shoulders and let the towel drop to pool at her feet. She tried squelching the burbling rise of panic that flared up with Xavi's echoing words when explaining the realm's laws and the banishment or slaying of witches.

"What kind of specialties?" Fee asked.

"Oh, menders can do anything from manipulating light or water or heat to things like secreting smoke or shifting objects— even molecular combustion."

Fee shook her head. She was not like them. She was not one of them.

Mistress Goodsong was not deterred. "What do you know of your birthmark?"

"This?" Fee turned up her wrist. "Only that it's very peculiar." She pulled it close to her chest.

"Did Savva lead you to believe a union with Prince Rye would have been agreeable?"

Fee's stomach lurched with a somersault of emotion. She shook her head.

"Well"—the healer raised an eyebrow—"in case there is any need for clarification—it is *forbidden*."

Fee pulled back. "Why?"

"'Tis an archaic Aethusian law regarding whom those with magic may marry."

"A law?"

Mistress Goodsong nodded gravely. "Mixing certain bloodlines can create wretched and tragic results." Her features softened and she added, "It is a lamentable experience, giving up someone you love. But Aethusian law is strong, and ultimately for the greater good—all before one. You must remember this."

She moved toward the door and paused. "One more thing. Where is Savva now? Does she know you've escaped with the prince?"

Fee shook her head. "Savva is unconscious—she was injured in a fall, and as we rushed off in search of Xavi, I could not come to her aid. I am uncertain as to whether she is alive or . . ." Fee faltered. "Or not, at this time. Might you be able to help?"

Mistress Goodsong's features went bleak. "Oh, dear. Not until the quarantine has been lifted, I'm afraid."

She opened the door. "I will return shortly with food and medicine. Stay put until then." She raised her head slightly and added, "Also, it's best, for your safety, that you're aware of Rye's opinion on witches. He has been schooled—as has most everyone here in Gwyndom—to see them as something that needs . . . eradicating. Like a pernicious weed, they will pull you out by the roots and destroy you. Keep your secret close, for your enemies are all around you."

CHAPTER
TWENTY-FIVE

WITHIN MOMENTS OF MISTRESS GOODSONG LEAVING Fee's room, the door between the two chambers echoed with Rye's rapid knocking.

"Ophelia? May I open the door?"

Fee pulled her head out of a stupefied haze and moved to let Rye in. He'd bathed and changed clothing too, and now sported a jade-green velvet jacket, expertly cut to fit his long, lean torso, and belted with a braided black rope. He seemed slightly taken aback at finding her in a dress, and Fee could see he was nervous.

"I've been given an audience with Queen Islay—and Quinn is to be there too. Hurry and toss on your robe. You're to accompany me—you'll need a layout for that region of the castle."

Fee nodded and lowered the robe over her head. Rye grabbed the hood and pulled it past her ears so that her face was recessed and covered in dark shadow. "There. You're hidden." He paused. "Are you all right? You seem uneasy."

She shook her head, but decided not to speak, as she believed her voice might betray her and then everything would come spilling out: a torrential fountain of worry, confusion, and remorse. Now was not the time. And perhaps Rye was not the person. She had to keep reminding herself that they didn't really know one another anymore.

He looked at her with one wary eyebrow cocked. But if he had been wrestling with questioning her, her silence won out. He took her elbow and guided her to the door leading into the hallway.

The corridors were a complicated maze of twisting, carpeted pathways lined with jeweled glass lanterns, heavy doors of wood and iron, and a clog of exquisitely dressed people slowly muscling their way forward like heavy-footed cattle funneling through the aisles of a barn.

The citizens of Gwyndom were resplendent. Their clothing sparkled: glittering with sequins, twinkling with jewels, and dusted with shimmering fabrics. The people were walking treasure chests. Their hairstyles were equally elaborate—twisting, piled-high braids; bountiful, buoyant ringlets; and shiny, slicked-back waves were fashionable designs Fee had never viewed on the people in her kingdom. Even their faces and hair were adorned with ornaments. Eyebrows were outlined with tiny ruby beads, beauty marks were emeralds or sapphires plastered on cheekbones and chins, and gold threads or strands of pearls were woven into lengths of hair. Even men's beards and mustaches winked with tiny studded gems when the light caught them.

Fee's skills of assessment needled at the back of her brain, but she did her level best to keep her head low and not stare. Both she and Rye were desperate for sleep and food—and Rye needed medicine—but apparently his determination was equal to hers.

She simply wanted to find Xavi.

And go home.

Ten minutes later, after wending their way through several arched hallways and serpentine passages, they came to a part of the castle where the extravagance exceeded Fee's imagination. Gold washed over everything, and onyx punctuated its gleam. The rooms were adorned like crowns, gold slathered over every fixture, wall, and ceiling. If there was fabric, it was plush and velvet—crimson, mulberry, jade, or blue. The colors dazzled in their opulent hues and were outlined in deeply radiant jet-black gemstones. Candles flickered in crystal chandeliers, throwing rainbow sparkles across the walls, floors, and ceilings. Pearled onyx vases exploded with every bloom imaginable, flawless flowers and vines tumbling onto the tables and floors with exquisite and dramatic abandon.

Sculptures grew out of every corner, and massive, gilded frames housed oil paintings of a woman Fee assumed was Queen Islay. She posed in myriad styles: seated, reclined, and standing. But in all of them she was stately, and her likeness oozed with power along with the one other thing the painters always seemed to highlight: the black gemstone hanging around her neck. Her eyes were everywhere, her attention focused as if she were constantly searching. Fee's insides pitched with upheaval as she passed by each one, following Rye to the queen's chambers.

He stopped just out of earshot from the two beefy guards who stood on either side of an intricately carved set of mahogany doors, inlaid with the same glistening jewel-toned stained glass Fee had admired in the hallways. Clearly, they had arrived, and this was where they'd part.

"I'm uncertain how long I shall be. Perhaps mere seconds, which means they've ordered me out of Gwyndom and now find me an enemy of the kingdom. Or I may never come out, which means they've managed to silence me permanently. Either way, I expect I'll face a struggle. Just don't wander off. We may have to dash—or you alone will be forced to. We'll know soon enough."

Fee looked up into Rye's face and tried to erase his worry with a look of encouragement. "Breathe, Rye. Don't forget to breathe." She hesitated before adding, "And whatever you do, don't ball your fist."

He pulled back with a look of surprise, but Fee shook her head and pushed him toward the doors and the men who guarded them. "I'll be waiting. Good luck."

She watched him approach the sentries, saw them bow their heads before granting him access. And then she felt her heart thrum with growing panic at the thought that the guards might have just served the answer to Gwyndom's prayers upon a silver platter straight into the queen's lap. Fee glared up at one of Queen Islay's imposing portraits and hissed from beneath her great hood, "You have one of them already. You may not have both. In fact, I believe you have more than your fair share of absolutely everything Aethusa has to offer. It's time to return what never belonged to you."

Fee stood out of sight from the guards, counting the lamentably mushrooming number of minutes Rye had been inside with the queen.

Perhaps she should try to find her way back to Rye's room or search for Mistress Goodsong. The healer had agreed to help—and it was clear she would come to Rye's aid whenever beckoned. But as the minutes accumulated on the other side of the door, Fee believed that Rye was in trouble and her only option was to trick her way past the guards, feigning some emergency message that needed to be delivered to the prince.

Summoning all her courage, she took a step out from behind her hiding place at the same time as the doors burst open. She rushed toward it, but having made her way halfway down the hall, she realized that the man who had come through the ornate double doors was not Rye but Lord Drachen, and he was thundering down the very passageway she stood frozen in.

His head was down, and long wisps of his silver hair had come undone from the tight clubbed queue he'd used to hold it in place. Fee sucked in her breath as the man barreled closer. He looked up suddenly, catching sight of her robe, and abruptly stopped.

"What are you doing in the queen's quarters?" he demanded, his jaw jutting out, thrusting the words as if he were kicking them out of his mouth. Fee was paralyzed, her muscles seizing and her brain gone blank. His eyes narrowed. "Who are you?"

Lord Drachen grabbed her arm and pulled her closer, reaching a hand toward her hood. His fingers brushed against the brown woolen fabric just as Rye's clear baritone voice sailed down the hall. "Brother Chorster!" he called from the doorway. "There you are! I need to see you immediately."

Fee started, and nearly answered him by crying out his name, but she caught herself and tried to wrest her arm free from Lord Drachen's grasp. The muscles in his jaw twitched, and he cast a glance over his shoulder, tightening his hold. "Just a moment," he growled.

A searing hot panic flushed through Fee's body, simmering from a source deep within her. Unable to pull her arm out from Lord Drachen's clutching grip, she instinctively used her other hand to grapple with him. Her fingers slipped up inside the sleeve of his shirt. Her own wrist slid over his, and the two of them jolted with the contact. Lightning-fast, it felt as if her arm had melded into his, her bones fusing to the fibers of the muscles along his ulna and radius. Broken images flashed before her eyes: a boy with a bow and arrow, a stolen kiss behind a tree, a humiliating rebuke in front of his elders—fragmented scenes of someone else's life, someone else's joy, someone else's pain.

Fee jerked her hand out of Lord Drachen's clench, gasping for air and stumbling backward. Lord Drachen echoed her movements but fell against the wall, eyes bulging, his body sliding toward the floor. She bolted for Rye, and he grabbed her by the elbow, rushing her headlong down a separate hallway.

Rye repeatedly scanned the area behind them hawkishly, to see if anyone followed. They slowed their rapid pace once sharing the passages with other castle inhabitants, and Fee kept her head lowered, her eyes glued to the back of Rye's legs so she wouldn't lose him in the mix of people.

Several torturous minutes later, they arrived back at Rye's apartments and hurried through the great wooden doors, bolting the locks securely behind them. Rye turned to Fee as she cast off her hood, his eyes filled with alarm. "What happened, Ophelia?"

How does one explain that you had found a door into another

person's soul—if that's what it was? Fee had no words to answer that question, so she bolted forward with her own urgent worries. "I am to ask you the very same thing. And broadly speaking, your event is much more pressing than mine. Tell me."

He looked at her curiously but then began pacing, running a hand through his burnished-copper hair. "As soon as I entered, I rushed for Quinn, expressing as much concern as I could muster. I said I'd been given word of some great emergency in Gwyndom but, being bedridden with whatever dreadful affliction I had, I could do little about following her until I could stand again."

Rye picked up his measured steps. "I said that I intended to pursue justice for Xavi until I draw my last breath, if need be, but at this moment, Fireli was in dire straits. Especially now, with a growing fear of some unusual rash of witches appearing."

"How did they respond?" Fee asked, wondering if her own last breaths were drawing near.

"Quinn said we should not wait to hold our wedding until we both returned to Fireli but instead should have it immediately here in Gwyndom."

Fee held back a gasp. "Immediately?" she whispered.

A heavy frown swept across his face. "In three days' time."

CHAPTER
TWENTY-SIX

FEE WOKE TO THE SOFT CRACKLE OF A POPPING FIRE, her eyelids lifting slowly to reveal the quiet flames of a well-tended hearth. Her head was fuzzy, thick with fog. She closed her eyes again, abandoning herself to the magnetic pull of slipping beneath the muddled surface, when, all at once, the sharp prick of reality thrummed through her body and forced her to bolt upright.

She was on a couch—the soft velvet cushions in Rye's antechamber—in his apartments within the lush and lavish Gwyndom Castle.

"Good morning, Ophelia."

Fee jumped and turned to see Rye sitting in an armchair beside her makeshift bed, his face unreadable and remote.

"Morning?" Her voice croaked, parched with disuse.

Rye glanced toward the heavy, drawn curtains. "Despite the black of night, it is a few hours into the new day. You've not slept long, and I'm sorry it cannot be longer, but now is our best chance to move about the castle with less company."

Xavi. Yes, of course. Her head buzzed with a disturbing racket. She grasped at the threads of wakefulness, but the effort was like slogging through one of the old salt marshes, dense with grass spears and tangled with weeds. She swallowed and tried again. "Have you slept at all?" She saw on the table in front of him a goblet of ruby-colored wine, half drunk and standing next to a decanter that was nearly empty.

"For a short while; enough, I suppose."

She straightened and pointed at the glass. "You shouldn't be drinking that just yet. The lining to your stomach is likely still tender and inflamed."

A small puff of air was Rye's response, along with one arched brow. "I didn't. *You* did."

"What?" Fee brought her hand to her head.

"Precisely," he answered wryly. "Moments after I told you about my audience with the queen, and Quinn's resolute plans, Mistress Goodsong came in with a tray of food, medicine, and wine. You wanted to start the search for Xavi straightaway, but she and I agreed that it was better to wait until most of the castle went to sleep. You were clearly upset, refused the food, and skipped right to the wine. Three glasses in somewhat quick succession. Then you"—he gestured at the couch—"passed out on the cushions."

Her mouth fell open. "I what?" But even as the words of surprise tumbled out, clarity and recall began to fill in the cracks. "Oh God. I did, didn't I?" She wasn't used to drinking such potent liquids, as the wine barrels in Fireli were thoroughly watered down to make them last. "Did I . . . say anything?"

"Enough." Rye's expression hinted at alarming possibilities.

Did she tell him of Savva's deception and suppression? That Mistress Goodsong had deemed she was not just a healer but some form of witch, as well? Or had she spilled forth with the unexplainable, utterly ridiculous heartbreak she felt when he'd announced the wedding to Quinn? *Again.*

Her heart hammered a rapid drumbeat clear up through to her ears. "Rye," she began, "I imagine there might be some things we should talk about...."

His gaze pierced straight through hers to a tiny, fragile place she'd been desperate to protect. He rubbed his hand across his chin and said, "There are. But for the moment they'll have to wait.

"Let's go find Xavi."

Fifteen minutes later, and clutching a rolled-up sketch of the castle, Fee worked her way toward one area Rye had circled for her to search. They'd agreed that splitting up would double their chances of success, but it also put Fee at a disadvantage with her unfamiliar surroundings. The lower-ranked monks of Gwyndom had taken a vow of silence, so it would not be unreasonable for her to refuse to speak if questioned by a guard, but it would raise suspicion if she stopped to ask anyone for directions. She was on her own. At least, until she found Xavi or met back with Rye in five hours' time.

No one was about. Following the long, twisting passages oddly felt like she was moving through the small blood vessels of a larger organism; the greater the size of the thoroughfare, the closer she felt to the queen's quarters, as if the queen herself were the steady throb of a mighty heart.

Fee came to a cluster of rooms circled on the map.

Bartering power. It is the only reason I assume they'd keep him alive, Rye had said. *Once they have what they want it will be easy enough to snuff him out. The four kingdoms already believe he is dead.*

Fee believed Rye. He'd spent the last three years in this kingdom and sat on the queen's council. He knew precisely what was important to her and her ministry.

Putting a hand on the latch of the first door, she found it locked, as was expected. So she pulled the intricately carved bronze key Mistress Goodsong had provided out of her robe's deep pocket. She fingered the sculpted engraving on its bow and came to rest on a small black stone embedded within it. Surely Gwyndom's core stone, as the entire castle was decorated with replicas.

The latch gave freely, and she swung the door inward, cautiously stepping into a darkened chamber, cool and smelling of dust from disuse. She pressed a small button on the wall just inside the door—a button, Mistress Goodsong had assured her, that when pressed, would ignite a spark and light the gas lanterns in each chamber.

She heard the *whuff* of flames come to life and looked about at a room empty of everything apart from cobwebs and a broken chair. She moved to the next set of rooms, and the next, and the ones after that. She found nothing but replicates and the same echo of disappointment.

She scanned the empty hallway and darted across the corridor to one last room. Inserting the key, she nearly jumped out of her skin as someone tapped her on the shoulder and called her name.

"Ophelia, I'm so sorry," a tiny woman with a great cloud of alabaster hair whispered. "Harold *tried* to get there in time, but the prince had already been taken."

Fee spun round and pressed her back up against the door. "Who? What are—?"

She raised a finger high in the air to punctuate her statement. "But do not fret over Savva. We're doing the absolute best we can." She stopped, eyes widening. "Good heavens! Someone's coming. Hide—quickly!" The woman's small hand shot past Fee, pressed the latch, and then pushed Fee inside.

She was gone in an instant. Fee cracked open the door, but the voices outside were nearly on her threshold. She again pressed herself to the wall, but a thud behind her made her jump. She heard a woman giggle, "So, pinning me up against a wall in a deserted hallway is your way of greeting me hello, is it?"

A man's voice answered in a low growl, "You know it is. But something has come up, and I'm afraid the rest of my greeting shall have to wait. I shan't be too tardy."

Fee's throat constricted with dry panic and a niggling recognition. The woman spoke again.

"Rolly," she said with a pout, "you say that every time you come to the castle. When will this all be over? When will you stop having to answer to that woman?"

Rolly? Fee wondered. *As in Sir Rollins?*

"*That woman* is integral to our well-being, darling."

"But look," the woman tittered, "an opportunity has fallen into our laps—the door to this room is open and inviting us to use it. I say duty can wait." The woman made a tiny squeal, as if being pinched.

Fee saw a man's hand dart out and grab hold of the door's latch, a familiar, ivory-colored opal on his middle finger. She pulled in a breath and tried inching farther away.

"You are tempting, but if I don't go now she may revoke my shares—despite the fact that I delivered what she wanted. She is scrupulously rigid. Meet me back here in an hour. I'll make it up to you. I have been promised a great reward in exchange for my loyalty this last long decade. I plan to bank on it."

Fee watched Sir Rollins's hand slip from the latch, and she heard the swishing of fabric as it brushed against the wall. The sound of their footsteps was smothered by the plush carpeting, so Fee waited a full minute before peeking through the door and into the empty hallway.

Leaning back against the wall, she finally released her breath. Fee was certain it was Sir Rollins. *He's been visiting Gwyndom during the epidemic,* she realized, a passage which was forbidden. And who was the woman he was referring to? Was it the queen? For if Queen Islay had taken over Fireli's mines, it would be crucial to ensure Xavi "opened" them—starting them up again when in fact they'd been working all along.

And who in the world was that tiny, lily-white-haired woman? And Harold? Clearly they both knew about Xavi and Savva.

Fee worried the hem of her voluminous sleeve, growing more fretful and utterly confused. They had less than three days to find Xavi. Then they would deal with Gwyndom—with the queen and her plans, and with Quinn.

Fee pulled out the map and sorrowfully crossed off the section that had produced nothing. Her entire life had been built upon saving people and yet, right now, she felt an unwieldy weight of dread proclaiming that she could not save Xavi or Rye from either of their fates. And if this turned out to be true, then there was no point in even trying to save herself.

CHAPTER
TWENTY-SEVEN

FEE SAT ON THE FLOOR IN HER ROOM, HER BACK against the bed, her monk's hood still drawn over her head, but she closed her eyes to further shut out the creeping fingers of gloom that threatened to engulf her. She had spent five hours hunting for signs of Xavi. Room after room produced only empty chambers, dashed hopes, and the daunting possibility that Sir Rollins—Fireli's regent—was in league with Gwyndom's queen and advancing her plans.

Fee felt hope slipping away. She was letting Xavi down. And with this realization, hot, heartrending tears began to slide down her cheeks.

She heard the connecting door to Rye's room open. She sensed two footfalls coming toward her before stopping. "Ophelia?" he said softly. And when she didn't answer or raise her head to acknowledge him, he came and slid down the bed to sit beside her.

"We *will* find him."

"I promised him, Rye. I promised I would come for him and make him well. I promised I would care for him. And, as horrifically selfish as this sounds, I am equally dejected for myself, as he is the only person who cares for me." Try as she might, she could not keep her voice steady.

Rye pulled back Fee's hood and turned her face toward his. Her eyes were brimming with tears, and he wiped away the streaks from those that had fallen. "*I* care for you, Ophelia."

"You can't," she whispered, shaking her head.

The look on his face was a mixture of bewilderment and compassion—a look that moved Fee to wrap her arms around his neck and pull him to her, embracing him tightly and murmuring into his shoulder, "I'm so sorry, Rye," again and again.

Swept up with the emotions of bitter defeat and overwhelming injustice, she did not notice that they were both pulling back, their cheeks grazing one another, their foreheads brushing, until, at last, Rye's mouth found hers, and she pressed her lips into his with a gasp for breath.

"Well," someone said brusquely, "apparently just like your mother."

Rye and Fee pulled back sharply from one another and turned to see Mistress Goodsong standing at the door that connected the two rooms. "I believe I informed you, Fee, that this could *not* happen."

Fee felt a wave of hot shame flood through her body as Rye leapt from the ground and grabbed her elbow to help her stand.

"It was my fault," Rye said briskly, rubbing the back of his neck. "I . . . I *did* tell her about Quinn—marrying in two days—and apparently, you've discussed that with Fee too, but"—he shrugged uncomfortably—"I suppose . . . I suppose it just hasn't sunk in yet. That is . . . how I should now behave. My apologies to you both."

Mistress Goodsong stared at Fee with raised eyebrows that sent an icy shiver up her spine.

Fee dropped her guilt-ridden gaze to the floor, and Mistress Goodsong continued. "The two of you need sleep—and Rye, more medicine. Come with me." She motioned to Rye, directing him into his adjoining suite. Just before shutting the door, the healer turned and said, "For your safety and well-being, I expect you to stay put, Fee. Do not disturb Rye, for as a mender you are fully aware of how precarious his situation is. Follow the codes of conduct as a caring healer . . . and follow the letter of the law as it now specifically applies to *you*.

"I shall return to assist you both in the search after you've each had a chance to rest and think more clearly. Good night."

She closed the door, and Fee heard a bolt slide into place, unmistakably barring her access to Rye.

Fee sank onto the bed, but did not get beneath the covers—only pulled the rough monk's robe tightly around her to ward off the chill of Mistress Goodsong's ominous words. The bed was too lavish for someone of her insignificant status, and Fee felt the notion emphasize itself everywhere she looked.

She did not belong here. This much was clear. But neither could she leave. She *knew* Xavi was here. The only way she was stepping foot outside the walls of this kingdom was either riding behind Xavi on his horse, or walking behind him in his casket. And if the latter option came to light, she would not rest one hour until those responsible came to pay for their crimes.

Fee's head was muddled with lack of sleep, a deficit of nourishment, the unnerving behavior of Rye and herself, and something else that niggled at the edges of her consciousness as her lids grew heavy and lost the battle to remain alert.

Something Mistress Goodsong said when she first walked in. She would recall it after a few hours of rest. Would remember it soon...

When Fee woke, the first thing she noticed was how she was in precisely the same position as when she'd first closed her eyes. And because of it, she was stiff and sore, her muscles aching from remaining in the cramped and paralyzed position of an animal spiraled in on itself. She unfurled her limbs and rubbed at her neck, sitting up and taking in the details of the room.

The second thing she grasped was the remarkable light that entered the room from the gauzy-curtained windows. Nearly ethereal, the sunlight spilled in like liquid gold, melding with and dissolving into each object it brushed against. The chamber glowed. It must be nigh sunset, she thought, gauging the slant of the shadows.

She quickly washed and changed frocks, putting the monk's robe over a chair until she needed it next. And surely that must be soon. Could it be that she'd been sleeping for nearly twelve hours? Scanning the room, she found evidence that Mistress Goodsong had returned to provide food. A small table by the window held a tray filled with bright, colorful berries, wedges of pungent cheese, fragrantly herbed bread, a carafe of wine, and one of water.

She started tentatively with the water and found her hunger had returned with a vengeance. She'd nearly cleared the tray when she heard the muffled sound of voices from behind the connecting door to Rye's room. Pressing her ear to it, she found the wood too thick to make out anything other than the cadence of speech. But a moment later, the door opened, and Rye stood on the other side of it, looking surprised to see her, but well rested. The high color had returned to his cheeks.

"Ophelia," he said by way of greeting, and then pressed his lips inward. "Are you rested?"

She nodded and looked beyond him to Mistress Goodsong, who stood as observant as ever, her face placid and smooth as polished stone. "Thank you for the food," she said to the healer. "Is it time for us to go?"

"Not quite," answered Rye. "I am to meet with Quinn and Queen Islay to hear of the wedding plans, as apparently they've finished organizing." He looked down to fiddle with the cuff of one sleeve. "It's nothing more than the formality of apprising me of details, I assume. I have little to do with it."

"And I suggest we not keep them waiting, milord," Mistress Goodsong said. "Fee, I'll return in an hour to provide you with a new map of areas to canvas. I think you shall have a modicum of time to safely move about whilst most residents are in the Great Hall for the evening's entertainment. Stay here until we return." She stepped forward, closed the door, and slid the bolt back into place.

It was an isolating sound. One of being trapped.

And Fee didn't like it.

Nor would she allow it. Anymore.

For ten years she'd snuck out by picking the lock Savva had on the stillroom door. And countless times she and Xavi had crept about the vast, desolate spaces and hollowed-out castle rooms. One needed to know how to break out and how to break in. They'd grown capable and quick, therefore Fee saw no reason she should remain sealed within this room one moment longer.

She had her disguise. And a small amount of practice to draw from. She would be gone no more than an hour. And one more hour of hunting for Xavi was a better choice than a miserable sixty minutes pacing the floor and wondering what Rye was thinking as he planned his wedding.

She threw on the monk's robe and retrieved a hairpin from the small bag that contained her herbs and medicines. She kneeled before the door that led to the corridor. Then she twisted the thin piece of metal and inserted it into the chamber, listening and feeling for the sounds and movements that said she'd shifted the lock's pins into the correct position so that she could slowly turn the barrel. Within seconds, the handle turned freely, and access to the rest of the castle was hers.

Hastily, she fled down the hallway, trying to memorize markers to aid her way back. She had no idea where she should go. But her costume would aid her if need be, along with the knowledge that no one would question her and expect a response.

Descending several sets of stairs, she found herself merging into a stream of people moving purposefully in one direction. There were others like her—hooded monks quietly traveling among the chattering palace inhabitants. Caught up in the flow, she drifted with the crowd as they poured through the hallway and headed toward several sets of large double doors—likely the Great Hall, where the evening meal would be served.

Peeling off from the multitude, she paused at one of the great onyx vases filled with spilling flowers and greenery. Something was off. She touched a petal from one of the stems. *Nothing.* She felt nothing beneath her fingertips and then suddenly realized the vase was filled with an arrangement of silk and plastic.

"You'll not draw vim from anything here, Fee," someone said from behind her.

She whipped around to stare into a broad-smiling, affable face—a woman with two contrasting-colored eyes. "'Tis all synthetic in Gwyndom. Mistress Goodsong has used every last ounce without replenishment." The woman tenderly patted the arm of her monk's robe and was quickly swallowed up by the crowd rushing into the dining hall.

Panicking that someone had recognized her, Fee raced to another set of stairs leading to a balcony that circled the lengthy dining tables stretching across the hall. Her heart thumped with anxiety, but how could she have been discovered? The robe she wore covered every inch of her. She stared at the people below filing in from all directions and finding seats. Was the woman there now, and staring up at her? She could find no upturned faces in the crowd.

There was no formality about the meal, as the service simply began immediately. Trays heaped with steaming food came in a steady stream from one end of the hall, where Fee assumed the kitchens must be. Hundreds of people sat eating beneath her, and when they had finished they gave up their space for somebody else. Most people did not leave the hall, she noted, but instead stood milling along the walls and clustered in corners with others who had finished.

They were waiting for something.

And a few short minutes later Fee realized what it was:

The queen, the princess . . . and Rye.

They entered from a double set of stained-glass doors, the jewel-toned designs catching the light from the crystal chandeliers and golden sconces scattered about the hall. Fee felt her breath catch at her first glimpse of Queen Islay. The monarch moved with stately presence, with steady grace, and with quiet but compelling strength. Her gown was not like the lushly color-drenched fabrics of her constituents, nor the luxurious feminine silks, pleated and gathered, that her daughter wore, but was a simple sheaf of pearly satin that fell in a straight line to the floor. It flowed like water, cascading to meet the smooth stones beneath her feet. As bejeweled and dazzling as the castle appeared, Queen Islay was the definition of simplicity, unaffected in her form.

Princess Quinn came to stand beside her mother on the raised dais at the front of the great dining hall. Her face—even from where Fee stood—revealed itself as puffy and red-eyed. Rye, Fee noted with a catch in her throat, followed Quinn and then crossed to stand on the other side of the queen. His face was staid—cryptically calm—but his left hand was balled into its telltale fist. A moment after Fee noted this, she saw his long fingers stretch out and compose themselves at his side to match his other hand. She breathed a word of thanks.

No one shared the upper balcony with Fee, and she sank to her knees to peer from between the wooden bars of the railing, knowing no person could see her but wishing to hide the emotions on her face, nonetheless.

The crowd hushed, and the queen smiled serenely.

"Good evening, lords and ladies, gentlemen and gentlewomen. I am here to make a brief announcement—one I'm certain has made the rounds to most of your doors and tables by now." She paused to give a small smile of acknowledgment at the ripple of excitement that ran through the assembly, when a man shouted from the crowd.

"When will you put the witch to death?"

Fee pulled in a sharp breath and glanced over her shoulder to check for some sudden rush of guards coming to seize her. Reassured to see she was still alone, she let her eyes fall back to the queen.

Queen Islay's smile had vanished, and she raised a hand to still the murmuring. "You've nothing to fear. We're attending to the matter. But I've other news—that of the heartening kind.

"My daughter, Princess Quinn of Gwyndom, and Prince Rye of the Kingdom of Fireli, are to be wed. I know we all share a great sadness and send our deepest sympathies to the prince after hearing the lamentable news of his older brother's passing. We shall grieve together over Prince Xavi and help him bear it.

"And it is with this same intention that we shall unite our two kingdoms through marriage—to strengthen and rebuild a community that has suffered terribly.

"The ceremony shall take place in two days' time, here in Gwyndom in the great castle courtyard, and I invite all of you to take part. Shortly, we'll be welcoming people from across the realm of Aethusa—ministry leaders, government officials, and, of course, the kings and queens from our two remaining sister kingdoms. We shall celebrate a new union and future. Let us shine the best of ourselves onto our guests and, most important, Prince Rye, and give him the confidence that he, at last, has joined our family in earnest."

Fee's fingers curled around the wooden spokes of the banister, tightening with each word the queen spoke.

This queen had stolen Fireli's king. And she was scheming to take over their kingdom just as she surely had taken over their mines. Heat poured from Fee's arms and flowed into her hands as her knuckles grew white and her breathing, labored. The heat morphed into a tempestuous tingling, shooting outward from the center of her chest and down through her arms into her fingers.

All at once, the wood that she clutched disintegrated in her hands, falling away like grains of sparkling sand toward the tables full of diners below. Her head thumped heavily on the railing as her arms slipped through, nothing to hold on to except air. Pulling up with a start, she fell backward and stared at the empty space where the two spindles of railing used to be.

Her mouth dropped open, and she sat up to stare at her hands, a film of sawdust covering her skin and the front of her frock. She breathed out a gush of surprise and then felt a tight clutch of chest-gripping panic.

Backing farther away from the railing, she scrabbled along the floor until she came to the stairwell. She rushed down the stairs toward the safety of her room. She heard the words of Mistress Goodsong take root in her head:

Hermetical menders have an unusual ability to . . . shift energy.

She was a hermetical mender, according to Mistress Goodsong.

According to the banisters, the horse, the sunflower seeds, and all the plants and flowers she'd touched within Fireli.

No matter her desperate wish to do so, Fee could not claim the woman had made an inaccurate diagnosis. She could not ignore the pulsing, throbbing waves of heat that prickled along her arms, determined to support the healer's firm words. And she could not deny the realization that had been looming mercilessly on the edge of her thoughts:

Fee was, indeed, a witch.

CHAPTER
TWENTY-EIGHT

SHE PUSHED THROUGH THE DOOR, RUSHED INSIDE, AND hurled it firmly closed behind her, bolting the lock with trembling, agitated fingers, still dusted with fine fragments of decimated wood. Fee sat panting and clutching at the fabric of the monk's robe, worrying it within her hands.

She squeezed her eyes shut. *What do I do? Rye must never find out!* She chanted these phrases repeatedly, trying to slow her breath and calm her hands. She spread them out before her, palms facing up, stretching her quivering fingers widely to study them. What Mistress Goodsong had said was true. And without Savva's antidote, her "skills" were recklessly leeching through.

She massaged her temples. "I am sleep deprived—surely suffering from hallucinatory stress." Crawling to the small bag that held her medicines, she wondered if she'd packed oil of lavender and the crushed heads of chamomile, as their volatile oils and medicinal compounds would aid most any stressful situation. She searched, but then came upon a vial even more promising: *Valeriana officinalis*— valerian.

She often made up large batches of the tincture, and Savva doled it out with regularity to the elderly residents who suffered from sleep disorders. It would be calming, without overtaking her body as a sedative, and would be the equivalent of sliding a soft, warm blanket over her autonomic nervous system. A mild tranquilizing effect. She would rid herself of the prickling tension, return back to normal, be *herself* again.

Or . . . would she simply be masking that which refused to be suppressed? And wasn't this what she'd wanted? To no longer feel benumbed? Hadn't she detested that daily sensation of clockwork-timed perfection when, within minutes of drinking Savva's tonic, the world went fuzzy and torpid, her limbs molasses-thick and her mind dull and leaden?

She stared at the vial in her hand, contemplating the choice, when she heard voices in Rye's room next door. She pressed her ear to the wall and found that although she still could not make out the words, she *could* determine that the female voice in the conversation was not that of Mistress Goodsong. It was too high.

Princess Quinn.

Her fists curled, and her gut knotted with unruly hostility. Fee immediately felt the resurgence of the tingling in her fingers. She tried to shake the frightful effect out of her hands, but, failing, paced to rid herself of the burgeoning energy.

A few minutes later, Rye knocked softly on the door between their two rooms.

"Come in," Fee said, rushing toward the sound.

The door cracked open, and Rye looked in, his features almost apologetically abashed. "The door was bolted from my side. Did you know?"

She twisted one hand around the other, hoping they did not appear queerly conspicuous, and gave him a simple nod.

"I can't imagine why—" he began, then stopped and shrugged one shoulder. "Well, yes I suppose I can, but you needn't worry—"

"I'm not," she said, meeting his eyes.

"Apparently *someone* is."

Fee took a step forward. "They should actually be worried for *you*." Seeing his look of surprise, she continued. "Don't you think we should be taking into consideration that you've been poisoned once already, and that a second attempt on your life is not without reason?"

He chewed on his lip. "The thought has crossed my mind. I suppose I shall have to watch my back."

"It helps to have others doing that impossible task for you, but"—she pointed at the door's bolt—"that's proving to be a challenge. Has Mistress Goodsong not come up with any ideas?"

Rye turned to look back inside his room. "None that she's shared, although she's just come in, so perhaps we'll have a better plan for tonight."

Fee joined him in his suite, nodding to Mistress Goodsong as she took a seat beside Rye on the couch.

"I trust you weren't too unhappy with the inconvenience of waiting whilst we were away, Fee. How I wish I could *permit* you a bird's-eye view of what's going on outside." The healer's statement made Fee's stomach twist in on itself.

"We certainly didn't have to bar the door to my suite, leaving her trapped only in her room, did we?" Rye said offhandedly while spreading new maps out on the table in front of them.

"A simple mistake, I'm sure," Mistress Goodsong answered in even tones. "A cleaning maid is overly concerned with your security, perhaps?" She pulled a pencil from her pocket and began marking one of the maps and then slid it toward Fee. "Now here," she pointed, "is where I suggest you search tonight, Fee. It is a large block of rooms beneath the kitchens that normally house the cookery staff, but they have recently been moved elsewhere, as the rooms are being treated for an infestation of rodents finding their way into the kitchens above. The key you possess will work as well as it did yesterday, but you'll need a torch, as the gas has been shut down."

Fee shivered with the thought of having to hunt through dark and pest-ridden rooms, but then immediately dismissed her uneasiness when thinking about poor Xavi being kept prisoner in one of them.

"And where will Rye be?" Fee asked.

Mistress Goodsong turned to Rye. "I suggest you search the five towers on the north and west sectors of the palace—the guards will not question your presence if they run into you, as most of the ministry council chambers are within those two quarters."

Rye nodded, and Fee quickly pulled the hood of her robe back over her head.

"Be back before sunrise, and both of you wait in your *separate* rooms until I return. If either of you come upon Xavi, find the first guardsman you can, alert him, and he will immediately locate me. Fortunately, over the years, they have developed a dependable routine and will always come to me first before going to the queen."

Why? Fee thought, wishing to ask but holding back. *Whatever would make them do so?*

Almost as if she'd heard Fee's question, the healer straightened the front of her already pristine skirt and added, "Generally, they have found their queen to be distracted and I, on the other hand, respond immediately to their needs. I've informed them that it is best to filter most requests for attention through me first so that we do not burden the queen with more than she can handle."

They both nodded and crossed the threshold into the corridor, but Mistress Goodsong put out a hand to stay Fee.

"Has Savva told you much about your parents, Fee?"

Fee looked at her quizzically. "Well, I was with them until I was eight—until the plague. And she has explained the importance of summoning their memory to—to keep their spirits with me. Why?"

Mistress Goodsong smiled wistfully. "You do look so much like your father."

"You knew him?"

"I thought I did," she responded before giving Fee a gentle pat down the hallway. "I thought I did."

The first thing Fee detected was the smell. The heavy whiff of garlic mingled with the fragrant scents of fresh, pungent herbs, and the high, tangy notes of yeast.

Next she noticed how damp and cold it was below ground, especially as, exactly like Mistress Goodsong said, the gas had been shut off, leaving the floor without light or heat. The torch Fee carried produced a small circle of illumination but provided her with no more than a paltry few feet of visibility.

The corridor was lined with doors, a few long strides apart from one another. Unlocking the first door, Fee peeked inside and took in a few pieces of sparse furniture: a thin, metal-framed bed, a straight-back wooden chair, and a washstand in the corner. There was no window, just a gas torch sconce on the wall. The room held very little invitation.

The second and third rooms were duplicates of the first. When she'd reached the fourth room, she expected much of the same, but upon looking in, she spotted a book lying open across the sagging bed.

Is someone here?

She stepped inside and moved toward the cot and then whirled around, clutching her heart as the door slammed shut behind her.

"So sorry! I only meant to close it—not fling it shut."

Fee dropped her torch with a start and gasped, scrambling to the floor for her light.

"Oh good God, I've done it again. I've scared you half to death and didn't mean to," came the voice once more.

From her knees on the floor, Fee looked up into the apologetic eyes of a teenaged girl—a teenaged girl she recognized as the one who'd tumbled to her and Xavi's feet the night they had escaped to their cave.

The girl hunched her shoulders and brought her fists beneath her chin, a clear posture of contrition. "Are you cross?"

Fee stood slowly, raising the torch with her. "Am I *cross*?" she repeated uncertainly. "I am dumbfounded. And now terribly confused. Who are you?"

"Dumbfounded and confused I can deal with. I only fret when people are cross." The girl exhaled an enormous sigh of relief and patted down her clothing, doing her best to smooth out wrinkles that did not exist. Her skirt was made from tubes of clear rubber hosing, sewn together in concentric circles from her waist to her knees, and her blouse looked as if it had been constructed from thinly sliced sheets of cork and, to Fee, appeared wholly uncomfortable and stiff.

The girl put a hand to her hair and, for a few brief seconds, fingered her silver-dipped dreadlocks, making them tinkle when she moved them. Then, as if she'd nearly forgotten about Fee's presence, she finally made eye contact with a tiny start of recollection.

"Oh dear, right. Now that I have you, you're to come with me."

Fee narrowed her eyes. "Who *are* you?"

"Oh, sorry." The girl rolled her own eyes skyward. "The name's Kizzy. I told them I could do this. That they should trust me. That I'd not bumble the whole thing, but I guess they knew better. They always do. Trust me to bite off more than I can chew!" The girl stared at Fee, as if Fee understood and would mirror the girl's humorous disposition after her good-natured self-criticism.

Fee peered at her, growing frustrated. "Who are *they?*"

Kizzy nodded. "*They* are the menders. And healers—although mostly menders." She looked to the ceiling. "Come to think of it, I don't think we have any of the Ordinary with us today." She met Fee's gaze and nodded. "Yes, just menders—who are waiting."

Kizzy then jumped. "Oh, good golly, let's go. They're waiting for *us.*" She grabbed Fee's hand and rushed her out of the door and started down the dark hallway.

"Wait!" Fee pulled back, trying to wrestle her hand free.

"Stop—I'm not going with you. I—I'm searching for someone," she finished lamely.

"I know that," Kizzy said with a face that expressed she was somehow in on a secret. "Come on. You won't be sorry."

Fee hesitated.

"You know what would be worse than *you* being cross? *Them* being cross. Now come on—chop-chop!"

One minute later, the girl paused by an unmarked door, placed her hand upon the latch, and then looked over her shoulder at Fee. "Are you ready?" she asked, her eyes alight with excitement.

"For what?" Fee's nerves roiled in her stomach in an endless, twisting knot of discomfort.

Kizzy smiled delightedly and leaned in, unlatching the door. "For your first hermetical huddle."

CHAPTER
TWENTY-NINE

THE YOUNG GIRL PUSHED OPEN THE DOOR AND STOOD aside, clearing her throat to get the attention of those in the room. Fee felt her mouth slacken as she took in the sight before her. A dozen pairs of eyes swiveled toward and focused on her.

The room was warmly lit; long, tapered candles and pearl-washed gas lamps glowed on all the tables and shelves around them. A fire crackled in the corner, spitting out sparks from the fresh, dry wood it burned. Deeply cushioned chairs and sofas were drawn together, forming a large oval. Sitting upon these upholstered tufts were twelve people she'd never met, and one she knew intimately well.

Savva.

Fee stood blinking bewilderedly for only a moment before she grabbed hold of her senses and rushed toward her mentor. "My God,

Savva!" she cried, putting her hands out to grasp the old healer. But they landed on nothing and just whisked through air until they brushed against the back of the chair.

Fee pulled up with a gasp. "Savva?"

The elderly woman shook her head and closed her eyes.

"She is not *really* here," an older man said, his cultured voice oddly familiar. He was one of only three men sitting within the ring of this conclave. He put a gentle hand on Fee's arm. His smile was sympathetic.

"Then where is she?"

The woman next to him—a tiny, plump, pearly-white-haired woman Fee recognized from the hallway last night—raised a finger and spoke in a way that brought to mind a seamstress's precise and even stitches. "Harold, that's not entirely true either. She's both here and not here. It's more appropriate to say that she is not *fully* here." She turned to Fee. "This is an astral projection of Savva. She is still in Fireli, unconscious, but appears to have enough strength left to be present for now."

"For now?" Fee echoed, looking back at Savva.

Another hand across her shoulder had Fee turning to face someone else. A woman who was as slim and willowy as the tall marsh grasses back in Fireli. "Fee? It is so good to officially meet you at last. We feel greatly honored"—and she gestured at the circle of people— "as the first to welcome you to a menders' meeting." She paused to give Fee's hand a gentle squeeze. "I know it must be a lot to absorb, and I do apologize if Kizzy did not adequately explain the situation." The woman glanced back toward the sheepish-looking teenaged girl, who simply shrugged and took a seat, her rubber-tubing dress squeaking against the wood.

"Why don't you sit down, Fee." She gestured toward a chair beside Savva. "My name is Mistress Merrybird, and here, around us, are some, but certainly not all, of Aethusa's hermetical menders."

"Do you mean you're all . . . witches?" Fee asked, lowering herself into the chair and feeling the hair along her arms prickle with alarm.

There was a ripple of unrest among the seated people, along with a few polite coughs, before Mistress Merrybird handed Fee a cup of steaming tea from the teapot she held. Her nose wrinkled slightly. "It is an antiquated term, Fee, and one that tends to stir up unnecessary anxieties among the people we attempt to serve."

Fee looked about the group and recognized the woman with the dual-colored eyes—one green, one yellow. The same woman who had spoken to her as she was touching the vase of silk flowers. "That's what Mistress Goodsong said. She insisted that you were . . . well, that you were real. And that you all have some sort of *specialty*."

Fee saw most of the faces suddenly crease with worry lines, and Mistress Merrybird said quickly, "She knows you're in Gwyndom?"

"Yes," Fee said. "And revealed *many* things I found alarming—in particular, that Savva was a wi—" She stopped, looked about, and began again. "That Savva, too, was a . . . *hermetical mender*. I denied it. But at this moment, seeing you . . . here," Fee said weakly, gesturing to her mentor, "I feel I can no longer defend that statement. Forgive me. My head spins. What exactly is going on?"

Harold nodded and put up a hand. "May I take a swing at this?" he asked the others. When no one objected, he placed his teacup on his knee and looked to Fee. "Do you read much realm history?"

"Not unless it pertains to herbs or healing." She stole a glance toward Savva. "And even then . . . not really," she finished sheepishly.

Harold made a small sound of acknowledgment. "Well, much of it is fabled now anyway, but close to a century ago, our kingdoms were vastly different—insofar as those who inhabited them. There was a time when magic was a moderately common practice, and having the ability to wield it was considered as categorical as whether you had the trait to curl your tongue, or possessed dimples, or . . . or had short thumbs," he finished with a flick of his hand. "It was tolerated, as most of it was put to structured and beneficial use. But then there grew a great campaign, which, over the course of a few short years, reached a fever pitch. A few fearmongering individuals—green-eyed zealots who held no magic and who desperately wished to have it—riled up a great body of people within the realm and wreaked havoc by stimulating their base anxieties. People developed an inexplicable fear of anyone possessing an uncommon ability to manipulate their surroundings with supernatural talent."

He shook his head. "Our people were forced out of the realm—"

"Or burned, or dismembered, or poisoned, or buried alive, or—"

Harold held up a patient hand. "Thank you, Kizzy. I think you've driven the point home."

Fee looked to Kizzy, sizing up whether she was enthusiastically reporting or growing panicked herself.

"The choice was to flee, or go underground and live quietly until it was safe to reenter the realm," Harold continued. "Magic was expelled from everyday life, and those who held any ability soon learned to pretend they didn't. As *healing* is a practice where the results are fickle and unpredictable, it was a safe enough vocation—and a place where we could do the most good."

The look of confusion across Fee's face must have been enough for Harold to cut to the chase. "You are a descendant of one of those people, Fee."

Her forehead creased with impatience and frustration. "If that were true, why wouldn't Savva have told me?"

"Fee, Savva could not reveal certain things to you. It was an agreement—a *bond*—in order to protect you," Harold said.

Fee turned her face. "What other *things* could you not reveal, Savva?"

The healer's watery eyes, clouded by cataracts, searched Fee's for understanding.

Mistress Merrybird picked up the thread. "Conversation may prove impossible for Savva, Fee, so I'll try to explain. The people who first raised you were not your birth parents, but loved you none-theless."

Fee's mouth fell open. "What?" she tried to whisper, but no sound came out.

"Your true parents were very much in love, but it was an illicit affair for your mother—a powerful liaison with a man full of extraordinary magic. Marrying him was prohibited. Still, it did not keep them apart, and your mother became with child. When she gave birth, it was to two children. And one had magic, just like the child's father. There were rules in place for a situation such as the one your parents faced that forbade them from keeping the child. There was her forbidden lineage—and the dangerous potential it held—so it was deemed that the child . . . *you* . . . must be put to death lest you misuse the powerful skills you'd inherited.

"It was one of the rules the realm established long ago—an anti-quated and disastrous decree—that there could be no mix of magic and—" Harold put up a hand to warn Mistress Merrybird, and the woman took a breath before continuing. "There could be no mix of *certain bloodlines.*

"Your mother fought for your life, Fee, but the law prevailed. One of our own was bent on seeing you . . . well"—she swallowed—"destroyed."

"Who wanted this?" Fee whispered, perusing the sea of wary faces.

"Mistress Goodsong," the woman beside Harold said quietly. "She, especially, wanted your life extinguished."

Fee shivered. "Why?"

Mistress Merrybird's face altered to express a note of pity. "She has become a most vengeful woman. She was scorned in love."

Fee's eyes locked with hers. A puzzle piece clicked into place. "She was in love . . . with my father?"

Mistress Merrybird nodded solemnly. "When Evanora . . . rather, *Mistress Goodsong* found out that your father was in love with another—and that the other woman was pregnant—she used an unyielding dark magic to ban him from the realm, and punished him further by removing his access to both his offspring and the woman he loved. Claiming she was fulfilling the realm's rule against mixing certain bloodlines, she persecuted your father.

"But Savva fought for your life too. She stole and hid you, Fee. She found suitable parents in Fireli and kept you safe from the realm's rule but, mostly, safe from Mistress Goodsong. At least until you were eight."

"Wait," Fee said suddenly. "You said there were two of us. What happened to the other baby?"

Mistress Merrybird's hands came together in front of her lips, poised in prayer position. "I'm afraid I am not at liberty to reveal the fate of the other child." Fee felt the breath in her chest catch.

Mistress Merrybird went on. "Mistress Goodsong threatened to tell the other menders of the realm that Savva had betrayed them by concealing you."

"Her fear and wrath came down hard," Harold added. "Evanora's madness became the kingdom-wide epidemic of Fireli."

Fee's stomach contracted with the wretched grip of fear. "You're—you're saying that all of the deaths in Fireli were at the hand of . . . Mistress Goodsong?"

"Well . . ." Harold began, and looked to Savva.

The persnickety woman beside Harold put a hand on his arm and said, "Do you think she's had too much to take in? She looks awfully pale. Perhaps we should wait."

Harold shook his head. "There is no time, Rosedriah. Fee will have to bear up well beneath this burden of information, as Savva does not have time to spare—and we owe her this."

Fee stole a glance at Savva and saw her face crumple with pain and her appearance flicker with uncertainty.

Harold looked gravely back toward Fee. "Savva *eventually* halted the blight, and to stop Evanora from attempting to take your life, she made a covenant."

Harold cleared his throat and looked toward Savva. "Perhaps it would be easiest if you *showed* Fee what happened?"

Savva silently beckoned Fee to kneel beside her. With an invisible touch, Savva clasped Fee's hand and slid her own upward until her wrist pressed against Fee's. Fee felt herself yanked into a merciless spin, cast through a whirlwind of baffling scenes—all of them too fast for her to focus on until one skidded to a halt and filled her vision, crystal clear and all-encompassing.

There they were—the two healers—versions of their younger selves by a decade at least. Savva looked beaten—exhausted and frail. They stood in Fireli amid shattering devastation. Fee heard Mistress Goodsong bellow, "Hand her over, Savva. Tell me which one she is."

Savva pointed. "Your charm of carnage failed to hit the mark but has done monstrous damage. Isn't that enough?"

"The realm needs to be rid of that child. And you know it."

Savva gave the younger mender a glare full of warning. "If you do that, you'll destroy any chance of seeing Azamar again. I know you are filled with regret. Do not further your anguish and crush our one last filament of hope."

Mistress Goodsong's features darkened. "The child is of a forbidden bloodline—a danger. *Rules are rules.*"

"Every hermetical mender has heard you utter that vexatious phrase a thousand times. It is your signature slogan and bone-deep belief, but surely there should be exceptions, Evanora, especially if there is a child's life at stake!"

Mistress Goodsong put up a hand to silence her. Savva refused to heed the gesture.

"She is no threat if she is ignorant of her breeding and abilities. I will make a pledge to you—I will train the girl myself—train her *only* in the art of medicinal healing. She would learn no magic—from me or other healers. I will continue to hide the child from her mother and the entire realm."

Mistress Goodsong closed her eyes and rubbed at her temples. "If I agree to this, I will need to think of what to tell the others to slake their fears. Likely they will come after her themselves." The healer suddenly paused and, glancing to the window, her eyes came to rest on the hills in the distance. "I will tell them she is dead— to protect you and the child. But in exchange, Fireli's metal mines become mine."

"Whatever for?"

"If I am to save Azamar, I need another origin of vitality—a magical strength that may overcome the spell's iron-fisted muscle and break it. This will benefit us both, as I know you want him back just as I do."

Savva's features fell open with shock. "If you use the metals as your derivational source, your work will be blackhearted and injurious. *You* will become malevolent. They are not meant to be used in such a manner. Plus, you've already plundered what Gwyndom has to offer—you've stripped your lands clean and cannot replenish them."

"My work reverently transfigures our kingdom."

"It is a shiny veneer."

"It is what the people of Gwyndom wanted, Savva."

"You indulge them like children for the assurance they will remain devoted to you. It is the antithesis of how a clear-sighted healer would behave."

"They will survive as long as they are guided by my words."

Savva pulled back. "Your *words*? I have just scrambled to create an antidote to inoculate our remaining residents against the black cinders of the hexing spell you cast. Your *words* killed countless people."

"They were misdirected, weren't they?" Mistress Goodsong's eyebrows rose.

"And how shall we feed those that remain? Without the mining, you'll remove our only source for bartering. The people will surely go hungry. Think of the children."

"You're right. We cannot have the innocent suffer so cruelly." Mistress Goodsong tilted her head. "Disperse the children throughout the realm."

"But, you would tear them from their homes?"

Mistress Goodsong smiled. "You could always give me just the *one* child."

Savva said nothing.

"Fine. The eldest prince and the child can remain. That will make for a cozy *threesome*."

Savva looked at her coldly. "It astonishes me how much you wish to make Azamar suffer. You thrust the child beneath his nose to make him grieve?"

Mistress Goodsong did not smile. "I am trying to clean up *your* mess, Savva. And I find myself bending to help someone who not only boldly broke Aethusian law, but is determined to continue doing so." She narrowed her eyes. "I just don't *trust you*."

They turned to see Prince Xavi come across the littered threshold of the stillroom door. "Savva, Sir Rollins has asked to see both you and Mistress Goodsong." His voice was small, tragedy fresh on his eleven-year-old face. He looked up toward Gwyndom's healer. "I thank you for all your efforts thus far, madam. You have been kind."

Mistress Goodsong put a hand on the young prince's head, bent down, and whispered into his ear. His eyes were glassy and fixed, as if the words she spoke traveled through him like a vessel and held no meaning. When she rose, Xavi left, and she turned to face Savva again.

"There. I feel more assured that you will adhere to our bargain."

"What have you done, Evanora?" Savva asked, her face filling with alarm.

"A tiny spell. A deterrent so that you will not secretly allow the young witch to develop her skills."

"What hex is this?"

"Every time she uses sorcery, the prince will feel its effects. Each little charm will strip him of life. Bit by bit."

Savva gasped. "I've said I would not teach her magic, but still it sometimes spills out of her unbidden. She cannot control that!"

"Then drug her—drug them all, for that matter. Tell them the caves are contaminated. Fireli must be quarantined. Tell them they must *all* take a tonic until they are better. What a convenient excuse to keep your people close. They'll not be given leave to see that some-one else has taken over their mines. Figure it out."

"Evanora," Savva said, her livid voice just barely above a whisper, "I shall remind you again that the girl—not *you*—may be the only way to bring Azamar back—and he holds what you want most of all."

The younger woman's jaw went rigid. "I had no idea he held Fireli's core stone on his person. But I will figure out a way to retrieve the opal."

Savva's face was ominously grim. "It is crucial that you do."

"There is ample time to reverse the banishment spell. Lastly, as part of our bargain, you will cease your efforts to rescue him as well, understand? *I* will be the one to save him."

"Perhaps it would be best to find a way to save yourself, Evanora. You have so much to give to the people of Gwyndom. You are meant to be their healer. Why not focus on—"

Mistress Goodsong raised a hand and cut Savva short. "Send away the children. Hand over the mines. And deal with the girl. I shall take care of the rest."

Savva pulled her arm away from Fee, breaking the memory, and Fee found herself toppling backward onto the floor beside her mentor.

Kizzy jumped up to help Fee find her feet. "Bit of a shocker, isn't it?"

Fee scrubbed at her wrist, trying to quicken the rhythm of intelligible thought and slow the pace of her racing breath. Mistress Merrybird topped up Fee's already full teacup and said, "Now you see. Savva was forced to suppress your magic to spare your life. Your kingdom has lived ten years in solitude whilst Mistress Goodsong tried to undo this banishment spell. You were altered greatly, and for that Savva has suffered immeasurably. She hopes one day you will forgive her."

Fee looked at Savva and blinked back angry tears. "Why would you have gone to such great lengths for *me*, Savva?"

The healer's spectral form wavered and thinned. She looked down, her voice strained. "I would do anything for you, Fee. You are my family, my life, my blood."

"What?" Fee said incredulously. "We're related? But through whom?"

Savva's eyes met Fee's. "Azamar. My son."

CHAPTER
THIRTY

A TINY RATTLE SEEMED TO RADIATE FROM SOME-
where close by, and Fee could not locate it until Mistress Merrybird
put a calming hand across her own. The rattling stopped, and Fee
looked down to see it had been the teacup shaking in her hand,
vibrating against the saucer she held beneath it.

Fee put the cup and saucer down and turned to Savva, fumbling.
"You? My parents are not—? And Azamar"—she looked around the
large circle of worried faces, remembering her conversation with
Xavi in the garden, remembering the name—"the man who was
Fireli's *gardener* was my father?"

"*Is* your father, Fee," Mistress Merrybird corrected.

"Is?" Fee pulled back. "Where is he then?"

"Locked away. Banished from a physical life," Rosedriah muttered bitterly.

Fee looked beside the woman to Harold. "Locked away where?"

"He does not so much reside within a place, as he resides within a ... *person*," he said carefully.

"And who would this person be?" Fee said, growing nervous of the answer.

"Azamar was banished by Mistress Goodsong with a dark spell cast off the back of her rejection. He resides *within* Prince Xavi. The spell must be broken."

"Or what?" Fee cried out. She looked to Savva and heard the mender speak to her inside her head. *Or all we love will wither and vanish.*

"All this time," Fee asked her, "Xavi has been thinking you were somewhat off-balance. And you've been speaking to Azamar—within him?"

The healer nodded.

"Can you see him—does he answer you?"

Savva shook her head.

"And now—" Fee looked around the room, her mind coming to grips with her situation. "—I am here—*working* with Mistress Goodsong to *fi-find* Xavi?"

The room was silent.

"Don't you think she's probably already found him and ... killed him?" Fee trembled with the words.

Harold rubbed at his temples. "We all agree, it stands to reason that Mistress Goodsong is the one who has kidnapped Xavi, as she needs access to him, but killed him? It's highly unlikely, Fee, as Mistress Goodsong wants Azamar back."

"*And* your kingdom's core stone," Kizzy piped up. "If she can get her hands on that little gem, well, there'll be a new king in town for sure."

She scrutinized Kizzy. "I—I thought—no, I was told that the kingdoms' core stones were just folklore."

Kizzy's face lit with impish delight. "You didn't know that the realm is full of sorcerers, either."

Rosedriah gave Kizzy a face full of censure, and the girl scooted back in her chair with a pouty shrug.

"Well"—Harold looked toward the ceiling—"they very much are a reality, and worth protecting."

"Protecting . . . or possessing?"

Mistress Merrybird's voice was soft but firm. "For centuries, menders have been the guardians of them. The stones are a source of energy. Mistress Goodsong has depleted that which her kingdom's core stone provided, and very much wishes to get her hands on Fireli's."

Fee closed her eyes to the hum of worried chatter and began to think. "So the only reason Mistress Goodsong has not polished me off is because she has not been able to free Azamar and claim the stone . . . and I am somehow now her only hope?"

"Yes. Time is running out for Xavi and Azamar. The prince's illness advances every day. Mistress Goodsong may be growing desperate," Harold said.

She began to laugh. "Are you sure none of you want to throw in a dragon—or a minotaur, for that matter? Someone please point me in the direction of the nearest fire-breathing creature so that I might prepare myself for the next onslaught of ludicrous unveiling."

Kizzy tittered in her seat, and Rosedriah clucked her tongue at the teenaged girl.

Harold leaned forward. "Fee, I know this must seem utterly absurd, but surely this is all beginning to make sense. Especially since you've been off your . . . your tonic for some time."

Fee looked down at her lap and began to pick at the threads of her robe. As much as she wanted to rush from the room, to leave this *nightmare*, she knew there was nowhere she could run to where the truth wouldn't continue to reveal itself.

She glanced up to lock eyes with Savva. "Where is my mother?"

The healer's dry and cracked lips rolled inward and she looked toward Harold. He sighed and brought his hands up to prayer position in front of his lips. "It pains me to say that there is some information we are bound within Savva's oath not to reveal."

Mistress Merrybird clasped her hands in front of her chest and said, "Fee, it's not that we do not *wish* to tell you everything, but we are bound to the oath with our lives. There is only so much we can divulge without immediately meeting our fate."

"We're not even supposed to be here. Our excuse is that we're in town for the wedding," Kizzy piped up. "Poor Prince Rye."

Fee looked at the girl miserably and, then, after Rosedriah tsked at her again, she murmured a small apology.

Harold glanced at his watch. "You really shouldn't be down here much longer. We're all in grave danger of being found out."

"And now what? I have a million questions, and you're telling me you can provide no answers? For even the simplest of quandaries— like if I'm able to give Mistress Goodsong what she wants, would she still wish to kill me? Or is there a way to stop the bits of—of *magic* that are leaking out of me? More important, what in the world happens when I link arms with people? I saw my whole life flash before my eyes.

When Savva did the same, I saw a piece of *her* past. It even happened yesterday, when it seems I accidentally did it to someone else!"

The circle of menders looked at one another, the flash of worry heightened on each face.

"Oh dear," Rosedriah said, leaning toward Harold. "It seems she can appraise."

"I can what?" Fee asked warily, looking from one face to the next.

Mistress Merrybird looked to the ceiling. "It's officially referred to as a *subcutaneous appraisal*. Not many menders possess the aptitude. And it's not a joining of the arms but a binding of wrists.

"Gifted menders are given a peek into the history of all their patient's pain—both physical and mental—and use it to find the most efficacious method of treatment available."

"Wait," Fee said. "How was Mistress Goodsong able to determine that I held magic if the appraisal is only providing information on my pain?"

Harold nodded with understanding. "I would assume she was able to quickly ferret out a moment or two when something unusual happened to you—magic-wise—that produced some unwanted emotional results. Perhaps, as we said before, something that took place before you were required to drink the daily tonic, or maybe on a day"—he glanced to Savva—"when you were determined to . . . skip it?"

Fee's face flushed hotly. "What about seeing future pain?"

Rosedriah shook her head quickly—like a tiny rattle. "No. Menders have no prescient abilities."

Fee swallowed. "I do."

"What?" Harold and Mistress Merrybird said in unison. The room tittered with conversation.

Harold put up a hand to quiet the group. "Before we move too quickly with our interpretations, why don't you explain, Fee."

"It's only happened twice before this meeting—the appraisal thing. Once by Mistress Goodsong, where I saw my own life— mostly my history—but also a brief scene of something that hasn't happened yet." Fee felt a tiny twist of anxiety, recalling Rye's face and his look of betrayal. "And the second time, which was accidental, I saw not only the man's past, but his future too—all his pain and pleasures. It went by very fast so I—"

Mistress Merrybird put a hand on Fee's arm. "You said you saw his joys as well as his sorrows?"

Fee nodded and looked around the circle. Everyone went silent.

"What does this mean?" Fee asked the room.

Harold answered. "It means your brand of magic is . . . well, not one we've come across—perhaps not fully understood yet, but additionally, it means you are, more than likely, a burgeoning concern for Mistress Goodsong."

Fee noted the tips of her fingers and toes were growing numb with a creeping sense of dread. "How so?"

He sighed. "Up until now *she* has been the most powerful mender in our realm. You are a person she believed to be dead, and then agreed would be stifled. The fact that she is aware of your presence here in Gwyndom and also has insight into your skills is worrisome."

"You supplant her, my dear, as the most powerful mender known," Rosedriah stated.

"Shouldn't we tell the queen? Alert the guards? Surely the

people of Gwyndom must know what she has done—and moreover what she is trying to do."

The room reverberated with objection.

Harold looked dismayed. "She's far too powerful for those without magic."

"One wave of her hand and Gwyndom's whole herd would be toast." Kizzy spun her hands above her head.

For once, no one chastised the girl. "My advice to you is to stay on her good side," Harold added.

Fee gave him an incredulous look. "How does one stay on the good side of a person whose wish was to see you murdered?"

Harold was dour but sympathetic. "Make sure it doesn't become a present wish."

Savva tapped on the arm of her chair. "Tell her the most important thing, Harold."

He sighed. "Yes, of course." He turned to Fee. "You have a monumental task ahead of you, Fee. You must find Xavi, figure out how to release Azamar from within him, and reclaim the stone for Fireli.

"It appears that you are the only other person capable of doing this—for this particular situation. To reverse the dark curse of banishment, one must back out of the spell—you must perform a *sacrifice* for friendship—to replace that which was harmed. And since the two friendships to work with here are either Azamar's or Xavi's, it would seem the burden falls upon you. Your relationship with the prince."

Fee looked overwhelmed and said in a voice deadened by numbness, "Monumental doesn't begin to describe it."

His face filled with pity. "Sadly, Fee, that is not the challenging part."

Fee looked about at all the menders. She wanted the nightmare to end. "Then what is?"

"Each person's skills—their *magic*, per se, must be generated from some foundational source. Yours comes mainly from nature, but, as is not uncommon within families who have an exceptional depth of skill, they also come from your magical bloodline. That means that whenever you draw from your skills, you deplete your source. Normally, this should not be a cause of concern. You have been drawing from Savva and your father for years whenever you've had a slight, ah . . . awakening, shall we say. But as Azamar is imprisoned within the prince, you essentially have been drawing upon Xavi as a resource as well—perhaps Savva revealed that to you just now?" He tapped his wrist, then looked up at Fee and then around at the others.

"With each day that passes, the spell depletes the prince's life source. He is, after all, carrying the weight of two people's lives. So when you use your skills . . . understand that you have been weakening the prince. Therefore, it is highly advised that you refrain from using magic, if at all possible."

Harold's gaze locked in with Fee's. "As it is, the prince may not rise to see himself as king. If we do not find him soon, he may not rise to see the dawn."

CHAPTER
THIRTY-ONE

FEE COULD NOT BREATHE. HAD SHE NOT BEEN SITTING, she would have buckled at the knees and fallen to the floor. Her mind raced back to the stillroom, weeks ago, when Savva had made the bone-chilling announcement that it was not the lack of an effective tonic that was killing Xavi, but rather that Fee was.

Fee was.

She was killing her best friend.

The one person she cared about more than anyone she'd ever known.

She was awash with guilt over her bitter complaints at taking her tonic, and for all the times she'd poured it out simply so she could sprout seeds faster, or make a vine ladder, or cheekily trip Rye with moving tree roots. All these things had been making Xavi ill. Her "special skills" were destroying him—each green shoot like a poisoned arrow to his heart.

She clutched her own chest. "Oh God, I'm a monster."

Kizzy fetched her a cool cloth to put over her forehead and stood beside her as the other menders gathered their things to leave. "You never knew," she cooed gently. "You cannot blame yourself, Fee."

Fee stared up into the girl's face, mindlessly registering that the tinkling silver tips of Kizzy's dreadlocks sounded like tiny wind chimes. "He even told me not to," Fee murmured. "Xavi told me not to do all the quirky little things I did because he was worried I'd get caught and horrifically punished." Her stomach suddenly lurched with a somersault. She closed her eyes. "And Rye!" she whispered. "What would he think if he found out I was the one making his brother ill? He'd . . . he'll never forgive me."

Fee buried her head into her hands and groaned whilst Kizzy rubbed her back. "Surely Prince Rye would understand. You hadn't truly meant to do anything. He seems the type to be most forgiving, isn't he?"

Fee shook her head, feeling faint, the muscles of her body tightening, gripping the edges of her bones. "I don't see how he could be. He . . . I've heard his thoughts on . . . on hermetical menders. He believes them to be abhorrent. No. He mustn't find out."

Fee stood and reluctantly tore her gaze away from Savva. It landed on the woman with dual-colored eyes. She smiled warmly at Fee, glanced around at the rest of the witches within the circle, and then glanced at the ceiling and blinked twice.

The room went pitch-black and then was immediately lit again. Fee inhaled sharply. The witches . . . had vanished.

* * *

Fee had so many questions. But there was no one to answer them, and she was forced to find her way back upstairs.

She needed to find Rye. She pulled the hood of her cloak over her head and fled down the hall toward the first set of stairs she could find. She had a general idea as to where he was, but the palace was huge and the area he was to canvas, substantial. Five towers he'd be searching. How in the world could she locate him?

After an exhausting climb and a hunt through three of the five, during which she wrestled with silencing the myriad mind-blowing revelations the menders had unveiled, Fee found the entrance to the fourth tower.

Following the spiraling staircase to its highest landing, she arrived in a spherical hall with four large wooden doors outlining the curved walls within the circle. She dashed across the rich, ruby-colored carpet to the first door on her right and pressed her ear to the wood.

Hearing nothing, she placed a hand atop the latch and felt it give beneath the pressure of her palm. The door opened to reveal a room that took up one-quarter of the tower. Slim windows lined the outer wall and allowed the yellowed light from the torches outside to spill into the room and across the carpeting in long, thin, wavering shafts.

She pushed the door closed and turned to face a circular table with ten matching chairs in the center of the room. Books and papers littered the surface as if a meeting had been interrupted.

Two doors flanked a large bookcase. Fee assumed they connected to the next room in the tower. She tried one of the doors but the handle was locked. She suddenly heard voices in the hallway and the sound of the latch giving way on the main door.

Gasping with surprise, she turned toward the other door on the opposite side of the bookcase but startled as someone grasped her arm. A hand covered her mouth, stifling her sound of alarm, and pulled her backward into the space of a dark cupboard. A closet.

The door closed in on her and she heard the hand's owner warn her with a whisper to be silent.

Rye!

His hand fell away as she turned toward him, relief flooding through her in a cool rush of waves. He held her still as the voices grew louder, two men entering the meeting room whilst they argued.

"Why didn't you lock the door when you left, Drachen?"

"I thought we'd be returning in a matter of minutes."

"Good God, if *she* had been the one to walk in here and find it open, our heads would now be resting on a pike somewhere on the high bridge just over the moat. We are lucky—and I don't like relying upon luck, understood?"

"Do try to temper your authoritative tone with me, Rollins. We both know what's at stake."

Sir Rollins? Fee thought. *Again?*

"Have you seen him?" Sir Rollins asked.

Lord Drachen grunted. "Only twice. Certainly not long enough to discern what he knows from what he suspects. He's kept a very low profile since returning."

"And you say the wedding has been pushed forward?"

"Tomorrow. Queen Islay announced it at yesterday's evening meal."

"And how does she appear?" Sir Rollins asked.

A loud puff of air escaped through Lord Drachen's lips. "If she was surprised to hear the princess's report of Prince Xavi's death, then she did not show it."

Fee sank to her knees and Rye dropped to her side, pulling her head into his chest to stifle the cry that demanded escape. He shushed her again with the barest of whispers and held her tight. The pain in Fee's chest had her believing that her heart had been punctured. The wound felt deep and ragged. She wanted to keen with grief, but bit down on the fabric of her robe to keep from making a sound.

No, no, she kept repeating in her head. *Xavi, how could they have done this to you?* Fee felt Rye's fingers thread through the strands of her hair, as if he were trying to hold on to them like dissolving filaments of hope. They remained silent, suffering in unbearable stillness.

"Where has he been put?"

"Apparently somewhere he cannot be heard."

Heard? Fee stiffened, and she felt Rye's fingers freeze in her hair.

"You've not seen him?" Sir Rollins asked.

"No. I've only been told that he is a treasure she may need to bargain with at some point. Apart from that, little else."

Fee and Rye grabbed each other's hands and slowly rose to stand.

"Listen," Lord Drachen said. "It is nearly daybreak. Gather these papers. We're expected to return here in an hour to speak of the mining operations. Your report will go first—she'll want to know the latest progress—and then we'll have the *official* meeting, where the others will join us. Including Prince Rye. And I'm sure I do not have to remind you of what to report during *that* gathering, correct?"

"Rest assured, everyone will hear exactly what they're supposed to."

Lord Drachen clucked his tongue. "What a mess this has become. Kidnapping the prince."

"I had nothing to do with that, Drachen. And I've no idea what she plans to do with him now that she has him," Sir Rollins said tetchily. "I was contracted to deliver the monthly supply of metals. My allegiance has always been to coin and not king. Now I will likely need to settle in one of the other two kingdoms once this is all sorted out."

Fee closed her eyes. Finally, one more piece of the puzzle clicked.

"That all matters little now," Drachen continued, still chafing. "Just meet back here in an hour—at seven. And don't forget to lock the door."

Fee remained still and listened to Lord Drachen leave. She heard Sir Rollins collect the scattered papers across the table, and a moment later, he, too, exited the room. The last sound she heard was the lock sliding into place. But she was amazed she could hear anything at all over the emphatic pounding of her heart as it thumped with clamorous joy in her rib cage.

Xavi was alive!

They waited another full minute before cracking open the door to the closet and assessing if it was safe to come out. The room was filled with sumptuous, rich hues of peach and pink from the approaching dawn. The highly polished round table gleamed with the sunrise's colors reflecting off its empty surface.

Fee and Rye stepped from their hiding place and finally saw one another's faces. Fee knew her expression must be one that mirrored

Rye's, and it felt as if a thousand balloons had been released within her chest.

"He's here, Rye. He's alive and in this castle."

Rye's smile softened, and he looked off into the corner of the room, thinking. "Well, yes, we definitely know he's alive, but Lord Drachen said Xavi had been put somewhere he could not be heard. That could mean anywhere here within the palace, or perhaps outside of it. Somewhere else within the kingdom—or out of the kingdom altogether."

Fee felt the wind sail out of her lungs.

"They also said Xavi was a treasure they may use to negotiate. What do you think that means? Negotiate with whom? With Fireli, for his return?" She thought about Azamar and the stone . . . and how much Mistress Goodsong wanted it. Did Rollins and Drachen know what she'd done?

Rye shook his head. "I'm not sure"—he looked around the room—"but I *am* certain that we need to leave here immediately. If there are to be ministry meetings held here shortly, we'd best get back to my room and parse all this information—perhaps connect a few more dots."

He gave her a small smile and nodded toward the door. "Come on, Ophelia, we've got a lot of work to do."

Fee looked up at him, wishing she could tell him how finding Xavi was going to be the easiest part of the task set before them. Unfastening a spell, extracting Azamar, and rescuing the fate of their kingdom would all fall in line shortly thereafter. Somewhere in between, she'd have to do the most difficult thing of all and tell Rye she was a witch.

* * *

Once safely back inside Rye's suite of rooms, Fee tossed off her robe and gathered up ink and paper to spread out on the low traveling chest in front of the sofa and chairs. There was so much she needed to tell Rye but she was filled with indecision over what she should and should not expose.

But how *could* he believe any of those things? They revealed that secretive sorcerous workings were all around him, right beneath his nose. And after hearing his previous position, it would be absurd to believe he'd suddenly welcome this unearthly new status of the world.

Rye sat across from her, scanning their notes, and Fee stared at him miserably. Was there a way she could lead Rye into realizing that Mistress Goodsong was the mastermind behind all their troubles?

"I'd forgotten to tell you that I'd run into Sir Rollins last night, or rather hid from him when I was searching my wing of the castle. I overheard him say he was about to be rewarded for his decade of loyalty."

Rye looked at her quizzically. "For the last ten years?"

"That would take it right back to the beginning of Fireli's plague."

His face sprouted confusion. "Queen Islay has been plotting a takeover of Fireli for *ten years*?"

"What if it wasn't Queen Islay?" Fee said slowly, and observed his brows drawing closer together.

"Who else could it be?" He snorted. "Quinn was much too young at the time, so it would be ludicrous to lump her into this scheme. There are a few individuals within Gwyndom's ministry cabinet who would likely wish to have greater power—like Lord

Drachen, but I can't imagine him having the gumption for such a coup. He's more lamb than shepherd."

"But it couldn't be Lord Drachen—he was in the ministry room speaking with Sir Rollins about *the woman* who would be angry with them for not locking the door. Someone is controlling *both* men, Rye."

He rubbed at his chin. "I'm convinced it's the queen. She is the only one with motive. She's called two separate meetings about the mines just this morning."

Fee stared at him, trying to mentally flick on a lightbulb of awareness in his mind. She pushed forward. "What do you think will be discussed at the first one—the one where you are not present?"

"I would assume you have a hunch that matches mine, Ophelia. Lord Drachen said she wants Sir Rollins's report on the status of the operations. Since I'm not invited to that one, chances are they're not planning to reveal to me the seizure of the caves until after I'm—" He stopped and looked up at Fee. "Well, after the wedding, I assume. And by then, perhaps they'd feel I'd believe it was too late to do anything, since our two kingdoms would be already joined."

Fee glanced down and studied their notes. "That's tomorrow, Rye."

"No, Ophelia. Because we'll find Xavi before that."

"Where could they have possibly put him?" She rubbed at her temples and then felt a niggling itch in the back of her memory. "Xavi sent the princess letters every month," she began slowly.

"So?"

"So when she first arrived in Fireli, Xavi mentioned his letters."

Fee closed her eyes and concentrated. "She said she prized them all—or something like that—and kept them . . ."

"Yes?" Rye pressed.

"Kept them . . . in a vault or a safe . . . or, no—she said she kept them in her *treasury*." Fee opened her eyes and stood up. "Do you know where that is?"

Rye looked befuddled. "I don't even know *what* that is, Ophelia. I've never heard her mention it."

Fee deflated, but then looked up quickly as they both heard a tap on the door and the sound of a key being inserted into the lock. She quickly dashed behind one of the long, floor-puddling draperies as Rye moved toward the door.

"It's just me," Mistress Goodsong said, coming in. Fee moved out from her hiding spot and watched the woman warily, suddenly very afraid the healer would know she'd met with the menders and immediately be able to discern exactly how much Fee now knew— and decide to do something crippling about it.

She felt a billowing wave of coolness come from Mistress Goodsong as the healer looked at the connecting door, which was still bolted and shut.

Stay on her good side, the menders had warned.

"We had a great deal to talk about following our searches," Fee gushed, swallowing uncomfortably.

Mistress Goodsong tilted her head. "To talk about?"

Fee's heart fluttered uncontrollably in her chest like a trapped bird, and she fumbled for something to say when Rye stood and broke in with "Xavi is alive."

The older woman's head spun toward Rye. "You've found him?"

"No—not yet," he said.

"Tell Mistress Goodsong what you overheard upstairs in one of the tower rooms," Fee inserted. She tried not to make it obvious that she was emphasizing him being alone, but Rye appeared to understand.

Once finished, he added, "Then I came back, and Fee and I have been trying to sort everything out. Thus far, we think we might know at least the *name* of the place where Xavi is being kept. Do you know where Quinn's *treasury* is?"

Fee was growing used to Mistress Goodsong's self-possessed style, and her face revealed nothing of surprise, but she did sit up a little taller in her chair. She sat silently for only a moment or two and then nodded, a terse smile curling the edges of her mouth.

"I know exactly where her treasury room is."

"Is it in the palace?" Fee asked, dangerously pushing for information in front of Rye and knowing that this was a most treacherous route.

Mistress Goodsong nodded slowly, and Fee's heart acted like a coin with two faces, one half singing with rapture and the other feeling the viselike grip of creeping fear. She stood again and tried to be bold. "Then let's go get him. Please. You must take us there."

The healer raised her finger again but waved it back and forth. "Not so fast. We must think this through very carefully. There are things to consider."

"Like what?" Rye asked.

"First, it is locked—and with a key I do not possess."

Fee shook off the fabricated roadblock as, in her mind—even if there was any truth to it—it would not be an issue. She'd yet to find a lock she couldn't pick with the aid of a hairpin.

"Second," the healer went on, "two guards stand on either side of the entrance, and I believe it is their habit to allow admission only to the queen, the princess, and those who accompany them. They may be an obstacle."

Rye and Fee looked at one another, Rye's face filled with discouragement, but Fee wondered if Rye was growing at all suspicious of what the healer was saying.

Mistress Goodsong stood. "Never fear. I will think this through and find a quick solution, for time is of the essence. But right now"—she turned toward Rye—"you must appear at the ministry meeting and act as if you know nothing of what you've discovered. The queen and princess will be attending as well. Do you think you can keep your cover whilst I come up with a plan?" She stared hard at Rye and then her gaze flicked over to Fee. "Your brother's life depends upon it."

Rye looked up, his face firm with resolve. "Of course."

"Then you must be off immediately," she said, pointing toward the door. "They are expecting you. And Fee," she said, turning back with a raised eyebrow, "there is absolutely no reason for you to leave the room now that we've discovered where Xavi is. It would be far too risky to have you get caught outside these chambers. Things could go disastrously wrong—understood?"

"Yes," Fee said, and blurted out, "Rules are rules."

The healer's eyes shot to lock with Fee's and conveyed the unmistakable message of *And so now we stand on the same page, do we?*

Prickling fear shot up Fee's spine. This was as strong a threat as the woman could covey. "Absolutely," she added obediently. "I'll stay right here until you both return."

The healer led Rye toward the door and turned back. "Rest assured, Fee, I *will* have a solution. And all of these problems? . . . Soon resolved."

After hearing the lock bolt, Fee sank down to the edge of the sofa, her whole body trembling with a jumbled maelstrom of dread and alarm.

Was the taste of rejection still so bitter on Mistress Goodsong's tongue? Was she still, decades later, acting against the love who spurned her, and any and all affiliated with him?

Yet Fee couldn't dismiss the involvement of Queen Islay and Princess Quinn. Perhaps Mistress Goodsong was also a pawn of Gwyndom's royal family and was acting out directives from a monarch who wished to reign over more than one kingdom.

She thought about Savva and felt a heaviness in her chest—like she'd capsized and her lungs were filling with water. Her *grandmother*!

And the news of her parents?

She thought of the two people who she'd known for eight years, loved deeply, and mourned to this day—but now there were two others who existed. Who was her biological mother? Was she alive? And how was she to free her father? A coiling thread of uncertainty unraveled within her body.

She wanted to tell Xavi—to expel everything and have him help sort it out. He would know exactly what to do. But Xavi wasn't an option.

And the imaginary scenario of telling Rye proved devastating.

Revealing who she was would instantly change how Rye looked at her. How he felt about her. Fee shook her head. How *did* he feel about her?

And with that question, Fee plummeted into a mournful fit of misery. For even though it seemed possible that they might rescue Xavi in time to save Rye from the ruinous wedding to Princess Quinn, Mistress Goodsong had made it abundantly clear that Rye and Fee could never be together. The law categorically forbade it.

CHAPTER
THIRTY-TWO

WHEN SHE OPENED HER EYES, FEE TURNED HER HEAD to find Rye staring at her. Several sheaves of paperwork lay spread out before him on the low table, and he held a stack of them in his hand, but they lay ignored on his lap. Instead, his head rested on his fist, his gaze falling on her.

Caught unaware, he looked down at the papers and mumbled a greeting.

"When did you get back?" Fee asked, sitting up and now feeling wholly self-conscious.

"An hour ago, but I figured you'd appreciate if I didn't wake you until Mistress Goodsong returned. Sleep seems so hard to come by lately."

He was wrong. Fee would have welcomed nothing more than time alone with him. But she couldn't tell him this—she refused to make the situation any more awkward for both of them.

She patted down her hair, realizing it had come out of her neat braid. It was a tangled, dark mass, unruly as her thoughts. "Tell me about the meeting."

His eyes fixated on her hair, and when she pulled her hands down to her sides, he suddenly reclaimed his scattered attention and sat up. "Pretty much as we'd expected. Sir Rollins gave some bogus report about the caves being ready for inspection.

"I said nothing to the contrary, and when Queen Islay questioned me as to whether I had any misgivings, I simply answered that we would need to put our trust in the upcoming results of the inspections but that the people of Fireli were in desperate need of rejuvenation, regardless of those results. She did not appear displeased with my statement."

"And what of the princess?" Fee asked, her eyes concentrating on the gilded frame of a painting on the wall behind Rye so she wouldn't have to interpret his expression. "Do you think she believes you—have you been . . . convincing enough?"

"Ophelia?" Rye said.

Fee turned to face him, his eyes serious and questioning.

"What did you mean yesterday . . . when you kept . . . apologizing?"

Fee felt the fire of a hot flush race to her face. How could she tell him? Now, after she'd found out there was no future for them? What would be the point—apologizing for who she was?

Even if everything fell into place—the rescue of Xavi, the cancellation of Rye's wedding to Quinn, the retrieval of Azamar and the stone—it would do nothing but harm her to tell Rye this secret,

and harm him to discover it. Fee was born an agent of witchcraft—
or whatever placating term everyone felt necessary to bind to it. She
would need to hide it, as it appeared this was the norm for all menders.

"I suppose it doesn't matter now. I really shouldn't have—" She
paused and chewed on her lip.

"Shouldn't have what, Ophelia? Kissed me?" His deep, jade-
colored eyes were filled with pained curiosity. "In truth, it should be
me expressing remorse. When I think of all I put you through when
I first returned to Fireli. God, I was awful. I was beside myself with
grief and an uncontrollable amount of anger." He shook his head
with remembrance. "I felt so cheated. Being without you and Xavi—
along with the confusion with what I took to be a punishment—an
expulsion from my home." He looked up at her. "And then to be
told that you were responsible for Xavi's murder . . . I couldn't think
straight."

Fee knew her expression was reflecting the same pain Rye was
speaking of, but he went on. "I'd been told lies—and obviously you
know I struggle with"—he picked up his left hand, made a fist, and
shrugged—"*this*. But now we know the truth. And doesn't that
change things for you?"

"We can't, Rye," Fee said in a whisper. *You* don't *know the truth*.

"We *couldn't*. Past tense, Ophelia. I believed I'd have to marry
Quinn to somehow save our kingdom—but a great deal has happened since that announcement was made."

"Yes, but—" she began.

Rye rose from his chair and swiftly moved to the sofa beside Fee.
"But what? Are you saying you feel nothing for me? Will you turn
me away—ignore me?"

Fee shook her head at the words that fell from Rye's unguarded heart, and she felt a tear spill down her cheek. "I'm not ignoring you, Rye. I'm protecting you."

"From what?"

"You wouldn't understand. I only know that we're not supposed to be together."

Rye put his hands on either side of her head, forcing her to look at him. "We were bound together, Ophelia, from the very beginning. Back before you or I can even remember. Savva was wrong to keep our letters from each other."

Fee tried shaking her head. "It wasn't just Savva."

"It could be the whole damn kingdom and I wouldn't care. Why can't you see that?" His finger moved to trace along her eyebrow. "I have followed an endless list of rules since told I had to leave Fireli. The only commandment I wish to fulfill is the one given to me by my parents—the one that matched the two of us." His eyes met hers. "Are you saying you will defy your king and queen?"

"I'm saying we will be forced to," she said, looking up at him.

"Ophelia," he said, drawing her face closer, "I have never held on to something with as much faith and confidence as I have the words of my parents. I believe they would never steer us wrong, and I cannot convince myself that what I feel for you should be resisted. What have I missed? Is it Xavi? Have you fallen in love with my brother?" His features prepared for a painful truth.

Fee quickly shook her head.

"Then what? If there is something out there that persuades you to reject me, tell me now—but if not . . ."

Fee stared into his eyes, glittering with invitation, and then acted instinctively. In one swift movement, she pulled his left hand down from her face and slid her hand up his sleeve, binding herself to his wrist.

Locked in a fixed gaze, she felt an upheaval of consciousness rush in to overtake her senses. Her brain exploded with an onslaught of images. Her body was engulfed in a surfeit of emotions. Breath rushed out of her and she was filled by someone else's memories, sensations, beliefs, and behaviors. Fee was submersed within the catalog of another human's life. The roaring swirl of tumultuous visions and vibrations radiated brilliantly around her, and she knew with certainty that, despite the pain Rye carried with him, she was a lifeboat he clung to and refused to abandon.

Up to this point.

Fee would not look into his future. It was there, and she could hasten toward it, but she'd made time stop, and she did not want to see the face she'd been given a glimpse of earlier. Instead, she wanted to stay in this moment—forever, if possible. The one where Rye pleaded for Fee to see things as he did. To accept what made perfect sense to both of them.

She could not refuse. Stubbornly muting Mistress Goodsong's and the menders' worrisome words that still echoed in her head, she focused instead on the breathless, braiding magnetic pull between them.

She released the grip on Rye's arm and watched him blink back with uncomprehending bafflement, pulling in a gasp of air as if he'd just resurfaced from beneath the water.

Feeling nearly drunk with hope, she threw her arms around his neck and pressed her lips into his. All thoughts emptied her head as

Rye tightened his grasp, moving his hands from her head down her back to bring her closer. She had nothing to compare these feelings to—the desperate urge to meld against him—and she was shocked at the force of her grip.

His hands were wrapped within the tangle of her hair, and he pulled at her, tipping her head upward to meet his mouth. He pressed the two of them together into an unearthly stretch of space that held no room for thought.

Fee heard him groan, the sound of his voice so foreign and intoxicating it alarmed and thrilled her to where she would do anything to hear more of the tones that reverberated roundly against her own chest.

"You smell of lilacs, Ophelia. Every time I walk into a room you're in . . . I smell lilacs. It drives me mad," he breathed into her hair.

No one had ever spoken to her of sex. And any vague recollections of books she'd read that told of intimacy between two people—the polite, chaste kisses of genteel romance or the old-fashioned courtship the elderly people of Fireli recalled while Savva treated them—could not possibly compare to the ravenous want that rose within her.

She toppled Rye backward onto the floor, clutching at his shirt as they fell. His thigh pressed between hers, through the layers of her skirts, and with one sharp inhalation, her mind swiftly formed a breathtaking new awareness.

Her laughter spilled into his mouth, and he looked up at her with a mixture of wondrous joy and unexpected hunger. Fee grabbed at the silk and velvet fabrics of his shirt and vest, unraveling the fastenings to reach his skin beneath them, thrilling as they fell away from her fingers. And then, staring at his bare chest, she felt her breath catch at the beauty of it, as the muscles and bones expanded and contracted, his lungs in search of air.

She gasped with widened eyes as his hand slid along her leg beneath her skirts and pressed into her thigh, grabbing it almost painfully.

Hell, yes to skirts, she thought suddenly.

She'd never seen his face so high with color, or his features so focused. She raced her hands down the front of his chest and caught the fabric of his breeches. He pulled up to sit so that she straddled him and brought her lips to meet his again, a wild strain of abandonment and desperation flooding through her chest and glittering over her skin.

Suddenly, the room exploded with sound. Every door around them slammed. One of the windows on the far wall shattered and glass shards flew at them. Rye covered Fee's head with his arms just as a second window detonated and spit sharp fragments in all directions.

They sat, raggedly breathing and trying to be still, listening to the tinkling of glass fall onto the floor.

They raised their heads and looked at one another, blinking back the shock and disbelief. Fee dazedly put a hand up to Rye's cheek and, with the delicate pinch of her fingers, removed a small shard of glass that had wedged itself into his skin.

Without a sound, the diaphanous shroud of joy that had enfolded them disappeared as if nothing more than a popped soap bubble.

Rye's eyes searched her face. "Are you all right?"

She raised herself up from his lap and helped him stand. She could barely catch her breath, but managed to nod.

They glanced around the room, taking in the broken windows.

He put his hand up to his cheek where the glass had grazed his skin and then glanced back at the empty casements. "Ophelia . . . did you . . . do—"

Fee shook her head in panicked denial. He knew! But whatever this was, it had not been some working of her hands.

There was a familiar knock on Rye's door.

Mistress Goodsong.

Rye quickly pulled himself together, lacing up his shirt and moving toward the sound. He looked back at Fee. She smoothed down her skirts and tucked her wild hair behind her ears. He opened the door.

"You need to make a short appearance at the noon meal before the three of us—" The healer stopped short. Her eyes scanned the room, scooping up information from every corner and crevice. "What?"

Rye took a step backward and put his hands up, shaking his head. "I've no idea. All at once everything suddenly . . . shattered."

Mistress Goodsong looked quickly from Rye to Fee. "Are either of you injured?"

They both shook their heads and Fee secretly wondered if the healer had been hoping Fee would have been.

Mistress Goodsong frowned and at last said to Rye, "Hurry. We've not much time. You will show up at the queen's side, address the princess, and then we will go to get Xavi." She turned to Fee.

"Stay here whilst I accompany Rye down. I shall be back for you in a matter of minutes."

Fee nodded and swallowed, still too uncertain to use her voice.

They left and Fee studied the wreckage. She needed to sit, to still her breathing, but every surface was covered in shattered glass.

She stepped carefully over the debris and moved toward the door to Rye's bedchamber. The latch gave freely beneath her fingers. A chair had been placed beside the entrance, and she lowered herself slowly to sit on its surface, her hands shaking on her lap. She clutched at her skirts to stay them, and cast a measured glance across the room. A large armoire stood in the corner, a beveled mirror beside it. A writing desk, a wall of books, a table with a pearled gas lamp, and his bed.

Rye's bed.

Fee could not make sense of what had just taken place. One moment they were thoroughly entangled with one another, feverish hot with the world blotted out by their breathless need, and the next they were taking cover from some unexplainable piercing attack.

Rye's suspicions about her were made crystal clear. He thought her capable of the explosion. Had she been? Would he shy away from her with alarm? Or bring reinforcements to arrest her because he could not be dissuaded about his hunch any longer?

She walked toward his bed. She let her fingers trail along the bed linens, rumpled from whenever he'd found time to be in it last. The sheets were petal soft in her hands, like silk and water, sleek against her skin. She pictured him lying here, as he was just minutes ago in the other room, looking up at her, dizzy with heat and hunger and need.

"Oh, Rye," she breathed out, brushing her fingertips across his pillow.

They trailed along the edge of it and caught on something hard. A book. She pushed the pillow aside and saw Fireli's *Book of Denizens* staring up at her. She raised the heavy tome in her arms and then turned to sit on the edge of his bed, settling the volume into her lap. A thrill of possibility skittered up her spine as she ran her fingers over the book's edging of opals. She closed her eyes and contemplated giving in to the tremendous temptation of finding herself within the pages and uncovering the names of her parents—her *mother*.

That's all she wanted.

She'd not look at anything else.

Why did you even bring this here, Rye? Fee pulled the book to her chest and clutched it closed with both hands, resisting the overwhelming urge.

"It's time you earn your keep, Fee."

Fee wheeled around to see Mistress Goodsong standing in the doorway, and hurriedly shoved the book beneath the pillow. She leapt up and pulled her hands away from the bed as if she'd been scorched, holding them close to her chest.

"What?" she asked, alarmed.

The healer's face was serenely still—despite the fact that she'd just walked through a room that resembled the floor of a battlefield. "No more games. You know what I need, and I bar the door from getting you killed. Let us enact this quid pro quo and be done with it, shall we?"

Quid pro quo? Fee thought, trying to hold her features steady. "You're going to take me to Xavi?"

"Follow me."

They moved through the warren of hallways, empty of people as this was the hour of the midday meal and everyone was in the hall with Rye, the queen, and Princess Quinn. The route was unfamiliar, but she kept in step with the older woman as they climbed the stairs and made a series of bewildering turns. The palace was a vast and towering fortress, an institution that dwarfed her own home, and the more Fee traversed throughout it, the more inconsequential she felt.

At last Mistress Goodsong slowed and they stood before a large wooden door bookmarked by two immaculately pressed sentries. Not a word was exchanged as she pulled a key from her pocket, twisted the latch, and opened the heavy portal. She nodded at Fee to step through. Fee was not surprised to discover that the healer had lied about access to Quinn's treasury room.

It was a small, dark antechamber. The only other significant thing in the vestibule was another door on the opposite side of the one they'd just entered through. Mistress Goodsong followed Fee in and shut the door behind her. But instead of opening the second entryway, she came to stand in front of Fee, silent and appraising.

She shook her head. "I told you the rules, Fee. And yet, you—just like your parents—ignored them. I cannot understand your streak of insolence."

Fee felt her brows furrow. "I beg your pardon?"

"I will not give it," replied the healer. "For your transgressions persisted even after my admonishment. Did you think I was ignorant of your behavior?" she asked. "I believe I sent a clear enough message as to Aethusian rule, but it seems that for some, nothing but an *earth-shattering rebuke* will make an impression."

Fee took a small step backward. "Are you speaking of Rye?"

Mistress Goodsong's chin stiffened. "Much of the blame lies at the feet of your father and of Savva, but you carry their habit of defiance as well. It stops here. And I intend to see to it—for the good of all. I must protect the people of Gwyndom from you. *You* should not *be* here."

"Be here, or be alive?" Fee asked wretchedly.

Mistress Goodsong scrutinized Fee's face. "Savva really has told you nothing, has she? Are you at least aware of the origin of our ancestors? The two strains of descent?"

Fee nodded weakly.

"Your side is less than shiny—their traits far from admirable."

"I mean no harm to anyone."

Mistress Goodsong puffed. "You are a ticking time bomb. And one I've tried to keep defused."

She turned to unlock the second door and Fee reached out an arm to stay her, to ask for clarification, but the woman jerked and twisted back sharply, blowing a gush of breath at Fee's chest. A sharp wall of wind wrenched Fee's hand from the healer's arm and shoved her against the wall behind her. Fee's head hit the wall and the gust slackened. She came back, blinking away the stars in her vision. "Wait," Fee whispered. "Please. Just answer me *why*? Why, if you so desperately wanted what Xavi held within him, would you try to kill him?"

"I am not trying to kill Xavi," the healer huffed. "I am merely loosening the bonds of life that hold Azamar bound to him. You see, I know of only one way to reverse the banishment spell—it requires an act of sacrifice. I've tried. Xavi voluntarily ingesting the poison should meet the criteria, but Azamar steadfastly refuses from where he stands. So now it rests in your and Xavi's hands."

Fee peered at the woman. "Are you saying my father's preference is to remain trapped over forgiving you?"

Mistress Goodsong turned and leaned in, narrowing her eyes at Fee. "Give me Azamar and the stone and I will agree to hold back your undesirable ancestry from Rye. Do not, and your secret shall be secret no more."

Fee knew from what the menders had said that even if Rye decided to take pity on her, there were scores of others who would line up to see her suffer the death sentence pronounced upon her at her birth—simply motivated from the fear of who she was.

Fee staggered forward. "Perhaps I would find my life an equal exchange for keeping you from trying to possess a man who does not love you and a kingdom which does not belong to you."

Mistress Goodsong's face curled with the smallest of smiles. "Then I shall up the ante. Instead of allowing the realm to finish the ruling of ending your life as we were instructed to do long ago, I would make the same *mistake* I made with your father but amplify its agony. In place of death, I'd grant you life. Perhaps one inside of Quinn, where you could experience your true love . . . secondhand."

The healer pushed open the door and stared hard at Fee. "Now go to work. And make some magic."

CHAPTER
THIRTY-THREE

FEE RUSHED AT HIM. HE WAS SITTING ON THE FLOOR, surrounded by books, and his head was tipped back, resting on the wall behind him. His eyes were closed, and his face was as pale as bone. He was thin, and drawn, and clearly exhausted.

"Xavi!" she said, reaching his side and grasping his shoulders.

His eyes fluttered open, and he stared at her uncomprehendingly. He squeezed them shut, and murmured, "No. I do not see you. You are not real."

"Xavi, please. It's Fee. I'm here!" She shook his arms.

He pressed his dried and cracking lips together and opened his eyes again. "Fee?" he croaked. The door behind her shut and a clank of the bolt bounced off the walls.

He pulled forward to sit up straight and grabbed her arm, feebly pressing his fingers into her flesh. "Is it really you? Fee, say something I can believe."

She held his face between her hands and looked into his eyes. They were glassy, his pupils enlarged.

"Xavi, Rye is here. We've come to get you out."

"Really?" he asked, his expression leery and unfocused. He leaned in to scrutinize her face. "It's very possible I'm having a conversation with the air at this moment, as most of the time I believe I'm just moving from one hallucination to the next." He moved his hands to rub at his eyes. "I must concentrate," he murmured to himself before dozing off again.

Fee got up and looked around, the wheel of worry churning about in her stomach spinning impossibly fast.

She scanned the room. Plain white walls with no windows, a thin pallet in the corner covered with one wool blanket, and hundreds of boxes stacked along the far wall, some three or four boxes deep. Fee moved to inspect them. A few had been opened and their contents scattered across the floor—like the books that surrounded Xavi—but most of what Fee could see hadn't even been unfastened.

Clearly, this must be Quinn's treasury room. And even more evident was the fact that Quinn had more treasures than she was interested in acquainting herself with.

Xavi mumbled, "Am I dreaming, Fee?"

She put a hand across his forehead. "Not this time." She struggled to make sense of it all.

Just how deeply were the queen and her daughter involved in the kidnapping and takeover of her kingdom? Even if Fee did figure out how to do what the healer wanted, what kind of fate would she be unfolding? If she retrieved Azamar and the stone, Gwyndom would be in a very powerful position to control half the realm—with leaders who were willing to assault anyone standing in their way from accumulating that which they wanted. Xavi would not be king—or he'd be forced to marry Quinn and be controlled by Gwyndom's rulers—a figurehead at best. Azamar might be forced to cooperate with Mistress Goodsong so that he'd not suffer the same fate in the future. And Fireli's people—or what was left of them—would find themselves living under the thumb of a new oppressive regime.

And if she didn't complete her task—what then? Would she face her own demise at the hands of the witches most fearful of her existence—or forever suffer like Azamar?

A slow drizzle of cold sweat fell between her shoulder blades, the prickle of fear climbing around her neck, its fingers constricting tightly.

The familiar metallic noise of a key in the lock jolted Fee where she sat, and she leapt to her feet and rushed to the door.

"Rye?" she called out as the door swung open. The face that greeted her was not one belonging to the emerald-eyed young man she wished to see, but rather to the young woman who wished to take him from her.

Fee grew tall and livid as Quinn entered the room.

Quinn rapidly looked about the room, taking in the boxes, Fee's presence, and finally Xavi. Her eyes filled with horror. "My God. What has she done?" She twisted her hands together in front of her and took a step toward him, but Fee swiftly blocked her path. Quinn pulled back and raised her hands. "This was not me—you must believe it! I had no idea. I simply followed you both here. She does not know I've discovered this—and she mustn't find out."

"You're trying to recuse yourself of blame?" Fee breathed out a puff of hot hair. "You come to Fireli, poison Xavi with the intent to kill him, then kidnap him, and now state you are innocent?"

Quinn reached out a shaking hand. "You have no idea whom you're dealing with. Mistress Goodsong is a . . . a . . ."

"A witch," Fee said plainly.

Quinn nodded, clearly astounded that Fee knew, but she continued, her voice barely above a whisper. "She is in charge of everything here—directs every*one* here. You must understand—I had no idea where Xavi was. And I did not try to kill him—at least"—her features collapsed with pain—"at least not knowingly."

"You fed him your tainted confections. Poisoned with the arsenic I gave you for the rats."

Quinn's eyes pleaded. "I was given a special box from Mistress Goodsong to give him once I'd arrived at Fireli—one I had not made myself."

"But you put them into his tea after he stopped eating the sweets, did you not?" Fee said bitingly.

Quinn drew in a sharp breath. "Simply to sweeten the bitterness he could not stomach from Savva's herbs. *And* I did the same for Rye. I—I had no idea they contained the poison. I would never have tried to kill Xavi—I am . . . I have been . . . in love with him for years," she finished meekly.

Fee studied her, tried to assess her level of truthfulness. "So you thought *I* was the one who had been poisoning Xavi?"

"Yes," Quinn said in a timid voice. "I *wanted* it to be true."

"What? Why?"

Quinn looked at her miserably. "If it wasn't, then it meant Mistress Goodsong had been feeding me lies for a very long time."

"Is your mother trying to conquer our kingdom?"

"There are days when the queen isn't even aware of her *own* kingdom. She hardly has a thought for anyone else's." A heavy frown swept across Quinn's face. "I'm sure, if given the option, my mother will be more than pleased to see the back of me. She hopes that I will be absorbed into someone else's lands, as I am too painful a reminder of what she does not have."

Fee studied her. "Are you saying your mother possesses no feeling or affection for you at all?"

"None." The frown was replaced by what Fee had long ago noticed when reading her body language. A tiny, nearly undetectable squint that appeared when the girl uttered a falsehood. "It feels like none."

Fee wished for an explanation but, glancing back at Xavi, knew time was running out. She asked one more question. "Do you truly care for Xavi?"

The princess's face brightened like the sun as she glanced down to the sleeping figure against the wall. "Yes," she whispered.

Fee saw no evidence to indicate the princess was lying. "Will the guards listen to you? Do as you ask?"

Quinn shook her head. "Mistress Goodsong has measurable sway over important people in the kingdom. She promises them wealth from your mines."

Fee thought quickly. "Then fetch Rye. Find him, and bring him back here so that we can get Xavi out and far away from Mistress Goodsong. We cannot allow her to follow through with her plans."

Without even asking what they were, Quinn gave Xavi one last glance before nodding and dashing out the door.

"Fee," she heard Xavi say softly, "I've not much time, and you have much to do."

Fee looked worriedly at him and moved to his side. "Much to do?"

His eyelids fluttered as he mumbled, "Find Xavi's bulla."

Fee pulled back sharply. "Azamar?" She blinked back the tears that fell down her cheeks and called for him again. There was no response from Xavi's fretful form. He wrestled for breath. She swiped at her eyes and moved to his side.

"Xavi, lie down. You'll breathe easier if you don't struggle so." She helped him settle onto his back and drew the old wool blanket to cover him whilst he slept. She kneeled beside him, staring at the pitiful rising and falling of his chest—a chest absent of his talisman.

Where could it be?

Fee stared at Xavi's wrist and swallowed. Should she, she wondered? It might reveal where the bulla was.

But what if there were things he knew that she should not— information like everything found within *The Book of Denizens*?

Fee squared her shoulders. "This is nothing like the situation with Rye. This is the common practice of many menders throughout the realm. I am doing nothing wrong," she finished in a low mumble.

She grasped hold of Xavi's hand and slid hers along the inside of his arm until, almost magnetically, their hands clasped and met wrist to wrist. The sudden jerk of feeling like she'd been thrust forward out of her skin and had fused with another person's bones was not as jolting as the first few times. Although it still stole her breath and left her dizzy with the intensity.

And yet, there was something very different about this experience. Even as the measurement of time—the temporal length of the common dimension of past and present and future—slowed to a crawl, Fee found herself leaning in to study the images as they presented themselves and was beginning to detect she had an element of control regarding the speed at which she viewed another person's life.

She had, in her prior experiences, watched a band of light, a bending, curving tube of cosmic brilliance, spill forth in front of her. This shaft of illumination contained the pictures, emotions, and all their memories. Their story unfolded in the space of a few heartbeats. It was a transfer of a near memoir that happened at lighting speed.

But this . . . This was not what Fee had expected.

She quickly identified the chute through which Xavi's information traveled, but in and around it, sometimes through it and merging with it, was another—a twin thread of dazzling light, oftentimes much more intense than Xavi's.

It belonged to someone else.

Fee felt an uncontrollable shaking overtake her body—even as she had no sight to witness it and an unreliable form of consciousness with which to interpret it. She felt spellbound—hooked and lured from following Xavi's illuminated images toward the other, stronger band of light. She was roped in and captivated by a thrumming, vibrating source of energy and strength.

She examined him—Azamar—and found him oddly familiar, as if she were seeing a piece of herself she did not know had been missing. She saw him standing in the Fireli gardens, his eyes closed in reverence. A flashing image of him appeared as he embraced a young woman—fair and refined. In another scene, his hands and face conveyed apology; Fee felt his sadness, but it was directed to yet another woman—a distraught and aching one. A wrathful, vengeful one.

The next thing Fee witnessed was a very young Xavi with Azamar and the agonized woman in the same garden, filled with a fresh carpeting of forget-me-nots. It was where the two beams of radiant light joined fast and fused. Fee watched as the woman pulled a vial from her pocket, emptied a glittering black powder into her hand, and blew it toward Xavi and her father. Azamar had tried to shield the young prince, but the dark, crystal dust swirled through the garden bed, snaked around their feet, kicking up the flaxen pollen, petals, and leaves from the flowers, and finally twisted upward to their faces. They breathed in the dust and pollen and, a moment later, the man seemed to merge with the little boy, drawn inside his form, disappearing from his side.

The woman threw her head back with a pained expression—anguish making her form crumple, and it was then that Fee could see it was Mistress Goodsong. Behind her, in the distance, stood Savva, bearing witness to the event.

The pictures and emotions matched the story from the menders. So she forced herself farther back into the past, back where this man stood again with another woman—the one Fee knew better than anyone else. Her mentor and grandmother. Savva placed a stunning, fiery, crimson-colored opal—the kingdom's core stone—in his hand, a look of maternal affection and faith ever so slight but undoubtedly present upon her face.

And then those faces turned to look directly at her, shocking her with a penetrating glance that not only reached through time and space, severing the bond she had with Xavi's wrist, but one that conveyed a message that surged like a bolt of lightning up her spine.

Hope.

CHAPTER
THIRTY-FOUR

FEE SLUMPED AGAINST THE WALL, HER MUSCLES finally releasing from the rigid strain of being tethered to another person—or in this case, two others. She thought about how awful it must have been for Savva—to know her son had been trapped for seventeen years and she was powerless to release him. Fee looked skyward, remembering how Xavi told her that for years Savva would say the strangest things to him—statements that made no sense.

But they would now. If Xavi knew that Savva had actually been speaking *through* him, to her son.

Both she and Azamar counted on Fee. And somehow, strangely, the talisman Xavi had been given. Savva had refused to allow him to give it to Rye as a remembrance when the two brothers parted. And now . . . it was missing.

Could Xavi have dropped it within the room? Taken it off and cast it aside unknowingly in his haze? Perhaps tossed it in a box? Fee moved to inspect the area around the cartons and then began pulling the lids off box after box, finding trinkets and toys, jewelry and ornaments—games to amuse, books to inspire, and letters to persuade.

Fee stared at the many gifts. *What a waste,* she thought, picking up a box of colored chalk and small pots of paint. "A wealth of riches. Xavi and I would have been thrilled to have had some of these things to entertain ourselves."

She went to Xavi and kneeled beside him, gently shaking him. He was out cold, and his breathing was nearly imperceptible. Oh God, he looked like he did when she and Savva had faked his death.

It gave her an idea.

She could not wait a moment longer for Quinn. She pounded on the door. She heard the bolt slide and clank and watched the door open a sliver, the guard's chary, bloodshot eye peering through the crevice.

"What?" the guardsman asked gruffly.

Fee conjured her best rendition of total panic. "The prince is dead! I must tell Mistress Goodsong. Give me leave."

The door opened suddenly and widely. "The prince is dead?" the guard asked in alarm.

"See for yourself." Fee gestured with a shaky hand toward the floor where Xavi lay, still and pale. She hoped a panicked once-over from the guard would be enough to fool him.

The guardsman rushed in, with a second one turning to gawk from his post at the main entrance. Fee moved past the guard who now hovered over Xavi and rushed toward the second one outside.

"Do not move or touch him," she said sharply. "Mistress Goodsong will want to see him as he is—to assess what went wrong."

Fee moved swiftly out the second door and started down the corridor from the direction she remembered Mistress Goodsong bringing her. After only a dozen steps, she heard the outer guardsman shout, "Mistress Goodsong! The prince is dead—what are we to do?"

Fee glanced over her shoulder and caught the sharp, assessing gaze of the healer as she made her way toward the treasury room from the opposite end of the hallway.

Fee was nearly paralyzed as Mistress Goodsong's eyes held hers.

For one infinitesimal second—one second that held what felt like a thousand thoughts to Fee—she paused and considered running back to Xavi. She couldn't carry him out on her own, plus the guards would stop her. And she knew she couldn't convince Mistress Goodsong to give up and leave them be. The only choice was escape. She must find Rye. With him, and now maybe Quinn, they could work together. If she could act quickly enough. For it was clear that Mistress Goodsong did not know how to release Azamar. And without Azamar there would be no opal.

Mistress Goodsong *needed* Fee.

Fee sprang into action, fleeing through the hall toward a spiral set of stairs. She raced down the steps and through a labyrinth of passageways, searching for familiar markers—anything that sparked a thread of recognition. She passed few people, but those she flew by simply stepped back with a gasp and did not offer aid or resistance.

After ten minutes of desperate flight and myriad wrong turns, Fee dashed up the stairs that led to Rye's suite, a razor-sharp ache in her lungs, which felt near to bursting. She made the final sprint to Rye's room and rushed through the door. He was there, bending to pick shards of glass off the floor.

Rye turned with a start as she called out his name.

"We have to hurry. I've found Xavi." She grabbed Rye's arm. "You will never believe all that I tell you, but you mustn't trust Mistress Goodsong—*she* is at the helm of all our troubles—all Fireli's troubles as well. Hurry, Rye. We have to get back, as the woman has just discovered I've escaped!"

"From what?"

She tugged at his sleeve. "I will fill you in as we make our way back." At this last statement she stopped cold. "But no . . ." She looked down, her eyes darting back and forth across the floor. "We will need help. There is no way you and I could overpower the guards and Mistress Goodsong. And I've no idea where Quinn has gone. Who can we call upon?" She looked up into Rye's confounded face. "Oh God, Rye, we need help desperately—we'll never make it on our own!"

Rye grasped her by the shoulders. "I am at a total loss as to everything you're saying. I don't know what to believe. I came back after meeting the queen, expecting to find you here with Mistress Goodsong, but she announced you'd suddenly turned upon her, acting deranged and desperate. She said it was as if you'd lost your senses— that you began throwing things at her and crying out how you were planning to frame her for Fireli's destitution and ruin."

Fee glanced quickly about the room. Its state of disarray was far worse than when she'd left. Lamps had been murderously smashed, paintings ripped through, the curtains stripped from their rods, and chairs upended.

Fee shook her head rapidly, denying the disaster. "No . . . no, Rye! It isn't true. You must believe me. And there is no time to explain. I'm not sure what she'll do to Xavi if we fail to get there in time!" She pulled him toward the door. "Who can you call upon?"

Rye closed his eyes in frantic thought, his hand automatically grasping at his other wrist. "I don't know—maybe a few of the guards who have spent the last three years with me? But even they may be under the control of the queen."

Fee took hold of his clenched fist and uncurled the fingers bunched with tight distress. "It is *not* the queen, Rye. It is Mistress Goodsong. And we shall have to take a chance, as these soldiers are all we've got. Just *trust me*."

He looked at her for merely a moment's hesitation, and nodded. "Okay."

"Find the guards and tell them to take you to the princess's treasury room on the eighth floor in the West Tower. I will do my best to fend off Mistress Goodsong until you arrive."

She looked back at him from the doorway. "Hurry, Rye. Everything depends upon it."

Fee tried retracing her footsteps, flying through the maze of corridors and praying she would not only arrive back where she believed the treasury room to be but also arrive in time. Twice she'd lost her way and found herself in the wrong tower, losing precious minutes.

With growing panic, she finally located the correct staircase and tore her way up the final flight of steps. As she raced down the hallway, she could see no guards standing outside Quinn's treasury room, and found both sets of doors wide open.

Bolting inside, she came upon a scene giving rise to a terrifying wail that slipped from her lips. The heady scent of flowers was over-powering—their perfume intense and dizzyingly strong. Her blood sang with the understanding that they were real and covering the floor by the hundreds, flower blossoms scattered from one end to the other. "Xavi!" Fee cried, rushing in and falling to her knees at his side.

He lay on the floor, slumped against a wall as if he'd crumpled there from standing. In his hand was a piece of red chalk, the dust covering his fingers and the front of his shirt where it appeared he'd slid down the wall against the words written upon it.

Fee looked up and read them.

Prince Rye—traitorous brother—slayer of kings.

She gasped and fell backward. What had Mistress Goodsong done? Was she framing Rye to keep herself free of suspicion? Fee fumbled for the chalk, frantically wiping the remnants of bloodred dust from his hand, when she heard the great haste of heavy foot-steps rush into the room. She twisted to look up and found Rye, his features in open shock, his skin draining of color, and his rapid assessment of the floor, the wall, his brother, and Fee.

His eyes met hers. She knew this face. It was the one that cried out with betrayal, deception, and abandonment.

He made one last glance to the chalk she held in her hand.

She dropped the chalk and quickly found her feet. "Rye," she breathed out.

He looked crushed. "No."

CHAPTER

THIRTY-FIVE

QUEEN ISLAY'S DAY CHAMBERS WERE LUSH AND OPU-
lent. Rich, jewel-toned fabrics covered the furniture, spread across
the carpets, threaded through the tapestries, and hung from the
windows. Gleaming gold paint outlined the edges of everything
that could be gilded. Crystals sparkled inside sconces and chandeliers, scattering a rainbow of colored rays across the floor and walls.
Fee thought it must be like living within a prism, constantly being
bathed in sumptuous hues.

Queen Islay sat placidly upon a large chair made of dark
mahogany wood, its armrests curved and carved with deeply incised
designs. Her body was so still, one might logically mistake her for
being part of the sculpted throne.

Fee stood off to the side of the throne, her hands bound behind
her back and her elbows in the firm grips of two soldiers. Her gaze

fell back and forth between the queen and the three people who stood before the monarch: Princess Quinn, Mistress Goodsong, and Rye.

The princess swiveled her head toward Fee and said a little breathlessly, "The chalk was in her hand, and Rye said when he entered the room he found her spreading the red dust onto Prince Xavi—to make it appear as if he'd been the one to write the damning graffiti."

Fee's heart skipped a beat, knowing just how close she'd come to losing Rye's confidence in her. When he'd found her on the floor with the chalk and she'd seen the look of utter betrayal on his face, Fee had scrambled to her feet, pleading, "You *know* this wasn't me. This was Mistress Goodsong. It's what I've been trying to tell you. She isn't who she claims to be!"

She'd watched Rye struggle, teetering on the edge as he sorted through the last three years. Rye's hand uncurled and Fee knew he had chosen to trust *her*.

Even though she, too, like Mistress Goodsong, was not who she claimed to be.

Immediately after that, they had scrambled for a plan. Fee rapidly convinced Rye that he would have to work with the feeble threads of a design she'd cobble together. She needed time—not to mention a strategy that could somehow disable Mistress Goodsong and keep her from Xavi.

She'd grasped his left hand and curled her fingers around his, intertwining them. "Right now, you must take a leap of faith. My whole aim is to keep Xavi alive and salvage what's left of our kingdom. This is the only way you can reclaim watch over Xavi and get him out of Mistress Goodsong's custody. She is a—" Fee paused. "She holds magic, Rye. A very dangerous kind."

She'd looked back at the drugged and recumbent figure of her best friend. "You must take him someplace safe. He is very ill. Allow Quinn to help you—you can trust her. Then tell Mistress Goodsong that you believe him to be dead, and I am the one to have killed him. She'll know it's not true, and won't correct your error, as she will want private access to him in order to obtain that which she is after. But keep her away from him—*however you're able to do it.*"

Rye had reluctantly nodded.

"You and Quinn must act innocent of Mistress Goodsong's turpitude. Then at least she will not feel threatened. If she is exposed as a witch, the people of Gwyndom will rise up against her, and she will unleash her depravity upon them in return."

Rye's features had stretched with alarm, but he followed her plan and had her taken by the guards to the queen's antechamber to wait. Mistress Goodsong had appeared and worked to further build her case against Fee. "She'd sat at Xavi's feet for ten years, Rye—had been his constant companion, learning everything one would need to know about running a kingdom. Including that it was sitting upon a mountain of wealth—something she'd never had a taste of. But after coming here—and seeing all of this? It is easy to see how she would be green with envy and entitlement.

"Earlier today I came into your chamber to find Fee in your bedroom, rifling through Fireli's *Book of Denizens*. How much more evidence do we need to determine that she cannot be trusted and will break any law to achieve her ends?"

Fee had dropped her eyes. She hadn't looked at the book, despite the fact that she had desperately wanted to.

Mistress Goodsong cocked her head. "And where has your brother's body been taken?"

Fee held her breath, praying the healer's words had not now swayed Rye against her.

Rye rubbed his temples and answered distractedly as he made toward the door. "I'm not sure. Perhaps your infirmary. I can't recall what instructions I gave them." He gestured at the guards and rapidly left.

Shortly thereafter, they stood before the queen, the cabinet of ministers, and all the castle's officials. Those who would determine Fee's fate.

"The girl is rife with deceit, Your Majesty," Mistress Goodsong announced. "From the moment we were introduced she was intent upon doing her utmost to sway Prince Rye away from his betrothal to the princess."

The queen did not move as Mistress Goodsong spoke.

"And even after I informed her that a match between them was prohibited, she persisted and pursued." Mistress Goodsong gave Fee a sideways glance. "She is devious, untrustworthy, and ambitious."

The queen's eyes shifted to Fee. "Prohibited?"

"Your Majesty," Sir Rollins interjected swiftly, standing from his chair within the large cluster of cabinet members and council. "Regardless of this young woman's future, I would urge you to follow through with tomorrow's wedding, as the situation in Fireli proves desperate."

"What a powerful voice we will possess within the realm after this union takes place," Lord Drachen added.

The queen stared gravely at the two ministers. "I am aware."

The princess stepped toward her mother, attempting to display a confidence that Fee could tell was shaky, at best. "I hold no objections and wish only to help the people of Fireli."

It was a long moment before the queen answered. "I can appreciate everyone's determined enthusiasm. Sir Rollins, your kingdom has suffered immeasurably. Lord Drachen, it is obvious the benefits will be mutual. Quinn . . ." The queen took a long, slow breath in and blinked back the moment of sadness that emerged in her eyes.

"Quinn, if you are content with the match, I will not defer the marriage ceremony. It shall take place tomorrow afternoon as scheduled."

The queen then turned to Mistress Goodsong. "Take the Fireli girl to the South Tower. She will stay there until we've arranged her trial. I will see to the details shortly and let the cabinet know of them."

Queen Islay held up her hand with a rueful expression. "Alas, I have neglected an important party. Prince Rye, I have known you for three years. I have seen you grow into a young man of great contemplation. As both these matters hold paramount importance to you personally and to the kingdom you shall shortly govern, do you agree to this?"

Rye's gaze moved from Mistress Goodsong—his longtime trusted, matronly advisor—to Fee. His look was forlorn and full of wretched confusion. He needed to be convincing—to fool Mistress Goodsong. He gave her an almost imperceptible nod and then looked up to the queen.

"I will do what is best for Fireli, as my brother would have wanted, and set aside the emotional upheaval determined to have me waver with indecision." He looked down and said quietly, "I will do as our kingdom's council and ministers have recommended and as *you* have granted as the right path as well."

Queen Islay stared at Rye for a long moment and then closed her eyes before saying, "Let it stand, then. Take the girl to the South Tower."

The healer cocked her head and said, "Are you sure, Your Majesty? The tower with all the windows?"

"Yes. She'll have an opportunity to see the wedding take place in the courtyard beneath her and come to terms with the knowledge that she was unsuccessful in her attempt to obstruct it."

Then Queen Islay addressed the rest of the room. "We have a wedding to prepare."

CHAPTER
THIRTY-SIX

FROM THE MOMENT FEE STEPPED ACROSS THE THRESH-
old and into the South Tower, her senses heightened almost to an
ungovernable state. The spindly candle she'd been handed before
the guard closed the door behind her illuminated a tiny pool of
light, but her eyes could see beyond the circle and moved from the
puddle of soft gold into a deeply rich and lustrous black—a carpet of
textures she somehow understood internally.

She recognized the scents of loamy soil, of newly turned damp
earth, of crushed green leaves and sharp pine sap. She heard the
growing sound of a buried hum, a resounding vibration that filled
the space and air she breathed. It rippled through her lungs and
made her tremble.

Her tongue took in the sugary-sweet floral notes that spoke
of exotic perfumes and lush ripe fruits. The room held an invisible

prism of odor and taste—the sparkling essence of flavor, but no tangible source.

As impossible to comprehend as each marvel was, the phenomenon she found most unexplainable was the curiously bizarre notion that she felt alive.

No—not alive. She felt . . . life.

Her fingertips tingled. Her skin prickled with goose flesh. Her heart thumped with a reverberant beat, accompanying some ancient, muted song, but it was a melody as sweet and intimately known as the surety of her name.

This room was home.

Unexplainably, mystifyingly home.

She stood in the center of the tower and made a slow swivel to take in the contents of the room. All around her, tumbling in an elusive cascade of patterns, Fee felt the room's throb of metabolism. A presence, a vitality, a spark. It echoed off the floor and walls and ceiling.

The circular room was almost entirely enclosed in glass, apart from a three-foot panel that connected the tower room to the rest of the castle through a large wooden door. Floor-to-ceiling transparent walls met high in the center of the room, sharp with crystal clarity— nearly making the room appear to be a simple disc of flooring jutting out above the courtyard below. The only thing that confirmed the existence of solid walls was a line of window boxes attached to them, waist-high and running along the entire circumference, apart from the door.

The boxes contained dried-out soil. Deprived of water, the rectangles of earth had pulled away from the sides of the boxes, crumbling between Fee's fingers as she broke off small chunks to examine them.

The room had been a greenhouse at one time, and although currently barren of plant life, the space spoke of past lives of living organisms and was an oasis of thrumming energy. Fee stared with wonder at the empty room, marveling at the thrilling sensations that blanketed her body.

She glanced to the bolted door. If luck was on their side, Xavi was someplace safe, although if Rye had been overcome by Mistress Goodsong, Fee could only imagine the wretched things the healer might attempt: dark spells and gruesome magic employed in order to release Azamar and Fireli's core stone from within the dying prince.

Fee turned to stare out the glass at the winking lights of the castle and suddenly pulled back, seeing Savva's reflection in the window. She whirled to look over her shoulder to find empty space.

"I'm here, Fee. We must speak quickly." Before Fee could respond with her relief at seeing her grandmother, Savva rushed on. "Magic can be complicated. If it is performed with ill intent, heinous results materialize. Mistress Goodsong cast a spell using dark devilry. There is an *expiration* date for the spell. Azamar and Xavi will be bound until his twenty-second birthday."

Fee brightened. "Wonderful! His birthday—and his coronation—are in five days' time."

Savva's face looked pained. "You don't understand, Fee. The host will have exhausted his ability to continue the taxing effort of sustaining two lives at the time of the spell's cessation."

A chill raced through Fee's body. "Are you saying if we are unsuccessful, Xavi will . . . die?"

"And Azamar will perish along with him."

Fee looked to the ceiling.

"There is more, Fee. Each kingdom's core stone is vital to keeping the realm healthy. If our stone is lost within this dark spell, it will die along with Xavi and Azamar. The stone is the kingdom's source of wealth and magic. Fireli will rapidly wither without it—become extinct."

Fee gasped.

"The remaining three kingdoms will suffer greatly. A rip in the fabric of the realm will have taken root. Magic will dwindle immeasurably, and the lands will grow barren. The realm will deteriorate into a sickly state of existence. Many will perish."

Fee turned back to see Sava's reflection again and heard her own breath coming in fits and starts. "What am I to do? How do I save them all? Because if you think I have any knowledge or control over this . . . this m-magic I'm now told I possess, I assure you *I do not*. I could make *seeds sprout*, Savva!"

"And while I am desperately trying to save other people's lives, I remain in the dark as to why other people would want to take away *mine*. Why?"

Savva's voice sputtered. "You and I descend from a dangerous line of magic, Fee—one not easily mastered but rather directed by passion and temper."

"According to the other menders, *you* were the most skillful healer Aethusa has produced, and you were able to bridle it—why not me?"

Savva shook her head. "I was not. I . . ." She faltered. "I took the life of many others. Mistress Goodsong may have uttered the spell, but I was the one who cast it across our kingdom in a cloud of uncontrollable anger, knowing she'd already taken my son. I went black with madness at the thought of her taking my son's child as well."

Fee felt her arms prickle with gooseflesh. *"You?"* she whispered. "You killed all those people in Fireli? My parents? The king and queen?"

Savva closed her watery eyes, pain radiating from her features. "Your magic is dangerous, Fee. As you are a product of banned mixed bloodlines, the combination you carry within you is a deadly concern, and everyone knows it."

"Deadly?" Fee asked, shaking her head.

"Power and rage, Fee. As fatal a combination as can be."

"What power do you speak of? No one would define my talent for seed-sprouting as potent."

Savva opened her eyes to find Fee's. "Your skills are latent, not inaccessible. But that is not the power I refer to. I speak of monarchial privilege."

"And why would you do that?" Fee held her breath.

"Because, Fee, you are next in line for the Gwyndom crown. Your younger twin sister, younger than you by mere minutes, is Princess Quinn. And your mother is the queen."

Fee could say nothing. She was utterly dumbstruck.

"Time is running out, child. You are capable of sprouting more than seeds. You have spent a lifetime planting a garden of knowledge. Reap it."

The old witch's form vanished, and Fee was left staring at air. She sank to the floor and stared up through the glass-paneled ceiling. Stars winked across the inky black sky, far away and as unreachable to her as any help down on the earth, where she sat in an inconsolable panic.

Finally rising, she paced the small tower for minutes—or hours. There was no way to track time apart from the stars—a talent she did not possess. But her thoughts were interrupted by a tapping at the door. Quinn. Princess Quinn. *Sister* Quinn.

The young woman raised the silken band around her wrist, pushing it farther up her arm. It revealed an identical birthmark to Fee's—a symbol of infinity. "Did you know that we are . . ."

Fee's eyes widened at seeing an identical imprint to her own, but she nodded, wary of saying anything more.

Quinn took a large breath. "I imagine that it is impossible for you to comprehend how much she had wanted you and not me."

"Who?"

"Our mother . . . the queen." The two words were said coldly, detachedly. "Mistress Goodsong told me stories right from the beginning—that I'd had a twin—one who had been blessed with everything my mother wanted—which was everything my father had. And then he left her. Cruelly and without a word. And you were the thing that was his carbon copy—dark and magical."

"Do you hold magic too?" Fee asked, glancing down at her wrist.

"No. Not all who are born from a magical bloodline carry it within them." Quinn was silent for a few moments before saying, "She believes you to be dead. As I did until I saw your birthmark on the first evening we met. It's impossible to live up to the person my mother wished I had been. I can never compare."

Fee felt something within her twinge with sadness. "Was it you who found Xavi in the cave?"

Quinn nodded. "Rye was growing sick, and I knew he could no

longer care for Savva. So I tended her. She woke for a few seconds, mumbling. She said you and I are sisters, but I'd already known that. She begged me to trust you—to get you to the cave. Savva said that Xavi's life was the lynchpin that would either keep Aethusa alive or destroy the entire realm."

Quinn looked up into Fee's eyes. "But I was convinced you were trying to kill Xavi. I despised you. Because of you I could not have my mother's love, and quite possibly not Xavi's either.

"So I brought him to the best healer I knew. Mistress Goodsong. Except it appears she wishes him ill and weak. I don't understand."

Quinn raised her shoulders an inch. "You must save him, Fee. He is the only thing I have—the only thing I need."

"I cannot do it from here," Fee argued.

"I'll get you out."

"How?"

"I'll tell our mother what she has longed to hear for eighteen years: *something magical has just happened.*"

A slow creep of warmth slid across Fee's cheek, and the incremental flush of heat pulled her sluggish mind up from the rooted depths of slumber. She kept her eyes closed, wishing that when she'd open them, she'd find herself slumped over the distillery room's scarred wooden table, having fallen asleep at her studies.

The scent that filled the room was overpowering but familiar. It had been in the bouquet of perfumes her nose had been greeted with when first entering the South Tower last night, but it was a thousand times greater this morning and finally convinced Fee to open her eyes.

She blinked back the picture in front of her, stupefied. The room was filled with lush greenery and the heady, bud-bursting stalks of periwinkle-blue lilacs. They spilled out of the window boxes onto the floor and along the glass ceiling. Sun-dappled, peach-colored rays of light sparkled across the waxy green leaves and winked upon the glass surfaces.

Fee sat up with a gasp, her eyes saucer-wide and uncomprehending.

"I wanted it to be you," she heard someone say from behind her, and she spun to see Queen Islay gazing out across the green valleys in the distance, her back to Fee.

Fee scrambled to stand. "Your Majesty?" She fumbled with words, still believing the scene was the creative delusion of a fractured mind.

"You look exactly like him, but I could not trust my eyes, because for more years than I can count I have wished for nothing other than to see his face appear before mine once more."

Queen Islay turned and met Fee's gaze. "I had to be sure, which is why I had them bring you here."

"I'm at a loss for words, Your Majesty. This"—she glanced about in scattered fashion—"this feels like some elaborate mirage—soon I will wake to find myself in the same wretched state I fell asleep in last night."

The queen's features softened and the corners of her mouth curved slightly. "You even share the same frown lines—lines I'd traced a thousand times." She closed her eyes briefly. "No, Ophelia, this is not a dream—although it is a dream come true for me."

Queen Islay pulled a lilac stem beneath her nose and took in a deep lungful of air, smiling in reverie. "Do you know the meaning behind this flower?"

When Fee shook her head, the queen pressed her lips inward with a private smile. "First love. That is what they depict."

Fee stood motionless.

"This tower was where I first met your father—which is why I felt certain the room would definitely answer the question that rose to my lips and quickened my heart when I laid eyes upon you yesterday: Were you our child?

"Did you know of it?" the queen asked, leveling her soft gaze on Fee.

"It is a recent discovery, Your Majesty. I still cannot believe it and am convinced there is some error."

The queen raised an eyebrow and gestured at a wall of blossoms. "And this did not confirm it for you?"

"These flowers? The lilacs, you mean? How could they? Did you bring them?"

"*You* did, Ophelia."

Fee pulled back with shock. "Me? Oh . . ." she breathed out.

"Your father explained to me that magic was nothing more than the drawing and using of energy. Everyone has it, or access to it. And the type of magic one has can be defined as symbolic—or reflective. You do not invite and command the kind of energy that you *want*. You invite and command the kind of energy that you *are*."

"Mistress Goodsong used her energy to unleash the wretched epidemic on Fireli—or at least part of it. The plague that killed my parents." Fee looked up. "Rather, the people who I believed to be my parents. She drove out the children, and took away our mines. She forced Savva to drug us all to a numb and befuddled state. And all because of greed."

The queen's face went ashen, and only her eyes revealed the true horror Fee knew she was experiencing at hearing the news. "Mistress Goodsong loved your father too. But it was not meant to be, and no other love could tear your father and me apart."

"I think she did," Fee argued. "Do you *know* where he is?"

"I have not seen nor heard from him in over eighteen years. And I could tell you that for every day, or week, or month that goes by, there is not one moment that I do not feel his absence. There has never been another."

The queen moved to where Fee stood in the middle of the room—her eyes moving across each of Fee's features in what was likely a studied comparison. "He'd only just discovered I was with child. But when it was learned by others, my world fell apart in horrific fashion. Hastily married off to another, the births bound in secrecy." Queen Islay's face could not hide the revisiting pain. "The consortium of witches determined one of you held magic and the other was bereft. You were taken from me. The kingdom was told I'd had one child, but to me . . . I had nothing.

"Every time I saw Quinn it was a reminder that I was unfit—that if I could not save one of my children, then I had no right to raise another. I could not bring myself to grow attached."

The queen shook her head with heavy sadness. "By the time I realized how selfishly I was behaving, it was too late. Any attempts to bond with my tiny child were thwarted."

"By whom?" Fee asked.

"Mistress Goodsong. She'd taken over the maternal role and sabotaged my efforts, convincing Quinn that I believed her a mistake. She has suffered for it terribly."

"Why could you not get rid of Mistress Goodsong? Cast her out of the kingdom?"

The queen's brows pinched together. "I was afraid. Azamar had warned me. This woman—although most everyone in the kingdom did not know—held powerful magic. Sorcerous skills far above one monarch's feeble ability. I feared that if I were to make such a ruling, she would surely have made the people of Gwyndom suffer.

"No"—the queen smiled ruefully—"I have been a shell of a monarch as much as I have been a hull of a person.

"But seeing you . . . seeing this—" She looked all about her. "It was like opening the door that had held captive the very essence of who I was.

"Do you see that large oak tree on the grounds? The one with all the acorns scattered beneath it?"

Fee glanced outside and saw myriad people setting up garlands and massive vases full of flowers for the wedding. The tree the queen stared at was colossal and towering, its branches spreading out to create a canopy where the prince and princess were to be wed.

"It is the only living thing here on the castle grounds. Everything else—the grass, shrubs, and flowers—they are all manufactured. It seems we cannot grow anything anymore. Our soil is infertile—or so I am told—and can sustain nothing, apart from the one remaining tree. Once, Azamar told me I could never fully understand the essence of any life unless I was fully immersed within it—and to make his point, he grew a tree around me. Just like that." The queen snapped her fingers.

"In the blink of an eye, I was at the heart of this wood, bound by it, enrobed within it, and wholly consumed. Looking back, I suppose I should have been mad with hysteria, but the feeling wasn't one that evoked suffocation. Instead, it made me feel what the tree felt: solid, vital, safe." She looked up at the ceiling. "The truest empathy for another living thing. And sadly, our kingdom has lost its own vitality. We are gutted out and stand as hollow representations for the truth."

Fee seized the moment with a rush of boldness. "Your kingdom has been overtaken by an individual who has lost this empathy you speak of. She will snuff out any form of life—but currently an innocent and honorable one—to achieve her wants. I beg for my release to save it."

The queen turned to look out the window again. "Xavi is safe," she said quietly.

"He is?" Fee's lungs filled with the sweet relief of a full breath of air.

"For now." She nodded. "Rye instructed the guards to bring Xavi's body directly to my private chapel and not to Mistress Goodsong's infirmary. Although he could not give me the illuminative details as to why you begged the healer to be barred from Xavi, Rye appears to put a great deal of worth behind your words."

"And how is Xavi?" Fee feared the answer as much as she needed to hear it.

The queen shook her head. "He has only come awake just before sunrise—a great shock to me, as I spent the night on my knees praying for his soul, for proof of who you are, and for any guidance I could be afforded. He is recovering in my chapel—safely, but I would not say resoundingly."

"I have some news that may bring both joy and sorrow to your heart, milady. Regardless, I feel certain you would want to know of it."

The queen's features opened with curiosity.

"I know where my father is."

Nothing about Queen Islay's face altered apart from the high spots of color that flushed her cheeks.

Fee swallowed uncomfortably. "He has been bound. Condemned to live his life *inside* another, and has been doing so for those last many years you speak of. It was both a spell and a curse cast by Mistress Goodsong when he rejected her affections."

The queen's nose flared slightly at this revelation.

"I've only discovered it yesterday, but I am afraid that I have no idea how to release him from where he resides."

Queen Islay steeled herself. "Where is he now?"

Fee looked toward the door. "Currently, he is inside your chapel."

CHAPTER
THIRTY-SEVEN

"NEARLY EIGHTEEN YEARS?" XAVI REPEATED, HIS
hands coming to clutch at his chest.

Fee nodded and handed him another cup of steaming broth—a
mixture of things she'd requested to be put together in the kitchens
and brought up to the queen's private chamber to aid Xavi's sluggish
recovery.

"How? I mean, I can't even contemplate the act of such a thing—
nor do I have any recollection of it occurring." He looked down at
himself with confusion. "Wouldn't I . . . *feel* something if what you
say is true?"

Fee shrugged. "You have. Many times, Xavi. Like when you've
felt someone was nearly steering you, or when you found the notes
with the unexplainable argument against reopening the mines."

The queen, who sat rigidly in a chair close to Xavi and Fee, pulled back with a countenance of utter surprise.

Xavi looked off in the distance and paused, taking in yet another of the countless, staggering revelations Fee had reported to him. "Yes." He nodded. "And this explains the myriad exchanges with Savva that made absolutely no sense. Fee and I used to think her positively balmy when she would put a hand on my shoulder and apologize, or pray that I was at least not losing hope."

The queen leaned in closer to Xavi. "She . . . spoke to him?"

"Or tried to. I have no idea if she received anything back, as no communication came through me, but—"

"Actually, it has," Fee said.

"What?" both Xavi and the queen said together.

"Twice—both times you were nearly unconscious, Xavi. Azamar said we needed to find your pendant. Where is it?"

"I—I don't know." Xavi fumbled beneath his shirt. "Someone took it. I think I remember that, but I had been planning to give it to Quinn—as an engagement gift."

"What? Why?" Fee asked aghast.

"Well, it was going to be a romantic gesture. You've seen the amulet, right, Fee?"

She nodded. "It has a carving of a small flower on it."

"Yes, and a few Latin words on the back. The first word was *abjungo*, and since that means 'bind to' I thought it would be fitting for her to see it as a token of our impending union."

Fee cringed. "Xavi, *adnecto* is the word you're thinking of. *Abjungo* means to unharness or separate. What were the other two words?"

Xavi's face fell. "I don't know. They weren't at all familiar to me."

"We need to find that amulet," the queen said, her eyes set on Fee, and then she turned to Xavi and finished, "We *must* have that amulet."

Xavi and Fee looked at one another. They both knew she wasn't speaking to the prince.

They needed a plan. Fee felt as if she'd thrown a dozen balls into the air and had now been informed that none of them could touch the ground.

She stood at a small sideboard in the queen's private chamber, putting together a few sachets of herb packets to brew to ease Xavi's malaise. She needed time to think her way through the riddle of this proposed unbinding spell.

To reverse the dark curse of banishment, one must back out of the spell—you must perform a sacrifice *for friendship—to replace that which was harmed.*

This was what Harold had said. But what was a sacrifice for friendship?

"Have you read it?" Xavi asked, glancing to where *The Book of Denizens* lay on the table in front of him. The queen had convinced Rye the tome would be safest in her guarded chambers, and was keeping it here until his return to Fireli.

Fee swallowed the small lump of guilt lodged in the back of her throat. "No . . . but I nearly did. Only because I'd just been told about my parents. I only wanted to discover my mother's identity, Xavi. Nothing else. Do you believe me?"

"I trust you more than I've ever trusted anyone, Fee. And it seems only right that you have access to it now." He gestured toward the book. "You have my permission."

She slowly reached for the book, sliding it toward her until the tome sat heavily in her lap. Opening the hefty binding, she heard the spine crack. She turned to the title page and saw the long list of names and ornamented signatures of Fireli's monarchs. The dates beside their designation went back hundreds of years.

"Xavi, this book can't possibly contain all the names of everyone who has ever lived and died within Fireli, can it?" She let the pages slip through her fingers with a soft *whir* of sound.

"No. Every one hundred years, fresh, blank, new leaves are inserted, and a sizeable number are removed. The old ones are archived and kept in Aethusa's Great Realm Library—a place I hope to visit one day. But you'll find *our* pages here, if you want to view them now."

She flipped through the tissue-thin sheets with trembling fingers until she came to the section heading that displayed last names beginning with the letter *D*.

A small list stood beside each name, revealing their most personal details. The inky, tremulous handwriting of Savva revealed the known and unknown of each person within their kingdom. And there she was. Ophelia de Vale.

Fee scanned her record. Under "Parents" it identified the two people she'd spent the first eight years of her life with, Peregrine and Annabelle de Vale. Not the truth. Not the secret.

Then: *No known allergies apart from susceptibly reactive birthmark. Treat with tonic.*

Her shoulders slumped. "This fails on such a grand level," she said, and watched Xavi sigh with a hint of humor.

"Why don't you look at *my* page?"

She glanced up with uncertainty, the old vellum sheets filling her nose with the scent of expectation. "Are you sure?"

He smiled, but it was a gesture tinged with melancholy. "You really have no choice if you hope to properly treat me for any deadly disorders, now, do you?"

Fee scanned the words beside Xavi's name and read aloud one entry under "Allergies." "Hay fever?" She snorted. "I've always known that—simply from the millions of times you used your sleeve as a handkerchief."

She skipped down to read farther on. What caught her attention sent a jolting shock through her body.

Phobia: Fear of death

She looked up and saw Xavi's eyes locked on hers, waiting for her reaction.

"What?" she whispered. The weight of a thousand stones fell to her stomach. "Why wouldn't you tell me of this? Why did you allow me to . . . to nearly *kill* you with Savva's death tonic?" She thought about the terror he must have suffered at her hands.

"Xavi," she began tentatively, "you've always known I was . . . a . . . a witch, haven't you?"

He nodded.

"Savva told me that *I* was actually killing you—whenever I . . . Could you feel it . . . when I used some skill?"

He nodded again, and she wanted to curl in upon herself with guilt.

"Why didn't you tell me?" Her words were barely audible.

"I figured it out long ago—that there was *some* sort of connection, but I wasn't sure why. Yes, I wanted you to stop, but only because I didn't want anyone to discover who you really were. At least until I was in a position to do something about changing the laws."

"I was hurting you—it must have added to your fear."

He closed his eyes and drew in a long breath. "Yes, I have a fear of dying—pretty much like everyone else . . . Mine is maybe a *little* stronger."

She could tell he was lying. She knew him too well.

"But," he went on, "it isn't just corporeal death I fear. It's more the death of my success. The possibility of failing my kingdom, our people, my obligations. It is probably more relevant to my anxieties over the death of these *things*, than the demise of myself." He looked at her solemnly. "I would do anything to save our kingdom—given the chance."

Fee put the book down and crossed to where Xavi sat, kneeling beside him. She grabbed both his hands. "Xavi, you *will* be one of the greatest kings our realm has ever seen."

Xavi shook his head. "Just as much as we'd like to believe that love can move mountains, Fee, this woman has a personal vendetta against the queen and"—he gestured to his chest and looked down at his body—"the man who shares breath with me. We may be foolish to think we can overpower her and gain back our kingdom."

Fee stood and moved back to the book, picking it up again. "No, Xavi, she may have done everything she could to weaken us, but she has been unsuccessful thus far. We may not have strength, but we possess determination."

Fee's finger skimmed through Xavi's page in the book and came to rest on another notation under his known allergies. She glanced up at him. "You aren't allergic to peonies."

"No. I'm not."

"Then why is it—" Her eyes suddenly went wide with knowing. "Oh," she breathed out. "So this is like bait?"

Xavi made a small nod.

Fee suddenly looked inspired. "You see this entry? Next to your allergy? It says *restituo*: see bulla." She looked up at her best friend. "The English translation for *restituo* is restore. And that's precisely what we're going to do—even if I must break every rule in the rulebook to do so. We're going to take it all back. And *not* die trying."

CHAPTER
THIRTY-EIGHT

THE LATE-AFTERNOON SUN SPILLED DAPPLING RAYS OF soft yellow light through the broad branches of the great oak tree the prince and princess were to be married under. The wide expanse of emerald-green artificial grass, stretching from the tree to the castle, held hundreds of people who were there to witness the ceremony. A buzz of energy threaded through the crowd like a current of jittery tension, a tightly trussed string, freshly plucked and wildly vibrating.

Queen Islay climbed a set of stairs to stand upon a raised dais beside a white-robed monk whose face was nearly covered by a low-drawn hood. Monarchs and ministry leaders from each kingdom sat in two straight rows behind the queen, ardently observant. Rye, in a resplendent emerald long-tailed coat, stood one step below the queen and next to the princess, whose ivory gown glowed with the reflection of the golden sun. Mistress Goodsong fixed the last of its folds into place on the grass, tossing aside a few stray acorns that crunched underfoot.

The queen raised her hand toward the impatient crowd, calling for silence, and offered a face full of apology. "My fellow citizens and honored guests of Gwyndom, I have an unexpected announcement." The people quieted.

"It brings me a touch of sadness to announce that the wedding between Princess Quinn and Prince Rye of Fireli shall not take place today. And as bitter a pill as this is to swallow, knowing Prince Rye will not be joining our royal family, it is sweetened by the fact that at least I am able to hearten him by providing the gift of full pardon to one of his kingdom's citizens for a serious crime she has been proven innocent of committing."

A great wave of murmuring chatter skated through the crowd like a stone skipped across water. Mistress Goodsong moved forward toward the dais and questioned the queen, wholly astonished. "Ophelia de Vale has been declared blameless for the murder of Prince Xavi? Surely, Your Majesty, I must assume you are in error."

The queen's face brightened. "I am pleased to say that I am not. We must thank God for miracles or medicine, for Prince Xavi is recovering his health, and we have high hopes that he will continue to do so."

"Recovering?" Mistress Goodsong sang out, half addressing the crowd. "Welcome news, yes, but the fact that the girl did not *complete* her task to assassinate her would-be king does not call for absolution."

"I would agree, Mistress Goodsong, had that been an accurate assessment of what took place. But the one we blame for the attempt on the prince's life lies elsewhere, closer to home, and, in fact," the queen said, one eyebrow raised, "stands before me now." Her words were crisply punctuated.

Mistress Goodsong's eyes narrowed to a scathing glare. "Me?" she said. "Prince Rye will vouch for my innocence. He revealed to *me* the murderous scenario created by the girl—where the flowers were strewn about the floor."

"Flowers?" the queen asked.

"The peonies. That are toxic to Prince Xavi. Does this not point a damning finger back at the girl, as she is one of Fireli's healers and would know his pernicious allergies?"

"It might," Rye interjected, "had I *revealed* the bloom that caused this pernicious allergy."

Mistress Goodsong turned toward Rye, startled.

The tension in Rye's left hand was palpable but controlled. "I never indicated what flower had been strewn across the floor where my brother lay dying, only that there *were* flowers. Therefore, one must grievously deduce, Mistress Goodsong, that your sharp eye and thirst for details came from a source other than myself."

"I am a healer," she spat. "It is not unusual for one such as myself to discern any individual's hypersensitivity to some food or material."

"Not unusual," the monk in the white hood standing beside the queen announced, pulling the cowl from his head to reveal his face, "if it had been a real one."

The crowd gasped at seeing the pale face of Prince Xavi.

"It is a red herring, revealed within Fireli's *Book of Denizens*— meant to smoke out would-be assassins. In this case, an untruth indicating that I am deathly allergic to peonies." He paused to catch his breath. "It was my parents' deathbed effort—protecting me from anyone who gained access to our kingdom's private book with bad intent."

"And," continued Queen Islay, putting a hand on Xavi to indicate he should rest, "although the unauthorized examination of another kingdom's *Book of Denizens* is an act of prosecutable behavior, it is not as felonious as an assassination attempt on a soon-to-be-crowned monarch. This, I fear, is handled with capital punishment."

Mistress Goodsong whipped about in a circle and bellowed out her rebuttal to the guests around her, "I shall fight this wrongful charge! Take it to the highest court!"

The queen shook her head dolefully. "I am afraid this is why we have gathered in such important numbers here today, Mistress Goodsong." The queen made a sweeping gesture behind her to the rows of monarchs and ministry cabinet members. "These are the members of the highest court—individuals who deemed the matter of such great consequence that they insisted it be dealt with at once."

Mistress Goodsong fumed. "The people of Gwyndom will not allow it. They need me—they *rely* upon me. You will have a revolt of mutiny upon your hands."

The queen nodded. "It is not inconceivable that many people of Gwyndom will be in uproar. But"—she held up a hand, seeing the groundswell of disquiet growing within the crowd—"the realm's governors have discussed the situation and are willing to reduce your sentence. They will spare your life if you cooperate."

"I have no fear for my life. But I am curious to hear what you ask of me." Her smug words were marked with crisp acrimony.

"It is believed that you possess something of Prince Xavi's. A talisman from his own kingdom's healer, given to him when he was a boy. We want it returned. We *insist* it be returned. Immediately."

Mistress Goodsong pulled back. "I have no such trinket." She gestured down the length of her person. "Search me—search my infirmary. You'll find nothing to back your claim of theft."

The queen's face blanched white with worry. "Withholding this amulet will lead you to a certain irreversible end, Mistress Goodsong. Perhaps you should rethink your denial."

The healer thrust out her jaw. "I tell the truth! I do not possess—"

"I do," Princess Quinn said to her mother, her expression pained and fearful. "I have Xavi's charm."

"The bulla?" Xavi asked.

Quinn nodded and put a shaky hand to her chest. "You gave it to me, Xavi—when you were ill and I attended you. You were feverish and ailing—and you asked—n-no—*insisted* I take the charm from around your neck and hold it for you."

Mistress Goodsong grasped the princess by the arm and turned her. "That's it. That's what I need, child. It is what *we* need. Give it to me."

Quinn pulled her arm out from the healer's clutch and backed up a step. "There is no we. You attempted to poison the man I was betrothed to."

The healer stiffened, her eyes glittering like hardened jewels. "It was you who fed him the toxic substance!" Mistress Goodsong suddenly took another tack. "Quinn, you have been overlooked and ignored your entire life. The good people of Gwyndom know that I have been here for them when their queen was not. This is *your* kingdom, Quinn.

"Your mother has abdicated the government—because of the melancholy brought on from her past. You must demand that she step down. And this, Princess, will render the throne vacant."

Queen Islay moved toward her daughter. "Please, Quinn. Return the pendant, for possibly it holds the key to the recovery of your father."

"Recovery?" She glanced up, surprise replacing her anguished features.

"Mistress Goodsong has grieved him with her dark magic, fastening his soul . . . to Xavi's." The crowd rippled with panicked expressions of alarm, the whispered word *witch* tumbling out of people's mouths. "He has been banished to this place for the last eighteen years as punishment for spurning her love."

Quinn traced a finger beneath the neckline of her shimmering gown and caught hold of the thin chain that rested on the inside of it. As she gently pulled, the tiny links emerged one by one until the round amulet materialized. She looked down at the thin disc.

Mistress Goodsong clutched again at the girl's arm. "Give it to me, Quinn. You have no magic, and it will mean nothing to you. I am the only one who knows how it can be properly used."

"Apart from me."

Everyone looked up as Fee leapt down from one of the broad branches of the great oak tree, landing by its trunk. The crowd undulated with soft exclamations, like the whitecapped wave of an ocean tide, rippling with unseen energy. They searched the tree's branches, wary of other people ready to drop from its limbs—an unexpected windfall of fruit.

"I can release him. I can help *our* father."

Again there was a billowing response from the flood of people on the lawn.

Without looking, Mistress Goodsong thrust her palm out toward Fee—a punch of wind shoving and brutally pinning her to the broad tree trunk.

"The woman is a witch!" one man shouted, pointing at the healer.

Fee struggled against the invisible hold. And the frenzied crowd panicked. Shouts of *Capture the witch! Get her before she escapes!* filled the air.

The mob surged forward like a living, cresting wave. Mistress Goodsong skimmed her hand from where she'd held Fee at bay in a curve along the front of the press of people. Their forward movement halted.

"Listen to me, Quinn," Mistress Goodsong said, taking a cautious step toward the girl, as if she were stalking prey. "You already know that some of Gwyndom's most influential citizens are devoted to me—"

The crowd fought their restraints, crying out in fear, but the healer continued. "If you give me that amulet, I can ensure you protection—cooperation from *all* the realm's governments."

Quinn clutched at the bulla, frozen in place as her eyes darted from the people back to the healer. She stole a glance at Xavi on the dais and pulled the charm from around her head, then held the necklace out. "*Do* something, Fee."

All at once the healer shouted out to the soldiers near Quinn, "Grab her. And get hold of that pendant!"

Three men rushed forward, and on instinct, Fee looked to the ground toward their feet. She flicked her finger in a quick upward swoop. Roots from the great oak split through the earth, catching the toes of the guards and tripping them to sprawl on the artificial turf.

"Toss it to me, Quinn," Fee shouted.

The princess pitched the amulet into the air, propelling it in a high arc over the heads of the people between them.

Mistress Goodsong thrust out her hands in a swirl of movement, summoning the strength of a fundamental force—a silent spell in the making. A great gust of wind caught the necklace midair, redirecting it toward the healer's outstretched, waiting hands.

But suddenly the world went dark. Like someone had flicked a switch on the sun's bright rays, the crowd was plunged into blindness.

And then, in the space of a heartbeat, the sky's illumination returned, and on the dais stood a dozen witches. Savva stood in the middle of them all, unshakably resolute. They were primed for battle.

The crowd called out in alarm, many falling to their knees. The blackout had caused Mistress Goodsong to lose focus and loose the hand that held the people trapped.

It had also obscured the trajectory of the pendant.

Fee watched Mistress Goodsong scuttle along the ground to locate the necklace.

A man stood and thrust his fist into the air. "I've got it!" he yelled.

Mistress Goodsong's eyes locked onto him. Pointing with two forefingers at the man, she then swept her arms across the heads of the people surrounding him. They fell flat to the ground, leveled by her gesture. The man stood alone, rooted and fixed, his eyes wide with fear.

Again, the healer motioned with her fingers, a simple twist, and the pendant caught on her current and sailed toward her hands.

But a mass of leaves suddenly fell from the oak tree, stitching together to form a wall of obstruction. Fee turned to see Harold, his outstretched hands shaking with effort.

Mistress Goodsong blasted through the leafy structure with a fist that motioned like a hammer. The green fragments flew apart and fluttered to the ground.

Many Gwyndomites fled from the unfolding havoc, alarm creating a chaotic flurry of bodies.

But Mistress Goodsong was not deterred. She dove into the leaves, her hands scattering them to clear the ground for her search.

Laboring against the bolting crowd, Fee wrestled to get closer and looked over her shoulder again to the dais to see Mistress Merrybird raise her hands. Two purple balls of thermal heat shot through the air and exploded into an umbrella of pyrotechnic brilliance. The tiny sparks caught the swirling leaves and fire rained down around the healer.

Mistress Goodsong immediately twirled in a simple circle and the flaming foliage was cast out over the heads of the fleeing Gwyndomites.

At last spotting the amulet, she reached for it, but suddenly found it encircled in a hard bubble of pearled iridescence. She could not break the globe. Mistress Goodsong looked up to see Savva, her eyes closed in arduous concentration.

Fee propelled herself toward the opalescent balloon, but all at once felt something close around her throat. Her eyes popped wide as she could no longer draw breath. Mistress Goodsong held her hands in a circle as if she herself were choking the life out of Fee.

"Your choice, Savva!" the healer shouted out as Fee clawed at the unseen grip around her neck. "The old charm or the young charmer!"

Savva's eyes flew open and she collapsed to her knees, popping the impenetrable film that sheathed the bulla.

Mistress Goodsong released her hold on Fee, who fell to the ground as well, heaving for great lungfuls of air. The healer grasped the pendant and held it up, the chain wrapping itself around her fingers.

Quinn's face blanched with shock, and Xavi's eyes closed as if he was absorbing a deathly blow. The queen cried out, and the remaining Gwyndomites hastened back to their feet.

The healer closed her fingers around the disc and held it in the air, smiling triumphantly toward the heavens. Her gaze then swept across the stunned remaining few.

She laughed and said, "Savva. I know how much you like your orbs of protection—hiding yourself, your granddaughter, and now this little pendant. But surely you can see how they've all come to such bad ends. Even your son suffers in the bubble he lives within.

"People who break the rules *always* experience misfortune in the end—it cannot be escaped. And the consortium of your comrades—those witches who signed a pact long ago—must be punished as well."

Savva held up her hands and croaked out a plea. "None of them tutored Fee. Not one endeavored to help release Azamar."

But Mistress Goodsong pulled a vial from her pocket and continued. "I do not like the flailing hands of bedlam. And this kingdom is on the cusp of a feverish infirmity. As the healer of Gwyndom—and the protector of the health of this kingdom—my diagnosis for it is a dire one, which can only be cured by the strongest of actions—*disinfection*. I must root out that which causes the kingdom great upset.

"Gwyndom needs my help. I will make it a better version of itself."

She raised the vial. "A little cure for what ails us!" she shouted above their heads, and then whirled the hand holding the pendant about in a circle. The wind first rose straight from the ground beneath them, as if a great hand had pinched together the fabric of air around their bodies. Then it changed directions and swept in and around the people in a roiling, eddying flurry. Leaves spun above them in a growing circular current, clothing snapped in the reeling gusts, and the breath of the sudden squall exhaled a daunting cadence that grew to a fevered pitch.

Everyone was frozen with horror. Fee's heart hammered in her chest as she looked up from the ground and took in the fate of the people around her. The fear-stricken face of her sister; the pained expression of her helpless mother; Xavi, who had been through more cruel pain than was fit for an entire kingdom; and Rye. She met the jade-colored eyes of the boy she loved and the man she longed for and heard him shout a surprising statement. "Use your *magic*, Ophelia!"

Her fingers stung with a searing heat, and she tore her gaze from Rye to Xavi—the person who would suffer the most if she did.

All before one, she remembered the wicked healer lecturing.

Everything burned within her as she glared at the woman whose rules were forcing her to choose. A frenzy of volatile emotions churned uncontrollably within her body.

Mistress Goodsong pulled the cork stopper from the vial.

Fee grabbed handfuls of acorns and suddenly felt Savva's past words fasten themselves like a sharp pinprick onto her consciousness—*Funnel your anger into focus.*

She dismissed them. Anger was the only thing she had.

Taking aim, she threw the acorns at the witch's feet, blisteringly fast, and shouted, "No! Never again!"

With the amulet in one hand and the vial in the other, the witch looked down at the earth around her and saw the clutch of acorns sprout green shoots and stalking spears. In the blink of an eye, after encasing her feet and fixing her in place, they snaked up her legs and swallowed her waist, thickening and reaching higher toward the sky, a growing, green, woody serpent slithering upward at lightning speed.

Mistress Goodsong's eyes were two round moons as they watched the rise and spread of unfolding growth, and then in a wave of rapid panic, they found and fixed on Fee's. Fee saw the woman's mouth form some unidentifiable word as she realized her ripening fate.

Thick slabs of bark covered the outside of the oak as it sprang from the ground and encased the witch. The wood grew, cracking and groaning past her head in the direction of her hands, outstretched toward the sky, still clutching her poison and the pendant.

The queen cried out with an anguishing wail as the tree burst forth, upward and outward, enveloping the witch and burying the key to Fee's father's release along with the woman who'd imprisoned him.

The tree unfurled its branches and spread its girth, staking claim to new earth and an increasing patch of sky. In mere moments, it had reached the height and breadth of the oak that had given it life, the oak from where the acorns had fallen. A mirror of its father, the hardwood stood firm and stout and, finally, silent.

The air around them had gone eerily still, the wind extinguished along with the witch. They all stood blinking, mouthing soft and silent words of surprise, like fish in a shallow pool peering up to the surface through a thin film of water. Stunned, they kept their eyes fixated on Fee.

She moved in slow motion toward the dais full of people and witches. The platform where the queen remained bent and wretchedly despondent. Where Quinn stood aghast, her bottom lip quivering. Where Xavi clutched at the fabric on his chest and fell to his knees, a thick sheen of sweat glistening on his ashen face. Fee rushed to his side but he raised a trembling hand, taking in slow lungfuls of air as if he'd just been racing uphill. She helped settle him on his back to make his breathing come easier and he squeezed her hand to reassure her.

Fee looked up and took Rye's outstretched hand. He helped her to her feet, and she read the expression on his face, one that held equal parts compassion, comprehension, and worry. She turned and took a few tentative steps toward the queen to address her.

"I am so sorry, Your Majesty."

Rye's hands came around Fee's shoulders, their strength a balm against the icy bleakness before her, and solid proof he would stand beside her despite the unnerving, harrowing spectacle of sorcery she'd conjured at his bidding.

Queen Islay pulled herself up with a breath that seemed to zipper in the spilled emotions that had brought her to her knees. Her gaze landed upon Fee, and her face filled with practiced benevolence.

"You have nothing to atone for, child. In fact, the people around us must express a depth of gratitude for that which you have accomplished. Mistress Goodsong meant to do us great harm. Had you and the others not acted in the manner and speed you did, none of us would have breath to draw nor a future to build upon."

Fee looked up into her dispirited eyes. "But . . . the amulet," she whispered.

Quinn came forward timidly. "Had I known of its importance . . ."

The queen tried to smile at Quinn. "How could you? No one told you the significance of its carved words."

Quinn gave her a questioning look. "On the back? The three Latin words?"

Xavi raised a desperate gaze toward Quinn at the same time as the queen grabbed her hand, and Fee blurted out, "Do you know them?"

The princess looked from one face to another and knelt beside Xavi, putting a handkerchief to his brow. "Yes," she said. "I think."

"Quinn," Xavi said, his voice cracking with urgency and hope, "what were they? And in what order?"

She swallowed, her eyes revealing a fear of misremembering. "The first word was *abjungo*," she said slowly.

Fee nodded with encouragement. "Yes, it means 'to separate'—and the next two words may reveal the key to unharness Azamar from Xavi." She whispered, "What are they?"

"*Myosotis sylvatica.*"

Fee blinked. "Are you sure?"

The queen leaned forward and gripped Fee's arm. "What does it mean?"

Fee looked up at the woman, her eyes surely expressing the defeat she felt as a heavy weight in the pit of her stomach. "It is nothing more than the Latin name for a flower—the forget-me-not."

CHAPTER
THIRTY-NINE

"SO," XAVI SAID, CLEARLY RATTLED BUT TRYING TO show a measure of composure, "one of two things must occur. Either Fee discovers some bizarre but effective sacrifice for friendship, or we create an elusive flower potion. But one of them must be deemed worthy of reversal by the spell, correct?"

Harold and Mistress Merrybird nodded. "We all agree," Mistress Merrybird said, signaling toward the other menders who had gathered in the queen's private chambers, "that a simple distilled tincture of the blossoms will be the easiest treatment. Since Savva witnessed the path of Mistress Goodsong's powder, she may have concluded the flower's pollen—from the bed of forget-me-nots Azamar and Xavi were standing in—was accidentally inhaled as well. Perhaps it has medicinal counteragent qualities."

Harold added, "It's likely she may have only come to this

conclusion *after* she made the bargain with Mistress Goodsong, as even if Savva was with us right now, her oath remains intact. She could not aid this desperate quest."

"The tincture should be easy enough," Fee said dispiritedly, but felt the muscles in her shoulders clench, knowing failure would be catastrophic.

The queen put a hand to her heart. "Then we mustn't tarry." She looked pleadingly at the three menders. "How quickly can you make the tincture?"

Rosedriah shook her head dejectedly. "I'm sorry, Your Majesty, but like Savva, we signed a bonding pledge that as part of the agreement to protect Fee, we'd neither teach her magic or attempt to unbind Azamar."

Xavi struggled to sit and wheezed out, "I suggest you break the pledge! For as Fee has explained it, you will either find death by helping to save the realm now, when other angry menders discover your actions, or death will find you after a wretched and slow march toward starvation once we lose Fireli's stone. It's only a matter of choosing the better of two bads, is it not?" He clutched at his chest to catch his breath, and Fee moved to his side, trying to calm him.

Harold shook his head. "Believe me. We would choose to break the pledge if it meant saving Fireli and the rest of the realm. But our skills toward this endeavor have been rendered impotent with our signatures. There is nothing we *can* do, even if we wanted to."

The queen looked aghast. "Well, then who will make the remedy?"

Mistress Merrybird announced, "It will have to be Fee."

Fee realized she'd exhaled with a whimper, then took a solid breath and said, "I'll need the flowers, obviously." She refused to think past the task at hand.

Queen Islay's eyes held a strong note of alarm. "As you've surely come to see, apart from the one—er, rather, *two* oaks—nothing surrounding the castle and its grounds is from the natural world. We are a kingdom surrounded by a manufactured landscape."

"Then what shall I use?" Fee said, her voice coming out strangled.

"You can sprout them yourself, can't you?" Kizzy asked.

Fee eyed the candid young hermetical mender, her dreadlocked strands of hair sporting large ceramic clacking beads, her skirt with strips of each kingdom's flags fluttering around her legs. "Not without harming Xavi further. I won't take the chance."

The queen's features pleaded with the menders. "What are we to do?"

Fee thought quickly. "I think we should return to Fireli and find the flower there—the one that Savva carved into the disc."

Xavi pulled himself to sit straighter—a little unsteadily. "Then I suggest we leave immediately. Time is running out. And hope is running short. But I will not waste either one of them when they are still accessible. Fireli awaits."

CHAPTER
FORTY

WITH EACH PASSING HOUR ON THE THREE-DAY JOUR-
ney back to Fireli, the stress Fee cradled grew in heft like an
unanchored ballast that caused a ship to falter. But the strain was
present in the faces of the rest of the company too.

Late on the second night, Fee woke with a start from an unsettling, horrifying dream.

Savva had come to her. The old healer, her shaky, skittering
hands placed on either side of Fee's face, held a world of apology
as she pressed the images of Xavi, Azamar, and the kingdom's core
stone into Fee's head.

Determined to believe it was the symptom of a wearied mind,
spinning within a half-conscious nightmare, Fee went to the nearby
icy stream and scrubbed her face, callously rubbing herself raw of the
unwanted suspicion of what she might soon be asked to do.

When they reached Fireli, the first thing she learned was that Savva had died three days prior. The citizens, everyone Savva had ever treated, had given the kingdom's healer a worthy and honorable funeral. Astonished to find herself buried further beneath a mound of new emotions, Fee stood in the center of the stillroom and quietly wept, her heart aching for being robbed of the knowledge of their kinship.

"I'm sorry, Fee," came a voice from the doorway.

She turned quickly, swiping at her tears, and saw Xavi, his face full of tenderness. She walked to him. It must have required all his strength to make it to the stillroom. She felt his arms struggle to wrap around her, but she sank gratefully into the familiar comfort he'd always provided. And she did not for one moment lose sight of the notion that it must have required another source of great strength on his part—a *different* source of strength—knowing his own death was potentially only two days away.

She had no more time to grieve. She looked up into his face and said, "It's time I get to work."

The castle inhabitants gathered baskets full of forget-me-nots, and once Fee and Kizzy had sorted them all, Fee counted four different species among the mounds. *Myosotis decora, Myosotis scorpioides, Myosotis arvensis*, and *Myosotis alpestris*. None were the species carved onto the back of Xavi's pendant. Their differences made her anxious, but she refused to take a chance, and decided to make medicines from them all.

As soon as one batch was finished, they rushed to Xavi's chambers, gathered everyone, and waited to see the results. In the space of thirty-six hours, Xavi had been given twelve different extracts and tinctures and, by the end of it, the only thing apparent was that the medicines weren't working.

Not only were they ineffective in freeing Azamar, but now they were making Xavi increasingly ill. The medicines were poisoning his liver.

His skin took on a yellow tinge. He lost his appetite and was nauseated. Fatigue had overcome him on the second day, in that he grew so weak, he could only recline on the settee and wait hopefully for the next treatment.

Xavi asked if he could speak with Fee alone, and everyone filed out of his study, somber and respectful. His old maid, Mistress Kemble, stood mindlessly dusting his desk and shuffling papers from a neat, tidy stack. Fee met her eyes and then glanced toward the door. The old woman nodded, took the papers in her hand, and quickly shelved them between two large books within the stacks behind Xavi's desk.

Mistress Kemble left and Fee quickly moved to the shelves to pull out the papers. Xavi's notes. Azamar's arguments about compounds Xavi had no knowledge of. The papers they'd both been certain had been stolen had been mindlessly and effectively "tidied away."

She put them back and decided against letting Xavi know. There was no point. Instead, she knelt down beside the settee and stared into a pair of jaundiced eyes that pleaded with her for the truth.

"Fee?" he whispered through cracked lips and a parched throat. "The sacrifice."

"What of it?"

"You've figured it out, haven't you?"

"What would make you say such a thing?"

He gave her a small smile. "I know you. You're a worrier. Up until about two or three days ago, it was something that had you pacing the floor. But now"—his voice wavered slightly—"now you're not speaking of it at all, which tells me you've discovered what would work and don't want to face it. Am I right?"

Her vision blurred with bitter heartbreak. She made a slow nod.

"Tell me," he said.

"Savva came to me—in a dream on one of our nights of travel. She said that the healer was right. That all she had to do was weaken you to the point where the bonds to your life were threadbare and frail. Mistress Goodsong tried binding your wrists, reaching in, and offering Azamar the hand of forgiveness. He refused, knowing her gesture was hollow. One of gain, not gift.

"And now, Mistress Goodsong is not an option. It is down to us. Savva said I had to give you what you wanted most."

Xavi would not break his gaze. "I want to save Fireli."

"I realized"—Fee swallowed—"that our sacrifice for friendship would have to be . . . you."

"Me," Xavi said at the same time.

She nodded.

Xavi's eyes remained locked with hers.

Another tear rolled down her face. "The magic I would draw from you when binding our wrists to reach my father would be enough to pull him out, but more than you could bear. It would be the ultimate sacrifice for both of us." Fee whispered her last sentence. "I would lose the greatest friend I've ever had, and Fireli would lose the greatest king they'd never known."

"But Fireli *would be spared*." Xavi swallowed and reached to squeeze her hand. "Promise me, Fee. Promise if the last batch does not work you *will* do this. You'll bind our wrists and do what needs to be done."

Fee closed her eyes, wept, and bowed her head. It seemed as if her whole life had been nothing more than one effort after another in an attempt to kill the person she loved the most.

Queen Islay and Mistress Merrybird came to Fee in the still-room. They sat around the large, old wooden table, where the few remaining scraps of seeds, petals, leaves, and stems were scattered. Fee was distilling one final batch of medicine—a combination of all the remaining species, in the hope that some sort of crossover complementary action might occur if the components were brought together.

The queen's words were sobering. "By daybreak tomorrow we will know whether the castle will celebrate Prince Xavi's corona-tion . . . or his funeral. It is important that we plan for both.

"The ministries of our kingdoms have been expunged of cor-ruption."

"And is yours also expunged of witches?" Fee asked, worried for Gwyndom's plans.

"There are very few worthy of pursuit, so have no fear for Gwyndom's witch hunts, Fee. Those, like Mistress Goodsong, *must* be found and dealt with. On this I'm certain we now agree."

Fee said nothing, but lowered her head.

The queen continued. "Mistress Goodsong stole a great deal

from Fireli by pirating the mines, and she used the profits to gain favor in Gwyndom. It will all be returned. After many hours of discussion during these last few days with those who remain in government—but more important, with Xavi—we believe that Quinn was unknowingly manipulated by Mistress Goodsong, and that no punishment should be pressed upon her.

"If your last remedy should prove potent enough to release Azamar and your kingdom's core stone, but toxic enough to kill Xavi, Prince Rye will take his place as the next king of Fireli. But I will not ask that we bind our kingdoms—between Quinn and Rye," she finished quietly.

"If Azamar should be rescued, I will abdicate." Her eyes met Fee's. "I will pass the crown to Quinn and help her become the queen I know she has the aptitude to be.

"Regardless, I'm powerless to give you what you truly want. A life with—" She stood abruptly, placed a trembling hand upon Fee's head, and then quickly kissed her cheek. "I'm sorry, Fee," she whispered before moving swiftly out the door.

Fee looked to Mistress Merrybird.

"As you may have already deduced, Fee, *you* are a member of the royal family of Gwyndom. The crown would traditionally pass to the child who is eldest in birth—you. Except, again, as you have been . . . blessed with magic, you are prohibited from ruling a kingdom. And forbidden from marrying someone who may soon rule one as well."

Fee looked down to see her hands trembling in her lap. She thought about Savva, and how even though she had been touted as the most capable mender of the realm, she'd not been able to resist the overwhelming reflex of her emotions. They were dangerous and uncontrollable, and because of it, Fee would suffer a lonely, loveless life.

"No," Mistress Merrybird said, clearly reading Fee's mind. "I believe we are more than the design of our biology and have the ability to overrule our passions with the actions of our reason.

"I am only sad there is not another alternative for you should Xavi fall victim alone, for to deny someone the very source of their vitality is to offer them a shell of an existence." She squeezed Fee's hand. "My hope is that Rye is *not* your one true love."

Fee was numb with her words. She nodded mutely and then, at last, said, "I must finish my work."

Mistress Merrybird stood and paused at Fee's shoulder. "If by some miraculous chance your last remedy prevails, and Azamar is released, you must immediately provide an antidote to Xavi, otherwise, that which is meant to cure him will instead kill him."

The crickets chirped in a low, mournful chorus outside the window of the stillroom. It was full dark, and the warm breeze that floated through the open frame brought with it the heady scent of night-blooming jasmine. Fee had sent Kizzy away and wished for only the mournful silence of the insects and the tiny click of the second hand as it acknowledged the passing time until sunrise. The last brew still had a couple of hours before it was ready, and the great copper pot sluggishly distilled her ingredients.

There was a soft knock at the door, and it creaked as it opened. As she had both hoped and feared, Rye stood on the other side of it. He held up a sturdy mug with a less than steady hand. "I've brought you some tea. I thought perhaps . . ."

Fee shook her head. She could not look at him. She wished for blindness in this cruel reality. She longed to close the door, push him back, keep him from coming across the threshold. But this was utterly impossible. She could not keep Rye from entering the still-room, just as she could not keep him from occupying all the space within her heart. She steeped in pain like the leaves of her brews.

"Your mother has spoken to you?" he said quietly.

She nodded.

"So you know . . ."

She nodded again, looking up.

Rye pressed his lips inward, and Fee watched as his gaze left her eyes and studied her face. It traveled to the dark hair that spilled across her shoulders, swept to her hands, and then down to the floor before returning to rest on her mouth.

He spoke softly. "How are we to do this, Ophelia?"

She stood stock-still, listening to her heart thud within her chest, and then felt compelled to ask: "You know you are the only one who calls me that? Why? Why not *Fee* like everyone else?"

His eyes crinkled before the barest of smiles curled the corners of his mouth. "Because your name is music—every syllable—and I cannot bear to deny myself the joy of hearing each blissful note." He put his hand up to her face, one finger tracing her features. "Your name paints a picture in my mind, and I see you come alive—the curve of your brow, the angle of your cheekbone, the jut of your chin."

His fingers slid along her skin, and she shivered. "I want to memorize this. I want to know the shape of your ear beneath my fingers, the scent of your hair when I breathe you in, and, more than anything, I want to know the curve of your mouth as it fits onto mine.

"Ophelia. I love you. I have always loved you. And no matter what happens to us, I will never *cease* loving you."

Fee could not breathe. She could not think, or move, or speak. But she could feel.

And every nerve in her body shimmered with attention. And when Rye brushed his lips along her forehead and down to her ear, her body responded with a ripple of gooseflesh. And when he skimmed his nose along her jaw and traced it down her neck to place a kiss within the hollow of her throat, she thought her knees would give out beneath her. And when he threaded his fingers through her hair and moved her head so that her eyes met his, she knew the question he wanted answered.

"Yes," she breathed out. "Yes."

Fee woke sometime later and stared at Rye's face as the candlelight flickered across his skin. She, as well, was determined to fix every detail of his features into her mind. It was easier to study them when his eyes were closed, as his dark, emerald gaze usually left her dizzy and befuddled.

She felt his breath on her face, a faint trace of a breeze, and then felt her vision go blurry, realizing she would never feel it there again. A tear trailed down her cheek onto the pillow, and then another, and another.

Rye's eyes opened, and he put a hand up to her face, brushing the streaks away with his thumb. "Your eyes are so beautiful,

Ophelia—even filled with glittering tears. The color is unlike anything I've ever seen. Except perhaps the tiny flowers you gave me when I was ten. Remember? The ones you found in my keepsake box. They match them precisely."

Fee's heart stopped with a quick jolt. "The flowers?" she asked, sitting up and clutching at the sheet that wrapped around them. "Do you still have them?" Her mind whirled, pitched into sudden action.

Rye nodded, raising himself to sit beside her.

"Here?" she gushed. "Do you have the box here?"

His eyes grew wide. He threw the sheet back and leapt up from Fee's cot, rushing to slip on his breeches and snatching the linen shirt that lay at the bottom of the bed. He slid down the ladder from the loft and dashed out the door.

Fee gathered her clothes and hurried down the ladder, seizing every item she'd require if Rye came back with exactly what they needed. She looked at the clock and started to pace.

Four hours.

That's all they had, and she would need every second of it. She peered up to the ceiling and clasped her hands. "Please, Savva," she begged. "I will read all your books. I will work for the rest of my days to heal this kingdom and treat every person in it—to become as capable and masterful as you were." She squeezed her eyes shut. "I will make you so proud . . . just . . . Please, help me help them."

Rye burst through the door, clutching the box. They rushed to the table and lit the lantern. Rye threw back the lid and picked up the dried flowers, presenting them to Fee across the spread of his palms. She bent to study them, and then pulled back with a gasp.

"*Myosotis sylvatica*!" she said in a rush of breath.

Suddenly she panicked. They needed to be fresh—to flow with life so that she could draw out the oils and essence. She had no choice. She'd *have* to use magic. Fee's heart filled with a thrill of hope, but she also noted the bright taste of fear in her mouth. She knew what she had to do—despite the strain on Xavi. She prayed she would use just enough to cure him—not enough to kill him.

She placed her palms beneath Rye's, touched her thumbs to the flowers' stems, and closed her eyes. She did not need to see to know what was happening within Rye's hands. She could feel the flood of life grow through her fingers and into the stalks. She knew the blue blossoms were mushrooming before them, spilling out in rich abundance over their hands and onto the floor. The tiny woodland flowers filled the space around their feet and, at last, Fee opened her eyes to see Rye's—marveling and dumbfounded—looking back and forth between hers and the flowers before them.

"Put the kettle on to boil," she said, shining with hope.

CHAPTER
FORTY-ONE

FEE STOOD OVER THE COPPER POT THAT HELD ALL THE flowers immersed in water. It burbled softly on the stove, boiling to create a steam that she collected and then condensed. The distillate dripped with agonizingly slow speed.

Less than thirty minutes earlier, she'd sent Rye to gather everyone in Xavi's chambers to be present for the last attempt to save his life and free another's. They were waiting for her. Counting on her. And the fear and anxiety were colliding in such a way she believed she'd aged ten years in the space of the last few hours.

She'd prepared the liver tonic—the antidote that Xavi would need if he survived ingesting this last tincture. It stood on the scarred wooden table in a brown glass bottle—potent, but potentially pointless.

Fee stared out the stillroom window, a sliver of the horizon announcing the coming dawn. The clock on the wall declared its arrival with a fevered pitch of foreboding agitation.

She tried closing her eyes and ears to every sight and sound and was greeted by the only other thought that pursued her attention. *Rye.*

She drew in a long breath—the air she believed somehow still contained the memories of their last few hours together. The blissful, heady moments where they came to know each other in ways that made her heart pound with the memory of discovery. It wasn't enough.

She opened her eyes and knew at once that her batch was finished. After she'd filtered it through finely woven cheesecloth and funneled it into another vial, her shaking hands wedged a cork into the opening. She glanced once more into the rafters of the thatched roof. "If knowledge is power, why do I feel so hamstrung and helpless? I'm begging you, Savva. Please be here with me. Please."

She dashed out the door toward Fireli's future king. Toward the precarious fate that awaited them all.

Harold's face appeared as he swung open the heavy wooden slab of Xavi's door, his features drawn tight with worry, which he tried to hide beneath a veil of encouragement.

Fee rushed through to the sitting room, where everyone gathered around Xavi. The prince was on his back, his eyes fluttering open and closed whenever someone whispered to him. Quinn sat at his side, holding his hand, gently stroking it with a mixture of comfort and apology.

Fee kneeled down beside him and brought her face close to his.

"My good and noble Xavi. My best friend. I cannot believe how cruel this life has been to you."

"Cruel?" he repeated, opening his eyes and mustering a small smile. "No. For I have spent so much of it with you. And we have made the best of it. And the best of it has been cherished beyond measure."

Fee felt her chin tremble and the rush of hot tears spring to her eyes. She tried to smile, holding out the bottle. "I truly believe this will be the one to free you, Xavi."

He took a shaky breath and replied, "Yes. A tonic that will either free me of this spell, or free me of this life." He placed a hand on her arm. "But understand, I *know* that you have done more for me than any one friend could expect. And I love you for it, sweet Fee." He made a feeble attempt to squeeze her arm before adding, "Remember your promise . . . if this does not work."

She nodded.

A tear rolled down his face. "Now . . . hand me the bottle before I either lose my nerve or lose my chance."

Quinn helped prop him up and, uncorking the bottle, put it to his lips and tipped the contents into his mouth.

Everyone gathered in a tight circle around him: Kizzy gripped the hands of Mistress Merrybird and Rosedriah on either side of her, Harold bounced nervously beside Rye, their grim faces mirroring each other, and Queen Islay stood in the center: tall, determined, and expectant.

Thirty seconds went by, and the only obvious sign of the medicine taking any effect was the further yellowing tint that seeped through Xavi's skin.

The queen closed her eyes. Hope seemed to bleed from the room as a single ray of sunshine crept over the windowsill and shone on the tips of the furniture.

The precious seconds ticked by loudly, and with each click, Fee felt Xavi slipping away from them, and then heard him whisper, a barely audible *Fee*.

Fee shook her head over and over again with defiance at the bitter realization of what she had to do next, her hand trembling uncontrollably. She ground her teeth. She would do this for the kingdom. For her king. For her friend.

She took hold of Xavi's arm and pushed up his sleeve. For a brief moment, Fee thought her eyes had grown blurry with the wateriness of tears, doubling her vision. Because another face seemed to share the outlines that belonged to Xavi.

Wavering and thin, the edges grew more sure, and slowly the contour and shape of another man gained solidity.

Quinn gasped, and the queen cried out. Kizzy drew in a wheezing breath of surprise, and everyone standing took a step back.

The silhouette separated itself from Xavi, rising from a prone position to a seated one, with arms outstretched to both Quinn and Fee.

They each grabbed an arm and helped pull this tall dark man up to stand, his form growing firm, sound, and substantial. He drew them both in toward his chest, toward the fiery red opal that hung at his collar, clutching at them for strength and to convey a desperate emotion of elation.

"Azamar," the queen breathed out in an awestruck whisper.

The man stumbled forward into her arms, and what felt like a thousand years of grief and longing seemed to lift from both their faces.

Fee looked back to Xavi, who was as still and pale as stone. "Quinn," she cried. "Quickly, the other bottle. Give him the antidote!"

The princess uncorked the vial and, again, raising Xavi's now lifeless body a few inches, put the bottle to his lips and began to pour the contents into his mouth. Much of the liquid dribbled straight down his chin, benefitting no one, and Fee felt her heart seize with a fist-like sense of fear.

"No," she cried, grabbing the bottle from Quinn's hand. "You will bloody well drink this, you stubborn fool!"

Fee tipped the remainder of the antidote into his mouth, holding his chin high so the rest couldn't trickle out.

Nothing happened. He was still. Waxen. Breathless.

Fee felt a wave of fury thrum through her body and vibrate in her bones. Her breathing grew suddenly ragged. Her vision sparked with pinpoints of blinding light.

This could not happen. She would not lose it all. Not Xavi. Not Rye. Not every reason for drawing breath.

The sounds around her were a scattering of fading, frantic voices among a vortex of rushing wind, at once volatile and violent. The only voice that came through the cacophony—the roar of noise—was Savva's.

Funnel your anger into focus, Fee.

She had another chance.

Fee pressed their wrists together and propelled herself into the darkness of Xavi's life, toward the fading beam of light that now retreated alone and stood unshackled.

Arms outstretched, she reached toward the paling shaft—his history. Fee shouted for him, crying his name, calling him back.

Fragments of their lives whipped in a frenzy all around her—the years they'd shared, the strength they'd provided, the friendship they'd created.

Fee saw so many faces. The people of Fireli, her parents, the king and queen, the consortium of witches—and Savva. Her eyes bright and brimming with tears. The witches held hands, embracing one another and conjoining their powers, a vortex of thousands of lives and the vigor of their voices blossoming with fortitude around them.

There was so much warmth and courage here. So much life and strength from these souls. "Use them," she shouted at Xavi. "Use *me*!"

Seeing Xavi's dimming features, she reached out, her fingertips barely brushing and then finally grasping hold of the one thing that appeared to have the most substance. The bulla around his neck.

Upon touching the brilliant golden disc, Fee was flooded with a world full of knowledge. Savva had left the bulla brimming with her magic like a tome saturated with wisdom. In a flash of heat and light, crossing all time and space, Fee suddenly understood how she was connected to everything: to the earth, to all people, to friendship and love. Nothing, not even death, could separate her from the threads of this tapestry.

But she would not let death work its dull knife just yet.

Directing every emotion she felt—every ounce of rage and grief, joy and passion that raced through her veins, she pulled them both toward the surface, away from the magnetic draw of a cold grave and its inky depths.

And like the crack of a whip, they were propelled backward, snapped as if they were rubber bands, and thrust back through to the world they'd just left.

She fell back against the floor, heaving and stunned. And then saw Xavi lurch upright. He bucked and coughed, spluttering for breath. His forehead was slick with the sheen of sweat and his eyes bulged with the effort Fee had dragged from him. He squeezed them shut to counteract the ray of bright sunlight that struck him in the face and fell back against the pillows, gulping for air. Moments passed before he breathed out in a gushing exhalation. "Dying would have been *so* much easier."

Fee looked about the shattered room—at the chaotic disarray, the result of the force of her desperate measures—and at the faces within the room, displaying wide-eyed shock and unmistakable apprehension.

The witches all stood, hand in hand, closely huddled. Mistress Merrybird at last broke their depleted bonds and heaved out the words "Are you all right?"

Fee nodded mutely and then looked about the room. "Did *I*…?"

Harold stepped forward. "It was magnificent, Fee. I've never seen anything like it. Yes, it was savage, but only at first. Then something happened. We all saw it. We saw everything."

Azamar moved toward her, his voice warm and resonant. "You need not be afraid, Fee. You've been controlled your whole life. You've had a tightly fitted lid pushing down upon you to suppress your magic, your emotions, and even one to hide your existence. This was an untethering, but one you governed yourself. Rest assured, you will learn, and you will manage your magic just fine."

Xavi blinked back the sunshine, and looked at Fee, forcing out raspy words. "I agree. You'll find no fear from this quarter. But you do realize that no one will come to you for treatment if all your medicines taste like fetid liquid mud pies, don't you?"

Fee's tear-stricken face beamed back at him, and she leaned over to grasp him in a fierce hug. "Happy birthday, you wretched fool."

Then Xavi turned to Quinn and said, "Perhaps you'd consider going into business with your sister? Fee can scowl at the ill and infirm and treat them with her vile potions, and you can reward them for their bravery with one of your curative confections and heartwarming smiles."

Quinn's face lit up, her eyes twinkling with optimism and mirth.

Rye came to stand behind Fee, his hand clutching her shoulder, his features expressing a great span of relief and joy. "Xavi, you have no idea how good it is to see you."

Xavi gave him a weak smile and chuckled. "Well, I couldn't rightly leave this poor kingdom in the hands of some lout of a rascal, now, could I?" Then he crooked a finger at his brother, and Rye leaned down closer to hear him.

Xavi made a small nod of acknowledgment toward Azamar. "You may want to introduce yourself to the man who will soon be your father-in-law. I have known him for a long time; a quiet fellow, but he may have a few things he's been itching to share."

Azamar raised a finger. "Well, firstly, Prince Xavi, if there be any hesitation in your heart as to the devotion of this remarkable young woman—our Quinn—rest assured, I can vouch for her. For the face that I saw countless times gazing into yours these last few weeks was a mirror image of her extraordinary mother's as she used to peer into mine. She is genuine. She is sincere. And you will be wholly fortunate to have her at your side as the two of you resurrect Fireli." He kissed Quinn's cheek.

Azamar then turned his attention to Fee. His eyes glittered and then swept skyward. "There are a thousand things I wish to say to you, Fee. And a thousand and one things I wish to teach you. If when I look at Quinn I see your mother, then it is no surprise to look at you as if I gaze into a mirror.

"Savva was fiercely proud of you. I will do my utmost to pick up where she has left off—if you will let me. And although your new monarch is determined to change the laws of our kingdom to make sure you and our kind are protected, until then, we are forced to hide the truth of who we are, but not the good that we can do. I am determined to unearth that which was hidden from you since birth. I want to introduce you to the person you truly are, and the great hermetical healer you will become.

"Xavi and Rye, I entrust you both to care for these young women. Their mother and I are certain they have been bound to two of the finest young men of the realm."

Rye gave Azamar a self-assured nod and then picked up Fee's hand, placing it upon his heart. "It matters little to me what you are or who you are. What matters to me is *where* you are. I want you by my side. Always. And despite my tests with certitude, there is one thing I have never doubted—it is the knowledge that no matter how much I may have complained about it as an insufferable ten-year-old, there is nothing I want more in this life than for you to call me *husband*."

Fee did not need the flush of heat that encircled her wrist to take pleasure in the accomplishment of saving these lives, nor did she need the power of magic to underscore the importance of each one of them.

All she needed was the surety that she would be part of the great restoration of her kingdom and her family. It was here that she would love them, and help them, and heal them.

ACKNOWLEDGMENTS

IF THERE IS ONE THING I HAVE COME TO RECOGNIZE after finishing a book, it would be that doing it alone, and doing it deftly, is well-nigh impossible. I think the two words that fall out of my mouth more often than any others would be "thank you." After that, it would be "I'm hungry."

But this page is about gratitude. And if I could make it the size of the sky, I would.

Thank you to my editor, Kristen Pettit. You have been a tremendous teacher. I have learned, I am learning, and I will forever continue to learn from all your immeasurable efforts. Jennifer Unter, my ambitions remain, as always, to find a path that will somehow catapult me over the standards you require (and so warmly assure me are possible). Finding an agent like you defines true felicity.

Christina MacDonald, you have six billion bits of knowledge squished into your body that I'd give my left lung to have, but I thank my lucky stars you are here to offer up yours. Alexandra Rakaczki, Jessie Gang, Erin Wallace—I'm fairly certain you all have found a powdery fountain of fairy dust somewhere and have sprinkled this book with much more than my fair share.

Elizabeth Lynch, just saying, or typing, or thinking your name brings me a warm glow of immeasurable and irreplaceable comfort. Okay, it's either you or a dram of twenty-five-year-old Caol Ila. Same cherished effect.

Kathleen Morandini, you are patient, and kind, and so generous with your time. Thank you for connecting me to the people who I'm trying so hard to engage with.

Huge hugs to Abby Murphy, who will doubtlessly find her name on every acknowledgment page in each of my books. Without your gentle hand, my stories would be unreadable.

My many thanks to Clare Vaughn, Lisa Perrin, Bill Bragg, Michael D'Angelo, and Megan Beatie. I am privileged to be surrounded by so much enthusiasm, talent, and dedication.

A massive hug to Rick Tevendale—because without your relentless nudging to come to yoga class at least once a week to master my miserable handstands, I'd likely still be sitting in my chair, stiff and woefully short of cerebral oxygen. Dave Gourley, someday I will return all your books. Maybe.

Chloe and Gabe, I miss you. I miss the noise you make whilst I'm trying to write. It's wretchedly quiet. But . . . the writing is going a helluva lot faster, so for that I'll send you extra food. And, of course, all my love.

Mom and Dad, I cannot say thank you enough for not only the genetics of perseverance—despite lack of aptitude—but for your unending patience as I pitch you story ideas to gauge just how bad they are in relation to the reactions on your faces.

And lastly, thank you, Dave Cuttino. Softly, softly, catchee monkey. I am forever grateful for your steadfast determination.